Lou took Rena's hand. "I don't believe you've seen the womb room yet." She led Rena upstairs to the corner room at the end of the corridor.

Earth-colored drapes of spun cotton wafted in loose folds to the thickly carpeted floor. There was a stereo, a fireplace, several soft inviting chairs, simple wooden tables, pillows and footstools, a contour lounging chair, and, under the wall-length windows, covered with the draperies, a square bed-size mat nearly two feet thick cloaked with a thick cotton comforter. The dim lighting cast a warm amber glow over the room.

Rena felt fluttery. Excitement and also that little edge of fear. "Womb room, huh?" She fingered the soft fabric of the comforter. "It's very sensual in here. Very well done."

They stood facing each other. Lou smiled but did not speak. Rena thought her the most striking woman she had ever seen.

"This is where we'll come," Lou said, breaking the silence. "You and I. When you're ready."

THE
SECRET
IN THE
BIRD

THE
SECRET
IN THE
BIRD

BY
CAMARIN
GRAE

The Naiad Press Inc.
1988

Printed in the United States of America
First Edition

Cover design by The Women's Graphic Center
Edited by Katherine V. Forrest
Proofread by Sidney Abbott
Typeset by Sandi Stancil

Library of Congress Cataloging-in-Publication Data

Grae, Camarin.
   The secret in the bird / by Camarin Grae.
     p.   cm.
   ISBN 0-941483-05-3
   I. Title.
PS3557.R125S4 1988
813'.54--dc 19   87-31181
                                         CIP

Books by Camarin Grae

Winged Dancer
Paz
Soul Snatcher
The Secret in the Bird
Edgewise (forthcoming)

CHAPTER ONE

Rena Spiros did not see the appalled looks of the crowd as the attendant led her away. She went passively. Casey Grant went too, her heart pounding violently. "She hasn't been well," Casey murmured, but no one heard.

They were taken to the zoo office and soon a policeman was there. Casey held Rena's bloody hand as they questioned her. Rena's eyes were glazed; she did not speak.

The police were ready to take her to Read Zone Center but Casey intervened and they ended up at Ravenedge, a private hospital near the lake on Chicago's north side. While Casey talked with the psychiatric resident, Rena remained slump-shouldered and mute.

Forms were filled out. Passively cooperative, Rena signed the papers and let herself be led upstairs and deposited in a room with two beds and two closets. The police officer left.

Dr. Terri Kepper, the ward psychologist, questioned Casey. "There's been no other violent or bizarre behavior that you know of?"

1

"Never," Casey replied. "Just the depression, since Pat's death, but never anything like this."

"They were lovers, you say, Rena and Pat."

"Yes, for the past two years."

The psychologist jotted notes as they spoke. "How did they get along?"

"Pat and Rena? Fairly well, I guess. Actually, Rena never talked much about their relationship, but when I saw them together they always seemed to get along OK." Casey hesitated. "Pat dominated Rena."

The psychologist tilted her head. "How do you mean?" She was a small woman in her mid-thirties with wavy hair and large teeth. Her eyes were soft and deeply inquisitive.

"Rena did whatever Pat wanted." Casey looked out the uncurtained window. "She catered to her. I don't know why."

The psychologist waited.

"It doesn't fit her personality. Rena's a real strong woman. But with Pat, I don't know . . . and then after Pat's accident, Rena changed drastically. She stopped going to her job. Stopped going out with friends. She even dropped out of Wommin Line — that's a women's crisis network she'd been active in for years."

"Did she talk about feeling sad, depressed?"

"Not really, but it was obvious. When I tried to get her to talk about it, she evaded." Casey's smooth forehead formed a questioning frown. "Do you think it's like a . . . some sort of an exaggerated mourning reaction? I've heard that happens sometimes."

"It could be." Dr. Kepper set her pen down. "The depression may have been set off by her lover's death but there's clearly more to it than that. The bird . . . well, who knows what that's about? We'll try to find out." She reflected a moment. "You say they were supposed to go to a barbecue together the day of Pat's death and that Rena was late."

"Yes, so Pat went alone."

"And on the way to the barbecue, she had the accident."

2

"Yes." Casey pushed up her glasses with her middle finger. Her cherubic face was lined and worried. "Do you think Rena might be blaming herself for the accident?"

"Perhaps." The psychologist wrote something.

Casey shook her head. "I tried to get her to go into therapy, to get help."

"Well, she did now, didn't she?" The doctor smiled her large warm smile.

"I guess." Casey drew her lower lip into her mouth. "From what you know so far, what do you think it could be? What do you think is wrong with her?" There was a note of desperation in her voice.

"I don't know," Dr. Kepper said calmly. "Not yet. Depression, clearly, and anger. Probably guilt. Possibly there's some delusional thinking going on that led her to kill the bird at the zoo, but at this point, Miss Grant, I'm afraid we're still pretty much in the dark."

Rena remained nearly mute. Dr. Kepper tried repeatedly to get her to talk but had little success. When Casey visited the next day, Rena was remote and barely communicative.

"Is the food any good?"

They were sitting on the dayroom porch. The summer sun shone cheerily through mesh-screened windows.

Rena took a long time to answer. "It's OK." Despite her gloominess, she looked very attractive, with her clear skin, straight narrow nose, large dark eyes. And she looked younger than her thirty-seven years. Her tall frame hung loosely on the green plastic chair.

Casey nodded. A few minutes went by. "How's your roommate?"

Rena stared at the wall. Thirty or forty seconds passed. "She screamed last night."

"Screamed? What do you mean? At you?"

Rena shook her head. "No, just screamed — in the middle of the night."

3

Casey tried to laugh. "I'll bet a lot of weird stuff goes on here."

Rena did not answer.

"Well, what did you do today?"

Slowly Rena shook her head.

Casey's eyes filled with tears. "Do you want me to bring you some books or anything?"

Rena did not answer.

The next day, Casey came again, but again Rena hardly spoke. Casey had to leave because it hurt too much to see her friend this way.

Dr. Kepper found Rena where Casey had left her, sitting impassively in the rear of the dayroom. "You visited with Casey?"

Rena glanced at her, then looked away.

"She's a good friend of yours, hm?"

Rena stared silently.

"She seems like a nice woman."

Rena made no response.

"Of course, it's hard to tell. There's something about her. The way she dresses, maybe. Those boyish clothes. She's obviously over thirty, but trying to look younger. Yes, I think she's a bit . . . phony, perhaps."

Rena started to say something, but stopped.

"Now I don't hold that against her. She's probably got problems. Covers them up with that fake smile of hers."

Rena turned her head sharply. "What are you talking about?" she snapped. "Casey's not at all phony."

"Oh."

They remained silent.

"Some psychologist." Rena scrutinized the smaller woman through the corners of her eyes, really seeing her for the first time. "You're just egging me on, aren't you?"

Dr. Kepper flashed a wide smile. "I guess. Say, Rena, do you mind if I tell you a story?"

Rena shrugged.

"It's a true story. About me."

4

Rena didn't respond.

Dr. Kepper looked intently at Rena as she spoke, as if trying to draw Rena's eyes to her own. "Whenever I used to set the table for dinner," she began, "I'd always place something on each corner first, plates or glasses, forks. There always had to be something, and then when the table was set, I'd put the corner pieces back where they belonged."

Rena was listening.

"My husband called me on it several times, asked my why I set the table that way." Dr. Kepper stopped speaking, still looking at Rena.

"Mm-hm," Rena said. "And?" She faced the psychologist.

"I had no idea. In fact, I hadn't really been aware of it until he pointed it out to me. It felt uncomfortable, to be doing a behavior that seemed to make no sense and that I had no explanation for."

Rena nodded. Her thoughts had gone inward.

"Like you and the bird," Dr. Kepper said. "You don't know why you killed it, do you?"

"No," Rena replied painfully. It was the first time she had responded to any questions about the bird.

"Finally I figured it out," Dr. Kepper continued. "But I had to go back in years to do it, remember things I had forgotten."

Rena glanced at her. "What things?"

"Our summer cottage at Bass Lake, the picnic lunches and dinners we had on the big redwood table under the oak trees. I was eight years old when we stopped going to the cottage."

Dr. Kepper leaned back in her chair. Rena waited for her to go on.

"The cottage burned down. Everything was lost. We were all inside sleeping when it started. It was very frightening. I had forgotten the details. It was too upsetting to remember, and that's probably why I forgot about setting the table." She and Rena were looking at each other now. "You see," Dr. Kepper continued, "I would often set the table at our outdoor meals at the cottage, and because of the breeze, mother taught me to put something on each corner of the tablecloth so the cloth couldn't blow."

Rena almost smiled. Just then they were approached by a rail-thin man.

"Can I get a pass?"

Rena had noticed him earlier, pacing the room, back and forth, never altering his pattern.

"Possibly so, John," Dr. Kepper said gently. "Bring it up at the ward meeting tomorrow."

"OK, doctor." He did an abrupt about face.

Rena watched him resume his pacing. She turned back to the psychologist. "How did you finally remember? About the tablecloth."

"I was determined to. I kept working on it. Thinking of anything in my life connected with setting the table. Finally, I got to the cottage and the memory of setting the outdoor table." Dr. Kepper laughed. "It was a relief to make the connection. I don't set the table that way any more."

"A relief."

"Yes, but it was painful to remember the fire and everything that was lost."

Rena nodded. "I have no idea why I kill birds."

"You've killed others?"

"Yes."

"It's not meaningless, Rena. See what happens if you let yourself think about it. See what comes."

Rena felt frightened.

"Give it a try."

She closed her eyes, biting her lip.

"What comes to mind?"

"Nothing."

"About birds in general. Any associations at all?"

Rena let herself think about it. After a few moments, a memory came. "Setting hooks for them, to catch them."

"Hooks?"

"Yes. In the hills, early in the morning when it was still dark, baiting the hooks and placing them around the trees and bushes where the birds came."

"Hm-m. Where was this?"

6

"In the country. I'd go with my cousin."

"I see. And what happened?"

Noises from a group of patients at one of the card tables interrupted them. There was a heated argument. One of the women was yelling in Spanish, another simultaneously cursing her in English. An aide came and quieted them.

"So, you'd go with your cousin and bait hooks, and what happened?"

"Nothing. We'd set them, then come back a few hours later to see what we'd caught."

"And what would you do with the birds?"

"Take them home to Mom. She'd cook them."

"I see. And how did all that feel to you?"

"OK. I liked it. I liked eating them. I liked catching them."

"How old were you then, Rena?"

"Young, seven — eight."

"It was in Greece?"

Rena felt the pain. "I guess so." She looked at the psychologist. "How do you know about Greece?"

"Casey told me you were born there."

"It must have been in Greece." Rena turned away.

"What else comes to mind about catching those birds?"

Rena nodded. "Recent ones. It's . . . I . . ." Her eyes were wet. "I don't know why I do it." Tears moved down her cheeks. "I feel like I have to."

"Have to what?"

"Kill them. Cut them open, cut their guts out." She was crying freely now.

Dr. Kepper put her hand on Rena's shoulder. "Would you like to come to my office, continue our talk there?"

"No." Rena shook her head vigorously. "I just want it to stop! I want the pain to go away."

"What pain, Rena?" the doctor asked gently.

"Inside, in my gut, in my heart."

"What does the pain say?"

"It tortures me."

"Since when?"

7

Rena covered her face with her hands. Her thick black hair fell forward, the ends resting on her shoulders. "Since she died. Pat. My . . . friend." Rena looked into Dr. Kepper's eyes. Concerned eyes. "Do you know about Pat?"

"Yes, Casey told me. Was it after her death that you started killing birds?"

Rena nodded.

Neither woman spoke for a while, then Dr. Kepper said, "Pat was very important to you."

"I despised her." The words were said coldly. Half a minute passed. "She was everything to me. I loved her," Rena said sadly.

"Do you understand it?" Dr. Kepper asked. "The two feelings?"

"Not really."

"Maybe if we talk about it, we'll come to understand it."

Again Rena looked Dr. Kepper directly in the eyes. She hesitated briefly. "Do you really think Casey is phony?"

"No."

"She's not."

"I didn't think so."

"Maybe talking would help."

"It's worth a try."

Rena rose and so did Dr. Kepper. They walked together down the corridor and into Dr. Kepper's office.

CHAPTER TWO

Rena was discharged after eleven days at Ravensedge. Her first night home, Casey brought Chinese food and Rena again tried to teach her how to use chopsticks. Casey ended up using a fork.

Later they sat in the gazebo in Rena's yard. It was a clear, balmy Chicago evening.

"Mary Ellen and Beck are having a party Saturday night," Casey said. "You think you might be up for it? They asked me to be sure to invite you."

Rena tried to imagine herself at a party. She used to enjoy them. "I don't know. I might be. I haven't seen Mary Ellen in ages."

A crackle of firecrackers sounded in the alley, the neighborhood kids using up their leftovers. It was July 6th.

"Most of the women from the coffeehouse collective will be there," Casey said.

"Maybe, Case, I'll see how I feel."

"I'm glad it's working out with Dr. Kepper."

Rena nodded. "So far, so good." She took a drink of iced tea. "We talk about Pat a lot."

Casey shifted her lithe athletic frame on the cushioned lawn chair. "Is it helpful?"

"I don't know yet. Pat and Rebecca. Did I ever tell you about Rebecca?"

"No."

"She was the first," Rena said.

Casey pushed her hat back. "First what? Not lover?" She had taken to wearing a cap lately and Rena told her she looked like the little Dutchboy.

"No, the first woman who had that strange power over me."

"Oh?"

"You know what I mean."

"Like Pat."

"Mm-hm."

Casey nodded. "No, you've never talked about Rebecca."

Rena lit a cigarette and blew a fat cloud over her head. She watched the smoke drift through the slatted roof boards. "I was living with Evie when I met her. You know Evie, the artist."

"Yes, abstract expressionism."

"Evie and I were like peas in a pod. I thought I had found *the one.* You know. But then I met Rebecca." She shook her head. "Two weeks later I moved in with her. It was a very rotten thing to do to Evie. I can't forgive myself and I can't explain it. I just had to be with her, with Rebecca. I had to. I couldn't resist."

"Sounds familiar," Casey said.

Rena nodded. "I know. Only Evie . . . well, she and I never had any more contact after it happened . . . after Rebecca and I got together."

"I guess I'm more resilient." Casey reached and pulled a long weed from the ground. "Or persistent. Of course, our relationship had barely begun when Pat came along. Well, anyway, tell me about Rebecca. What was she like?"

"Like Pat in a lot of ways." Casey nodded.

"Very self-assured, strong . . . kind of egocentric. Arrogant. But very kind and loving too. Sometimes she was almost cruel." Rena crushed out her cigarette in the flower pot she used as an ashtray. "She didn't always treat me real well . . ."

10

"Mm-m."

"But I had great sex with her."

"Oh?" Casey looked very uneasy. "So was that the main attraction? The sex?"

"It was part of it." Rena repositioned herself on the lounge chair, wedging her heels between the webbing. "Until Rebecca . . . with Evie and with women before her . . . with you . . ." She looked tenderly at Casey, "and with men, years ago, I had never . . ."

Casey nodded.

"I can't believe I'm talking about this." Rena pushed her fingers through her thick, shoulder-length hair. "Maybe I can because I already did with Dr. Kepper and it doesn't seem so . . . so weird now, or shameful, or whatever. Anyway, I never had orgasms with anyone until Rebecca. And then, after Rebecca, nobody else until Pat."

Casey nodded again. She hooked her feet around the chair legs. She was wearing hiking boots. "I wonder why," she said. "Do you know?"

"Well, when I talked about it with Dr. Kepper, I ended up connecting it with the fact that Rebecca was so . . . that she was both powerful, you know, like dominating, but also gentle and loving. She was both. The others, you and Evie and the rest, well, they were caring enough and nice — you certainly were — but, like . . . well, *too* nice, in a sense." Rena suddenly felt intensely uncomfortable. "Do you know what I mean?" She looked searchingly at Casey.

"Not exactly," Casey said.

"It's something about needing the person to be a little rough or controlling or something for me to get . . ."

"Turned on?"

"Yes. I mean really turned on. Otherwise, I'd enjoy making love, but . . ." Rena looked into her friend's eyes. "I'm sorry, Casey, I know . . ."

"It's OK. Go on."

"It would be tender and soft and equal and I never came."

Casey nodded. "I never believed it didn't matter. It always matters. I thought maybe I . . ."

"No, it wasn't anything you —"

"So, with you and Rebecca, it wasn't equal."

11

"No."

"Or you and Pat."

"Right. I got so turned on with Pat. I mean, all she'd have to say was, 'Come here, woman', and I'd get all wobbly and wet."

Casey chuckled. "M-m. I'm not sure, Rena, but are you saying your relationships with Rebecca and with Pat were kind of S and M-ish?"

Rena laughed. "Oh God, serious political incorrectness! I hope not, Casey. I hadn't ever thought of it that way. I mean, we didn't use handcuffs or whips or anything like that. They never caused me any physical pain."

"But, they topped you psychologically?"

"I guess you could put it that way."

"And that turned you on."

"Mm-hm. I have no idea why. I think I need to know. Dr. Kepper and I are working on it, but we have no answers yet. It feels like we're making progress, though, like something's happening. We'll see where it goes." Rena drank the last of her tea. She stretched her arms over her head, then smiled warmly at her friend. "So how's your aerobics class going these days? You still jumping around like a madwoman with the other health nuts?"

They talked until the sun set and the yard was very dark, but did not mention Pat again nor anything related to Rena's troubles.

A few days later, Rena went for her first outpatient visit to Dr. Terri Kepper. They met in a small office in a building next to the hospital.

"How have things been?" the psychologist began.

"Not bad," Rena said. She looked around the room. "This office is much nicer than the one at the hospital. I can't tell you how glad I am to be out of there." She lit a cigarette. "Never again," she said. "You don't mind if I smoke in here, do you?"

"I don't mind. And does it feel good to be back home?"

"Yes." Rena looked out the window into the building next door. She could see a row of women typing. "I still feel kind of depressed but not nearly as bad as it was. I've even been looking over some

12

materials for next semester. I'll be co-teaching a new course, *Women and Society.*"

The doctor nodded. "Any bird problems?"

"I've been avoiding them — birds, I mean. I don't go into the yard alone. I don't trust myself."

"Not yet. Where would you like to begin today?"

Rena settled in the chair. Dr. Kepper seemed perceptive and concerned, she thought. She liked her. "That barbecue," she began, "you know, the day she died. I've been thinking about it. I didn't want to go." She was not looking at the psychologist now. "I couldn't just tell her, though. I guess I was afraid." She shook her head. "She could get so damned nasty. She'd been a bitch to me the night before. Well, not really bitchy, but standoffish and . . . Anyway, I was angry at her. I didn't want to go with her to that stupid suburban barbecue party." Rena stared at her hands. "That's why I was late."

"I see."

"I guess it seemed like a safe way to express my anger. I wanted to hurt her, but not . . ." She shook her head, her eyes were wet. "I thought it was safe, but it wasn't. I'm sure it pissed her off when I didn't show up and when she gets angry, she's so fucking aggressive. I bet she drove recklessly. I bet that's why it happened."

"That it was your fault in a sense?" the psychologist said gently.

Rena's hand covered her face. Dr. Kepper waited.

"I should have called, at least. It was selfish. She expected me home. I should have been there."

They worked on Rena's guilt for the rest of that session. Rena cried much of the time and kept blocking. "There's evil in me," she said at one point, and then, shaking, her mind blank, could not go on.

She arrived ten minutes late for the next session. "I saw a bird, a pigeon, on the way here. That's why I'm late. I watched it for a long time. I wanted to grab it."

"But you didn't."

"I tried. It flew away. I need my trap."

"How do you feel when you catch them?"

13

Rena's eyes gleamed. "Mm-m. I feel excited. Excited but also kind of cold and calculating. And I feel . . . eager. When I'm about to get one, I can't wait to cut it open."

Dr. Kepper nodded.

"Oh, God, isn't that disgusting! You must think I'm . . ."

"Let's try not to judge it," the psychologist said. "Let's work on understanding it, OK?" She waited a moment. "I'd like you to cut open a bird now, Rena, in your imagination. Imagine you just caught one and you knocked it out with the chloroform. Tell me exactly what you're feeling and what you do next."

Rena's breathing immediately changed, grew audible and labored as she pictured herself making the first incision. "I feel high," she said, "and at the same time like I'm in a trance, sort of. And I feel like I have to do it. I want to more than anything, even though it's sick and disgusting."

"Does it feel that way at the time? Disgusting?"

"No. I'm not aware of that until after. When I'm doing it . . ."

"Do it now."

Rena paused a moment. She closed her eyes. "I take the scalpel and make a deep incision."

"How are you feeling?"

"Eager. I can't wait to get inside."

"Why is that?"

"Why? I don't know. I have to see what's in there. There's something inside that I have to see."

"Inside the bird."

"Yes. I have to see it."

"All right, you've cut it open, what are you doing next?"

"I take out the parts, all the different organs. I'm cutting them in pieces." Rena's eyes were still closed, a slight smile on her lips.

"Why are you cutting them?"

"I don't know. I have to . . . to look."

"Look at what?"

"The insides."

"Why?"

Rena shook her head.

"OK, what happens then? What are you doing now?"

"Cutting and cutting and looking, placing each piece on the plate, cutting and looking." Her face fell. "But there's nothing . . ."

"Nothing?"

"It . . . it . . . I don't know. I cut up everything and then . . . and now I feel awful. I'm disappointed. Something's wrong. Oh God, look at my hands. The blood. This is disgusting. It's sick. Evil. What's the matter with me?" She held her hands away from her.

"You're feeling disgusted now?"

"Yes."

"Why?"

"Why? God, look what I did! I killed a poor bird. It's sick. It's stupid. Why did I do it?" She was crying. "I must be crazy."

"Remember the tablecloth, Rena?" Dr. Kepper said calmly. "The story I told you." She waited for Rena to look at her. "There's a reason you kill the birds, the way you search among the viscera. It means something very important to you. This was a good start."

Slumped in her chair, Rena sobbed softly.

"We'll get to it," the psychologist said.

At the next session, Rena talked of Pat again. "At times, I used to feel very safe when I was with her, but at other times I'd feel terrible, real uncomfortable, like she was dangerous, hurtful to me."

"*Was* she hurtful?"

"Yes."

Dr. Kepper waited.

"She made fun of me. A kind of teasing that I just hated. I asked her to stop. Many times. She'd say she was just playing with me, that I was too sensitive."

"It hurt, the things she'd say."

"Yes. She'd pick on the way I moved, on how I always used to wear this certain scarf around my neck, or the fact that I scrubbed the floors so much. Anything. She'd always have a smart-ass crack to make. It wasn't funny to me." Rena was crying.

"You've been teased before, haven't you?"

She continued crying.

"Can you talk about it?"

Rena shook her head. A long time went by. "Other times, she was very kind and loving."

15

"That's when you felt safe?"

"Yes ... and after sex."

"You felt safe then too."

"Yes. Before ... before we actually started to make love ... it was always the same, she'd always be in her ... I don't know, her *macho* place, you know, acting bossy and domineering. It would always start that way."

"How did you feel when she acted that way?"

"Part of me didn't like it at all. It was ridiculous, in one sense, and then it would be demeaning too, the way it went. But ... I know ... in some way ... for some reason ..."

"It aroused you."

"Yes." She looked at the psychologist. She saw openness, concern. "Very much. I'd feel all tingly and ... I don't know, I'd feel like ... like looking up to her, like she was powerful and large and I ... I felt *adoring* towards her."

"I see. And that would happen before you had sex."

"Yes. She'd ... she'd say something like, 'Take your shirt off, woman, I want to look at you.' It would often begin that way. I'd get a rush and ... and I couldn't resist. I didn't want to. I'd do what she said. I'd be so turned on, just by an interaction like that. I'd feel overpowered and overwhelmed by her. I'd do whatever she'd tell me to do."

"You got pleasure from doing what she said."

"Yes."

"From obeying her."

"Yes, I did. Isn't that strange? I felt sexually turned on and ... and very wound up and ... I don't know, just full of feelings."

"Very exciting feelings."

"Yes."

"And what would she tell you to do?"

"Oh, different things. Like, 'Go up and lie on the bed now with all your clothes off. Spread your legs and stay that way until I come up.'"

"Mm-hm."

"I'd do it. I loved it. And I'd wait there for her, excited ... just all ... like full of ... these feelings ... like anticipation ... and like edginess, but a good kind of edginess. Sometimes she'd make me wait a long time. It would grow, the tension, excitement. When I heard her coming, I'd . . . I'd writhe with delight, and . . . I'd be so excited, so eager."

"Mm-hm."

"Then she'd come into the bedroom and stand over me for a while, just looking." Rena's breath was audible. "She'd make love to me. Very forcefully, possessively. It was . . . it was great!"

"And you'd be orgasmic then."

"Oh yes!" Rena took a deep breath and sighed.

Neither woman spoke for a while. Rena stared blankly. Dr. Kepper watched her, frowning pensively.

"What about other people who've had power over you?" the psychologist asked.

Rena shook her head. "Just Rebecca. She was the only other one."

"I mean like parents, teachers, bosses . . ."

"Oh, people who've had authority over me? What about them? What do you mean?"

"Does anything stand out about any of them? Early in your life, especially."

Rena thought. "No, not really. I don't remember anything unusual about any of them. There was my mom, of course. My grandma. Aunts. Teachers in grade school. No, nothing stands out."

"What about your father?"

The muscles around Rena's mouth and eyes tightened. "My father?"

"Mm-hm. What memories do you have about him?"

Rena folded her arms. Her whole body was tight. "I don't. I never knew him."

Dr. Kepper looked puzzled. "I thought you said he died when you were ten."

"I said that's what they say. That's what my mother says. I have no memory of him."

"Hm-m. You don't remember him at all?"

Rena shook her head and stared at the arm of the chair.

"You lived with him, didn't you? In Greece. Your parents weren't separated?"

"That's what they say."

"And when you were ten, he died."

Rena said nothing.

"How did he die?"

Rena winced. Her heart was pounding. She answered as if feeling nothing. "A hunting accident. He and my uncle, on the same day. I have no memory of it."

"You were ten at the time."

"I guess." Rena twisted on her chair. She couldn't seem to find a comfortable position. Her hands were cold, palms clammy wet.

"It upsets you to think about him," the psychologist said.

"There's nothing to think about!" Rena said sharply.

A long silence followed. Rena cried softly. At last she spoke. "There's a gaping hole in my life. The first twelve years . . . all I have is a few scraps of memories. I sometimes think that I . . . that I never had a childhood, that my life started when I left Greece."

Dr. Kepper nodded again. "Well, perhaps we can bring the memories back, Rena."

Tears slipped in glistening lines down Rena's cheeks.

"But slowly," Dr. Kepper said. "There's no need to rush it. It's clearly very frightening to you. But maybe bit by bit the memories will come and then we'll understand about the birds and the other things, about your pleasure in being dominated, about your depression."

Rena nodded, but part of her knew that more than anything she didn't want those memories to come. She desperately did not want to remember and she had no idea why.

She cancelled her next session saying she had the flu. She missed the next two sessions as well and when she finally did return, she barely spoke. She felt afraid of Terri Kepper, afraid of their talk, afraid of something evil in herself that she would rather die than face. She missed the next session. She didn't answer the phone when Dr. Kepper called. She didn't go to the following session either. She sat alone at home, going nowhere, doing little, feeling barely alive.

CHAPTER THREE

Casey came to Rena's house frequently. She was growing more and more alarmed and discouraged by Rena's continued deterioration. "Maybe you should go back to the hospital," she suggested one hot, steamy morning. It was early August.

"No way," Rena snapped. "Not a chance."

They were at Rena's kitchen table. Rena had barely touched the sweet roll Casey brought her. On the wall next to the table Casey noticed a couple of dried red-brown spots. She said nothing.

After a few more attempts at conversation, Rena sighed. "I've got a headache," she said. "I need to lie down now."

Casey stood. "All right. I'll be back in a couple of days. Call me if you feel like it. Any time, Rena, OK?"

"Thanks, Casey." Her voice was flat, lifeless.

Rena closed the door behind her friend with a sigh of relief and went back upstairs to bed. The crying had stopped, but the sadness was becoming intolerable. Things will never improve, she thought. Nothing in my life has any value. I have nothing to look forward to and I can do nothing about it.

She felt hopelessly dejected, inadequate, confused. She didn't want to remember the past, felt absolute terror at the prospect, and didn't know why. She felt like a complete failure as a person and didn't know why. She would run her accomplishments over in her mind but they meant nothing. How minuscule they seemed compared . . . compared to what?

The feeling was guilt, terrible guilt, but Rena could not identify its source. She hated herself — more, it seemed, each miserable day. She had lost all interest in activities and in people. Even Casey's visits were a strain. She knew her friend meant well but she wished she'd accept that nothing could help. She had considered killing herself. It seemed the only thing stopping her was the birds. She had caught two already today and three the day before.

Casey came again the following Tuesday. "Dr. Kepper's been trying to reach you, Rena. I wish you'd answer your phone."

"I don't want to talk to her."

They were at the kitchen table again. Rena had on an old pair of blue jeans and a wrinkled T-shirt. It looked to Casey as if she hadn't combed her hair that day. "It's no use," she said. "It doesn't matter, Casey, don't you see that?" She sighed deeply. "I wish you'd just leave me alone."

Casey couldn't help looking hurt. Rena did not see it.

Both were silent, Casey wondering what to do next, Rena apparently lost in some sad private place.

"Would you like some coffee?" Rena said at last. She went to the stove.

"You can't just stay in this house every day and do nothing and see no one." Casey was looking at the wall. The spots she'd noticed the other day were gone. She turned to Rena. "Maybe you can afford to take the summer off from work but what about when fall comes? You have classes to teach, your research project to work on. You have to go on with your life."

"Do you want coffee or not?" Rena barked.

"Ah, shit! You're a mess, Spiros! A quitter! Copping out like this. It makes me sick." Casey did feel sick then. She wanted to bite her tongue. She went to her friend's side, put her hand on her shoulder. "I'm sorry."

her tongue. She went to her friend's side, put her hand on her shoulder. "I'm sorry."

"It's OK," Rena said flatly. "I hate me too."

Casey let that pass. "Will you do me a favor?" Her hand was still on Rena's shoulder and Rena did not try to move away. "Will you come with me to De Nova Saturday? Remember how many times you said you wanted to go and then something would always come up with Pat?" Casey feared it was a mistake to mention Pat but she went on. "Let's go this weekend. It would mean a lot to me. And you sure as hell could use a change of scene. Will you come?"

At least ten times before Casey had tried to persuade her. She feared this time Rena would throw her out and refuse to talk with her anymore. Instead Rena just shrugged.

"It'll be good for you," Casey said hopefully. "It's peaceful there, and beautiful. There's a big river and a pond. Lots of hills, flowers, bir . . . the women would be happy to have you." Casey was watching Rena's reactions closely. "But they won't bother you," she added quickly. "They'll leave you alone if you want. You can stay in one of the guest houses with me. They're real cute little cabins, real rustic. What do you say, will you come?"

Rena shrugged again. "I guess," she said.

The eight hundred acres of rich Wisconsin land were owned and worked collectively by about thirty women. The number varied as women came and went. They called it De Nova. A dozen buildings stood on the land — two houses, large and old, in various stages of renovation; five split-log cabins, all new, and two A-frames; a dormitory; two lavender barns. Grain, corn, and soybeans grew in the fields, rows of fruit trees in the orchards. The barns housed horses, milk cows, fowl. Beyond the fields stretched a beautiful forest cut by a winding river.

When Rena and Casey arrived, the sky which had been cloudy all morning was beginning to clear. They parked in the gravel lot and walked the short path to the *Big House* to check in. A group sat around the huge kitchen table. Rena struggled through the introductions, forcing a stiff cordiality. The women invited them to

21

sit. Rena was about to decline when her eyes suddenly widened and her jaw dropped.

The woman who strode through the door was tall — very tall it seemed to Rena. She had broad shoulders, a serious, almost stern face, and hypnotic gray eyes. She entered the room as if she owned it and everyone in it.

"Hi Lou, good to see you," Casey said. "I'd like you to meet a good friend of mine, Rena Spiros. Rena, this is Lou Bonnig."

Lou stretched out her hand. Rena was spellbound. She felt her face redden. Her arm lifted for the handshake. Lou's hand was strong and powerful.

"Welcome to De Nova," Lou said.

Rena remained standing, motionless, her eyes following Lou Bonnig's movements as she took a chair at the head of the table. Rena's breathing was suspended.

"Have a seat," someone said.

Mechanically Rena lowered herself into a chair. She was barely aware that anyone had spoken to her or that she had sat. Conversation resumed, Rena remaining transfixed, staring wide-eyed at Lou.

"You OK?" Casey asked softly.

"Huh? Oh, yeah." Rena made herself break the stare and tried to calm her heart.

". . . going through the photos again," Lou was saying. "It's a shame to leave them sitting around in a box."

"We should do something creative with them," a robust Asian woman said. "Make some kind of album."

Several women laughed.

"I agree," Lou said. "They're laughing, Janet, because that suggestion has been made many times."

"We agreed last year and the year before that and maybe the year before that too," a large red-headed woman said. "The pile of pictures keeps growing. The plan is to take some old prints and calendar art and integrate the pictures of people into them somehow."

"I've seen it done," Casey said. "It makes a great album. A lot better than just rows of photos."

"But we haven't been able to get any volunteers to do it," Lou said, looking at Janet.

Janet shrugged. "I'm not very artistic."

Lou's understanding smile sent a tingle along Rena's spine. She wanted that smile to fall on her. "I could take a crack at it," she said. Her voice was hoarse. She was looking directly at Lou who returned the gaze. "I'd like to try," Rena said more softly.

"Wonderful," Lou said.

Casey stared at Rena.

Rena's eyes remained on Lou. She thought her face strikingly handsome, especially now with the smile.

"Let me know when," Lou continued, "and I'll go over the photos with you. Help you sort them out, get rid of the chaff."

Rena nodded excitedly. She could picture them sitting side by side. She wanted to please Lou, to do whatever it might be that she'd want Rena to do.

Frowning, Casey continued watching her friend.

"So? When?" Lou persisted.

"Whenever you say," Rena replied softly.

"This evening then. I'm coming back after dinner for some poker. We can do it before the game, around seven. How's that?"

"Fine."

Casey noticed the glow in Rena's cheeks, and thought she looked better than she had in many weeks.

Later, at their cabin, Casey watched Rena carefully groom herself. "You seem rather taken with Lou."

Rena didn't answer right away. "Yes, she seems . . . interesting."

"Hm-m."

"Does my hair look all right?"

"It looks fine," Casey said crisply. She took her jacket from the door hook. "I'll see you over there."

Lou had not yet arrived when Rena got to the *Big House*. She sat restlessly at the window of the large, sparsely-furnished living room while a number of other women, including Casey, talked in the kitchen. At ten after seven Rena saw her coming up the path. Her heart began to pound. She fluffed up her hair and, once again, straightened the collar of her shirt. She could hear Lou greeting the women in the kitchen. She waited breathlessly.

"There you are." The voice was deep and rich.

Rena squirmed. "Yes . . . uh, I've been waiting for you." She looked around the room. "Where are the pictures? I . . . uh . . ."

"You make a rather striking picture yourself."

Rena hoped she didn't blush. Pat had made her blush more than once and Rebecca had too. "Oh, thanks, uh . . . should we get started?"

Lou was standing quite near her. She wore a loose flowing cotton blouse and black cotton pants. She was quite tall, five-nine, at least, and moved with swift sureness. Rena watched as she went to a large cardboard box on the sideboard.

"Here they are, hundreds of them. It'll be a challenge." Lou carried the box to the coffee table in front of the well-used leather couch. "Come on over here."

Rena slid onto the couch next to Lou.

"You live in Chicago?" Lou asked, scrutinizing her.

"Yes."

"Have you known Casey long?"

"A couple of years."

"Are you and she lovers?"

Rena was taken aback. "Lovers?" She felt her cheeks reddening.

Lou laughed a hearty laugh. "None of my business, huh? I'm insatiably curious about who does what with whom and why. Character trait. Can't seem to break it."

"We're not lovers," Rena said. She was working furiously to calm herself and have a normal conversation. "Do you live here, at De Nova?"

"Next door." Lou stretched her arm out along the back of the couch. Her hand rested very near to Rena's neck. "But I spend a fair amount of time here. De Nova's quite a place. Do you know our history/herstory?"

"No, not really. Casey told me a few things." Rena brushed her hair back nervously.

24

"You're very pretty, Rena, do you know that? You have kind of an exotic look." Lou squinted. "Wild inside, but subdued for some reason. Definitely exotic. What do you do in Chicago?"

"Do?" Rena tried to make sense of the simple question. Her madly rushing blood seemed to be skipping her brain. "Oh, do. Yes, I, uh, teach. I'm a teacher. Sociology. At a Junior College." She was operating on automatic now. "And I've been doing some research. Studying formerly rural women, women who relocate to urban areas and . . . well, I was . . . I suppose I will again. I've been taking it easy lately."

"I see. I'd like to hear more, but not now. I want to get you going on the album before the game starts." She scooped a pile of photos from the box and spread them on the table.

Rena tried to focus on Lou's comments about the people and scenes in the pictures, but was repeatedly distracted by the way Lou's mouth moved as she formed words and how her gray eyes sparkled.

A half hour later, when the poker crowd gathered around the dining room table, Lou joined them and Rena stayed with the photos, trying to match pictures of women in various poses and attire to the background scenes from the calendars Lou had given her. She got involved in the project, yet not for a moment did she lose awareness of Lou in the next room. From time to time, she could make out her deep voice among the others.

Casey was in the game, declaring twenty dollars her absolute limit.

"Now don't be hasty," Marta said, scooping in a pile of coins and several bills. "Everything I win over a certain amount goes to the fund."

Sharon laughed. "Right. Would you like to tell us what the *certain amount* is?"

Marta smiled. "I haven't decided yet."

"What fund?" Casey asked.

"For the farm. The mortgage payment and equipment loans. Didn't you hear what's happening?"

"No." Casey's sweet full face darkened.

25

"We got so little for the crops last year that we're having a hell of a time raising the money for our loans."

"Oh, you're kidding." Casey was alarmed. "De Nova is the best thing that's happened in the Midwest for years," she said. "What will happen if you can't meet the payments?"

"They'll repossess. The fuckers," Marta said. "We'll lose this place. Lou already put up ten thousand. We owe her that. We're still fifty thousand short."

"Shit. When's it due?" Casey folded, her second pair hadn't come in.

"Three months. We're having another fund raiser next weekend. In Madison. You should come. There's going to be some dynamite music. Lou's emceeing the show."

Casey dealt the next hand.

"*Hot Flash* from Chicago is going to play," Lou said, looking over her cards. "They're very amusing. And we got a couple of local singers, and a comic. Kate Clinton she's not, but you won't fall asleep and we're only giving her twenty minutes. I'll bet fifty cents. There'll be a dance afterwards."

"Sounds good." Casey gave each player another card. "I'll bet a dollar," she said to Marta who had two aces showing, "if you tell me what your cutoff point is." It had become a tradition at De Nova to tease Marta about her frugality.

Marta gave the question serious consideration. "Five bucks," she said at last. "That'll cover the gas I used yesterday. Anything I win over five dollars goes to the fund."

"All right! Same here," Sharon echoed. "How about the rest of you?"

Everyone around the table nodded. De Nova was home for some of them, a necessary re-fueling place for others.

"That doesn't include you, of course, Lou," Sharon said. "Lou practically gave us this place, you know." She directed her words to Marta.

"It includes me," Lou said.

"We'll have to have fund raisers for you pretty soon."

"I'm doing all right. I'll see your dollar, Casey."

"Lou's got plenty of everything," a very butch-looking woman said. It was the first time she'd spoken since the game began.

"Cool it, Kate," Janet said.

They played until well after midnight. Marta ended up the big winner, netting over thirty dollars. She didn't hide her dismay at her own generosity as she handed $25.85 over to Carolyn who was that year's treasurer.

When Lou entered the living room, Rena felt the atmosphere change immediately, as if the air molecules suddenly came alive. "How's it going?" Lou asked, leaning over her.

Rena's body temperature rose. She showed Lou the pages she had completed, three of them. Lou examined them closely for a long time without speaking. Rena waited for her reaction, feeling anxious anticipation.

"You're good," Lou said finally. She was looking directly into Rena's dark eyes, not smiling.

Rena felt fluttering sensations from her neck downward over her breasts to her belly. She broke the eye contact. "There's still a lot to do. It . . . it's fun, I'm enjoying it."

"Good." Lou was still standing very close to her, close enough for Rena to feel her body heat. "I'd like you to come to my place tomorrow. You and Casey. Around two. All right?"

Rena tried to sound casual. "Yes, I'd like to. I'm sure Casey would too." She kept her eyes on the pictures. After a breathless moment, she felt the touch of Lou's hand on her shoulder and heard the caressing words as in a dream.

"Good night then, Rena. See you tomorrow."

CHAPTER FOUR

The next afternoon, Casey and Marta were still tuning up Casey's car when it was time to leave for Lou's. Marta said she'd finish it up by herself, for a fee, and laughed. Casey borrowed a jeep to get them to Lou's.

The house was large and rustic, set far in, away from the road, surrounded by giant old trees and shrubs. Rena's excitement escalated as she and Casey approached the door. There was a note tacked to it. *Rena and Casey, I had to leave to help some neighbors with a stalled sump pump. Come in, get comfortable, sit, drink, explore the place. Be back ASAP. Lou.* Rena felt both disappointment and relief. As much as she wished to see Lou again the prospect made her very nervous.

"Quite a place, don't you think?" Casey said. They were standing in the center of the huge living room. She had been here a number of times before. "I love the spiral staircase."

Up to her bedroom, Rena thought.

They gave themselves a tour. Casey commented on the textured unpainted woods, the beamed ceilings and light and open

28

atmosphere, but Rena's enjoyment was coming from being in the home where *she* lived, seeing the objects *she* touched, the furniture *she* used.

They took their time looking around the house. Casey was very aware of how intrigued Rena was. They went out into the immense yard. Beyond the yard was the farm where they could see grazing animals and, beyond that, fields and orchards. Casey loved the garden. She commented on the variety of flowers and especially all the succulents. "There are four or five different types of jade," she told Rena, pointing them out. "Look how she did the annuals, some of them separated by color and then those over there, all mixed together like rainbows." Casey continued the exploration on her own when she saw that Rena had wandered away.

As Lou pulled into the driveway, she could hear the disturbed squawking of her chickens and geese. She went toward the coop. The door was slightly ajar. When she entered she was greeted by airborne feathers and the sight of blood and dead fowl. In the center of the carnage sat Rena Spiros, absorbed in what she was doing, oblivious to Lou's arrival.

Lou watched as Rena sliced through a section of goose tissue. The remains of a dissected chicken lay in a bloody pile next to her.

"Playing doctor or planning a big dinner?" Lou asked coolly.

Rena's head lifted slowly. Her eyes were glazed. She appeared not to recognize Lou.

"Hey, what's going on, girl?" Lou took a few steps toward her.

Rena jumped to her feet, the heavy carcass tumbling from her lap and plopping grotesquely onto the dirt floor with an oozy thud. Her eyes were strange. She held the paring knife tightly, staring hatefully at Lou. After a few seconds she blinked and let the knife fall from her hand. It landed next to the chicken's head.

"Rena! Oh, God!" Casey stood in the doorway.

Rena's lip quivered. Casey ran to her side, began talking to her gently, soothingly. Rena's red-splattered chest moved with her jerky breathing as she leaned, sagging, against a post.

29

"... get you back home ... to ... to where you can be taken care of and ... Are you OK now? Are you feeling better?" Casey turned to Lou. "She's been going through a bad time in her life. I thought being in the country would help. Oh shit. I'm sorry about the ... I'm sorry. I'll get her out of here." Casey began leading Rena away.

"Hold on." Lou looked closely at Rena whose head was hanging loosely. "Are you in touch? Can you speak?"

Rena shook her head slowly, not looking at either of them. "I'll go away." Her voice was barely audible.

"Not yet you won't."

"We'll pay for the birds," Casey said.

"I'd rather have an explanation." Lou gestured toward the door. "Take her in the house, will you, Casey? Get her cleaned up, and we'll talk."

"All right." Casey's arm was around Rena.

"My shirts will fit her, the pants will be a bit long and baggy, I'm afraid."

"Thanks, Lou," Casey said.

The trio made their way to the house. Casey got Rena to the john, laid out the clothes Lou brought, then joined Lou in the kitchen.

They were silent while Lou got the glasses and beers. After taking a long swallow, Lou looked at Casey across the table, waiting for her to speak.

"She's been a mess since her lover got killed in a car crash. That was a couple of months ago. Before that she was fine. She was her normal self — fun to be with, involved in all kinds of things, doing well in her career. Then after the accident ... ever since then she's been withdrawn, isolates herself. She stopped going to work." Casey wrapped her hand around her beer bottle. "Occasionally she kills birds."

"So this wasn't the first time."

"She doesn't know why she does it. She was hospitalized for a while. Got some therapy. It seemed to be helping but then she quit. She really deteriorated after that. I thought coming to the farm might help."

"Why'd she quit therapy?"

Casey rubbed her temples. "The most I could get out of her was that the therapist wanted her to remember some childhood stuff she'd forgotten and she didn't want to. She wouldn't go back."

"She needs to."

"I know."

"Is she psychotic?"

Casey looked at Lou with disgust. "I don't know," she said angrily. "I hate words like that. This is Rena we're talking about, my friend..."

"Your friend who butchers birds for no apparent reason. That's pretty crazy behavior."

Casey turned and looked toward the bathroom in the hall. "We're leaving. You don't have to worry —"

"Tell me more about her."

Casey raised her eyes. "Morbid curiosity?"

Lou let the comment pass. "What about this lover of hers who got killed? That's what set it all off, right? Tell me about her."

Casey hesitated, but then found herself talking, perhaps needing to. She told Lou her perceptions of the relationship between Rena and Pat and also what she had learned recently about the connection between Pat's dominating style and Rena's sexuality.

"That's very interesting," Lou said. She was looking pensively across the room.

Casey's arm was resting on the table, her hand tightly clenched. "I thought she had stopped that bird stuff. It's really...creepy." She began to cry. "I'm afraid she *is* crazy. I'm afraid for her ... what's going to happen. She's such a wonderful person ... so ..." She grabbed a paper napkin from the polished wooden holder and dabbed at her eyes. "She's not taking care of herself. She won't see any of her friends. She lies to her family. They have no idea what's really going on. She ... I think she needs to be in the hospital."

"Possibly. You say it seemed to help last time?"

"Yes. But she refuses to go back." Casey blew her nose vigorously. "Every time I've mentioned it, she absolutely refuses, gets pissed at me, won't talk about it."

"Well, if she won't go voluntarily ..."

Casey grimaced. "Oh God, don't you hate that idea?"

31

"Commitment? Yes, in a general way, I do." Lou handed Casey another napkin. "But in some instances, it's the only option. Making judgments for someone who isn't in a position to make them for herself."

"I don't know if I agree with that," Casey said. "Maybe." She wiped her eyes. "I just don't know. I don't know what to do."

"Are you in love with her?" Lou asked.

Casey looked down the hall. "That's not what's important," she said. A minute later she excused herself to go check on Rena.

She returned immediately. "She's gone."

"Shit! Let's go." Lou was on her feet. "Did she take the jeep?"

The jeep was still there in the driveway alongside Lou's maroon Volvo. They went straight to the chicken coop. There was no sign of her.

"You check the road back to De Nova, I'll try the woods." Lou didn't wait for a response but headed immediately with her long strides towards her fields, then into the woods.

She walked determinedly. One main path led to the river and a few smaller ones crisscrossed the woods. She took the main trail, stopping at each intersection to watch and listen. At the top of a small hill she looked in each direction. The river glistened in the sunlight to the east; no sign of her there. South was the little pond, surrounded by thick growth; she intended to clear that area some day and made the peaceful little pool more accessible. She did not see Rena in that direction. She headed toward the river then took the narrow uphill path northward toward the meadow. Rena was not there. Lou continued through the meadow to the thick clump of old oaks and maples surrounding the rocks where she often came to read or just to think. As she neared the rocks, she heard something. She tilted her ear toward the sound. She continued quietly, climbing the lower rocks then upward almost to the summit. Again she heard the sounds of movements in the brush. When she reached the top of the rocks she had a clear view of the scene below.

Rena stood beneath the best oak in the woods, where Lou had made a swing for her niece several years before; only the ropes remained. Rena had a piece in her hands, ten or twelve feet long. Lou moved forward, continuing to watch as Rena fingered the rope then tossed one end over the thick branch several feet above her head. A noose hung ominously from the stately old tree in whose shade Lou had spent many pleasant hours.

Lou started down, then stopped and continued watching, eyes glued on Rena, fascinated.

Rena had pulled several rocks under the hanging rope and was adding a log to the pile. She climbed atop the mound. Balancing herself on the makeshift platform, she held the loop of rope next to her head. Lou moved closer. Rena climbed down again. Lou was within six yards of her. Rena stared at the hanging, swaying rope. Lou leaned against a boulder and continued observing. Rena's hands opened and closed at her sides, then slowly once again, she mounted the platform.

"All right, that's enough!" Lou was still leaning solidly against the huge rock.

Rena turned sharply, almost slipping from the platform; she grabbed the rope for balance. "Leave me alone!"

"No." Lou's voice was calm.

"It doesn't concern you."

"On the contrary."

"It's my choice." Rena held onto the noose with both hands. It swayed inches from her head.

"You're not in any shape to be making such a choice," Lou said gently, somewhat patronizingly. "Come down from there."

Rena seemed uncertain.

"Come on. Now." It was clearly an order.

"My life is over, don't you understand? The evil . . . disgusting . . ." She was shaking. "Let me die. I have no reason to live. I need to be dead."

"I'm not going to let you kill yourself."

Rena let go of the rope but remained balanced atop the logs. "I'm not going to the hospital."

"You need help. That's one place to get it."

Rena shook her head. "I don't want help. I want it to stop. I want to die."

"Get over here."

Rena felt the unbidden rush. She climbed down from the platform.

"Sit here," Lou ordered.

Rena sat on the smooth flat rock, not looking at Lou. "I won't go to the hospital. If you force me then I swear I'll kill myself. I'll find a way. I'm done."

Lou took hold of Rena's chin, slowly pulling her face up. "You're not done at all, my self-destructive friend." She was looking into Rena's frantic black eyes. She smiled matter-of-factly. "You have a lot to do yet."

Rena shook her head, feeling the warm-cool fingers against her cheeks.

Lou let go of her. "But I think I'll let you do it here, not at a hospital."

"What do you mean?" Lou seemed toweringly tall.

"You're going to stay here awhile, at my place."

"Stay here?" Rena was breathing heavily through her mouth. Several seconds went by. "You can't make me do that," she said weakly.

"Yes I can." Lou pulled a pack of cigarettes from her pocket. "I'm not going to let you kill yourself," she said, striking a match, "so that leaves you two choices. One, stay on at my home with me. Two . . ." she took a deep drag, ". . . be committed to the loony bin."

Rena's head was whirling. "Why don't you just leave me alone?"

"Two choices."

Rena stood. She started forward as if to leave.

Lou grabbed her arm. "Uh-uh," she said. "You aren't going anywhere."

Rena felt her bones melting. She couldn't speak.

"Sit."

She sat again on the rock near Lou's feet.

"You like it when I tell you what to do, don't you?"

Rena said nothing.

"Answer."

"No. Yes. Maybe I do. I don't know."

"I believe I know just what you need, Rena." She chuckled.

Rena did not respond.

"Any idea what makes you cut up the birds?"

Rena's breath came in heaves. She shook her head.

"We'll find out," Lou said.

But Rena did not hear. She was distracted by the powerful closeness of Lou's body. The fabric of Lou's cotton pants was stretched taut over her leg muscles and Rena stared, fighting her impulse to stroke the leg and rest her head on it.

"You're going to stay with me and do as I say."

Rena sat up straighter, feeling torn. "Why?" she asked.

Lou hesitated a moment, smiling. "To free you," she said. She laughed. "You may consider yourself dead, if you wish. In a sense you are. Had I not found you, you'd be literally dead right now, wouldn't you?" Lou leaned toward her. "I'm taking charge of what's left of you."

Rena eyed her suspiciously. "Why do you want to get involved? What's in it for you?"

Lou laughed heartily. "That's something else to figure out," she said. "We have a great deal to do, you and I. I assume you've made your choice."

"What do you mean?"

"That what's left of you is choosing me rather than the mental hospital."

"I didn't say that. I . . ."

"All right. Let's go find Casey. I'll go along to Chicago to give my testimony for the commitment. I'll bring the rope for evidence."

Rena edged away, her back flush against the boulder. She felt the coldness of the rock along her spine. "No, I won't —"

"Then you stay with me and do as I say."

"I think *you're* nuts," Rena spat.

Lou laughed. "I'm going to have to watch you pretty closely for a while. Until I'm convinced you're not going to try something like this hanging stunt again. I have an investment in you now. So, are you staying or are we off to Chicago and the white coats?"

Rena looked into Lou's powerful gray eyes, then away. "I guess I'll stay."

CHAPTER FIVE

Casey opposed the plan. Rena rocked back and forth in the rocking chair. "I choose to stay," she repeated to every plea and argument Casey made.

Casey turned to Lou. "You have her in your power." Her usually soft green eyes were cold and hard. "I don't think you really give a damn about her welfare."

Footsteps sounded on the back porch.

"That's Darla and Trish," Lou said. "Come on in! The door's open."

Lou introduced everybody. The women nodded to one another, Casey remaining protectively at Rena's side.

"They're going to be staying upstairs with you, Rena," Lou said. "Your room needs a little work. I want you to go with them now and help them with it."

"What do you mean?" Casey demanded. "What's happening here?"

"Go on, Rena."

Rena accompanied the two blue jean-clad women up the curved staircase. Casey paced the room.

"Sit down, Casey. I'll explain."

Casey sat on the arm of the sofa. "Who are those women?"

"They're going to watch over Rena, protect her." Lou sat across from Casey. "Until I'm satisfied she won't hurt herself."

"You can't take on that responsibility."

"It's a big one."

"I don't like it. I don't like the whole thing. That power you have over her . . . it's . . . I'm not going to let you exploit her."

"You care about her, right? In love with her, maybe."

Casey breathed loudly through flared nostrils.

"I don't suppose you can have much of a relationship with her the shape she's in," Lou said.

"You know, I always liked you," Casey spat. Her eyes narrowed hatefully. "I never knew this side of you."

"What side is that, Casey?"

Casey looked away. She was uncertain. "I could have her legally removed from here and committed."

"Possibly," Lou said. She seemed very sure of herself. "In which case, I predict you'd lose a friend for good. Rena won't cooperate. Just enough to get released. And then what? I believe I can get her out of this. I want you to trust me."

Casey felt drained. She shook her head. "I always have before," she said sadly.

"I know."

"In your own way, you've done more for other people, for lesbians, than anyone else I know." She took her glasses off and rubbed her face. "I always thought you were a special person. Giving and generous, but hard as nails when —"

"Trust me then."

"Shit."

"Is the attraction mutual?"

"Huh?"

"You and Rena."

Casey put her glasses back on. "Before she met Pat it was." She shook her head. "You're like another Pat."

"This is different."

"Yes and no." Casey slid onto the seat of the sofa. She felt herself relaxing some. "I don't want my own feelings for Rena to get in the way . . ." She tugged at her lower lip. "I still don't see how you can do anything for her. I wish you'd level with me." The anger was returning. "I think you want to control her, like Pat did. I've heard a few things about you. That Rainshower woman or whatever her name was, the one with the pink hair who stayed at De Nova last summer. She was like a puppy dog to you."

Lou smiled. "We had an unusual relationship." She looked serious then. "It wasn't like Rena."

They could hear hammering from upstairs.

"What are they doing?" Casey demanded.

"Putting some mesh over the windows."

"Why are they doing that?"

"And installing some locks."

"You plan to keep her prisoner."

"I plan to free her."

Casey rubbed her temples. "I feel like I'd be wrong to leave her here, I mean, even if your intentions are absolutely pure. Like I'd be deserting her."

"I'm sure it's not easy for you."

"I've known you . . . what, almost three years now?" Casey had placed her cap on her knee and was twisting it around by the brim.

"Yes, since the first pumpkin festival."

"Right. I spent my thirtieth birthday at De Nova that year. I had a crush on you myself."

"I didn't know that." Lou smiled warmly.

"Well, it was no big deal. You were with Joanna at the time and besides it was soon after that that I met Rena." Casey paused. "You should have known her then, Lou. She was really something." Her eyes teared. "It's hard to tell now, she's so different, but she is such a neat woman. She's bright, I think brilliant sometimes, and she's strong. So self-confident and witty and interesting and deep-thinking and sincere and sensitive . . ."

Lou nodded. "I've had some training, you know. In California. I started a Psy.D. program there." She smiled. "I didn't finish. The

38

establishment and I didn't get along." Then she looked very serious. "I also have a feel for it, Casey, for ways of getting people unstuck."

"I don't know. I'm just worried sick about her."

"I know you are. I'll take care of Rena. Believe me. I'll send her back to you a new woman."

"That's what I'm afraid of. I want the old woman back."

"I'm not out to hurt anybody, Casey. Trust me."

"I'm going to keep in touch. I'll be calling. I'm going to come next weekend and see how she's doing — if she stays that long."

"All right. You may not be able to speak with her though. It depends on how things go."

"What do you mean?" Casey's eyes shot fire. "You can't keep her from me. Lou, this whole thing is —"

"Trust me, Casey."

Casey desperately wanted to. She could feel the pull of Lou's charisma. "I don't know." She ran her fingers through her hair. "You can't keep her against her will."

"I can if it becomes necessary."

"Lou, goddam it, you can't do things like that!"

Lou looked as if she could do most anything. "Call as often as you want, Casey. I'll keep you informed. Trust me."

When Rena awoke, the first thing in her mind was the image of Lou's face — the sharp squarish jaw and her penetrating eyes. Then she remembered the noose. She's right, Rena thought. I would have done it. In a sense, I *am* dead. I should be. I ought to be dead. She rubbed her temples. Oh, God. Am I crazy?

She sat up in the large bed. The two lean and wiry women had removed things from the room, the scissors and nail file from the dresser drawer, many of the objects from the bathroom medicine cabinet. Rena remembered watching them silently, from a fog, not knowing who they were or even if they were real, but at the same time aware of exactly what was going on.

Am I crazy? She tossed the covers aside. She was wearing only a T-shirt and underpants. The underpants were her own, the T-shirt someone else's. Lou's? Rena felt a shiver along the back of her neck.

She began to piece together the events of yesterday. Feeling excited in the morning, alive for the first time in ages, happy almost. She and Casey were going to Lou's house. Casey! Where's Casey? Oh, yes. We said goodbye last night. She left. She left me here with Lou. Two options: the hospital or Lou — doing what Lou says. *We're going to be spending a lot of time together,* Lou had said. *What's left of you is mine to do with as I choose.* Rena felt another tingle along her neck.

It was exciting when we first got here, being in Lou's house. Looking at her things. Then . . . all those birds. Rena felt anguished; her were eyes tearing. Why? Why? Why? What is wrong with me? The heaviness was there in her chest, the heaviness that had come when she'd learned of Pat's death and hadn't gone away.

She kept the shower water painfully cold. The bedroom door was locked. Lou had told her it would be. For some reason it didn't bother her. Was it really indifference? Or more than that? Did she want someone to take over for her? Someone strong and powerful . . . Rena turned off even the little trickle of warm and let the icy chill totally numb her.

Ten minutes later, wearing the loose jeans and T-shirt that were on the chair, Rena stood near the screened window looking down at the garden, the fields, avoiding the barnyard — looking past it to the woods, trying to catch a glimpse of the river, remembering again the rope hanging from the big, wide-branched tree.

A knock sounded. The door opened. "You're awake." It was Trish.

"Excellent observation."

"Ready to start your day?"

Rena sneered. "What are you, the recreation director?"

"You want some fresh clothes?"

Trish seemed undaunted by Rena's surliness, and Rena softened. "No, I don't need them. These are fine. Thanks."

"You sleep OK?"

She isn't going to stop, Rena thought. She seems so young and fresh, like a daffodil with dew on it. "How old are you, Trish?"

"Thirty."

"Really? You look younger."

40

"I know. How old are you?" Trish was sitting on the straight-backed chair near the window. She was slim and angular and her face reminded Rena of Mia Farrow.

Rena continued to stand. "Thirty-seven. Do you live here? At Lou's or —"

"At De Nova. In the dorm. I do field work. Outdoor type, you know." She laughed watching Rena's expression. "It's really fun. In college I was a Philosophy major and now I'm a philosophical farm hand. I love it. I'm going to show you the work I do. Teach it to you."

"Oh yeah? How come?" Rena realized she was feeling more responsive to Trish than she'd been to anyone other than Lou for a long time.

"Lou's idea. Exercise, then breakfast, then we'll go to the fields."

Rena smiled condescendingly. "I don't do exercise."

Trish held Rena's eyes. "You do here." She beckoned for Rena to follow her.

"Are you my bodyguard?" They had descended the stairs and were in the kitchen.

Trish nodded. "Yes, among other things. A glass of juice and then we're off for a jog."

"I'm not going running, Trish."

"Yes you are."

Rena laughed. "I don't like being told what to do. Seriously, I don't. So drop it, OK?"

"Hey, Lou," Trish called out in the direction of the living room. "Come with me," she said to Rena.

They found Lou in the study. "Good morning," Lou said, almost smiling. She looked closely at Rena, assessing her.

Rena felt herself flush and immediately was angry. She thought of Pat and the anger changed to heaviness again and that sickening feeling in the center of her stomach.

"She doesn't want to jog."

"That's OK. She doesn't have to want to." Lou rose. "I'll be right back."

She returned in minutes wearing a cut-off sweat shirt, loose shorts and running shoes. Rena thought she looked enticingly sexy

41

and was surprised at her own reaction. Until meeting Lou, she hadn't felt the least bit of erotic interest since two nights before the barbecue, the night Pat had held her down roughly on the deep pile rug and fucked her fiercely.

"Some warm-up exercises in the yard first. Stretch those muscles." Lou took Rena by the wrist. Trish followed them outside, climbed into the hammock and watched.

"Toe touches," Lou said. "Do what I do."

Rena imitated her half-heartedly.

"Bend, girl!"

After ten minutes of stretching, Lou headed toward the road. Rena followed and soon was puffing. She slowed down but Lou urged her on. "You can do better than that. Come on. I won't push you too hard. In a few days you'll be thanking me for this." She chuckled. "Well, maybe in a few weeks."

They ran what seemed like miles, but what Lou informed Rena had been merely one kilometer. "Good beginning, Rena. Good first day. Now you get a shower, a massage, and then breakfast."

As hungry as she was, Rena's thoughts were more on the massage than on food. Would Lou do it, she hoped, or would it be Trish or the other one, Darla? Rena thought of nothing else while she showered and put on clothes from her own bag which had appeared somehow in her room.

It was Trish who teased and kneaded her strained muscles and, despite the disappointment, the massage felt very good.

The three of them breakfasted together. "You do the eggs," Lou had said, "anyway you like," and Rena had scrambled them with cream cheese and cheddar cheese, enjoying the task though she hadn't cooked in weeks.

"Trish is going to take you to the fields today. There's a little more to do in my fields, then you'll go over to De Nova in the afternoon to do some plowing."

Rena had been eating heartily. She put the fork down. "I have no interest in farm work," she said firmly.

Lou smiled patiently. "Give it a chance."

"I'm not interested. I don't like physical labor."

42

Lou shrugged. "You're going to do it anyway." Her tone left no room for argument.

Rena stared at her plate. She could feel the hairs behind her neck standing up and that strange warm tingling sensation along her spine.

"Did you ever drive a tractor?" Lou's voice was light again.

"Nope."

"You'll like it."

"I doubt it."

"You'll like it. Trust me."

By evening Rena was exhausted and her muscles sore but she had to admit she'd had worse days. Trish kept her so busy she'd had no time to think about anything except how to keep the tractor on the right path, whether the payoffs of organic farming were worth the costs, and if the aches along her back and her leg muscles would ever go away.

Lou arrived home soon after Rena and Trish. Rena was collapsed in a canvas chair on the patio; she hadn't washed or changed her clothes.

"You look like a physical laborer," Lou said, handing her a tall glass. "So, how did it go?"

"Not bad." Lou looked magnificent in her tan linen blazer and wheat-colored slacks, and Rena had to turn away and take a sip of her drink to conceal her gasp.

"Tell me about it."

"I liked driving the tractor. You were right about that. There's a lot involved in farming."

"Helping things grow is very gratifying." Lou smiled. She pulled a chair next to Rena. "Did you ever have a garden?"

"I have one in Chicago. It can't compare to yours, though."

"Did you have one as a kid? "

Rena picked a piece of straw off her leg. "I don't think so. But my mother did."

"Oh yeah? Where? Was it in Chicago? Is that where you grew up?"

43

Rena felt herself tighten. "Yeah, right, the big city. So, where have *you* been today? It doesn't look like you've been playing farmer."

"I was at my office in town. What part of Chicago did —"

"You have an office? I didn't know that. What do you do there?"

"Talk with people. Help them make decisions."

Rena suspected Lou was teasing her. "Really? What kinds of decisions?"

"Various kinds. Relationships. Career. Mostly I teach my clients the process and they take it from there."

"I never heard of that, I mean . . . are you a counselor or trained to —"

"I've had some training. I'll tell you about it sometime, but right now I want to hear more about you. So your mother did gardening. Did you help her in her garden?"

Rena picked up her drink again. It was lemonade, she realized. "Sometimes. You know, *your* garden is really impressive. I've never seen such a big one with so many different things. It doesn't seem chaotic, though. Nice and orderly, like the Japanese." She couldn't look at Lou for very long. The sight of her made Rena light-headed.

"We had a little problem with the clutch on the tractor," Rena continued. "Trish was impressed with my mechanical ability. She says she's better at taking apart ideas and putting them back together than she is with things. I'm pretty good with cars, but Casey's the one who's really got the talent. You know about her shop in Chicago, *Save the Machines*. I love the name, don't you?"

"It's a cute name," Lou said. "So is yours. Spiros is Greek, isn't it?"

"Yeah. You know, I was wondering about the name, *De Nova*. A star, right? Or, the new . . . something. Anyway, the whole process of naming is fascinating. Have you read Mary Daly? I don't know . . . language has a tendency to impose meaning on —"

"Rena!"

"What?"

"You're babbling."

44

Rena stared at her ice. "I'm just making conversation." The animation had left her voice.

"I'm trying to learn more about you and you keep changing the subject."

Rena didn't answer.

"How come?"

She shrugged. "Why do you want to know about me?"

Lou slowly put her hands behind her head. "Because I'm in charge of what's left of you," she said. "I want to know what I'm dealing with. No rush though. In fact, I'd rather have dinner now. We'll talk later." She stretched her long arms. "There are some steaks in the refrigerator. You can cook them outside if you want." She motioned to the grill at the corner of the patio.

"I'm to do the cooking?"

"That's right."

Rena shook her head. "I don't get this. Do you just want me around to do your shit work?"

"Shit work? Girl, the way you talk."

Rena let her breath out in a loud rush. "I'm not comfortable with this."

"Hm."

"It's humiliating. Being locked in a room. Being told what to do. I don't like it."

"Really?"

"Why don't you just leave me alone. I'll go away and you can forget about me."

"Too late for that." Lou stretched again and rolled her head from side to side. "I'm responsible for you now. I'm going to take care of you."

"I don't need to be taken care of."

"You certainly do."

"Using me as a servant isn't taking care of me."

Lou laughed. "The road to freedom is a mighty twisted road."

"Bullshit." Rena set her drink on the table. "Look, Lou, I'm not sure what you're about. Maybe you *are* trying to be helpful. If so, I appreciate your concern." She was looking right at Lou now. It took a great deal of effort. "I really do, but whatever my demons are,

45

they're not going to go away by farm work and question-and-answer games. It's my problem and I just need to be alone to ... to ..."

"To get so depressed and self-contemptuous that you try to kill yourself again?"

"Yes," Rena said. "Maybe so. Maybe that's the script. I'm not what you think, whatever that is. You can't save me and you can't use me." She started to get up.

"Stop!"

She stopped.

"Where are you going?"

"I don't know. Out of here. To my room. Home. I need a ride to the train station." She stood.

"Wrong. You need to go take a shower then get going on the dinner."

Rena folded her arms. "And if I refuse?"

"You really need a shower." Lou was smiling, looking at Rena's dirty clothes and the smudges on her face and arms.

Rena stood fuming. "I'm serious. If I refuse?"

"Then we'll lock you in your room."

"Ah, fuck you! Do what you want. I don't care anyway. I don't give a shit what you do." She marched off the patio. Trish was immediately at her side. "What do *you* want?"

"Let's go upstairs."

Darla joined them. She stood on the other side of Rena. "Come on," she said. "Why don't you clean up. You'll feel better. Maybe we can all do the cooking together." She took Rena gently by the arm.

Rena jerked away. Darla took her arm again, the grip tighter this time. Trish took the other. They stood on the grass between the patio and the garden. Lou sat smoking, watching them.

"Let's go," Trish said.

Rena walked inside with her two escorts, but she would not take a shower nor would she speak to them. They left her in her locked room lying face down on her bed in her soiled clothes.

Several hours later, Terri Kepper called asking to speak to Rena.

46

"Ah, yes, you're Rena's therapist," Lou said. "Wondering about Rena, I assume. She's sleeping now. I'm Lou Bonnig."

"I heard about what happened up there," Dr. Kepper said. "Casey Grant told me. I'm quite concerned about Rena." For the next fifteen minutes, Dr. Kepper questioned Lou — about Rena's suicide attempt, her behavior since, and about Lou's motivations and involvement with her. Lou attempted to reassure the psychologist. It seemed not to work.

"I think she should come to Chicago and be evaluated," Dr. Kepper said. "Would you be willing to help arrange it?"

"Rena doesn't want that."

"Are you trying to persuade her to want it, to accept it?"

"Not at this point."

There was a brief silence. "What goes on at De Nova, anyway?" Dr. Kepper asked. "What kind of place is it?"

"It's a lesbian collective. A working farm. We raise soybeans and wheat, fruit, vegetables."

Dr. Kepper continued questioning Lou. She wanted to know if there were meetings, if the women shared a set of beliefs, if there was a leader, whether the people were free to come and go. Lou patiently explained the operation and some of the history of De Nova. "It's not a cult, Dr. Pepper."

"Kepper."

"Sorry."

The psychologist switched the topic back to Rena. "It's important that I talk with her. I have some free time tomorrow afternoon. Between two and four. Would you have her call me then?"

"I'll tell her you'd like her to."

"Ms. Bonnig, I want you to know I'm available for Rena. If you need to consult with me or if she wants to resume therapy, I'm here."

"That's good to know."

"She should be in therapy."

"Yes."

"Well, good night then. I'll be expecting the call."

Lou hung up and leaned her head on the back of the chair. The house was quiet. She could hear the crickets chirping outside.

CHAPTER SIX

When Rena awakened she was ravenous. It was pitch dark outside. She lay on the large old bed, on top the covers, still fully clothed, and thought about hamburgers and pancakes and piles of salad heaped with big chunks of cucumbers and tomatoes and full of olives, the tart Greek kind, and little bits of onions, all soaked and drippy with heavy oil and red wine vinegar.

She turned on the lamp, got up and checked the door. It was still locked. She made a quick trip to the john, then back to sit on her bed. She supposed she should wash but the food fantasies made her too impatient. It would be hours before the others awoke and she could get some food. She began to feel frustrated. Maybe I'll bang on the damn door and yell until they come, she thought. Suddenly she felt very strange.

Another time she had done that, pounded and called out for someone to come. When was it? She had pounded and pounded and yelled until her fists were red and sore and her throat raw. No one came. She was so hungry, she thought she'd die from the hunger, like the people in those camps someone had told her about. She was

49

a prisoner too. She had been bad and he locked her in the shed. There were tools and bags of things, fertilizer, and barrels, but nothing to eat. She banged and screamed some more. Finally, from the little crack in the shed door, she could see an arm. She could see the arm moving, unlocking the lock. The arm was hairy. She knew who it was and she had felt happy and relieved, but also frightened.

Troubled by the memory, Rena walked the length of the bedroom. She was sure it really had happened and yet she couldn't remember where or when or why, why she was locked up and who it was who came to free her. She pictured the arm again, the hairiness of it, and up near the elbow bend was the tattoo.

Revulsion and dread struck her like a physical blow. She was shaking. One leg gave out and she sank slowly to the floor, the feeling growing, the sickening fear and hideous guilt. Rena lay her head on the carpet and covered her face with her hands, willing the feeling to go away. She tried not to let herself think at all, to keep her mind clear and free, without thought, without feeling. Clear out the thoughts. Blank it out, go numb, make it leave.

The nausea receded but the heaviness would not go away. She remained on the floor, afraid to move, afraid to do anything that might bring back the horror and revulsion. A half hour passed. She still had not moved and finally the numbness and deliberate emptying of her mind brought an uneasy sleep.

To the east, outside her window, the trees were just beginning to become visible. Rena awoke with a scream, the resounding, bottomless sort of scream with no beginning and no end, coming from deep in her throat and deep in her psyche, a tearing, searing scream frightening to hear, terrifying to know it came from her.

Then Trish was there and the scream had turned to gurgling with raw labored panting. She couldn't be calmed until Lou came and held her head as she lay on the floor, holding her and stroking her cheeks, and even rocking her until she could breathe normally again. Lying there, held, eyes closed, she wanted this never to end, but Trish's voice brought her back, and suddenly Rena was extremely embarrassed.

She sat up, pulling away from Lou's kind warm arms. "Hey, uh ... wow ... I must have had a dream. Sorry. Did I wake you guys?"

50

She stood and stretched, trying to be the adult human being she'd been for years. She walked to the window. "Looks like the sun's on its way." The two women were watching her closely. "Sorry I woke you. I'm OK now. God, I feel silly."

Lou joined her at the window. "It's going to be a beautiful sunrise. I used to go down to the river to see them. The view is great from there. Hey, girl, you must be mighty hungry. What sounds good? I'll make you a big breakfast while you clean up." She took a step back and scrutinized Rena, smiling. "You do intend to bathe eventually, don't you?"

Rena managed a weak smile. "Did you save me any steak?"

"You got it. Steak and eggs. See you downstairs."

"And a salad."

Lou prepared a feast and Rena ate while Lou watched. "How are your muscles feeling today?" Lou asked.

"Sore."

"You have to keep at it. We'll let you digest awhile, then go for a jog."

Rena concentrated on the food. As soon as she finished, she started cleaning the kitchen. Afraid of the past, the future a fuzzy mist, she needed to stay focused on each moment. Lou drank coffee and ate some toast while Rena worked, then she helped Rena wash and dry the pans and large bowls that didn't fit in the dishwasher. Afterward they walked to the river.

It was a beautiful August day, warm but not humid as it sometimes became during Wisconsin summers. Rena was beginning to relax. She allowed her gaze to drift to Lou and enjoy the sight of her seated on the grassy shore, her head back, eyes closed, drinking up the morning sun. Lou's skin was country tan and flawlessly smooth except for the tiny wrinkles around her mouth and eyes and the little flat mole just below her lower lip on the left. That's where the movie stars used to put beauty marks, Rena thought. She felt comfortable and safe being there with Lou and as her eyes moved from Lou's face to her long neck and downward, she felt increasingly aroused. A vivid fantasy came. Her clothes tossed aside, Lou was upon her, her strong limbs and knowing fingers taking her, possessively, her body arching to the unspoken commands.

51

"What are you thinking?"

Rena blushed hotly, then laughed. "I'm glad I'm alive right now."

Lou took Rena's hand. "I am too." She stroked the fingers, along the back and then the palm. "Very glad."

Rena raised her chin for the kiss, but Lou only looked at her, intently, deep into her eyes. Finally, with one finger, she traced the outline of Rena's jaw from her ear to her chin. "I want you to tell me about the dream, the nightmare you had this morning."

Rena looked away, toward the slow-moving river.

"Tell me what you remember."

She wanted Lou to take her, consume her, thrill her, possess her, make her body pulsate and go wild. She did not want to speak of nightmares or anything that was of the black pain world she hated and that hated her. "It upsets me to talk about it."

"Yes, I know. Tell me what you remember."

At that moment, if Lou had told her to strip and climb the tallest tree, she knew she would have been naked and aloft in a flash. If Lou had told her to walk across the river, or to bring her a deer, or the moon, she would have hastened to obey. Lou wanted her to speak. "I was in a cave. It was dark . . ."

Lou waited for her to continue.

"The cave was dark, but I could see things dimly, the walls, thick walls with deep recesses. And it's cold. I'm trapped in there. It's so frightening. I'll never get out. I'm going to die here in this awful cave. It's damp and cold." Rena hugged her arms.

"Go on."

"I'm crouched in a corner. At one section . . . about . . . a few feet from me . . . up . . . over at the side, some pebbles begin to loosen from the wall and fall onto the ground. I hear scraping sounds and more pebbles fall and some bigger stones. The wall is loosening and then there are fingers. I can see the fingers digging . . . digging through the wall. Then I can see a whole hand. There's a thin stream of light coming in with it. The hole's several inches big now and the hand keeps making it bigger. It pulls away rock and the hole's growing and more light comes in."

Rena was not looking at Lou as she spoke. She was no longer at the river, safe with Lou in Wisconsin. Sweat coated her face, dampening the edges of her shirt.

"Then I can see the whole arm. It's big and hairy, black hair, a man's arm, thick and muscular. I don't know if he's going to rescue me or kill me. The hole is big enough for the whole arm to fit in now. It reaches toward me, the fingers moving, and I can see the tattoo — a vine winding around a rose. And then..."

She was swallowing rapidly. Her face was pale. "And then..."

"And then what?" Lou coaxed.

Rena's eyes were red, her face blotchy. "Oh God!"

"Tell me the rest."

Her eyes closed, she clutched Lou's hand so tightly that some of the pain may have been transmitted. The words came slowly. "The arm reaches into the cave almost up to the elbow... and then it... it falls. It lies there on the dirt and the rocks. An arm. Just an arm."

"Just an arm?"

"Yes, a disembodied arm."

Lou held her tightly as Rena sobbed. The crying went on for a long time and when it finally stopped, Lou continued holding her, strongly, gently. The sun was warm and a light breeze came through the trees.

"That's very frightening, a truly frightening dream. Do you know what it means?" The sun speckled the women's arms and backs. The river moved slowly on.

Rena shook her head.

"Anything at all? Does it remind you of anything?"

"This morning... I had a memory this morning. About the shed."

"Yes?"

"I was locked in the shed and then someone came to let me out. I think he was going to let me out, I'm not sure. His arm was... it had a tattoo and... it was just like in the cave."

"Just an arm?"

"No, no it was a whole person."

"Who?"

"I don't know. I don't want to think about it." Rena was shaking her head.

"Think about it, Rena. Who might it have been? Who might have been coming to the shed, to let you out or . . ."

Rena shook her head.

"Do you know when it took place?" Lou persisted.

"A long time ago." Rena was opening and closing her hands, staring at the grass. "When I was a child."

"Where was the shed located? Was it near your home?"

"It was in the back, where the sheep were, and Kitsos, the neighbor's mule."

"In the country then. When did you go to the country as a child?" Lou had let go of Rena and they were sitting side by side.

Rena placed her hand on her stomach. "I'm not feeling very well," she said.

"I know," Lou answered. "This is hard. Can you picture where the shed was?"

"It was behind our house."

"Where you lived?"

"Yes. I could see our house from the crack in the shed door."

"It wasn't in Chicago then."

"I guess not."

"Where was it?"

Rena turned away. She was crying again. "I don't know!" She rubbed at her temples. "I don't want to know. Oh God!"

"Can you picture it?"

"I don't want to."

"Do it anyhow, Rena. Picture the house and the shed. Tell me where it is and who's there."

"I don't want to, don't you understand? I can't think about it!" She turned her back. "Don't make me."

"You must. Let yourself do it. Go on, Rena. Try to remember."

"Noo-oo-o-!" It was more a howl than a yell. She sprang to her feet, flew down the river bank and in seconds was in the water, stumbling, banging against rocks, then down, fallen, and she did not try to rise. She lay with her face partially submerged letting the water take her on its course, dragging her body against the shallow, rocky bottom.

It was several moments before Lou got to her. She grabbed her under her arms and Rena did not help as Lou dragged her limp body to the shore. She tugged her halfway up the bank. "Come on, girl, a little leg power. I can't do it all myself."

Rena found her footing and the two women made their way up the bank, Lou supporting much of Rena's weight. They sat dripping on the grass, panting.

"I guess I can't rush you," Lou said, after a few minutes. She squeezed water from her pants cuffs. "Quite a block you've got there, girl. You've convinced me of that." She stood and pulled Rena to her feet. "You don't trust me enough." She smiled. "But you will. It'll happen. Come on, let's go home."

Rena walked numbly, still partially supported by Lou's arms. She felt ashamed and humiliated. Throwing myself in the river like a mad woman. What the fuck is wrong with me, she thought.

"Guess what time it is," Lou said cheerfully, when they were back at the house.

Rena glanced at the sky. "I don't know. Around nine-thirty, ten?" Her hair hung straight still damp from the river. Her jeans were soaking wet.

"It's exercise time."

"Oh no. Not for me."

Lou frowned. "Don't fight me, Rena."

Rena shrugged but her heart was pounding.

"Do you want to exercise or be locked up in your room?"

Rena laughed hollowly. "I suppose I could exercise."

"Good. Stay right there."

Lou returned quickly with two pairs of shorts and shoes. They dressed, then Lou began the routine, stretches first, followed by jumping jacks. Rena faced her, copying the movements, but with significantly less flexibility and enthusiasm. After the warm-up they jogged, a run just slightly longer than yesterday's. Again it seemed endless to Rena.

It was worth it, though, she thought afterwards, for it was Lou who gave her the massage this time. Lou's fingers rubbed and stroked and Rena loved each moment of it, her mind full of fantasies. Despite the horror of the nightmare and the scene at the river, Rena realized she was in a good mood.

She joined Trish on the patio for coffee. Lou came a few minutes later dressed in slacks and a lavender blouse. "Time to get to work," she said. "That means you too, Rena."

Rena pretended to be asleep in her chair.

"I'm off to my office," Lou said, ignoring Rena's silliness. "You farmers have a good day. Rena, I want to see you tonight at eight." She poked Rena's foot with her own.

Rena remembered the massage. She opened one eye.

"You dig?"

"Sure."

"And Dr. Kepper called. She wants you to call her this afternoon, between two and four. So, if you want to, you can take a break then. Goodbye, Amazons."

Rena watched her leave, openly enjoying the sight of her long legs moving loosely and easily.

CHAPTER SEVEN

Rena worked in the De Nova fields the rest of the morning, and in the afternoon went horseback riding with Trish. Off and on during the day she thought about Terri Kepper, knowing she should return her call but knowing also that she would not. She didn't want to deal with the questions, nor the concern. At six they went to the *Big House* for dinner. A muscular, jovial Japanese woman named Janet kept Rena laughing in the kitchen with her non-stop puns and twists of snide humor. Rena was in charge of the potato salad. After dinner, she and Trish remained with the group talking around the table.

"I think our mistake was to sell outside, to count on the outside market. What they pay us is barely enough to cover our costs and yet we keep selling to them and losing more money each year." The speaker was Alpha, a short round woman with short short hair who wore three scarves around her neck and four earrings in her left ear.

"What's our alternative?" Janet asked. "We need cash. How else can we get it?"

"Sell the crops directly to women. Cut out all the middle*men*."

"Great," someone said, "theoretically. But we don't have the resources nor does the rest of the women's community. We have no mills, for example."

"Lou says we should raise more fruit and vegetables and less grains."

"Yeah, and increase our production of milk and cheese."

"*Lou says, Lou says.* I think we're having trouble because of all the things *Lou says.*"

"We know your opinion, Kate."

"I'm the only one who has any objectivity. The rest of you are so under Lou's thumb, you can't see straight." Kate sat with one of her blue-jeaned legs thrown over the corner of the table. A toothpick bobbed in the corner of her thin-lipped mouth.

"Well, personally, I think we should be focusing on the orchards and vegetables and dairy products too. I think it's the direction to go but it's not so easy to convert —"

"We have to leave," Rena said to Trish. "It's getting late." The prospective meeting with Lou had been very much on Rena's mind all day.

Trish checked her watch. "In a little while."

They left ten minutes later. "What did Kate mean about Lou?" Rena asked as Trish drove the jeep to Lou's. "About everybody being under her thumb?"

"Don't pay any attention to her. She doesn't know what she's talking about."

"You're not under Lou's thumb, huh, Trish?"

"Of course not."

It was 7:45 when they arrived at Lou's. The house was well-lit but quiet. Rena assumed Lou was in her office. She started up the stairs to get ready.

"Where you going?" Trish demanded.

Rena stopped and smiled. "To my room, bodyguard woman. Relax."

"I'll go with you."

"That's not necessary, Trish."

"Probably not, but I'll go anyway."

In the bedroom Trish waited near the window while Rena looked at herself in the bathroom mirror and imagined once more, her body tingling, how it would be making love with Lou. She washed her face, ran the brush through her thick straight hair and looked at herself again. Before coming here, she hadn't really looked at herself for weeks, hadn't cared. How odd that she cared now. How odd that Lou was able to affect her so. She scrutinized her features. They seemed acceptable enough, the face narrow, the nose small, the teeth straight except for the middle bottom one which was a little out of line.

Darla came into the room. "Phone call for you, Rena. It's Casey."

"You only have a few minutes," Trish said. "Better make it short."

Rena used the phone in Darla's room. She sat on the bed. "Hello, you."

"Rena. Hi, you sound good."

"I am."

"Things are going OK?"

"Yes. Real well, in fact. It's amazing. I'm actually beginning to feel . . . *alive* again. Isn't that something? And it was all your idea, Case, coming up here."

"I'm glad. I've been worried about you."

"Casey Grant, I love you."

"What?"

"You are one wonderful friend and person."

"Are you stoned?"

Rena laughed. "I *am* high, Casey, but not from drugs. It just feels so good to be . . . to be tuned in again, to give a damn about what happens."

"That's great, Rena. Really. I like hearing you sounding like your old self. So, tell me about it. What have you been doing?"

"Not that much really, I mean, just farm-type things, but it's great. I want to tell you more, but I can't talk right now. We've got something planned at eight, so I only have a few minutes. Let me get back to you, OK?"

"Sure, OK. Hey, I'm really glad you're feeling better."

"Me too. I want to talk with you real soon. I'll be calling. Don't worry about me, OK? I'm really doing fine."

"What's going on at eight?"

"I'll tell you about it next time we talk. I'll call you soon."

Trish was right outside the door when Rena left Darla's room. "Go ahead. It's time," she said.

Rena hurried down the stairs. When she was almost to Lou's office, she stopped. It was hard to identify what she was feeling. Excitement? Fear? She knew she felt nervous. She went to the open doorway of the office.

"Come on in," Lou said, not looking up.

Papers were piled on the desk and Lou was writing. She had on her glasses, which Rena thought made her look even sexier, and she was wearing a jade-colored top and a thick silver bracelet with stones the color of the blouse. The few gray hairs along her temples matched the gray of her eyes. Rena guessed her to be close to forty. "What are you doing, writing out someone's decision for them?"

Lou raised her head, taking in Rena with a glance. "You think that's what I do?" She was smiling warmly.

"I suppose you let your customers think they're making their own decisions." Rena took the chair at the side of the desk and rested her feet on the arm of the sofa. She felt giddy with excitement.

After another minute or two, Lou switched off the desk light and rose. She took Rena's hand. "I don't believe you've seen the womb room yet." She led Rena upstairs to the corner room at the end of the corridor.

Earth-colored drapes of spun cotton wafted in loose folds to the thickly carpeted floor. There was a stereo, a fireplace, several soft inviting chairs, simple wooden tables, pillows and footstools, a contour lounging chair, and, under the wall-length windows, covered with the draperies, a square bed-size mat nearly two feet thick cloaked with a thick cotton comforter. The dim lighting cast a warm amber glow over the room.

Rena felt fluttery. Excitement and also that little edge of fear. "Womb room, huh?" She fingered the soft fabric of the comforter. "It's very sensual in here. Very well done."

They stood facing each other. Lou smiled but did not speak. Rena thought her the most striking woman she had ever seen.

"This is where we'll come," Lou said, breaking the silence. "You and I. When you're ready."

Involuntarily Rena's eyes went to the mat.

"I like the setting to be right," Lou continued. "This room is right."

"It's a . . . a very nice room." Rena's voice cracked and she felt herself blush. They were naked, in her mind, on the mat, Lou on top of her.

"Calm down, girl. I want you to pay attention to what I have to say." Lou laughed. "It's hard, isn't it? You want so badly to make love."

Rena blushed some more and Lou laughed again. "But you're not ready, Rena. Not yet." She stretched out on the lounge chair, gesturing for Rena to sit. "Now, listen."

Rena tried to shift gears and focus on Lou's words.

"The other day you tried to kill yourself. In a sense, you succeeded. You killed part of yourself that day, and then some more today in the river."

Rena did not want to hear this. It wasn't words she wanted, especially words about ugly things. She longed to feel Lou's body pressed against hers, feel the transporting power of Lou's strong hands, the magic of her sensual mouth.

"You killed the part you own," Lou continued. "Forfeited it. What's left, I own. I saved it and it's mine." She did not smile as she spoke. "I own you."

The words sounded strange. Frightening, but oddly exciting. Rena felt confused. She wanted to nod her agreement. "No one can own another person," she said instead.

"Sh-h." Lou's finger was at her lips. "Don't analyze it." She shook her head. "Stop being so literal. Just listen now." She folded her hands casually behind her head. "I own you and I will teach you exactly what that means. You will learn to let go, let go of your self, to lose yourself — in me."

Rena started to say something but Lou stopped her with a frown.

"You see, Rena my dear, you must lose yourself to find yourself." She was grinning. "Strange but true. It can be no other way. You proved that today by the river." The grin became a scowl. "I asked you to speak to me and what did you do?"

Rena looked at her hands.

"Answer."

"I couldn't . . . I couldn't do what you wanted me to. It was . . . I felt . . ."

"You were frightened."

"Yes."

Lou nodded knowingly. "That's because you haven't yet given yourself over to me. That's why you were so afraid. I will teach you to trust me absolutely. You'll learn to give yourself to me completely. Completely, Rena. Body, soul, mind. Everything."

The idea was absurd, Rena knew, but Lou's words brought a peculiar delight.

"Tomorrow it begins in earnest. Tomorrow you begin to learn about being owned, about total trust through total obedience." She paused, looking closely at Rena. Rena said nothing. "Unquestioning obedience. You will learn to put yourself in my hands completely. And you will come to like it. It will feel good to you."

Rena gave a zombie-like nod.

"It begins tomorrow," Lou repeated, looking at her watch, "and tomorrow begins at midnight. It's now eight-twenty-five. You may do what you like in the house until midnight, then you're to go to your room and sleep. Trish will tell you more. Just do what she says."

Lou stood and without looking again at Rena left the room. Rena remained in her chair. She felt disjointed, and a little lightheaded, but definitely intrigued. Don't analyze it, she thought. Let the feeling in. It was a good feeling, warm, safe, like the womb room, like a nest. She went downstairs and into the kitchen where Darla was playing with the cat. Beginning at midnight.

Scraping and banging sounds came from up above. "What's that?" Rena asked.

"Trish and Pete," Darla said. "They're rearranging some furniture. They'll be done in a minute then we're going to play cards. You want to play?"

"Sure." Rena went to the refrigerator and got a beer.

"You're a teacher, huh?"

"Yes. Sociology." Rena shook her head. "That seems so far away right now."

"Yeah, summers can do that. That was the best part of being a student I always thought. Summers off."

"I've never taken summers off," Rena said. "Not in years. I didn't plan to take this summer off, but I guess that's what I'm doing." She fingered the cap from the beer bottle.

"You were going to teach this summer?"

"No. Continue my research. I'm studying women uprooted from farm life to urban life. Well, I was. The project's at a standstill now. I haven't been much into it lately."

"I always lived in cities until I came to De Nova. Philadelphia, New York, Chicago. I like it here much better, at De Nova. We have some women who have jobs in town, in Madison. They live here and work there. So what are you learning about the women you're studying?"

Rena chased the rolling beer cap under the table. "That it's a difficult adjustment for most of them. They develop a lot of stress-related physical symptoms initially. Some experience anomie. Self-esteem diminishes." It all seemed so remote now, the teaching, the research. Another person living another life. She had been asked to teach two summer courses, but had declined. It was soon after that that she'd killed the first bird, she realized. "Oh-oo."

"What is it?" Darla asked.

"Nothing." The heavy feeling sat in her chest like an lump of iron. The cat which had been winding itself around Rena's leg suddenly sprang to her lap.

"I'll be damned! She never does that," Darla said.

Rena stroked the soft fur.

Trish and another woman bounded loudly down the twisting staircase. "All right, deal!" Trish said. "Rena, this is Pete Struthers.

Pete, meet Rena Spiros, budding farmer and all-around horsewoman." Trish plopped into the chair next to Rena.

Pete Struthers was a strikingly beautiful woman, tall and graceful, with tawny black skin and long delicate fingers. She was shuffling the cards.

The four women played noisily for the next few hours. Trish won as usual. She "shot the moon" four times and was very smug. "If you got it, you got it." She put away the cards humming happily.

Pete donned her red iridescent motorcycle helmet and said goodnight. They listened to the sounds of her roaring departure. Rena went to the john, then to the refrigerator for another beer.

"Bedtime, Cinderwoman," Trish said. "No more drinking for you."

Rena looked at the wall clock. It was five minutes to twelve. She stretched and yawned. Actually, she didn't want another beer. Sleep sounded much better.

"I'll walk you upstairs," Trish said.

Rena laughed and shook her head. "Do you get overtime?"

"I get all I need." Trish flashed a cocky grin.

When they were almost to Rena's room, Trish stopped her. "Take your clothes off out here."

"What!" Rena scowled. "Trish! I'm shocked." She enjoyed Trish. "I demand to know your intentions."

"I'm to help you learn what Lou wants you to learn." Trish was not smiling. "It starts now. She says you are to obey me as if the orders were coming from her. I order you to take your clothes off."

Rena was also no longer smiling. She felt uncomfortable, and confused. Trish waited. A strange feeling of alienation came, as if this were some bizarre dream, all of it, beginning from the moment she had first seen Lou and felt the first jolt.

"Take them off."

The voice was quite real. Rena unbuttoned her blouse, threw it on the floor. "Can I ask why?" She took off her jeans.

"Underpants too."

She took off her underpants. "All right, can I go in my room now?" Her nakedness in front of Trish did not bother her, maybe because it seemed to have no particular effect on Trish.

"Go ahead. Leave the clothes out here."

Rena entered the room, flipped on the light. She stopped abruptly, staring in disbelief. The room had been stripped. The mattress was gone from the bed; there were no chairs, tables or lamps. She heard the door lock behind her. "Hey, what the hell is this supposed to mean?" She pounded on the door. "Trish! Trish, dammit! This is nuts!" Rena shook her head. "They're nuts," she said. "I thought I was supposed to be the crazy one."

There was no carpet. The floor was shiny bare oak. The walls were empty and stark. Rena paced the room in her bare feet. Besides the bed frame, the only piece of furniture remaining was the dresser. Rena checked the drawers. Empty. Casey was right, she thought. I should have left with her. These people are insane. The room reminded her of the tour she'd taken to Alcatraz, the cold dark bare cells where they locked prisoners alone with nothing, nothing at all. At least there was light in here. She couldn't sleep like this, naked, on the floor. She went to the door and began banging and calling again. Nothing happened. Nothing would, she suspected. I'll get towels, she thought. She crossed the echoey room to the closed door of the bathroom. It was locked. Shit! How dare they! She began to laugh. God, what a trip.

She felt angry. She felt outraged. But she did not feel depressed. The room was warm. Rena looked out the window, the mesh-covered window. She was tired. She turned out the light, lay down on the cool floor, angry, puzzled, laughing to herself too, and then she was asleep.

CHAPTER EIGHT

Trish arrived very early the next morning. Rena was only partly awake and had just begun to remember how it came to be that she was sleeping naked on the floor in a nearly empty room.

"Thirty sit-ups." Trish had locked the door behind her and was leaning against the wall.

"Good morning." Rena sat up. Her neck was stiff.

"Start."

"Trish, are you trying to communicate something?"

"You're to do thirty sit-ups. Now."

Rena smiled. "Trish, why don't you just fuck yourself." She tried to stand. Her muscles screamed. She forced herself to her feet. "Open the john door unless you want me to piss on your pretty floor."

"You have to do the sit-ups first. Rena, you have to do what I say. Everything. Now, get started."

"You're beginning to get on my nerves."

"Do I have to get Lou?"

Rena feigned great alarm. "Oh no, not that!" Then she shifted her expression to exaggerated disgust. "Go on, get her! Get the big master, you wimp!" She was looking out the window. The morning was misty, but she wasn't thinking of that. Lou had said she owned her, that she was supposed to obey her. For reasons Rena couldn't understand, as much as she was fighting it, she was inexorably drawn to the idea. Part of her was. Yes, she wanted Lou to take over. Control her. Own her. But, no, she didn't want that at all. I'm Katerina Spiros, she thought, grown-up person, teacher, scholar.

Her ears began to ring; a loud, clattering sound filled her head. She was on the stage. Lights shone on her and she was beaming as the audience applauded. They liked the presentation. She knew it was one of her best, *Support Networks Among Farm Women.* The applause continued as she left the podium and joined the rest of the panel at the table on the stage.

The memory was from a conference of the American Sociology Association in Los Angeles less than six months ago. How far away it seemed now, locked as she was in a barren room and being ordered about like a vassal.

"Rena, I'd rather not have to. Now, why don't you just do what I say. Accept it."

"Accept it," Rena repeated flatly.

"Right."

Rena shrugged. She stretched out on the floor. "How did this happen?" she murmured.

"One . . . two . . . three . . ." Trish counted.

By fifteen Rena felt the strain terribly. She stopped.

"Keep going."

She resumed, more slowly, her fingers not quite making it to her toes.

"Eighteen . . . nineteen . . ." Trish was sitting now, on the floor by the door. "Good. Keep going . . . twenty . . ."

The muscles in Rena's abdomen protested. She took another break, then forced herself to make the final grueling effort.

". . . twenty-nine . . . thirty." She lay stretched on the floor. "Oh, poor me."

Trish chuckled. "You're going to end up fit as a fizzle."

The laughing hurt Rena's gut. "That's *griddle,* you stupid twit."

"Don't call me that. Did you get cold in the night?"

Rena rolled and lay on her stomach. "Are you supposed to be this nice to me?"

"Probably not."

"Would you open the john door now?"

"I'll have to check with Lou."

"Good grief! All right, go check with Lou. Make it quick, my bladder's bursting."

Trish returned in ten minutes. "Lou says not yet."

"Absurd!" Rena stomped her bare heels on the floor. "Hey, where you going?"

Trish locked the door behind her. Rena gave it a sharp crack. It hurt her hand. She fumed around, kicking walls, banging the window. The memory of being locked in the shed flashed through her mind. But, no, this was different, very different. She began to feel calmer. Despite her anger, she could not deny the strange pleasure she was deriving, an erotic-tinged pleasure. Lou is very powerful, she thought.

Several minutes passed. Rena wondered how much longer she'd be able to retain her urine. That would be humiliating. Lou came moments later. Rena opened her mouth to complain but nothing came out. Lou seemed huge, larger than a person, larger even than she had seemed yesterday. She wore faded jeans tucked into leather boots and a black T-shirt that hugged her chest. Rena remained speechless. She folded her arms over her breasts. She felt shy and vulnerable, different than with Trish. Lou walked to the john door, her boots thumping across the floor, unlocked it and gestured for Rena to enter. She remained in the bathroom doorway and Rena had to walk sideways to get past her.

"Can I close the door?"

Lou shook her head.

As urgent as her need was, Rena was sure she couldn't urinate in Lou's presence.

"Go ahead."

Rena sat, looking at the floor. When she finished, she still could not look at Lou. She washed her hands but there were no towels.

68

She shook her hands into the sink and then didn't know what to do with them.

"Trish tells me you have quite a mouth." Lou walked back into the barren bedroom. Rena followed. "I don't want you to speak anymore. Not without permission. You are to do nothing without permission." Rena stood uncomfortably before her. "Let that sink in a moment," Lou said.

Rena's eyes were locked on a slat of the bed frame. She could not look at Lou.

"You are not to question what I tell you," Lou continued, "or what Trish tells you. Remember, Rena, unquestioning obedience. You do what I tell you to do when I tell you to do it. Look at me now."

Rena moved her eyes from the bed to Lou's shoulder.

"And you get what I choose to give you when I choose to give it. Got it?"

Rena nodded. Against her will, she felt herself becoming aroused, very aroused. She even feared there might be dripping down her legs.

Saying no more, Lou left the room. Trish came a minute later bringing clothes, a pair of royal blue cotton pants with a draw string at the waist and a short-sleeve shirt of the same fabric. "Get dressed and come to the kitchen."

Rena was relieved to be covered. Part of her was convinced this treatment was nonsensical and intolerable and that she would have to leave. Part of her felt she deserved it, wanted it, needed it. That part knew she could not pull herself away.

In the kitchen, Lou and Trish and Darla were just sitting down to eat. There were eggs and pancakes, chunks of pink ham, milk, juice. Rena started to take the chair next to Darla.

"No, no, no," Lou drawled, shaking her head. "You're to stand. Over there."

"I can't sit down to eat?"

Lou held her finger to her lips. "Sh-h. No talking, my sweet. Try to remember." They were very sensuous lips.

Rena went and stood at the counter as Lou had directed.

"She's not doing very well so far, is she, Trish?" Lou put two eggs on her plate and a thick slice of ham.

"Not really."

"She doesn't deserve to share our food, do you think?"

"I think not, not yet, at least."

"I suppose she does have to eat though."

"I suppose."

"There's always grits."

The women ate and chatted, ignoring Rena. What would Casey think if she knew they were treating me this way, Rena thought, or Dr. Kepper, or any normal human being? This is sick. "This is sick," she said aloud.

Lou turned to look at her, seemingly aghast. "Amazing," she said. "How slowly you learn. Put you hand over your mouth, Rena."

Rena felt woozy. *Put your hand on the branch, Rena.* Her head was spinning. Who was saying it? *Do it, hold on, I'll reach you. Trust me.* And then the strong arms were around her, holding her, safe. She was safe and he was holding her and kissing her and she was safe.

"Do it, Rena."

She placed her fingers over her lips, staring at the floor, momentarily confused, not sure where she was or if she was safe or ever would be.

"Good. Stay that way."

Their conversation was an unintelligible buzz. Rena stood immobile, numb, her mind fuzzy, a ringing in her ears. At some point, a bowl of steaming mush was placed on the counter. She was told to eat. She lifted the spoon mechanically, tasting nothing, swallowing without awareness. Soon Darla left the kitchen. Rena started to leave also.

"You can't go," Trish said. Rena looked at Lou. "May I go sit on the patio," she asked softly.

Lou put her finger to her pursed lips again, shaking her head.

"You're not supposed to speak without getting permission," Trish said.

70

"Well, how am I supposed to ask for permission if I can't speak?" Rena pushed the half-empty bowl away. "Stupid twit," she mumbled.

"What did you say?" Trish demanded.

Rena glared at her.

"Very slow learner," Lou said, turning back to Trish. "This may take awhile." She finished off her ham and wiped her mouth with a lavender napkin. "How did it go with Freddie the other day? Can he get the fuel pump for you?"

The conversation continued but Rena had tuned it out. Lou's powerful and good, she was thinking, but nasty too. Too powerful. Sexy. She was remembering the womb room upstairs, how much she wanted Lou to touch her, take her, possess her, own her. Own her! Rena realized she felt even more excited and aroused with Lou than she had felt with Pat. With the thought of Pat, she began to feel sick. She rubbed her temple.

"Time to clean up, Rena."

"What?"

Trish was speaking to her. "The kitchen is a mess. Get to it."

Rena carried her bowl to the sink, looking at Lou who was sipping coffee. She caught her eye and Lou smiled. Rena remembered how Lou had held her after the nightmare and how warm and loving she could be. She continued working, scraping plates, rinsing out pans. She grabbed the little piece of ham that was left, wrapped it in a napkin and put it in her pocket. "Do you want me to save this coffee?"

"Rena," Lou said harshly, "ask permission before you speak. I'm getting tired of telling you that."

Rena felt as if she'd been caught sneaking a piece of baklava. *Rena, I'm surprised at you,* he had said. *That's for the guests tonight.* She had disappointed him. She was now disappointing Lou. "I'm sorry."

"That's better." Lou waited. "Did you want to say something?"

"May I?"

"Yes."

"Do you want me to save this coffee?"

"No, we're done with it."

71

It smelled very good. "May I have some?"

"No. Throw it out. That's enough talking now." Lou turned from her.

"I don't like this," Rena said angrily. "This stupid way of treating me isn't what I want. A person can't be owned. You're crazy!" She threw the sponge into the sink, so hard it bounced back out. "I'm leaving!"

Lou looked at her calmly.

"Did you hear me?" Rena's voice had a panicky edge.

"I heard you."

"I'm leaving."

"No you're not."

"I am. You can't stop me. I can leave if I want."

"You don't want to."

"Yes I do!"

"All right."

Rena stormed from the room and up the stairs. No one followed her. In ten minutes she returned to the main floor with her suitcase which she had found in the storage room packed with all her things. She was dressed in her own clothes. "Will someone drive me to the train station?"

Lou and Trish were on the living room sofa. "Trish?" Lou said.

Trish stood. "OK, I'll give you a lift."

Rena looked at Lou. Lou's expression revealed nothing.

"Are you just going to let me go?"

Slowly Lou reached for a cigarette. "If you stay," she said, striking the flame, "you have to stop fighting me."

Rena set her suitcase on the floor. A long time went by with no sound but her breathing and the ticking of the mantle clock. "It's not that easy," she said at last.

"I know."

"It makes me feel weird."

Lou shrugged.

Rena was close to tears. "Fuck you," she said.

Lou uncrossed her legs. "Rena, come here!" Her voice was hard, as were her eyes, the gray looking darker, almost black.

Rena approached her fearfully and stood before her at the sofa. Lou's anger frightened her. And she felt bad, guilty, for having evoked it. She remembered another angry face. A man. A hairy man.

Lou saw the fear. "Rena, let go," she said gently. "Quit fighting it."

"Don't make me leave!" Rena pleaded.

"You have to suspend that part of you that's fighting me. It doesn't have to be such a struggle. Shift your gears, girl. Get into it. Let yourself do what part of you wants very much to do and needs to do."

Rena felt herself trembling, deep within her core. She knew it was not only fear. "Let you own me?" She sat on the leather footstool in front of Lou.

"Exactly."

She looked at Lou's feet, at the boots.

"All right?" Lou said.

Still looking at the boots, Rena took several deep breaths. "All right," she said.

"OK, you can stay, but enough rebellion. Imagine you're a prisoner, if that helps, that you've been sentenced here and have no choice."

"Do I have a choice?" There was no defiance in her voice.

"No." Lou reached out and gently smoothed Rena's hair. "Go put the blue outfit back on now, then finish cleaning the kitchen."

Rena picked up her suitcase and went upstairs. The confusion was painful. She could not go away from Lou, couldn't bring herself to leave. The heavy feeling was returning. She thought of Pat. She thought of the arm. She thought of dying, and then she thought of Lou and dressed herself in blue and went back downstairs.

Lou and Trish were gone. She was sure Trish was nearby somewhere. She went into the kitchen and worked furiously. After putting the last pan away and turning on the dishwasher, she walked out to the patio. Trish was there.

"I'm done."

Trish started to smile, then cut it off. "You weren't told you could leave the kitchen."

"Oh, I should stay there?"

"Yes, of course. When you finish something we've told you to do, then just wait until you're told what to do next."

Rena returned to the kitchen. It's like brainwashing, she thought. She was reminded of the studies she'd read in graduate school about American P.O.W.'s in Korea. She began wondering again if Lou might be a little off. Was she some kind of a power-hungry sicko? Maybe De Nova was a cult. Maybe she was being recruited. Trish certainly seemed to be under Lou's spell. Maybe Lou was the guru and all these women were in her power. Maybe it was dangerous being here.

Rena leaned against the sink. No, no that's not true. They're treating me the way I deserve. The sick feeling was coming again. She rinsed her face with cold water.

From the kitchen window she could see the barnyard. A rooster strutted near the fence. She stared at it, her mouth open. That's why I can't leave. The bird. I have to get inside the bird. Her chest began to heave. Barely aware of what she was doing, she removed a sharp knife from the kitchen drawer and slipped out the side door.

CHAPTER NINE

Trish leafed through *Modern Farming,* but her mind wasn't on the magazine. She was thinking of her role in Lou's plan for Rena. She was to start Rena on painting the house trim next. It felt very strange — giving orders, observing Rena's struggle, trying to accept the wisdom of what Lou was attempting to do. She remembered when she first came to De Nova herself. She had stayed in the dormitory, but then she kept disappearing for days at a time — lost weekends — and would return strung out and ashamed and full of excuses. Finally Lou insisted she stay at her place. How patient she'd been. Trish remembered how Lou had gotten her to grow things, first the garden, then the orchards and fields. Bit by bit her love of the outdoors had returned, and her feelings of accomplishment and worth. She had attended A.A. meetings until she no longer needed them.

Trish's reminiscing was interrupted by the sight of Rena walking toward the barn. She jumped up immediately and was next to her before Rena had gone another twenty yards. Rena didn't seem to notice.

"Rena!"

Rena continued walking.

Trish quickened her pace and got in front of her. Rena's eyes looked strange, crazed. Trish's stomach tightened. She felt as if she had never seen this woman before. Rena continued walking, her eyes riveted on the rooster.

"Rena, stop!"

Rena looked to her right, staring at Trish as if she were an apparition.

"Please, Rena, just . . . just give me the knife."

Rena seemed dazed, confused. She looked down at the knife held tightly in her hand. "The bird," she mumbled. "I have to get the bird. Cut it. I have to get inside of it." She looked at Trish. "Get out of my way." The blade tip pointed toward Trish's abdomen.

Trish backed away. She felt chilling terror.

Rena looked past her, over Trish's shoulder.

"No, Rena," a voice said. It was calm and firm.

Lou was there. Trish continued looking at Rena. Rena didn't move.

"I don't want you to kill any birds." Lou moved in front of Trish, shielding her. "You're to do what I say, Rena. It's what you need." She kept her eyes on Rena's. "It's OK to let it happen. Listen to me! It's OK, you hear? Let it happen. Let me take over."

Rena's jaw slackened as she stared at Lou, but her eyes remained wild.

"Put the knife on the ground," Lou ordered.

To Trish, the next thirty seconds seemed to take a century. She stood to the side, her heart pounding, staring at Rena, at the knife. Lou remained directly in front of Rena. Rena seemed confused, uncertain. Trish looked from one to the other. Lou's gaze bore into Rena with such intensity it was as if her will emanated through her eyes into Rena's soul. She's weakening, Trish thought.

Rena felt the power, Lou's terrible power. And she felt the countering pull of a strong force within herself. The two powers ripped at her, fighting each other. Her grip tightened on the knife.

Lou's eyes bore into her. She's powerful, Rena knew. Her breath came in gasps. Very powerful. She's winning. Lou is winning. As the final turning came Rena could almost hear it happening inside her mind--a rending sound, a movement in her brain like something on an axis, tilting, then a sucking whoosh like air leaving a tube all in a gush.

Rena bent and lay the knife on the earth. Trish realized she had been holding her breath. Lou placed her hand gently on Rena's neck and spoke to Trish. "She'll be OK now. I think it will be easy sailing from here."

Trish looked at Rena and then at Lou. Rena's eyes seemed normal again. Lou hadn't seen them, Trish thought. Her heart was still pounding. She stared at Rena who watched silently as Lou strode through the yard and away.

Trish waited a moment. "Let's go inside." She tried to make her voice sound calm.

They walked toward the house, Rena looking straight ahead, Trish stealing furtive glimpses at her. "How are you feeling?"

Rena touched her temple with her fingertips. "Feeling. Yes, I am. I'm feeling fine. Are we going to the fields today?"

She seems almost like Rena again, Trish thought. She took some deep breaths. "Not today. Lou wants you to do some painting."

"All right."

"The outside trim on the house. You're feeling OK?"

"Yes, I'm fine. You keep asking that."

They were in the hallway near the stairs. "You're to stay away from the barnyard, Rena. Don't even look in that direction." She stared at Rena's eyes.

Rena nodded knowingly. "That's where the birds are," she said.

"Yes, you're not to go there. Lou doesn't want you to."

"I know about Lou." Rena nodded. "I do what Lou says. She owns me, you know. If I don't do what she says, then I have to kill the birds." She shook her head. "But that's not the way, no, that won't work. Killing them won't work. I know how it works now. It's Lou. That's how it works. Yes, yes, that's it."

Rena was staring straight ahead as she spoke. Her eyes had a glazed look now. Trish didn't like it. "Rena, are you all right?"

"I'm all right. It's all right to lose myself." Her eyes remained unfocused. "I'm losing myself. Lou knows what she's doing. Lou knows. She owns me, you know." Rena seemed very relaxed. "Lou knows." She was nodding her head. "Lou knows. Lou knows. Lou..."

"Shut up, Rena!"

"All right, Trish." Rena pressed her lips together.

"I'll help you get started with the painting. There are ladders in the shed."

Trish could not get the image of Rena's eyes out of her mind. She had seen that terrible look before. A cold chill shivered her skin again. She wasn't Rena then, Trish thought. It was as if someone else had taken over. Some level of Rena that was . . . evil . . . diabolical.

CHAPTER TEN

Rena painted all morning. As she glided the bright white over the dirtier white she thought about how clean and pure it looked. She thought about the little lines the brush bristles left and then how they disappeared. She thought about how the little dots of paint splattered here and there when she scraped the brush against the can. She thought about how white her fingers were getting and wondered how she'd look painted white all over. She thought about how high up she was and how things looked from up there. She looked around, but not toward the barnyard. It wasn't good to look that way. Lou didn't want her to. She wasn't allowed.

Over the next few days a peaceful contentment grew within her. She could count on Lou. Lou was the absolute. The yardstick. The rock.

She's wise, Rena thought. And generous. Letting me have a mattress again and even sheets and a pillow. Rena wondered why she used to want to speak so much. There was comfort in her silence and in knowing Lou knew when it was good for her to speak or sit or eat or work or rest and when it was not. It made everything simple and Rena felt the calm and peacefulness of it.

Occasionally she paused to think about what was happening to her. She would begin to feel uneasy then, even repelled. But it wasn't good to have those thoughts and so she would stop them. She grew more and more accustomed to looking to Lou or Trish for direction on when to do what and what to do when. It seemed natural that Lou should decide and that she, Rena, should carry out each decision Lou made.

Whenever there was time and Lou allowed it, Rena worked on the album, cutting out segments of the photographs, pasting them on background scenes, carefully matching content and color tones and size. She wasn't sure her work was any good until Lou told her how clever and creative she was, and then she knew. What she enjoyed most was doing the small things for Lou, things that seemed to please her. She brought her tea or a beer when Lou was working in the office. She served her meals at the table, happy to be in the same room with her, content to eat later when Lou said it was all right. Lou was patient and strong and kind and good. Rena knew well how fortunate she was.

Friday morning, Rena felt especially proud. She had jogged two full miles with Lou, almost keeping up with her all the way. You're doing great, Lou had said, and the words gave Rena a feeling of pure joy.

On Friday nights Lou usually went to Madison, Trish had told Rena, to visit friends, but tonight Lou would stay at home. Rena wondered why, but didn't ask. Lou did not like too many questions, even though Rena always asked permission first. Rena was thinking about this as she sat in the living room where Lou had sent her half an hour earlier. Lou and the others, Darla, Trish, and Pete, were still in the kitchen. Rena had tended them while they ate, eaten her brown rice and greens when they were finished, then cleaned up the kitchen. After that, Lou had told her to go into the living room.

Her eyes dreamy, Rena leaned back on the sofa thinking about how knowledgeable Lou was, how brilliant. I'm lucky she even bothers with me, Rena thought. How blessed to be owned by a perfect person. She's more than a person, she's . . .

". . . off in the ozone." Lou's voice startled her. Lou and Trish watched her from across the room. "I think she's re-entered," Lou said to Trish, chuckling. Trish did not seem amused.

"Where were you, girl?" Lou chided. Without waiting for Rena to respond, she walked on and disappeared into her office.

Trish remained a few seconds, continuing to look at Rena. Rena smiled at her. Trish did not return the smile. "See you later," she said and followed Lou into the office.

Rena wondered what was bothering Trish lately, why she kept looking at her that way. Then her thoughts returned to Lou. Lou looked especially attractive tonight, she thought. She loved the way the light caught the highlights in her hair, the silvery sparkles among the brown. Lou was part Indian, Rena had learned. I bet she's got magic powers from her ancestors. She pictured Lou on a horse, a sleek black mare, galloping, soaring over mountain crests, her headdress flying in the wind. Rena blinked. A glimmer of her adult self crept in and she scoffed at her silly thoughts. But then the sinking feeling came. Quickly, by an act of will, she cleared her mind and waited without thinking for what Lou would want her to do next.

Another half hour passed and Rena began to feel bored and sleepy. She knew, though, that sitting in the living room as Lou had told her was what was best. She was involved in convincing herself of this when Trish reappeared.

"Lou wants to see you in her office."

Rena went immediately. She was surprised to find Lou stretched out on the sofa. She waited for Lou to speak.

"You look tired."

Rena shrugged noncommittally.

"Are you?"

"I guess I must be if that's how I look." She was absolutely sincere.

Lou scrutinized her. "You've changed, Rena. Do you understand it?"

Rena was puzzled and more than a little uncomfortable. "I'm not sure."

"You're not sure of much these days, are you?"

81

"I don't know."

"Do you know who you are?"

Rena felt confused. "Yes, I'm . . . I live in your house. I'm your . . . I don't know. Who am I to you?"

"Come and sit down." She motioned Rena to the sofa, moving her feet to make room. "It happened very quickly."

Rena was staring at Lou's mouth and the little mole near her lips.

"How do you like the way things are for you here? Are you happy? Satisfied?"

"Yes." When Lou spoke, Rena noticed, little lines came and went around her mouth and her eyebrows moved.

"Is there anything you'd like to be different?"

Rena strove to extract meaning from the question. "Should there be?"

Lou took a deep breath. "Amazing," she said. "You let go faster than I predicted." She twisted her feet, grimacing. Rena looked at the soft rich leather of her shoes. "You like these shoes?" Lou asked.

"Yes."

"They're new. They're killing my feet. I'd give them to you if I thought they'd fit you."

"They wouldn't fit."

"No."

"Shall I take them off for you?" Rena asked.

Lou smiled. "Yes, why don't you."

Slowly Rena undid the laces and gently removed the shoes, cradling each foot caringly in her hand, smoothing out the socks. She placed the shoes on the carpet. "I like going barefoot."

Lou's eyes narrowed. "You're like a little child, you know. It's kind of freaky."

"I know how to give foot massages."

"Is that so?"

Rena looked imploringly at Lou.

"Go ahead."

The first strokes were light, cautious ones. Lou's feet were pleasantly warm. Touching them felt good, so very good. Rena kneaded the muscles of Lou's soles with her thumbs and fingers. She massaged the deep arches, the ankles, and toes, gently, firmly.

Lou leaned back. "Excellent," she said.

Because Lou's eyes were closed Rena dared to look closely at her face. Relaxed, Lou's features lost the sternness they often had, becoming soft, almost delicate. Her mouth looks sweet, even vulnerable, Rena thought, as her fingers, though still stimulating the muscles, now also included lighter touches directed at the skin. "May I remove your socks?" she asked softly.

Lou opened her eyes a slit and observed the glow of excitement on Rena's face. "Yes, do," she answered.

The massage continued, flesh-on-flesh. The touching became more and more sensuous and Rena's eyes more and more dazed. Her hands made occasional drifts upwards, her fingertips slipping tenderly along Lou's calves. Eyes closed, Rena was lost in sensation, her breathing heavy, her mouth loose.

Lou watched her. She observed the swaying of Rena's breasts and felt the quivering of her hands. Rena placed her head gently on Lou's ankles, her hair falling across Lou's feet. She cradled the lean, muscular legs and stayed buried in Lou this way until Lou spoke.

"You like being at my feet, don't you."

"Yes," Rena responded, without hesitation, her fingers softly stroking Lou's legs.

"Rena."

Rena raised her head, feeling awed when their eyes met.

"Get me some tea."

She left immediately, returning quickly with the tea and one of the blueberry muffins she had made for Lou at breakfast.

Lou was at her desk. "I'd like you to do some typing for me tomorrow. You do type, don't you?"

"I've got flying fingers."

"I know."

Rena smiled lovingly at her. "I like how you look in glasses."

"You do, huh? Do you think I'm attractive?"

"Very."

"Me too. I didn't used to be. I was an ugly kid and even an uglier adolescent."

"That's hard to believe. Did it affect your self-image?"

Lou laughed heartily.

"What, Lou?" Rena asked innocently.

"Your sense of self. Despite everything, it keeps popping up."

Rena turned her head away. "You don't want me to ask you questions about yourself."

"Not especially. By the way, did Trish tell you Casey's coming tomorrow?"

"No."

"She's coming up for the De Nova Benefit in Madison. And to see you."

"Do you want me to see her?"

"Sure, why not?"

"Right."

"And Dr. Kepper called while you and Darla were grocery shopping."

"Dr. Kepper?"

"Yes. You remember her, don't you?"

Rena smiled. "Barely. It seems like anything that happened more than a few days ago is . . . I don't know, kind of hazy."

"She was concerned that you never returned her earlier call. She'd like you to call her."

"Do you want me to?"

"Yes, I do. What will you say?"

"That you own me."

"Rena!"

"I shouldn't say that?"

Lou frowned. "I can't tell if you're kidding or not. Do you think you should say that? Seriously, what do you think?"

"Whatever you want."

"How do you think she'd feel about what's going on here?"

"She'd be glad, I think. She worries about me being depressed. I'm not depressed. She worries about other things too, but I can't quite remember what."

Lou looked worried. "Maybe you shouldn't call her."

"All right."

"No, you should call. Just tell her you've been feeling well, keeping busy. Don't mention the things she wouldn't understand. Don't mention that I own you. Do you know what I'm talking about?"

"Are you ashamed?" The moment Rena said it, she knew it was a mistake. "Just kidding," she said hastily. "I know how to handle her. She wouldn't think it's a good idea for you to control me like you do."

Lou looked surprised. "You're quite aware, aren't you? Your adult self is still partially operative." She smiled. "And what do you think of the idea? Of my controlling you?"

"I think it's fine. Much better than tranquilizers or anti-depressants."

Lou seemed to give that thought. She nodded. "All right, give her a call then, before it gets too late."

Rena called from the office and Lou listened approvingly to all she said. She told Dr. Kepper she was well, not depressed or suicidal in the least, still unsure of her future plans, but satisfied with how things were going for now. The conversation was brief and ended with Rena agreeing to call her again sometime.

Lou praised her for how well she handled the talk and Rena felt very peaceful and content.

CHAPTER ELEVEN

Casey arrived at noon. Rena greeted her in the driveway, hugging her with one arm, the other behind her back.

"You look healthy," Casey said, "better than you have in a long time."

Rena smiled. "Country air." She handed Casey a bouquet. "I picked these for you. Lou said it was all right."

Casey smiled, taking the flowers. "They're beautiful."

They talked for a while on the patio and then Casey suggested they go over to De Nova for lunch.

Rena felt flustered. "Um . . . maybe. Just a sec', let me check something." She went inside, found Lou on the phone, and waited patiently near the doorway until Lou finished. "Casey wants me to go with her to De Nova for lunch. Would it be all right?"

Lou had her feet up on the table. She swung them to the floor. "So, how's it going with you two?"

"Fine. It's good to see her. No problems." Rena gazed admiringly at Lou. She loved to watch her move.

Lou smiled. "You may go with her. Darla's over at the *Big House*. I'll let her know you're coming."

Rena beamed, feeling very appreciative.

There was a flurry of activity at the *Big House*. Hordes of people, not members of the collective, had come for the Benefit. Rena didn't like all the noise and bodies. She and Casey made themselves cheese sandwiches and went across the yard to the dormitory patio. Kate Gordon was there sunning herself. Rena would just as soon have gone somewhere else but Casey sat and started talking with Kate. Kate was a short, gruff, rather tough-looking woman and Rena didn't like being around her.

"Where are your keepers today?" Kate asked her. She was wearing faded blue jeans and a plaid flannel shirt rolled up at the sleeves.

Rena looked at her as she might a pus-oozing toad.

"Bonnig's got everybody convinced that Rena's a real mental case." Kate directed her comment to Casey. "You know she's experimenting with her, don't you?"

Casey's nearly invisible eyebrows lifted. "What do you mean?"

"Hey, Casey. Let's go for a walk or something."

"Wait, Rena, I haven't eaten yet." She turned to Kate again. "What do you mean, Lou's experimenting?"

"It's her hobby. She's always *experimenting* with people, messing with their minds. You don't know her very well, do you?"

"Lou? Yeah, I think I do. What are you getting at?"

"Nobody around here likes me to talk about it. She's got them under her spell too."

Rena pushed her sandwich aside. "Anyone got a cigarette?"

Kate tossed her a pack. "She's not a nice woman, Casey, but I'm not supposed to say so. Some of the *sisters* want to kick me out of the collective. Did you know that?"

"No."

"Everything's very private around here. Like how your friend there is treated like a slave. No one goes around talking about that. I'm not afraid to talk. I'm not intimidated by that bitch."

"Why don't you go do something useful," Rena said scornfully, "like move to Alaska."

"Right. Right. Anyone who dares tell the truth about *The Queen* is immediately at the top of the shit list. You're not the only one who'd like me to get lost, Rena."

"You have a vicious mouth."

"I have an honest mouth. Do you know how De Nova got started?" She was talking to Casey again.

"Not exactly. Some women got together and Lou sold them this land. Very cheaply. That's my understanding. They formed a collective."

"Lou started the whole thing. It's her baby. She recruited the women. They're all hand-picked. Don't think your friend there will ever go back to teaching college. She'll stay here, you just watch."

Rena had her back to them, smoking and looking into the distance.

Casey was feeling uneasy. "What do you mean, she recruits them?"

"Just that. In one way or another, every woman in the collective has a *special relationship* with Lou Bonnig."

"Oh really? And you too?"

"You bet. I did, that is. I'm one of her failures. Usually people like me — and there haven't been many of us, she selects well — usually they just split and that's the end of it. I'm the thorn in her side. I'm still here."

Casey scrutinized Kate. "Tell me more. What exactly does she do?"

Kate settled back, her feet up on the bench where Casey sat. "To start with, she's filthy rich. She wasn't before she went to California and when she came back, she was. You know about the California thing."

"No."

Kate tilted her head smugly. "Bonnig produced women's events out there — concerts, festivals, the usual. That was in the seventies, you know, when that kind of thing was new and exciting. I thought everybody knew about her role in all that. She was quite the wheeler-dealer. She was behind some of the camping festivals too. The first ones. Maybe you weren't out then."

"I was out," Casey said. "I just wasn't out and about much."

"Some people complained. They questioned Lou's handling of the finances. But it never went very far. She shut them up. She left California a rich woman. And then she comes here to create her own little queendom. Only, financially, this place is falling apart." Kate seemed pleased about that.

"Lou loaned the collective ten thousand dollars," Casey said.

"Right. Very generous. She's trying to save her empire."

"Oh really? And what does she get out of it?"

Kate leaned back, folding her hands behind her head. "Plenty. Look at your friend. A perfect example. She gets to control people."

Casey was beginning to feel angry. She didn't want to hear this. Kate's a hostile woman, that's all, she thought, with a special dislike for Lou for some reason. "I thought all the decisions were made collectively."

Kate laughed. "Right. By *consensus*. The only problem is, they don't have minds of their own. They'll *consent* to anything Lou wants them to consent to. Look, nobody who's here right now is that bad — I mean, that sucked in. I think Rena's the worst to come along in a while. The last one who was really completely under Lou was this young punky dyke named Itsy Rainflower. Can you believe that name? *Itsy!* Rainflower's bad enough. This one was so goo-goo over Lou, she ended up giving her her whole inheritance. Her father or somebody croaked and Itsy got a bunch a money. She didn't have it long. It all went to De Nova. She split, went to Colorado. She's lucky she got away."

"So you're saying Lou takes advantage of people."

"People who are fucked up in some way, or in a crisis, or whatever. Itsy was flipping out about some older woman who blew her off. Yeah, right, takes advantage of people. She's not just after their money, don't get me wrong. That would never be enough to satisfy Lou. She's after their minds. Did you ever notice how everyone here thinks alike? I mean about major things. They all agree on what's politically correct and what the no-no's are. They're brainwashed if you ask me."

Casey was becoming increasingly disturbed despite her skepticism about Kate.

"And they all fall in love with her," Kate continued, "or they think it's love. She uses them for a while, teases them, fucks them, then tosses them aside and goes on to the next one."

Rena turned around. "You're an asshole, Kate, you know that? You really are. Casey, let's go. Why listen to her stupid lies anymore?"

"And what's she doing to Rena?"

"From what I hear, she controls every breath that one takes. Anyone who controls your breathing controls your mind."

"I'm leaving. Are you coming, Casey?" Rena was on her feet. She saw Darla coming out of the *Big House*. "Hey, Darla!"

Darla joined them. "I was looking for you."

Darla was chatty at first, but Rena and Casey were so quiet, seeming so within themselves, that soon she fell into silence too. After a short walk, they went back to Lou's. Casey went to check out the garden. Rena sat on the porch watching her. Lies, she thought, all lies.

"Casey's really into flowers."

The voice startled Rena. She had forgotten Darla was there. "Darla, is Lou rich?"

Darla tilted her head. "I guess. Why?"

"Where'd her money come from?"

Darla frowned. "Do you think that's any of your business?"

"Kate says she rips people off."

"Ah, yes, Kate would say something like that."

"Does she?"

"Lou? Rip people off? No way. Not in my opinion."

Rena was silent.

"I know she was involved in some business thing in San Francisco in the early seventies. Something to do with electronics. She joined up with some faggot friends of hers and they did pretty well. That's what I heard. I never got the details. Apparently she got bored with it and went back into counseling."

"Does she have a degree in counseling?"

"Yeah, she's got a couple of degrees. She's an educated woman. She's got a master's in something — counseling psych, I think."

Darla looked uncomfortable. "I'm not sure Lou would want me telling you this stuff."

Both were silent for a while, then Rena spoke. "Why did you come to De Nova? In the first place, I mean? What made you come?"

"You're full of questions." Darla pulled at the tips of her short reddish hair. She was a thin, soft-spoken woman, with round eyes and bright rosy cheeks. "It was because of Lou, actually. She invited me, that is. We met in Milwaukee. I was mad at everything." Darla laughed. "I mean mad. I hated the patriarchal institutions of this country so much, I couldn't see straight." She laughed again. "I literally couldn't see straights without fuming and telling them what fucking oppressors they were. I was a separatist but my separatist friends weren't separatist enough for me. I was angry at them too. I kept getting into trouble, like with the cops and things. I got in fights. I mouthed off a lot. I couldn't keep a job. Lou came one night to this bar I used to go to. We played pool. She beat me. Nobody beats me at pool. I mouthed off at her. That was the beginning of our friendship. Anyway, she invited me here, said I might like living here. That's how I came."

"I see. You didn't have any money or anything when you came?"

"Why do you ask that?"

"Just curious."

"I had some."

"What was it like, I mean, you know, with you and Lou? Did you . . . I mean, were you involved or anything?"

"Were we lovers, you mean?"

"Were you?"

"None of your business."

Rena was quiet, almost pouty.

"What's with you today, kiddo?" Darla asked. "This isn't like you. Is it because Casey's here, is that it?"

Rena didn't respond. She was watching Casey examining a patch of marigolds. She thought of her own garden — the yard, the birds. Immediately she felt tight, heavy. The thought-shifting came automatically. "I'm looking forward to tonight. I'm kind of surprised Lou said I could go."

"She's real pleased with how you're doing." Darla had chewed a toothpick to bits. She tossed it in the ashtray.

"You think I'm doing OK?"

"I guess. I don't know. You seem to be doing fine to me. I'll tell you, though, I'm glad that strict part is over. I felt bad for you, I mean, you know, having to ask permission to turn around or take a breath or a shit. What a drag."

"It's what I needed."

"I guess."

Casey joined them and the talk turned to flowers and then to the concert in Madison and the dance that would follow. Rena realized why she was excited about going. She didn't care about the music or the comedy. She realized she'd been thinking all along about dancing with Lou, a slow dance, she imagined, her body held in Lou's wonderful arms.

The music, for the most part, turned out to be mediocre and so was the comedy, but there was a good turnout and everyone seemed to have a good time. Lou was the emcee. She kept the energy level up, even told a few jokes. Rena watched her admiringly. She can do anything, Rena thought.

After the show, the dancing began. Rena danced with Casey, fast and loose like she used to. Casey seemed very happy.

"This is like old times," she said when they went to sit awhile. "You know, way back, when we first met. We used to dance our asses off, remember?"

"Yeah," Rena said absently. She was looking around the room for Lou. It was nearly midnight and she hadn't danced with Lou yet. There had been several slow dances. Each time she looked for Lou, but each time, if she found her at all, she was with that tall woman in the red shirt, a Chicana who looked so serious and who Lou looked at so warmly.

"Remember that time at the Swan when Gerri and all those people were there and you got a little loaded? Remember that? You were so funny. God, I lo . . . Those were good times."

"Gerri's the funniest woman I've ever met."

"The two of you just never stopped."

The reminiscing was pleasant and for a while Rena forgot about Lou. She realized how much she cared for Casey, what a lovable woman she was.

"Remember the camping trip in Michigan, the time we went canoeing?"

"I never thought I'd enjoy tipping over in a canoe." Casey pretended to fall on the floor.

"It was fun."

"Yeah, but six times!"

Rena laughed. "Was it that many?"

"At least. My moccasins got ruined."

"So did my cigarettes."

"Rena." Casey's tone suddenly changed.

"What, hon." Rena was feeling very warmly toward her. Casey looked especially appealing when she was serious as she was just then.

"Come back with me tomorrow. Back to Chicago."

Rena's jaw tightened.

"You know what I was thinking? I could use some help at *Save the Machines*, you know, office stuff, accounts and all that. You're much better at that than I am. I'm offering you a job, for however long you want. I think it would be real good for . . . that it would be a good idea. What do you think?"

Rena shook her head. "No," she said. She was looking around the room for Lou. "No, I couldn't do that."

"Why not?"

Where's Lou? Where is she? "No, I have to . . . I'm going to stay here. Thanks about the job, though. I mean, thanks, but . . . no . . ."

"Do you trust her, Rena?"

Rena stopped scanning the room. "Absolutely," she said, looking directly into Casey's eyes.

"What about what Kate said?"

"Lies. Just lies." Rena was becoming agitated.

"I hope you're right."

"There she is. Excuse me, Casey." Rena darted across the floor bumping into people. "Lou. Hi."

"Well, hi. You having a good time?"

"Yes."

Lou was with a group of people. Rena remained standing there in front of her, saying no more.

"Is there something . . .?"

"No, I'm . . ." Her lip was quivering.

"Oh-oh," Lou said. "Come with me." She took Rena's elbow and guided her through the crowd. "We'll go to the john."

The john was full of women. They went to the men's john which was also full of women. Finally they found a deserted place in the hallway.

"All right, tell me, what is it? You look like you're about to decompose."

"I'm scared."

"All these people? I was wondering if it was a good idea for you to —"

"No, it's . . . it's what Kate said."

"Kate Gordon? What did she say? That I'm the devil and eat up pretty, delicate girls like you?"

"She said awful things." Rena was biting fiercely on her lower lip.

"Hey, you're going to hurt yourself." Lou touched Rena's lips with her forefinger, a very light, soft caress.

"I'm frightened."

"I'm here, Rena." Lou put her arms around her.

Rena rested her head on Lou's shoulder. "I know they're lies."

"But it still frightens you to hear them."

"I think Casey believes them."

"Oh, I see. That *is* scary."

"She wants me to leave. But this is where I belong, right?"

"That's right."

"I don't ever want to leave."

"You stay as long as you want."

Rena moved back a few inches. "Am I an experiment?" she asked.

Lou tilted her head the way she often did when momentarily puzzled or surprised. She looked directly into Rena's eyes. "We're trying something new," she said, "you and I. If that's what you mean."

"You would never mess with my mind."

"No, I wouldn't mess with your mind."

"Kate doesn't understand about you saving my life and about your responsibility and owning me because the part that's dead —"

"She doesn't understand any of that."

"I don't want to go away."

"And I don't want you to."

Rena nodded, a teary smile on her face. "I feel better."

"Good."

"Will you dance a slow dance with me?"

Lou hesitated, then shook her head. "No," she said. "Not yet, Rena. Not tonight. Be patient. Everything in its time."

Rena nodded. "OK. Thanks for letting me come tonight. It's all right if you don't dance with me." She was crying softly. Lou wrapped her arms around her again, holding her and wiping away the tears.

The following morning, Casey came to Lou's house. Rena seemed preoccupied and was cool towards her. "Do you want me to leave?" Casey finally asked.

Rena looked up from her magazine. "Maybe so, Case. There are some things I have to do today, some typing, and then Lou was talking about taking me . . . about going out with me someplace."

A jab of pain came. Casey looked out the window. "I think I'll head back to the city then. There's a million people over at De Nova and I'm not up for it."

"Yeah, I know what you mean." Rena's tone was flat.

"So when will I see you again?"

Rena shrugged.

"You don't care."

"That's not true." Rena seemed flustered. "I just don't know. I don't think about tomorrow much. I don't think about it at all."

On the drive back to Chicago, Casey reviewed and re-reviewed her impressions of the visit. She could not shake that uneasy feeling

95

she got about Rena at times, especially when Rena was in Lou's presence or talking about her. She seemed content, but it was almost a childlike contentment, and there was that uncharacteristic passivity. Casey wondered if Rena would ever fully regain her old self.

Later that afternoon after Rena finished typing some letters for Lou, they drove to the *Little Dells* so they could hike and Lou could teach Rena rock climbing.

The rope was wrapped around Rena's waist.

"Push off with your feet," Lou told her, "and let the rope slide between your fingers."

The drop was sharp. Rena felt a clutching fear, vertigo. "I can't."

"Yes you can. I'll tell you exactly what to do. Trust me."

The memory came again — his voice, calm, reassuring. *Trust me,* he'd said. *Hold on.* She had stumbled and rolled down the ravine, was clinging to a branch, terrified.

"Just do exactly what I say." Lou repeated in detail each move Rena was to make. She had Rena say back what she had heard. "Go ahead, now. Trust me."

Rena's feet were planted firmly against the smooth rock slope. Slowly she loosened her hold on the rope and simultaneously gave a push with her feet as Lou had directed. She was moving, hanging out in the air momentarily, re-contacting the slope with the soles of her feet, then out again and down, down, down, until finally she was on the ground.

Lou expertly made her way down the slope and was at Rena's side in a flash. She hugged her. "Very well done."

"I did just what you said."

"And you made it."

"I made it. I'm safe."

"Exactly." Lou wrapped her in her arms and Rena felt proud and free and safe, like she had when that kind man pulled her up the ravine and held her close to him.

* * * * *

On Tuesday, Rena finished the album. Lou arranged a showing that night at De Nova. It was a great hit. Many of the collage compositions were humorous — photos of familiar women, collective members and their friends, juxtaposed onto scenes of leaping whales, volcanic uprisings, close-ups of intestinal villi. In one, Lou stood majestically over the Grand Canyon, one foot on each side. That was Rena's favorite.

The days passed smoothly and peacefully. Rena now freely came and went in and around the house as she cheerfully carried out the activities Lou assigned to her. She still stayed away from the barnyard, never even looking at it. She exercised and did housework and worked in the garden. No longer was her door locked. Her room was again fully furnished.

Lou was often busy and away from the house but Rena was not dissatisfied. She knew Lou would return and ask how things were going and maybe even give her a hug. Rena longed for more, but she was patient. More would come. Lou had said as much.

Rena remained centered in each moment. She never thought about the past and never considered her future except to anticipate new contacts with Lou. She had no problems, nothing to worry about. Lou took care of everything.

Wednesday night, Rena slept deeply and long and woke up cheerful as usual. Lou had been out late the night before and Rena missed her. She was eager for the day to begin, and to maybe have breakfast with her. She dressed and was about to go downstairs when she heard Lou's bedroom door open and the sound of voices. From her doorway, Rena watched them walk down the hall. Lou had her arm around the woman and spoke tenderly to her. It was the tall one, the Chicana, from the dance. They did not notice Rena.

Rena stood rigidly in the hallway watching them, eyes narrowed in a hateful glazed stare, her body trembling. In a daze she descended the stairs to the kitchen. From the window she saw them passing the barn, strolling hand in hand towards the woods. She stared coldly, her breathing suspended.

* * * * *

Trish was on horseback, returning from an invigorating early morning ride in the woods. She waved as she passed the two women on the path. And then she spotted Rena. A cold chill shot up her spine and her taste buds picked up the metallic tang of fear. The knife in Rena's hand glinted in the sun. And her eyes, oh, God, that look was in her eyes. Trish's instinct was to get as far away from her as she could, but she knew Rena had to be stopped. The horse shimmied, sensing her tension. Trish reined in, hesitated, then spurred the horse forward, full speed, head on, right at Rena. At the last second, she swerved, sideswiping Rena, knocking her from her feet. She dismounted and ran for the knife. Rena tore off. Her heart pounding, Trish watched Rena until she disappeared down the road.

How she made her way away from the house and down the road toward the highway, Rena did not know. She became aware of where she was and that she'd been running only when she realized she could barely breathe. Her face was wet with tears. She had no idea where she was going. Away, that's all she knew. She had to get away. She slowed her pace, but did not stop. She could hear the traffic ahead. When she reached the highway, she sat on the ground, leaning against a post near the edge of the road. Her head buzzed. She couldn't stop her crying and didn't try.

After a long time of sitting in the dust, lost in her misery, a car stopped. Rena did not hear the man questioning her or even see him there until he shook her shoulder.

"Can I take you somewhere? Do you need a ride?" He was a big, red-faced man.

Rena looked up at him with her red-rimmed eyes.

"Are you OK, lady?"

She wiped at her face. She was wearing jeans and the checkered blouse Lou had said looked good on her. "Will you drive me to Chicago?"

The man took her wrist and helped her to her feet. "I can't take you that far, ma'am. I could give you a lift to Deerfield. Maybe you can pick up another ride from there."

They drove silently. Several times the man tried to converse with her, but Rena did not reply and she failed to thank him when he dropped her off at the gas station in tiny Deerfield.

Thirst seared her throat. She went to the pop machine but realized she had no money. She drank from the faucet in the dirty john and rinsed her face in cold water. Outside again, she began to walk away from the town, down a dirt road. She had no destination. After nearly a mile she came to a pond and sat at its edge. Her eyes were dry now. She was staring at the ducks.

CHAPTER TWELVE

A young couple, male and female, picked her up. If they noticed the blood on her, they didn't say. They were stoned. The music pounded all the way to Chicago. They dropped her off on Broadway in New Town and she walked home from there in a daze.

Later Casey found her in the gazebo. "Oh, thank God! Rena, are you all right?"

"I can't find my keys," Rena said flatly.

"You left all your stuff at Lou's."

The name made Rena flinch.

"They said you just disappeared this morning. Why, Rena? What happened?" Casey noticed the smears on Rena's shirt and jeans.

Rena rubbed her fingers along the wooden arm of her chair. "I found a duck. It had pretty iridescent feathers. I used a piece of glass."

Casey grimaced.

"There was nothing there, just guts."

Casey was perspiring. She unwrapped a piece of gum and bent it into her mouth.

"Casey, isn't life weird?" Rena reached over and picked a flower from the edge of the gazebo. "The way it goes up and down."

Casey sat. "Yeah, it sure is. Rena, why don't you come to my house. Have you eaten lately?"

"I don't think so."

Rena accompanied Casey without objection. She washed up in Casey's john, put on one of Casey's T-shirts, nibbled at the food Casey gave her then stayed seated in front of the TV where Casey parked her.

"I've got Lou on the phone," Casey called from the other room.

Rena stiffened.

"She wants to talk to you."

"No!" Rena crossed her arms over her chest.

"She said to tell you it's important and that you should trust her, that you have to trust her."

Rena's hands fell to her sides. She got up and started toward the phone, got half way across the room then stopped. "No, I don't want to talk to her. I won't!"

Casey came into the room. "It's OK, Rena," she said as she would to a child. "You don't have to."

The next day, at 2:00, Rena was in Dr. Kepper's office. Casey waited outside.

"Can you talk about it?" the doctor asked gently.

"I'm mad at her."

"At Lou?"

"Yes."

"She upset you."

"She's a bitch."

"Hm-m. She must have done something pretty awful."

Rena drooped in the chair. "It doesn't matter."

"No? It seems like it does."

After a little more hedging Rena told of the woman who had spent the night with Lou and how Lou seemed to like her so much.

"It's hard to share Lou, to see her caring about someone else," Dr. Kepper responded.

Rena nodded. "She wanted me to go away. She didn't want me anymore."

"What makes you think that?"

"I just know."

"Because she was with someone else?"

"Yes. I suppose I'm being childish." Rena looked at the psychologist for the first time. "I've been doing a lot of childish things."

Dr. Kepper's eyebrows rose. "Have you? What sorts of things?"

Rena talked about all of it, from the very beginning, when she first met Lou, to the chicken coop, and the hanging attempt, running into the river and then Lou's irresistible firmness and her declaration that she now owned Rena. "I wanted her to own me."

"It took a big burden off you. It sounds like she made you very dependent on her."

"Yes." Rena's eyes were angry slits. "She said I had to give up my self."

"It seems like that started to happen. I imagine that was very frightening."

Rena shook her head. "No, it really wasn't. It felt good. I felt very . . . very safe. I felt like I didn't have any worries. I never thought about the bad things anymore. I liked it."

"I can see why. It was a real escape for you."

"Yes."

"A temporary one."

"Why did she have to do it? *I* wanted to sleep with her. I've never even been in her bedroom. Never. I peeked in once. I was sure someday I'd be able to go in there, with her, and stay all night."

"That's what you wanted."

"Yes."

"And now you feel rejected by her."

"Yes."

"And angry."

"Very angry. She messed with my mind."

"It sounds like she did." The psychologist watched the desk lamp suck up the smoke from Rena's cigarette. Her eyes went back to Rena. "In a way it may be a very good thing that you saw her with a lover. It's hard to say what might have happened if you continued under her domination."

Rena was quiet for a while. "Does it remind you of Pat?" she asked.

"There are similarities." Dr. Kepper waited. Rena didn't speak. "Do you think so?" the doctor asked.

"Yes and no. Pat never . . . I never was so . . ."

"You regressed with Lou. She encouraged it."

"She's a real bitch."

They talked about it for the whole session, which lasted two hours, then scheduled another appointment for Monday. Dr. Kepper encouraged Rena to remain at Casey's and to work at the shop. She also persuaded her to contact her college and arrange to take the fall semester off.

For the next two weeks, Rena spent every day at *Save the Machines.* She had always liked being at the shop, had liked it from the first time Casey had brought her there three years ago.

Casey's fix-it work had grown from a hobby to a business. She had never liked what she called the *throw-away mentality;* she was devoted to salvaging things, whatever she could. She repaired broken objects, replaced parts that no longer worked, recycled what would otherwise have been discarded. Rena used to like watching her work, liked the purity of what she did, the concreteness. Casey fixed radios, TVs, clocks, stereos, toys, typewriters, toasters, power tools, innumerable other appliances and gadgets. She was the least enthusiastic about electric knives and can openers and toothbrushes, though she repaired those too when people brought them in and were willing to pay what she charged — twice her usual amount. Luxury tax, she called it.

Now Rena was helping her friend. She straightened out Casey's disorganized accounts. She designed an advertising flyer for her, got it printed and found some kids to distribute it door-to-door. She even repaired a toaster.

They broke a window to get into Rena's house and took clothes and other things Rena needed back to Casey's. At Casey's apartment they cooked and watched TV. Rena, though not very lively, seemed to be doing all right. Casey got her to go to a movie once, to play racquetball several times and to spend an evening with some old friends. Though agreeable to most suggestions Casey made, Rena showed little enthusiasm for anything.

Three times a week, Rena went for therapy sessions with Terri Kepper. She spoke of her daily activities, and of what had happened at Lou's and how she felt about it. Not once did she allude to anything that had occurred prior to her trip to Wisconsin, and Dr. Kepper did not ask. As time went on, Rena grew more and more detached from her feelings about Lou, and by the third week, seemed to have no interest in talking about her — or about anything else. Finally, Dr. Kepper confronted her.

"You've closed off much of yourself, Rena. I think it's time for you to begin opening back up."

"It doesn't matter."

"*You* don't matter?"

"Not really."

"Why do you think that?"

"It's true. Everything's just . . . empty."

"You've blocked out everything with any meaning."

"Nothing means anything."

"Do you think about Lou?"

"No."

"What do you think about?"

"Nothing. About organizing Casey's tools, about calling the people who owe her money, about what to buy at the supermarket."

"Do you think about how you used to be, before Pat died?"

Rena's eyes narrowed. "No."

"Think about it now."

"That Rena is gone. She's dead."

"She's hiding."

Rena shrugged.

"What's she hiding from?"

Taking in a long deep breath, Rena slowly exhaled. "Remember that feeling I told you about, that pain I used to get."

"Yes."

"I don't get it anymore."

"That's what you're hiding from?"

"Could be."

"It's time to stop hiding."

Rena did not respond.

"Are you thinking about that?"

Rena nodded.

Dr. Kepper waited.

"I had a terrible dream when I was at Lou's, when I was first there."

Dr. Kepper waited.

"I'm afraid if I talk about it the pain will come back."

"It probably will," the psychologist said kindly. "You can't do what you have to do without pain."

"I don't want the pain."

"Of course you don't. Do you really want to continue living the way you are?"

"I don't even feel like I'm living."

"You have to pay your dues, Rena. There's no way around it. You have to feel the pain to get past it, to be alive again."

"Maybe."

"Tell me about the dream."

Rena stared at the arm of her chair. Her voice was very low when she began to speak. "I was in a cave . . ."

By the time she finished, she was crying, for the first time since she sat on the side of the road a mile from Lou's house. She talked about her memory of being locked in the shed. And she cried some more.

"Think back, Rena, way back, to when you were a little girl. What's the earliest thing you can remember?"

"Do I have to?"

"I think you do."

Rena closed her eyes. She took several deep breaths. "I remember sitting at the dinner table. I was little, I don't know how old. There were lots of people there. My mother. My cousin, Taki. There was some lady in a green dress, and a man, and there was another man. He was big. He was the boss of the dinner. When he spoke, everyone listened. I was scared of him."

"Who was he, do you know?"

"No. He was there a lot."

"Was he your father?"

Rena's eyes were shut tightly. "I don't know."

"Can you picture him?"

"Just that he was big and he wore a white shirt."

"And you were afraid of him."

"Yes."

"Why?"

"Everybody was afraid of him. I wanted him to smile at me. I wanted him to like me. He *had* to like me."

"That was important to you."

"If he didn't like me . . ." Rena gripped the arm of her chair.

"What would happen if he didn't?"

"Sometimes I hated him. But I had to do what he said. Always. I had to make him smile or else . . ." Rena shook her head. "Do you think he was my father? I don't remember my father."

"You will, Rena. You're doing real well. What else about the dinner?"

"When I did everything right I would get a big hug. It felt so good."

"Yes. It felt good. Warm and safe?"

"Yes."

"Was it the big man who hugged you?"

"No!" Rena shook her head vehemently. "Sometimes he hugged me. I didn't like it but I wouldn't squirm away. I'd make myself stay."

"Because it was important to please him."

"Yes."

"Who was it that hugged you and made you feel so good?"

Rena's face muscles tightened. "I don't remember."

Dr. Kepper nodded. "What else do you remember from your childhood?"

106

Rena narrowed her eyes, thinking. "I remember the park by my house. I remember my cousin, Taki, being mean to me. I remember my grandma's house. I remember my mother brushing my hair on the balcony."

"All of this was in Greece?"

"It must have been."

"What was your mother like back then?"

"Oh, she was nice." Rena smiled. "She played with me and gave me toys and things and sewed dresses for me. One time when I fell in the gravel where they were building a new house, she wiped the blood away with a washcloth and told me how brave I was. She took me to the movies. She took me to the museum."

Rena felt the color drain from her face.

"What is it?"

"Daddy worked at the museum," Rena said slowly. Her breath came in rapid gasps.

"It's very scary to remember your father."

Rena's eyes were closed. "He hugged me a lot. He hugged me after I fell down the edge of the hill and he saved me."

"He was loving to you."

"Oh God!" Rena buried her face in her hands. "I have to leave."

"You don't have to leave. We'll go slowly. Tell me more about your mother."

Gradually Rena calmed. "My mother was a good person," she said. "Very sweet. She still is. I remember sitting in the kitchen with her when I was a kid, while she was cooking, and I'd pick the black grains out of the rice. I used to love to do that."

For the rest of the session Rena talked about her mother. There were many memories, most of them essentially positive. Some took place in a city, which Rena assumed was Athens because that's where her mother told her they used to live. Some took place in the country, where her grandmother's house was located, and where the balcony and the shed were, and the hills.

The next session was also filled with memories of childhood, mostly about school, friends, her mother. If she began to get close to anything connected with her father, she became distraught and could not go on. By the next session, her memories had run dry.

107

"It may be that you've talked about all the safe ones," Dr. Kepper said.

"I can't remember anything else."

"It's probably more that you *won't* remember," the psychologist said gently. "The other memories, those that have to do with your father and the other man, are the painful ones."

Rena sat quietly.

"Do you have any photographs of your father?"

"No."

"Does your mother?"

"I suppose she does."

"Could you get some and bring them here?"

Rena shook her head.

"You can't?"

"I never look at those pictures. Nothing from back then. I leave the room if my mother or aunt or anyone starts talking about Greece." Rena's voice was getting louder. "I don't want to look. Don't you understand? I don't want to know. If I do ..."

"If you do?"

"I'll have to ... I'll ... I won't be able to go on living. I'll have to ..."

"It's that bad?"

Rena was crying. "Yes it's that bad."

"Guilt? Connected with your father?"

"I'm evil." Rena's head was buried in her hands. I don't deserve to live. I'm ... don't you see?" She looked up Dr. Kepper. "I ... I'm ... Oh, God, I'm not a person. I'm not like you. I'm not like the rest of you." Her voice was getting louder and louder. "I'm not a human being. I'm a lizard. The devil turned me into a lizard. That's what I am! A LIZARD!" The words were a tortured scream. Rena staggered to her feet and ran from the office and down the stairs and kept running.

She cut the gizzard into quarters with a scalpel, examining each piece before pushing it aside. She started on the lungs next, slicing unhurriedly, looking carefully, then pushing the tiny chunks to the edge of the plate. She was much too involved to hear the doorbell.

Casey went to the back door and pounded loudly. She called out to Rena.

Rena continued her task, aware of nothing but the driving need to cut and keep on cutting until she was done. Perspiration glistened on her forehead.

Casey was cursing herself for having repaired the dining room window when she noticed the window was open. She got the ladder from under the back porch and in minutes was inside, in the kitchen, looking on with disgust as Rena continued slicing, oblivious to her presence.

Standing with her back against the refrigerator, Casey watched Rena clean up, scraping guts into the wastebasket, washing off the instruments, the plastic cloth, and her hands. Only when she was finished did Rena realize she was not alone.

"You saw what I did." Her face was white. "Casey, I think I'm crazy. I just can't help myself." She was crying.

They went back to Casey's and the next day Rena returned to *Save the Machines.*

On Monday she kept her appointment with Terri Kepper. The session dragged. Rena spoke sporadically, of inconsequential things.

"Hard to get started today," Dr. Kepper observed.

Rena didn't reply.

"Can you talk about what you said on Friday? Before you left?"

"What I said?"

"About yourself, what you called yourself."

"I don't know what you mean."

"You said you're a lizard."

"I said what?" Rena upset the ashtray balanced on the arm of her chair. She picked up the butts. "A lizard! How weird. I never said that. Lizard?" She looked suspiciously at the psychologist. "Why are you making things up? What are you trying to do to me?" Her agitation grew. "It's some kind of a trick." Her teeth were clenched in anger. "Or you're trying to torture me. You want me crazy, that's it. You want me to be locked up."

"You have no memory of saying that to me?"

Rena glared. "I never said it."

"I see."

Rena looked at her watch.

"We have a lot a time left," Dr. Kepper said.

"I worked on a radio this morning."

Dr. Kepper allowed Rena to change the subject and did not try to stop her the rest of the session as she spoke of programs she watched on TV, problems Casey was having with her sister who was contemplating divorcing her husband of six months, her phone conversation with her mother who talked about the restaurant and her new draperies and how tired she often felt.The following session, on Wednesday, Rena barely responded to Dr. Kepper's questions and volunteered nothing. She had stopped going to Casey's shop. She had moved back home, over Casey's objections. She continued killing birds. Much of the time she was in a daze. She ate very little. None of this did she tell her therapist. The following Friday she did not go for her appointment. There was no answer at her home when Dr. Kepper called. Dr. Kepper called Casey.

"I went to her house yesterday," Casey said, "when I couldn't get ahold of her by phone. She wasn't there. Her car was gone."

"Did you try Lou's?"

"That's where she is."

"You talked to her?"

"Yes, to Lou. Rena's been there since Wednesday night."

"Damn," Dr. Kepper said. "I don't know what else to do."

Casey's eyes were wet. "Nor I," she said sadly.

CHAPTER THIRTEEN

Trish was distraught about Rena's return. She argued and cajoled, even pleaded with Lou to send her away.

"You're wrong," Lou told Trish. "What you saw was her pain and her confusion. There's nothing *evil* about her."

"She was going to kill you."

"Nonsense."

Trish hissed in exasperation, "If you saw those eyes, Lou, you'd believe me."

"I believe she looked weird." Lou put her arm around Trish's shoulders. "Out of control maybe, crazed even. But it's not what you think. Trust me, Trish. Rena was on her way to kill a chicken, not me."

"She's dangerous."

"Calm down. If you're scared of her, stay away."

"It's not for me I'm scared."

* * * * *

Rena had been back for three days. She could not get enough of Lou. When Lou was away somewhere, she would feel uneasy. Knowing Lou was in the house or nearby brought contentment, and being with her filled Rena with a sense of completeness and meaningfulness. As enamored as she had been before, she felt many times more enthralled and devoted since her foolish departure and her inspired return. She could barely reconstruct what had ever led her to leave and what demented foolishness had kept her away so long. Something about Helena, Lou's friend of twenty years whom she loved and sometimes made love with. It was nothing to be upset about, Lou had assured her. Rena felt highly honored that Lou had chosen to speak of this with her.

They were in front of the fireplace, Lou on the sofa, Rena on the rocking chair. Rena was glad it was cool enough for a fire. She had pulled the chair as near the sofa as it would go. The nearness to Lou was her air. She rocked contentedly, watching the flames. "It's so good to be here. Did I mention that?"

"Once or twice," Lou said, smiling.

"You're really glad I'm back?"

"Of course I am. This is where you belong."

"It was awful being away."

Lou nodded. "I knew you'd return."

"I thought I never wanted to see you again."

"You made a mistake."

"I was like a zombie in Chicago." Rena shuddered. "Everything was so empty. I love being here with you, Lou. I just love it." Her eyes shone with adoration.

"Stand up, Rena."

Rena stood immediately.

"See that vase?"

"Yes."

"Go stick your hand inside of it."

Without a moment's hesitation, Rena took the vase, carefully placed the flowers on the table, and put her hand into it.

"What's inside?"

"Water."

"Drink it."

Rena brought the vase to her lips, drank until Lou told her to stop.

Lou watched with apparent satisfaction. "Tell me why you did that."

"Because you said to."

"Did you wonder why I told you to?"

"No."

Lou nodded. She gestured toward the fire. "And if I told you to put your hand in those flames."

"Do you want me to?"

"What if I did?"

"Then I'd do it."

"Would you get burned?"

"I'm not sure. Yes, I suppose I would."

"Knowing that, you'd do it anyway?"

"If you said to. If you wanted me to, then it must be what I should do, even if it would burn."

Lou smiled. "That's a lot of trust."

"Yes." Rena's eyes were round and guileless. "I trust you absolutely."

"I think you do."

"Whatever you ask me to do is what's best for me to do."

"Come sit on the sofa with me."

Rena moved hastily, settling herself as close to Lou as she guessed Lou would want. Lou touched Rena's knee and stroked her leg. Rena felt tingling shivers. She longed to crawl into Lou's arms and feel them around her. Lou looked at the fire and Rena continued looking at Lou. What she saw was not a mere human being: Lou's power and goodness seemed limitless.

With her fingertips, Lou caressed Rena's cheek softly, lightly. Rena turned her head to feel with her lips the touch of Lou's superhuman flesh. The magic of the contact stirred in Rena an overpowering sense of joy — total joy and awe. "You must be God," she said.

Lou smiled. "I am to you."

"I adore you. I worship you."

113

"I can see that." Lou's smile had faded. "Perhaps you're ready," she said. "There are some things I want from you."

"Anything." Rena was stroking Lou's hand, just barely touching the surface of the magic skin.

"I'll ask a lot from you."

"Anything." Rena touched her lips to Lou's palm. "Anything at all. I'm yours completely."

"I'd like you to be mine."

"I am," Rena declared with unreserved sincerity. "I feel like I'm part of you, like I don't exist separately from you. I *am* yours. Completely."

Lou pulled her hand away. "But that's not quite true, Rena. You say you're mine, that I own you, and yet you've kept part of yourself away from me." She touched Rena's temple. "Inside here. There are things in here that I don't know, that aren't mine."

"I'll give them to you. Anything you want."

"It won't be easy."

"I don't care." She looked at Lou with total adoration.

"To tell me what's inside there, you have to have the thoughts. With the thoughts come the feelings."

"I feel overwhelmed by you. I feel as if I've transcended being just a person, like you've lifted me into another universe."

"You feel that way?"

"Oh, yes." Eyes closed, Rena rubbed her cheek softly against Lou's hand and upward along her bare arm.

"I'll want to know everything." Lou ran her forefinger along Rena's ear and down her neck.

Rena could barely breathe.

"Would you like me to make love with you?" Lou asked.

Rena gasped. She closed her eyes again, nodding, and rested her head against Lou's chest.

"I will," Lou said, "when you give yourself to me completely and are free."

Rena's arms went over Lou's neck. "Yes, I'm free. You made me free and now we can —"

"But you're not free." Lou unwrapped Rena's arms from her neck. "We've just begun. We've taken only the first step."

"I'm ready now, I'm very ready to make love with you."

"No." Lou smiled knowingly. "But I do believe you're now ready for the real journey to freedom."

"I'm ready." Rena shivered from Lou's fingers stroking her back.

"When you tell me what's locked up inside that brain of yours, that's when you'll be free."

Rena looked down. "You mean the memories, don't you?"

"Of course."

She looked at Lou. "But I can't remember them. They're gone."

"Not gone, my dear, just hidden. From you as well as from me. We have to bring them out of hiding."

Rena's fingers picked nervously at the sofa. "I don't know. I don't know if I can."

"I say you can."

Rena looked into her powerful eyes. "I can, then," she declared. "All right. Yes."

"Good. Then we'll begin to *commune,* you and I, talk intimately together. I will ask you to look inside yourself and you will."

Rena nodded.

"You'll tell me everything that I ask about and you'll come to know everything that you need to know to be free."

"My father?"

"Yes."

Rena swallowed. "You want me to do this?"

Lou nodded.

Rena nodded in return. "I'll commune with you," she said.

Alone in her room that night, Rena sat on the chair by the open window and thought about the conversation. It was dark outside, the world barely illuminated by the stars and moon peeking through the clouds. A cool breeze grazed her cheeks. Her head felt very clear. The situation was very clear.

I have to do what Lou says. It's dangerous, what she wants me to do, but I can't do otherwise. She wants me to remember. I have to do whatever she wants. The horror. The evil things. If I remember, then surely it means death. Oh, how I adore her. It's so very dangerous.

After their two-mile run the next morning, Lou asked Rena how she was feeling about their talk yesterday.

"Kind of scared," Rena said.

Lou was on the sofa. "Come sit over here."

Rena settled comfortably under her arm.

"That feel good?"

Rena nodded.

"Remember that time we went rock climbing?" Lou asked.

"Yes."

"You were frightened then too, remember? And I told you how to handle it. You learned you could do more than you thought, didn't you? You trusted me and it turned out well."

"Yes, it did." Rena smiled. "I felt a sense of accomplishment. I didn't think I could do it."

"Fear," Lou said. "Then trust, leading you to stretch yourself, take risks. Then success and growth."

"I feel safest when you hold me."

"I noticed that." Lou put her other arm around Rena, holding her tenderly. "That tactile need, very basic."

"It's more than just the touching."

"Oh, I know, you horny tart."

Rena giggled.

Lou let go of her and moved back. "After you're done working in the orchard today, I want us to meet. In the womb room."

"All right."

"Do you know why?"

"To make love?" Rena smiled coyly.

"One-track mind. That's not what we're going to do in the womb room."

"We're going to *commune*."

"Right. See you at four-thirty. Clean up first, and wear something real comfortable."

* * * * *

116

Rena walked into the womb room at exactly 4:30. Lou was not there yet. She stretched out on the contour chair and looked around. It was indeed a very beautiful room. Warm. A feeling of softness. Pleasing to the eye, to the touch. She leaned back, immediately feeling very relaxed.

"Hi, sweetie." Lou had a tray with her. She set it on the table. "You chose the right chair. I want you to be very comfortable." She handed Rena a cup of tea. "Drink this, it'll loosen up your tight parts."

Rena took the tea. It was delicious, just slightly sweet and very aromatic, different from any she'd ever had before. They sat a few minutes, drinking and talking about the day. When Rena's cup was empty, Lou pulled a stuffed, armless chair next to her and told her to lie back. She sat at Rena's side near her head and began stroking her forehead.

"All right," she said, "let yourself relax . . . let go of any tension . . . just relax . . . breathing deeply." She kept stroking Rena's forehead with her cool fingers as she spoke in a purring voice. "Deep slow breaths . . . that's right, close your eyes and just let yourself relax . . . more and more completely relaxed . . ."

Lou continued the stroking and the soft words for another ten minutes. Rena was more relaxed than she could ever remember being.

"Now, I'm going to ask you some questions about your past, about experiences you've had, and I want you to remember them very vividly, as if you're living them now as you speak of them."

They went as far back as Rena's twelfth year. Rena had one memory after another. She recalled her first impressions of the United States. Arriving in Chicago. Her mother being frightened and very quiet. The vastness of everything. The dinginess. The newness. Rena remembered it all very clearly. "I felt like I was born again." She laughed. "Not in the religious sense. I don't know, something about coming to Chicago . . . that's when it seems my life began. I think I'd been . . . I don't know, very closed off to things before that."

The next *commune,* the following day, was similar. First the cup of tea, the deep relaxation, and then the memories. Again they did not go further back than Rena's twelfth year. Rena was enjoying the communing. It was very gratifying to have someone so interested in the details of her life. It was particularly gratifying that that someone was Lou Bonnig. Rena felt valued. Important. And she felt even more devoted to Lou. It wasn't frightening at all.

Once, when Lou told her to conjure up a more recent memory, she talked about Pat, of the day Pat moved in with her. She spoke of getting intense sexual pleasure with Pat, having amazingly powerful orgasms. When she began speaking of the last time they made love, she started to get upset. Lou stroked her and said soothing words and soon Rena felt comfortable again. They moved to other memories. Never did Lou ask her to remember anything before her move to the United States.

Trish was no longer staying at the house. She came by occasionally to visit with Lou and do odd jobs for her. She was cordial to Rena but no longer friendly. On Sunday, Casey came unexpectedly. She and Rena spent most of the day together.

"Well, I have to admit you seem happy here." Casey took her glasses off, rubbed her eyes, then put them back on. "Are you in love with her?"

Rena didn't answer right away. They were at the guest cabin at De Nova where Casey was staying. Rena had picked up Casey's hairbrush and was running her fingers over the bristles.

"You can tell me," Casey said.

"I don't know what to call it, what I feel for Lou. *In love* doesn't quite seem to capture it." She stroked the handle of the brush tenderly. "Enchanted, maybe. I'm enchanted with her. She's the most important person in my life — the only one, in a sense."

"Mm-m." Casey stared at her hands. "I probably shouldn't have come."

"Oh, I'm glad you did."

"I don't think I'll stay the night."

"Oh damn! It bothers you, doesn't it? That I'm so . . . that Lou's so important to me."

Casey stood and went to the window, her back to Rena. "I'm glad you're doing better. That's what counts." She turned, took the brush from Rena and put it in her bag. "I'm leaving." She walked to the door. "Call me sometime."

The next meeting with Lou, *tea and communing*, as Rena had come to think of these sessions, was more intense. Lou asked more questions, made Rena think more deeply about the memories and her feelings. It was hard, but afterwards Rena felt even more bonded to Lou. She talked in more detail about her attraction to dominating women and about her sexual experiences with them. Lou asked many questions, stroking Rena's face or arm or hand as they talked. Rena realized aspects of these experiences that she hadn't been fully aware of before. "It was as if I had no choice, once they were in my life — Rebecca, and later, Pat. I had to please them. I couldn't help it ... succumbing to them ... submitting. It gave me pleasure, but it was also like I owed it to them for some reason, like I had to make amends for something."

Lou let her speak, listening, encouraging, asking questions. "How did it end with Rebecca?"

Rena took a long time to answer. "She moved to Seattle. She fell off the scaffold. Rebecca was a painter, you know, painted houses. I used to help her sometimes."

"I see. No wonder you did such a good paint job here. Did she get hurt?"

"Broke her leg. She had a friend in Seattle. They'd known each other for years. They'd visit back and forth. I didn't know they were lovers but finally I caught on." Rena's face muscles tightened. "I remember when I found out. It was a Saturday morning. Later that day, I went with Rebecca to a job. She was doing the window trim on an old three-story house on Wilson Avenue. We were using three different colors, kind of like San Francisco houses. That's the day she fell."

Lou nodded. "OK, I want you to let go of those memories now." She frequently shifted the scenes Rena was to re-create, back and forth in time and place. "Tell me about your trip to the States from Greece. Picture it and tell me what you remember."

119

Rena had no trouble. She talked of the little children who sat behind her mother and her on the airplane, how fussy they got and how Rena had entertained them with crayons and books.

"And now a little earlier, the airport in Greece."

Rena spoke of saying goodbye to relatives and friends.

"And packing to leave."

That too was clear and easily recalled. It had taken place in 1962, in the summer.

"Now," Lou said. Her hand was resting on Rena's shoulder. Rena's eyes were closed. "I want you to go back earlier. Picture something that happened in the spring of 1962 or earlier."

Rena tensed. Usually she was quick in coming up with a memory. This time it took several minutes. "I'm walking home from school..."

Lou touched Rena's fingers. "Mm-hm."

"I have that feeling, that heavy feeling in my chest. I'm walking down the street near our apartment. Everything is white and bright. I'm wearing sunglasses. I'm thinking I wish the sun weren't shining. I feel very sad. No, not just sad, I feel ... really ... dejected. Heavy. I'm scratching my neck. It itches terribly. It's so ugly."

Rena stopped talking. Lou stroked her gently. "Go on."

"It's because of my evil."

Lou's eyebrows lifted slightly.

"That's why. My evilness made me ugly. Ugly like a lizard." Rena twisted on the chair.

"What does your neck look like?" Lou ran her fingers along Rena's long lovely neck.

"Rough and scaly, on my neck and behind my ears. It's my punishment but no one knows that. Taki calls me lizard, so do the other kids. I walk home alone. I go the long way so I won't see any of them. My head is down, my neck is itching, it's hot and sunny and I'm a lizard."

"OK, switch now, Rena. Back a little further. Picture when the rash first came, when you first got it."

Rena was silent a few moments. "I thought it was just an allergy. That's what my mother said. She said it would go away. I remember going to the doctor. Putting this greasy ointment on it. It didn't go away. And then I realized it was my punishment. It had to be. I was being punished!" Rena was growing increasingly agitated.

"Close your eyes, sweetie," Lou said. "It's OK. It's OK. Keep them closed." Lou stroked Rena's brow. "You realized it was your punishment. Tell me about that, how you came to realize it."

Rena took several deep breaths. "I'd had the rash a while, a couple weeks maybe. I remember one day . . . I was in my bedroom. My neck was itching so badly. I pictured myself getting Mom's big knife that she keeps in the top drawer and pushing it . . . into . . ." Rena's hands were fists, one atop the other, pressing tightly against her abdomen. Her eyes were still closed, the hair at her forehead wet and clinging to her face. "I have to die for what I did!" She was writhing on the chair. "My lizard skin isn't enough punishment!"

"OK, it's OK, hon. Stop remembering that now." Lou patted Rena's chest. "Take some deep breaths," she said. "Breathe deeply . . . slowly . . . that's right. Good, just letting yourself relax. Good. Breathe in. Mm-hm. Letting the tension go . . ."

Rena's hands rested loosely at her sides. Her face muscles had relaxed. Lou slipped her arms under Rena and cradled her, held her close and Rena became more relaxed until she fell asleep, held in Lou's arms.

The next night it was cool in the womb room. Fall had come. They built a fire and watched it as they drank their tea, and then Lou began the relaxation talk and Rena slipped comfortably into that very calm place.

The first memory Lou asked for was from Rena's high school days, the day she learned she'd won the scholarship. That was easy to recall and fun to talk about. Then Lou asked her to recall her eleventh birthday. That was a little more difficult.

"My mother invited people over. I didn't want them there. I didn't like being with people." It was a painful memory but Rena let herself recall it and speak of it. Lou remained right next to her, touching her reassuringly.

"And now your tenth birthday."

Rena was silent.

"Tell me when you have it in mind."

She did not speak. "Nothing comes," she said at last.

"Keep trying," Lou said.

Rena twisted on the chair and Lou spoke the words of relaxation, but the tension would not leave. Rena squirmed, her face full of pain.

"The morning of your tenth birthday," Lou said, stroking the soft skin of Rena's face. "You wake up and . . ."

"I don't know." Rena sat up. "I . . . I can't. I'm afraid."

Lou held her and Rena wept softly, but she could talk no more. She could not go on and so they stopped.

The next night at ten o'clock they met again in the womb room. Lou had just returned home from a dinner date in town. They drank tea silently. Everything seemed so safe and calm, yet Rena knew danger lay ahead. They finished their tea.

"All right, lie back, girl."

After Rena was fully relaxed, Lou asked her to talk about the rash again. Rena let her mind go back in time and immediately felt pained. "It was horrible," she said, "when I finally realized what the rash meant. I got this crushing heavy feeling. My punishment. My evilness."

"And what were you being punished for?"

Rena's eyes were closed. Lou was right next to her, her hand resting on Rena's arm. She felt safe. The memories kept coming, clearer and clearer. She could feel the itching. Her fingers went to her neck, her nails scraping the clear smooth skin.

"I don't think I should." Her eyes were part way open.

"Should what?"

"Remember any more."

"I want you to, Rena. Go on. Keep remembering."

"You really want me to?"

"Yes."

She closed her eyes again. Her lips moved. Her eyelids flickered. She let the memories emerge. A little moan came from somewhere inside of her, and then she spoke. "It wasn't a hunting accident." Her voice was low and scratchy. "That's not how he died."

Her chest was heaving. Lou leaned closer to her. Rena kept digging at her skin. Her neck was getting raw. Lou gently took Rena's hand to stop the scratching.

"That's why I had to be punished! Oh God!"

She writhed on the chair. Her eyes were open wide then. Raw pain took her. She was frantic.

"*I* did it!" she groaned. "I killed him! I KILLED MY FATHER!"

CHAPTER FOURTEEN

Lou's arms were wrapped around Rena's convulsing body. She pulled her to her lap and held her there as Rena moaned and cried.

"That's good, Rena, very good. You're being brave. You're letting yourself say it, those terrifying words, that's good." Lou rocked her, pressing her cheek against Rena's, rocking her and holding her for a long, long time.

"You have to go on, Rena," Lou said at last. "Tell me more. Tell me what happened."

Rena opened her eyes. She was panting. "I need to stand." She got up and paced the room, her breathing still labored. Her legs were wobbly. Finally she sat, not on the lounge chair, but on the upright one facing Lou. She was shaking.

"Can you go on now?" Lou asked.

Rena stood again. "No. Not now. I need to move, run. I'm going jogging."

"It's late."

Rena went toward the door.

"I'll go with you," Lou said.

Lou was panting with exhaustion long before Rena headed back to the house. They had gone over three miles and not spoken a word; Rena had stayed yards ahead of Lou most of the run. In the kitchen, she wiped her face and neck with a towel. "I'm going to sit downstairs by the fire awhile."

Lou took the towel from Rena's hand. "All right."

"Alone."

"I'll be in my office."

She watched the flames crisply whirl together, the blues, oranges, whites. She didn't blink, didn't move. She didn't think. Her face was expressionless, her brain making Alpha waves in the eerie reflection of the fire's glow.

An hour later, she went upstairs. Lou came to her in the womb room.

"How are you doing?"

Rena didn't answer.

"Are you ready to talk?"

"Yes."

"About your father?"

"Yes."

Rena was on the contour chair. Lou took her place beside her. "What comes to mind?"

"That I murdered him."

Lou took a deep breath. "What else?"

"Just that."

"How did you do it?"

"Hit him on the head."

Lou looked nauseated. "Why?"

Rena didn't answer.

Lou waited, staring at Rena. Finally she spoke. "What was he like?"

"Daddy?" Rena shook her head. "He was wonderful. Perfect." She looked toward the ceiling, biting her lip.

"Tell me about him."

She closed her eyes. "He was very handsome. He had a soft voice, smooth like flannel, like flannel on my cheek. He used to take

125

me places. Just the two of us. I loved him so much. We did things together, Daddy and I. He loved me. He loved me very much."

Lou nodded. "What things did you and your father do together?"

Rena's eyes were open now and had a faraway look. "Sometimes I'd sit on his lap. I loved being close to him. I loved it when he held me. He told me stories. He was good," she said dreamily, "Daddy was good. We'd be together in his little house."

"His little house?"

"Yes. Oh, God! Oh, no!" Rena's body was rigid with tension. "Oh, why did I do it! I never wanted to hurt him. I just wanted him to love me." She was clasping her head between her hands.

"Did something bad happen in the little house?"

Rena's eyes were shut again, tightly.

"What happened, Rena?"

"I loved him so much."

"Yes."

"He taught me about love. Uncle Stavros said he loved me too much."

"Too much? What did your uncle mean?"

Rena sat up straight. Her eyes were very clear. "I want another cup of tea."

"After you remember some more."

Rena looked directly at Lou. She did not seem at all like a child then, nor the least bit intimidated by Lou. "No, really, I'd like some now. I want to take a break and then I'll go on."

"All right."

"You make the tea, I'm going to make a phone call."

"All right, Rena."

Rena went to Darla's bedroom and dialed the phone. Lou went downstairs.

"Hello, Casey."

"Rena, hello! How are you? It's been a long time."

"I miss you."

"You do? Wow, I . . . well, that's good to hear. Is everything OK?"

126

"Yes, more or less. Casey, I just wanted to call and tell you that I ... that I think about you. I ... I really ... I want you to know how much you mean to me."

"Well, thank you, Rena. Really, that means a lot. More than you probably know, but what ... You worry me. Why are you telling me this now? What's going on?"

"Not to worry, worry-girl. An impulse, OK? I just needed to hear your sexy voice. You know, Casey, I may not show it sometimes, but you're very important to me. Very important. So how have you been? I hope you don't mind my calling so late. What's happening in Chicago?"

They talked for ten minutes, Casey filling Rena in on the latest happenings in her life, Rena talking about the good apple crop this year and sharing minor gossip about the De Nova women. Rena was very glad that they talked. The tea was waiting when she returned to the womb room. "How's Casey?" Lou asked.

"How did you know I called Casey?"

"I surmised."

"She's very special to me."

"I know."

Rena sipped her tea silently. She was strangely calm as she thought about it, about her father and about killing him. The truth was out at last and the truth would make her free. She laughed sadly at the cliche.

She was ready to continue. "On the last day," she said slowly, "in the village —it was a warm, sunny day — I ran to find him."

Lou settled in to listen, watching Rena closely.

"Everybody was crying. Uncle Stavros was dead. I ran to find Daddy, past the two hills to Daddy's little house. I knew he'd be there." Rena bit painfully on her lip. Her face was soaked with tears.

Lou waited for her to go on.

"The door was open. I went inside ..."

Lou waited.

Rena said no more. Her head was pounding.

Lou continued to wait, sitting tensely. "And ..." she said at last.

Rena blinked. "It was ... horrible!"

"What happened, Rena?"

127

She was staring straight ahead. "I remember the lamp . . . I was holding it . . . the brass lamp . . . I had it in my hand."

"And your father?"

"The lamp had blood on it."

Lou looked ill. "Was your father there?"

"Oh, yes. He's on the floor. He's lying there so still. Blood is all . . . all over and, oh God, oohh . . ." Rena was trembling, she held her stomach.

"Come on, let's get to the john."

Lou held Rena's hair back as she vomited. Afterwards Rena sat on Lou's bathroom floor, weak and exhausted. Lou coaxed her to her feet and laid her on the bed. She stroked Rena's clammy forehead until finally Rena fell asleep.

Rena awakened once in the night and didn't know where she was. Lou's bed, she realized. By herself, but safe in Lou's bed. She fell right back to sleep. In the morning, she still felt weak and shaky. She did not work that day. She stayed in the house. Amazing that she could have forgotten it and now it was so clear to her. She had killed him and soon she'd kill herself. She did not try to remember any more about it. She knew she would soon enough. She kept the thoughts away until after dinner when she and Lou went to the womb room and drank their tea and sat before the fire. Rena started talking without lying on the contour chair, without Lou giving her the suggestions to relax.

"My father was a gentle, loving man. I used to visit him sometimes where he worked, at the art museum. He would talk to me about the paintings and about sculpture. I've always loved art museums." Suddenly, Rena turned from the fire and looked directly at Lou. "I have no idea why I killed him."

"Come lie down."

Rena stretched herself out and Lou took her place at Rena's side.

"You're beginning to feel very relaxed," Lou began, "just allowing the tension to flow out of you . . . feeling very comfortable, very, very relaxed . . ."

Rena's breathing was deep and regular. Her eyes were closed.

"Are you ready?" Lou asked.

"Yes."

"All right. You're remembering now, going back in time, back to that day, the day your father died. You ran to find him. You ran to the little house. Something happened . . ."

Rena reached for Lou's hand and, finding it, let herself go back those twenty-seven years. "There was so much blood. He . . . oh, Daddy, oh, I'm so sorry." She was clasping Lou's hand tightly. "Oh, no, there it is!" Her voice quivered.

"Go on, Rena."

"Next to daddy, lying there all bloody and hideous . . . oh God . . . it's . . . ohh . . ."

"It's what, Rena? What is it?"

"The arm!" Her breathing came in labored gasps. "Uncle Stavros' arm!" She shuddered with revulsion. "It's all bloody, even on the tattoo. There's blood even on the tattoo . . . oh, God!" Rena clung to Lou's hand. Sobs wracked her body. She cried for a long time, the sobbing finally turning to whimpers. She wiped her tears away.

"Do you know how it happened?" Lou asked quietly.

"I did it." Rena's voice was low-pitched and cold.

"What did you do?"

"Killed them."

"You killed them? Both of them?"

"Yes."

Lou's jaw tightened. "How?"

"I shot my uncle with a gun. I hit Daddy with the lamp." Rena said the words flatly. "I cut off Uncle Stavros' arm."

"I don't believe it!"

"Uncle Stavros would never let me touch the chainsaw. He wouldn't let me but I did it anyway."

"How, Rena, how could you have?" Lou wiped perspiration from her forehead. "You were ten years old! It's impossible."

"I'm evil."

Lou flexed her shoulders, looking as if they pained her. "Rena, let's go back a little, OK? Are you OK?"

129

"Yes, I'm OK. I'm fine."

Lou did not look fine at all. "What happened before the killings, earlier that day? Can you remember how the day began?"

Rena took a deep breath. She was rubbing her hand along the side of the contour chair. "I remember feeling happy that morning. Daddy's coming today. I always felt happy when Daddy came. He's going to stay all weekend. He'll be here by lunchtime. That's what Mommie told me. *Agapo ton patera mou toso polie.*"

"Stay with English, Rena."

Rena opened her eyes. "What did I say?"

"I don't know, it was probably Greek. Stay with English."

"I never speak Greek."

"You were happy about your father coming . . ."

Rena let her eyes close again. "I looked at the sky. I knew it wasn't time yet but I went to the little house anyway. To wait for him. He always stopped at the little house before he went to Grandma's. He wrote poems and things."

"So you went to the little house."

"Yes. But I could see that the door was closed. I knew he wasn't there yet. He always left it open when he was there. I went to swing on the swing and wait until Daddy came. I started swinging and singing and then I heard something. I looked up and I saw him at the window. It was Daddy. He was in the house. I ran inside and . . . and . . ." Rena was sobbing.

"And what?"

Rena shook her head. She started to sit up.

Lou coaxed her back down. "Tell me, Rena."

"I don't remember. The next thing I remember is all the blood."

"Try to take it step by step. He was at the window. You went to the door. Was it locked? Did he open it for you?"

"I was angry." Rena's face hardened. "I felt crazy with the anger."

"Why? What happened? What made you angry?"

"I went inside and . . . I don't know. Oh, God, I felt terrible. Yes, now I remember. I remember running. I ran away. I ran until I was past the two hills and then I walked. I walked the rest of the way to the river. I went to the nest. My nest place. I sat there and then after a while I felt better. It felt good, what I was doing. Yes, I liked it when I rubbed myself like that. I liked that feeling. I never did it when anyone was around. Only at my river nest and sometimes in bed."

"You were masturbating?"

"I don't know how long I stayed there but I started to feel bad again. I ran to Grandma's. I found Uncle Stavros outside and that's when . . . when I killed him."

Lou was leaning forward, her muscles rigid. "You killed your uncle."

"Yes."

"Shit! Rena . . . all right, how? How did you do it?"

"With a gun."

"What gun? Where did you get a gun?"

Rena shook her head. "I'm not sure. Grandpa had a gun. He kept it in the closet."

"Oh, Rena." Lou seemed close to tears. Rena was crying silently.

"Oh, I'm sorry, Daddy, I'm sorry about Uncle Stavros. I'm sorry what I did."

Lou took a deep silent breath. "Does your mother know you killed them?"

"My mother?" It took a while for the question to register. "I don't know. I guess not. She never said anything. No, of course not. She couldn't possibly know."

"Who do they think killed them, your mother and everyone else?"

"They think it was a hunting accident."

Lou shook her head. "No, Rena, no. It doesn't make sense. It couldn't be the way you're saying. It couldn't be." Lou's face was flushed and lined.

"You're exhausted," Rena said calmly, "and so am I." She pulled herself up from the chair, sighed heavily, and then, without looking at Lou, walked leadenly to the door and out of the room.

131

CHAPTER FIFTEEN

Lou had trouble falling asleep. Alternative explanations scrambled around in her head. On one extreme was the possibility that it was *all* fabricated. For whatever twisted reasons, Rena could have created it all in her little ten-year-old mind and never stopped believing it. Maybe there was no "little house." Maybe there wasn't even an Uncle Stavros. And her father — who could tell? Maybe her father was a real creep, or maybe she never even knew him.

Lou realized she was perspiring. She tossed the covers off.

Maybe Rena had made up a wonderful fantasy father to replace the father she never had and then, as she grew older, she became more and more frustrated that he wasn't real and finally she killed the fantasy by imagining she killed the made-up father and the made-up uncle. Lou spent a lot of time on that possibility, elaborating on it until it was so complex and confusing that she laughed at herself for her own imaginative fabrications.

She was sitting up in her bed now, the pillow stuffed behind her back.

The other extreme was that *all* of it was true. Lou shuddered. Children certainly have committed murder, she thought. But, Rena! Could she really have such a dark violent part to her nature? Was Trish right? Shit! Maybe she'd bitten off more than she could chew with this one. Lou ran her fingers through her disheveled hair. Should she call Dr. Kepper? Maybe Rena got treatment back then. Maybe no one ever knew. This is getting freaky, she thought, twisting around until the sheet was hopelessly tangled in her legs.

Cut off his arm with a saw? Could a ten-year-old do that? Lou tossed some more. She seriously considered calling Dr. Kepper. Was she really a killer? A cold chill caught her insides. She had to talk with someone. She'd call Dr. Kepper.

But it was Trish she talked with instead. She called her at De Nova the next morning and they went to Mary's Kitchen, a truck stop near the highway.

"I found out why Rena feels so guilty," Lou said.

Trish listened silently as Lou told her the story. Lou told her everything she'd learned. When she was finished, Trish's face was drawn. "It's worse than I thought," she said, shaking her head. "Some people have twists in them that are almost impossible for us to fathom. They're missing something, conscience maybe, or compassion. Or maybe it's that they *have* something that the rest of us don't, some depraved part to their nature that makes them different. Aberrant. That makes them do things that would be unthinkable to most of us."

"Rena's not like that."

"I certainly didn't think so at first either."

"But now you do, I take it."

"Normal people don't have eyes like that, Lou. They don't get that look in their eyes." She paused. "It's creepy, but worse than that, frightening, very frightening."

"So you're saying you believe she killed them."

Trish looked extremely distraught. "Oh, God, Lou, what have you gotten involved in?"

"Trish, don't believe it! She couldn't have."

"I wouldn't believe it either if it weren't for what I saw with my own eyes."

133

Lou sighed. "I don't know why I thought I could talk with *you* about it."

Trish smiled sadly. "Because I'm the one you talk to."

"It always used to help . . ."

"This is no exception."

". . . to bounce things off you. Trish, you *can't* believe it! She couldn't actually have killed them."

"I know, Lou. I think I know how you feel. I agree it's mind-boggling, but she confessed, Lou. She admitted it. She told you how she did it and how people covered up, calling it a hunting accident. She told you what happened — that she got angry, flipped out or *in* to that part of her that's a killer, and she killed. Yes, I do believe it and it scares the shit out of me."

"She can't be a murderer."

"She is what she is. She's not a normal human being."

"They were killed in a hunting accident," Lou said quietly. "Rena feels responsible for it. That's all it is. We just have to figure out why."

"You don't get an arm sawed off in a hunting accident."

Lou's jaw was tight.

"On one level she seems like a really neat person. I'll grant you that." Trish accepted a refill on her coffee, pausing until the waitress left. "I was liking her a lot at first. You know that. But we didn't know about that other part of her then. When that other part . . . when I saw her with that knife . . ." Trish shuddered. "As far as I'm concerned, what she told you absolutely confirms it. Call it what you will — evil, psychopathology, brain damage. Whatever it is, she's got it. It's in her and when she gets enraged, it comes out. Takes over. Her father got her angry, and she did what she did."

"No." Lou was shaking her head vigorously. "No, you're wrong." The pain across Lou's shoulders was excruciating. Suddenly she remembered Rebecca. Her face fell.

"What? What is it?"

Lou absent-mindedly heaped sugar into her cup. "She had a lover once who was involved with someone else . . ."

"Yeah? So?"

"Rena found out. Some scaffolding collapsed. Rena's lover fell and broke her leg."

Trish rolled her eyes. "Oh, great. Was Rena..."

"Rena was working with her that day. Shit!"

"Sonofabitch! Damn!" Trish was tapping rapidly with her spoon. "It's not surprising though, you know. Very scary, but not surprising. So Rena messed with the scaffolding and..."

"No!" Lou clenched her teeth, shaking her head vigorously. "She couldn't have."

"She gets jealous, feels rejected, and then she totally loses it."

"It was an accident."

"Maybe she felt rejected by her father and that's what set her off." Trish pushed her coffee cup aside. "Lou, get rid of her. Please. She's dangerous. Get her out of your life before..." Trish shook her head, her eyes dark with worry.

"Nonsense."

"She tried to get you once."

"Right. Thanks for saving my life."

Trish's eyes narrowed angrily. "She's not like the others. You're not just dealing with some mildly troubled person here, Lou. What the hell will it take to convince you?"

Lou took a sip of her coffee. "A lot more than what we've got," she said.

"She needs to be locked up."

Lou was staring at the linoleum table top. "There's still so much of it that's a mystery."

"Curiosity killed the cat."

"Like the birds, for instance. Why does she kill birds? What does that mean?"

"It could mean anything. It doesn't matter. What matters is your safety. And other people's. She's a killer on the loose."

"The bird killing could be a form of self-punishment maybe — symbolic suicide."

"Or practice."

Lou ignored her. "One possibility I've been thinking of — it could account for the guilt and the anger — is that her father abused her, molested her sexually. That could be what happened in the little

135

house." She looked at her friend. "Think about it, Trish. It fits. They molested her, both of them maybe." Lou dug into the thought. "And maybe that's related to her sexual thing too. These two powerful men manipulate her, intimidate her, sexually use her and then as an adult she's only able to have orgasms with people who have power over her." Lou was squeezing her napkin into a tight wad. She pictured little ten-year-old Rena being sexually mauled by her father. A spasm of revulsion shook her. "They abused her until she couldn't take it anymore. She had enough and so she murdered them both."

Trish watched, saying nothing.

"No." Lou shook her head. "No, kids don't do that. Even if she wanted to, how could she have?"

"She could have." Lou crushed out her cigarette and lit another. "This is crazy. What the hell are we doing?" She tapped the cigarette nervously on the ashtray. "This is getting us nowhere. You and I don't know what really happened. You think she's capable of anything. I think she's fantasizing. But neither of us really knows. It's Rena who has the answers, not us."

"She's given you the answers."

"What she's given me is a guilt-produced fantasy," Lou said stubbornly. She leaned back in the booth. Her shoulders were unbearably tight. "But she knows what really happened. It's in there somewhere, in her mind."

"You're being very stubborn, Lou. Foolish, too, which certainly is out of character for you."

Lou was holding the wadded paper napkin in both hands. "OK, maybe she really did do it." She opened up the napkin and spread it flat. "All right, I'll try not to rule that out totally. But if she did, then there has to be a reason, right? A motive. Something to explain it. Something that makes sense."

"Bad seed," Trish said. "Twisted."

"I have to keep at it with her. We have to keep communing. It's frightening, believe me, but it would be worse to stop. She has to remember more."

"Let a shrink help her remember. Preferably one in a women's prison or psycho ward."

"That's not the answer. *I* can help her. I want to!"

Trish shook her head. "It's your life, Lou." There were tears in her eyes.

Rena awakened well-rested and calm. It was all making sense — the terrible guilt she'd felt, the sense of evilness. Knowing why brought relief. She felt the horror of it too, the absolute crushing horror, but also the relief. I'm almost free, she thought. Just a few more memories and it will be over. She felt calm, deadly calm. No longer did she feel compelled to do the remembering just for Lou.

Rena smiled thinking of Lou. In addition to remembering why she had killed, there was one more thing she needed to do. Why she had to do it, she wasn't sure. She smiled some more. Before she died, she would make love with Lou Bonnig — wild, fierce, uninhibited, passionate, evil, fucking love.

Oh, yes, I am evil, Rena thought. I am what I am. She jumped out of bed eagerly, ready to begin her day.

The house was empty when she went downstairs. She made herself a light breakfast then went outside. She hadn't been in the barnyard for ages, hadn't even let her eyes look in that direction. It was a cool morning. The light jacket she wore was hardly enough and she shivered as she entered the chicken coop. The geese honked at her, the chickens fluttered. Rena watched them peck and cluck. She felt nothing, nothing at all. Finally, bored, she left and went back to the house.

When Lou returned she wanted to have tea upstairs in the womb room. Rena, too, was anxious to begin.

After finishing her tea, Rena went to the contour chair. The room was warm. She felt very comfortable and was quite relaxed before Lou had said more than a few phrases about letting go of tension and breathing deeply.

"The day they were killed," Lou began, "you went to the little house. Now I want you to recreate it. Let yourself go back there and remember, remember all of it."

Rena nodded. She let her thoughts drift back in time, back to that summer day twenty-seven years ago. The memories came. She went to the little house to wait for her father. He was already there. She got angry. She went to the river, then later, to her grandparents' where she found her uncle. She killed him. She cut off her uncle's arm and took it back with her to the little house. She bludgeoned her father to death with the brass lamp.

Lou made her go over it and over it. "After your uncle was dead, you went back to the little house to find your father. Is that right?"

"Yes."

"And what happened then?"

"I killed him," Rena said coolly.

"All right. Tell me in detail how it happened."

"I went inside . . ." She was pushing hard, trying to remember exactly how it was. "He . . . everything had gone wrong. It was all wrong. I . . . that's when I killed him."

"How, Rena? How? How could you have? He just sat there and let you bash him over the head?"

"I sneaked up on him."

"Can you picture it? Are you really picturing this?"

"I wanted him to myself," Rena said in a very low soft voice.

Lou cocked her head. "So you didn't want to share him. Was someone —"

"I loved him so much. He was everything to me."

"Were you afraid you were losing him?"

Rena didn't answer. Her head was achy and she felt feverish. She told Lou she could do no more that day.

At the next communing session, the blocking continued. Lou decided to have her talk of other childhood memories. Through Rena's eyes, Lou came to know her family: Her father, Antoni — a kind, quiet, artistic, pensive man, devoted to his brother, Stavros; her mother, Maria — reliable, caring, agreeable, unassertive, devoted to her husband; her Uncle Stavros — a tyrant, a large, loud, hairy man who Rena had to please in order to please her father; her cousin, Taki, Stavros' son — a nasty, small-minded, competitive boy who mercilessly harassed Rena. The others — her grandparents, aunts, uncles — seemed to have played relatively minor roles in Rena's life.

Except for the meetings with Lou, Rena kept to herself. She worked in the orchards and read and went for walks. Trish no longer came by. Darla was there from time to time but Rena had little to do with her. Other people came to visit Lou but Rena had little interaction with them. Lou too gave Rena space. She did not tell Rena to work or exercise or to do anything, and Rena did not try to be with Lou. I don't blame her for avoiding me, Rena thought.

Thursday evening, on the way home from her office, Lou stopped at De Nova. She found Trish in the barn sharpening tools on the electric grinder. Trish hung the ax on its hook. "Let's go inside."

They had a snack, talked small talk a while. "You said you wanted to talk about Rena," Lou said.

"Mm-hm. How's it going with her?"

Lou shook her head. "Not much progress. She hasn't remembered anything new. You know, on the minute off-chance that she did kill them somehow, it's old history. There's no question of prosecution. Is there, do you think? I mean, assuming it was never reported. No, there's no worry about that."

They were in the living room of the *Big House.* Lou was on the old leather sofa.

"History repeats itself," Trish said. "It maybe already has."

Lou's face darkened. "I shouldn't be talking with you about this." She folded her arms. "I don't know why I keep trying. Your mind is closed. So what did you want to talk about?"

"My theory." Trish was sitting backwards on an upright chair, straddling it. "I called Casey. I was curious. You know what I found out?"

"What? What did you find out?"

"There was her father and uncle," Trish said slowly. "They were the first ones. They're dead. Then there was this Rebecca. It came close with her. And then Pat. Dead Pat. I was curious about her."

"What about? What do you mean?"

"I kept thinking about that scaffold business, and I kept thinking about how Rena went after you. I wondered about her and Pat, if she —"

"Shit!"

"So I called Casey. She didn't know anything. I was real subtle about it but it was pretty clear that Casey doesn't know that much about Rena and Pat. Rena never told her much. But Casey put me on to this friend of Pat and I called her."

"You're a regular Sam Spade," Lou said sardonically.

"Her name's Jessica. She was the one having the barbecue the day Pat got killed. She told me this woman named Dawn was at the barbecue. Dawn had a thing for Pat and apparently Pat was getting interested. Jessica didn't know if Rena knew about it or not. My hunch is Rena knew. My next hunch is that Rena messed with Lou's car that day . . ."

"You are flipping out!"

"Rena knows cars. She could have done something to the brakes or the steering or something."

"Trish, I'm worried about you."

"Lou, she's already confessed to two murders. And I know what *I* perceived. She's not normal. There's a sick twist in her."

"Someone's definitely twisted."

Trish rested her palms on the back of the chair. "Here's my theory in a nutshell." She waited for Lou to look at her. "Rena's first and foremost love object, Daddy Spiros, rejected her. That's what happened in the so-called *little house* the first time she went there. This totally undoes her — unleashes the evil in her. She gets him for it by offing and mutilating his beloved brother. She brings the macabre prize, Uncle's arm, to Daddy to torture him with it. Pops flips out, collapses in agony and grief. While he's totally vulnerable, Miss Rena conks him on the head. Afterward she blocks it all out. She doesn't remember she did it. Years pass. The evil part stays submerged. But then another love object rejects her. Rebecca. Rena tries to murder her by sabotaging the scaffolding. Partial success here. Next comes Pat, the next love object to reject her. You know what happened to her." Trish looked pointedly at Lou. "You're her love object now, Lou. Think about it."

140

"Lousy theory," Lou said. "I like mine better." She took a handful of peanuts and munched pensively. "It's nice and simple, with no need for evil twists or demons."

Trish cocked her head, waiting.

"Guilt and fantasy. The murder story is all a fantasy. A child's fantasy. The stuff about Rebecca and Pat is more fantasy. Yours."

"You're the one with the fantasy."

"Trish, you're beginning to annoy me."

Trish laughed. "I am, huh? Do you wish you never brought me here, never lured me from my dissipated life?"

"No."

"I'll drink to that." She raised her glass of lemonade.

Lou was serious. "I'm going to keep trying with Rena," she said. "I'm going to keep at it."

The next two communing sessions were fruitless. The block remained solid. Repeatedly, Rena tried on her own to figure out her motive. She wondered why she was what she was. Vile. Evil. Patricidal. What a twisted mind she had. Twisted person. She thought of Lou's garage. The Volvo. Carbon monoxide.

CHAPTER SIXTEEN

Days passed with no progress. No matter how Lou had her approach it, Rena could recall no more about what had taken place at the little house and was no closer to understanding her motivation for the killings.

Finally Lou asked her about Rebecca, about how she reacted when she found out about Rebecca's relationship with her Seattle friend.

Rena hesitated. "It was weird," she said slowly. "When I first learned of it . . . I don't know . . . I sort of . . . went numb. I know I was real upset and then . . . I don't know. There's a gap. I remember her getting hurt, being in the hospital a while, and then moving to Seattle." Rena was perspiring. "I never thought she'd do that to me. I thought . . ." She was crying.

"Be with another woman, you mean?"

Rena nodded. "She was getting ready to tell me about it, about Barbara, the woman in Seattle. I'm sure of it. She was going to break up with me. We never talked about it. After the accident, we just went our separate ways."

"Tell me more about the accident. How did she fall? Did she slip off the scaffolding or what?"

"A rope broke. She lost her balance."

"Were you there when it happened?"

"No. I was . . ." Rena inhaled deeply. "I was at the store. When I got back, she was gone. The people told me an ambulance came, the people who lived in the house we were painting. They called an ambulance."

"I see. And what happened earlier that day? Tell me about that."

Rena was opening and closing her hand. "In the morning . . . I remember I was cleaning up the apartment, straightening things in the bedroom. Rebecca's book . . ."

Lou watched Rena's hand.

"There was a book on Rebecca's dresser. It had a letter in it. I wondered who it was from so I looked at the return address. It was from Barbara. I put it back and kept cleaning up, dusting, watering the plants, but I kept thinking about the letter."

Rena said no more.

"And?"

"That's how I found out they were lovers."

"I see. And what happened next?"

Rena shook her head. Her teeth were pressed against her lower lip. "I . . . I don't know. I remember . . . we drove to that house, it was on Wilson Avenue. We set things up and then . . . I remember being at the store, feeling funny . . . feeling bad and then coming back and they told me she fell and that the ambulance had come. I . . . I went to the hospital. I felt terrible. I visited her a few times, but . . . I didn't tell her I knew . . . maybe she sensed it. Neither of us said anything. Before she came back from the hospital, I moved out. She went to Seattle then, soon after that."

"That was hard for you, painful, finding out about the woman in Seattle."

"I guess," Rena said vaguely. "Yes. I know I was upset. I thought we were . . . I thought we'd always be together. I don't remember it very well, how I reacted. It's fuzzy. I remember having a terrible headache that day . . . in the van, when we were driving to the job on

143

Wilson. And I felt kind of dizzy. Rebecca asked what was wrong. I don't remember much more . . . not until they told me she fell, except being at the paint store. I remember that."

"Do you remember setting up the scaffolding?"

Rena thought a moment. "Yes. We carried the boards from the van, then the other stuff. I took the paint. She had the ropes and brushes."

"Rebecca had the ropes?"

"Yes. She set up the scaffold. I went to buy another can of mauve paint. We had to get it mixed."

"I see. Did you handle the ropes at all?"

Rena hesitated. "No. Why?"

"Just wondering." Lou switched to what had happened earlier in the day, when Rena found the letter. Rena repeated what she had already said, adding nothing new. She was clearly becoming drained.

Lou shifted the topic. She worked on getting Rena to dislodge any new memories about birds or about her relationship with her father. Nothing new emerged.

"We'll stop for the day but I'm not ready to give up," Lou said.

"Nor I. To be continued," Rena said flatly, rising from the contour chair and leaving the room.

Lou went looking for Darla and found her feeding the chickens. She leaned against the door as Darla continued her work. "I'm more and more convinced that her *loving* father sexually molested her."

Darla nodded. "That can really mess people up." She found an egg hidden in the straw. "Ah, breakfast," she said.

"If she could only let herself remember it. Damn! We're just not making any progress."

"You sound frustrated."

"I've got to think of some way to get her past the block."

"You will, Lou. You've got a very creative mind." Darla gave her a friendly poke on the arm. "A little perverse and devious, maybe, but very creative."

* * * * *

144

The following evening, they were again in the womb room just finishing their tea. Rena was ready to begin remembering but Lou took Rena by the hand and led her to the thick foam mat by the windows. "Take your sweater off," she ordered.

Rena felt an immediate, delightful chill along her neck and spine. Her desire for Lou was as strong as ever. There was a tinge of fear which increased her excitement. She pulled the sweater over her head. She had a T-shirt on underneath.

"That, too."

Rena took it off. Her excitement rose as Lou lustfully scrutinized her bare breasts.

"Lie down now," Lou told her.

And then Lou was there with her on the mat, her mouth covering one of Rena's nipples, warmly, wetly, sucking it, her tongue going around and around. Rena writhed as Lou sucked harder, hard enough to bring Rena close to pain, just to the edge of it, where there was unbearable pleasure. Rena's head was back, her mouth open, hips raised.

Lou's hands tightly held Rena's upper arms as she continued sucking the hardened nipple, making occasional tongue tip trips around Rena's breast and under it and to her other breast and between them, licking softly, kissing and even nipping lightly with her teeth.

Rena was totally caught in sensation. Her hips moved rhythmically. Lou's hand went downward, to Rena's warm inner thighs, softly caressing along her jeans. Rena moaned with pleasure. Lou unfastened Rena's belt and then the button. Slowly she lowered the zipper. Rena burned with anticipation as Lou slipped her hand inside the pants and with one finger circled around the border of the hairs. Her mouth was on Rena's mouth, her tongue searching its interior. All Rena's nerve cells responded, sending heat over every part of her body. Lou's finger came nearer and nearer to Rena's cunt while her lips and tongue continued the kiss above. One more centimeter, one or two little vibrations with her knowing finger and Rena would fly, just one more second.

Lou stopped and pulled away.

Rena reached for her, trying to bring her back, clutching at her, pushing her pubic bone against Lou's leg, seeking Lou's hand, seeking the rest.

Lou shook her head. "No," she said.

"Yes," Rena pleaded.

"You know why."

Rena lay back, letting go of Lou. Her arms were spread wide. She was panting, and angry.

"You're holding back, my friend, fighting me. You still haven't fully given yourself to me." Lou was on her then, pressing against Rena's body, nibbling at her lips. Then again she stopped.

"Don't stop!"

"Don't you stop."

"I won't. Go on. Go on." Rena grabbed for her.

"But you did stop." Lou held Rena's chin in her hand. "You stopped remembering."

"This is vile."

"What happened in the little house, Rena?" Lou brushed her tongue over Rena's lower lip.

"I can't believe you're doing this."

Lou's face was a few inches above Rena's. "Tell me and then we'll go on." She flicked Rena's nipple with her fingertip. "Let yourself remember."

Rena exhaled with a hiss. "All right, I remember." Her eyes were fiercely angry. "He fucked me, all right? That's what happened."

"Sit up."

Rena sat, leaning on pillows against the wall. Lou sat cross-legged on the mat, facing her. "Do you remember it?" Lou asked.

"Actually, what happened is I wanted him to fuck me but he wouldn't. He was cruel." Rena's eyes glared.

"You're lying."

"You're cruel."

"Let yourself remember what happened and then you'll be mine, completely, like you're supposed to be, and then I won't be cruel."

Rena took a deep breath. Her face relaxed. "All right," she said. "All right, I'll try."

She did. She tried very hard to remember. Her eyes were closed. The pictures came. Seeing her father at the window. Going inside. And then . . . and then . . . and then it was blank. Nothing. The next thing she knew she was running. "It won't come, Lou. Dammit, it's gone. No matter how I try, no matter what you do, it's gone. I can't remember."

"You remember going to the river and masturbating." Lou caressed Rena along the jaw line as she spoke.

Rena reached for her, wrapped her arms around her, clinging to her. She tried to find Lou's lips, but Lou slipped away. She began fumbling with the buttons of Lou's blouse.

Lou held her wrist and, looking deeply into her eyes, spoke to her. "You remember that, masturbating by the river."

"Yes, I remember." Rena's breathing was labored. "Lou, come on. Come to me. Don't tease anymore, I can't stand it. Kiss me. Come on. Fuck me."

"No, my sweet. Not yet." She stroked Rena's face. "As soon as you remember."

"Maybe after." Rena was rubbing her palm along Lou's thigh. "I can't remember now, Lou, but maybe after we make love —"

Lou's laughter interrupted her. "You can't remember. What a shame."

"Lou, I hate this."

"I know. I'm terrible. You're all turned on, aren't you? You really do want more. You want it so badly."

"Yes, yes, I want —"

"Go ahead, then. You go on and take care of yourself."

"What?"

"Take off your jeans." Lou's voice was not soft. She rose from the mat and stood looking down at Rena.

Rena half sat up. She pushed her hair back. "No thanks. No way. That sucks. Forget it."

"Do it."

"Lou!"

"Now."

"But —"

"I own you, girl. Remember? That hasn't changed. You must still do whatever I say."

"Hey, but really it's OK, honestly. Don't worry about . . . I'm fine. Let's just forget it."

Lou shook her head. "I said do it, finish yourself." She smiled then. "I'm sure we'll both enjoy your coming."

"Lou, don't. I couldn't." If Lou so much as grazed her clitoris with a fingertip or tongue tip or even a breath of air, Rena knew she would come immediately. "I . . . I'm not into it anymore."

Lou laughed. "God, how you lie. You're going to do yourself."

"Lou, please, I'd be too embarrassed."

"Come on, off with the pants." Lou grabbed Rena's open belt and tugged on it. "Off." She stepped back and waited.

"I've never masturbated in front of anyone."

"You're going to now."

"Don't watch."

"Of course I'm going to watch."

Rena did not move.

"Do I have to take the pants off for you?" Lou said.

"I think so."

Lou laughed. She bent and tugged until Rena's jeans and underpants were at her knees. Unhurriedly she scrutinized the dark thick mat of hair and the slight bulge of Rena's belly. "Nice."

Rena felt the skin of her face and chest grow hotter.

Lou was sitting at the edge of the mat. She reached over and took Rena's hand and gently moved it to her crotch. "Go ahead, I'm waiting."

Rena's hand lay limply over the triangle of hair. If she were alone, she knew she would have a very good orgasm in seconds. "Would you turn your head?"

Lou laughed again, loud and throaty. She took off her blouse and laid it carefully over Rena's hand. "There, does that help?"

Rena stared at Lou's round full breasts as her fingers moved and her back arched. She closed her eyes and in a moment was moaning, peaking to a full and powerful orgasm. Lou's own breathing rate had increased somewhat. Rena lay motionless on her back and Lou continued to watch her, smiling lovingly. At last Lou spoke. "Was that a bad thing to do?"

Rena shrugged. She hadn't moved. Lou's blouse still covered her crotch.

"Does it make you evil?"

Rena did not respond.

"Did it feel like this at the river that time?"

"That was different."

"Tell me about it. Tell me what it was like then. Tell me what you were thinking."

Rena pulled up her jeans and sat up. She closed her eyes. She felt very peaceful as her thoughts took her back in time. "I was thinking about my father."

"Tell me."

"I wasn't angry anymore. No, not at all. I was feeling good about him. But then I thought of something and . . . and I got up and started running. I ran all the way to Grandma's."

"What was it you thought of?"

Rena's strained painfully. She made a tremendous effort to recall. "I want to, Lou."

"Keep trying."

Rena shook her head. "It's blank."

"All right, switch. Go back to what happened in the little house. You saw your father at the window. You went inside and then what?"

Rena strained to bring the memories back. She tried every way she could. Finally, sadly, she shook her head. "I don't remember."

"Keep trying."

She tried some more. "It doesn't . . . nothing more comes. I . . . I can't . . . oh, I'm sorry." She was crying.

"All right," Lou said sadly. "All right. And I'm sorry, Rena." She was rubbing Rena's bare back. "I thought it was worth a try."

Rena felt immediately aroused again. "I forgive you," she said. Her hand cupped Lou's breast lovingly. "Come on. Come to me."

Lou took her hand away. "No, Rena. It didn't work. We tried, but it didn't work. You're not free yet." She stood and put her blouse on. "Tomorrow we'll go visit your mother."

149

CHAPTER SEVENTEEN

The trees on the drive toward Chicago were beautifully orange and red and yellow. It was odd, Rena thought, that part of her was saying goodbye to all of this, to beauty, to life, to the people she loved, knowing that at the end of the search was the end of everything. Part of her felt as if she had just awakened and was saying hello again, I'm back.

She didn't like the idea of talking with her mother. Lou had insisted it was the next logical step; she was unmoved by Rena's protests. Rena did think there was a chance her mother could provide some clue to her motivation for the killings.

"She must never find out I did it," Rena had told Lou.

"That's right," Lou had said. "She'll never find that out."

Rena watched the passing cars. Her thoughts shifted to last night. What a bitch Lou had been. She looked at Lou from the corner of her eye and as always felt the strange excitement. She wanted her more than ever before, craved the complete combination of her power and sex. It would happen, Rena knew.

A half hour later they took the exit that would take them to Wheeling, Illinois, and to the home of Rena's mother and stepfather. Rena hadn't been there for months, since early summer.

"My mother doesn't know anything about what's been going on," Rena said. "About my being in the hospital, about the birds, none of it. She doesn't know I'm not working either."

"You're working."

"So keep cool."

"I'm always cool. What street are we looking for?"

"I'll tell you when we get there."

Rena had called her mother the night before. Ordinarily Maria Stamatis would have been at the restaurant by now but, as she had told Rena, she was very happy to stay at home for Rena's visit. She wasn't really needed at the restaurant, she said. Since they'd hired a manager, her husband wasn't particularly needed there either.

The greetings and small talk took about half an hour. They were in the living room with its huge lamps and velvet furniture and souvenir statues and vases from Greece. When there was a lull, Lou signaled her and Rena broached the topic.

"You know, Mom, I've been thinking a lot lately about Greece, about when we lived there and how things were."

"You have? I'm surprised, Rena." Maria was seated on the long white sofa across from Rena and Lou who sat in matching easy chairs. The coffee table was between them. Maria reached for her cup, realized it was empty and put it down again. "I drink too much coffee. All day at the restaurant." She spoke with a heavy accent. Rena liked it for some reason.

"A lot of things I remember but some of it is fuzzy," Rena said.

"Well, bygones are bygones."

"Mom, I want you to help me remember."

"Help you? How can I help? If you remember, you remember. If not, then that's all there is to it. You never wanted to remember before."

"I know. Why was that, Mom?"

"Well, you know, Rena. More coffee?" She directed the question to Lou.

"No thank you."

151

"It was a long time ago," Maria said. "Another life."

"What was life like back then?" Lou asked.

"Oh, it was a good life. Very good . . . until . . ." Maria took a deep breath through her nostrils, then raised her head. "Tell me more about what you've been doing at the college, Rena. She's a college teacher, you know. We're very proud of her."

"I believe it," Lou said. "Things were good until what?"

Maria was silent a few moments. "Very good. Rena's fa . . . oh, I'm sorry, Rena."

"It's OK, Mom. I want you to talk about Dad."

Maria's face had become clouded, her eyes moist. "He was a wonderful man. How he loved you, Rena. You were the biggest part of his world, you know, from the moment you were born. What a happy child you were. So smart. Always busy. Always into something."

Maria laughed. "Sometimes you would worry us, the things you did. Once when you were very small you went all the way to the monastery by yourself. Do you remember that? You wanted to see the sisters, you said. Because they always fed you sweets, I think. You were gone most of the day and when you came back and told us where you'd been, I wanted to scold you, but I couldn't. I was too happy to see you and that you were all right."

"One of my adventures," Rena said.

"Yes." When Maria laughed, her plump face became a mass of jiggling wrinkles. "You were always having adventures." She frowned then. "There was one time that was . . . oh, it was so frightening. You were gone all night. I thought I would die. We searched everywhere with lanterns and torches. I bet you don't remember this. You were only five."

"What happened?" Rena had only a vague recollection.

"It was at my parents' village, Trimata. We were visiting there. You were playing with a dog, somebody's dog. You went with it out into the hills. Someone saw you go. They told us later, when it was getting dark and we could not find you. You were with that dog somewhere and we were afraid you got lost. We gathered the villagers and we all went searching, but dawn came and still you were gone. The dog was back home, but you were not. I almost died with fear and grief. Your father searched all night and into the next day. He came home to see if you were back. It was almost noontime. He was about to go searching again when . . ." Maria smiled, shaking her head. ". . . there you were. There was our little adventure girl, walking slowly up the stairs. I ran to you. My ba-a-by! I screamed with happiness. When I hugged you and squeezed you, you didn't move. You were like a rag doll. You just stared straight ahead. I thought you must be so tired and I just put you to bed. You didn't say a word. You didn't speak. There was a little cut on your neck and some dried blood. I cleaned it up and put you to bed. You slept a long time and when you woke up, you were hungry and jabbering and lively just like always."

Rena was fascinated by the story. "Where had I been?"

"We never found out. You never told us. You said you didn't know, that you didn't even remember that you had gone away and that you were gone all night. You never remembered. You still don't, eh?"

"No," Rena said.

Maria laughed. "Villagers are very superstitious sometimes, you know. My friend, Panayiota, she was sure the Tribe of Darkness had gotten you." Maria made an attempt to assume a sinister expression. "You know, the evil ones," she said in a low voice, "the night wanderers." Maria shook her head. "My friend believed things like that, that there was a tribe of devil-worshippers who haunted the hills and grabbed little children. Many of the people of Trimata believed this. They told stories. You became one of the stories, I think."

"I never heard these stories."

"Some people would frighten their children with them. I never did. Foolishness, I thought. They believed the Tribe of Darkness would search for innocent blood for their ceremonies, their sacrifices. Or that they would take the children sometimes and do sorcery over them, put their mark on them, infect the innocent children with their evil, and then send them into the world to do terrible things and spread the evil ways." Maria shook her head, smiling. "So silly. The little cut you had, Panayiota thought this was their mark on you, their stigma."

Rena's finger went to the barely visible little scar just below her ear, a little *X* with two tiny dots beneath it. Could she actually have been taken by some *Tribe of Darkness,* she wondered. Made evil by their sorcery?

"And you never found out where she was all night?" Lou asked.

"I think she got lost in the dark. She couldn't find her way home, and slept somewhere in the bushes. I think some thorns cut her neck. Sharp ones. It never got infected. Panayiota kept waiting for Rena's evil to come out." Maria laughed again and turned to Rena.

Rena smiled weakly.

"Your father and I would tease her sometimes, about her ideas like that, but she never stopped believing in it. Your father used to say that nothing evil could ever touch his sweet angel."

"Right," Rena said numbly. "His sweet innocent angel."

"Could you tell us more about him?" Lou asked. "About Rena's father."

Maria's round face glowed. "Antoni was a wonderful human being. A wonderful father. The best." Her eyes had a faraway look. "How my life changed when I met him. I . . . the world lit up for me. I was so happy. He wrote poems for me, beautiful poems, and he could make me laugh. Such laughing we did." Her eyes danced through glistening tears. "When we were first married, we lived in my village. Did you know that, Rena? We lived in Trimata and I loved it there and so did your father."

"You always loved the country, Mom."

"And then you moved to Athens," Lou said. "Is that right? How come you moved to the city?"

Marie directed her answer to Rena. "Stavros," she said. She said the word strangely. Her head went up then down and her eyes shifted to the floor.

"Uncle Stavros? He got you to move?"

"Yes. He wanted us with him. He wanted Antoni with him, I should say. Stavros and I were never . . . well, it was your father he wanted. And Antoni wanted him. Like this, those two were." She held two fingers together. "So we moved to Athens. People always did what Stavros wanted."

"Why?" Rena asked.

"Why? Because he was Stavros. You just did it."

"Were you afraid of him?"

"Of Stavros? Yes, maybe I was. He was not always kind to me. He didn't think I was good enough for Antoni. I knew that because he told me so. I wasn't . . . what? Lively enough. I wasn't talkative enough, I was too shy. He told me all these things. Never in front of Antoni though. And I never told your father Stavros said such things. You could never say anything against Stavros to your father."

"How did he treat me?" Rena asked.

"Stavros? The same way. The same as me. He was very very stern with you, more than with Taki. You would get scolded for everything. And he picked on you all the time and teased you. I think he loved you, though. Do you think so?"

"I don't know." Rena's fingernails found her neck. "I mostly remember being afraid of him and having to please him. For Daddy, mostly. It was almost like for Dad to really love me, I had to have Uncle Stavros' love too."

"Yes." Maria nodded knowingly. "I felt the same."

The question clawed at Rena's mind. She forced herself to ask it. "How did they die, Mom?" She was gripping the arms of the chair.

"Oh, oh my!" Maria pulled on her ear, then fussed with her hair. "I don't think we want to talk about that."

"I want to know, Mom." She kept her tone flat.

Maria smoothed out her dress along her knees. "You do know. They died in an accident, a hunting accident, when you were ten years old."

Lou smiled and leaned back in her chair.

Involuntarily, Rena shook her head from side to side.

Maria looked at neither Rena nor Lou.

"Could you tell us more, Mrs. Stamatis?" Lou said after a while. "About how it happened."

"It happened in Kaftarei," Maria said matter-of-factly. "Antoni and Stavros went to hunt for rabbits. There were other hunters in the hills. It must have been the other hunters. They were both

155

killed." Maria pulled herself clumsily from the sofa. She was not a small woman. "I'll get us some coffee."

Lou and Rena waited silently until Maria returned with the pot. No one wanted any.

"And the hunters who shot them?" Lou asked.

"No one ever knew who they were."

"Did the police investigate?" "Yes, of course. They never found them. I wanted to leave Greece very badly after that. So did you, Rena. We wanted it more than anything and finally, because of Eleni, we were able to."

"Eleni is my aunt," Rena said to Lou. "Stavros' wife. She met a Greek-American visiting in Athens and they married and came here. Right, Mom?"

"Yes, and they sent for me, and they had John for me. He's a good man. A reliable man. He was good to you."

"Yes, he was." Rena's eyes penetrated her mother's. "Mom."

"Yes, *kukla,* what? You hungry?"

"It wasn't a hunting accident."

Lou scrutinized Maria, apparently assessing her reaction.

"What do you mean? Of course it was."

"It wasn't. That's not how they died. They were murdered."

Color drained from Maria's round face.

Lou gave Rena a sharp look. "Is there any chance it wasn't really an accident?" she asked Maria gently.

Maria's eyes were wet. "Why can't you just leave it," she said sorrowfully. "A hunting accident. A tragic accident. That's what happened. Why can't you just leave it at that?"

"Because that's not the truth," Rena insisted. Her throat felt tight.

Maria looked beseechingly at her daughter. "What makes you say that?"

"I know, Mom."

Maria shook her head.

"I know."

"She wants to know more about it, Mrs. Stamatis."

"There's no more to know. I told you what happened. They were hunting rabbits. They got shot." Tears rolled down her cheeks.

"Where did it happen?" Lou asked.

"Near Kaftarei. In the hills."

"They were together?"

"Yes. There were many hunters out that day. Sometimes they would be very careless."

Lou nodded. "I see." She turned to Rena. "You heard her, Rena. Let it in. What you thought just isn't so. It was an accident."

Rena was shaking her head.

"Maybe your mother can help us figure out why you believe otherwise."

Rena looked sadly at her mother and spoke very softly. "Mom, I know about Uncle Stavros' arm."

Maria's teeth grabbed her lower lip. "Oh, my baby!" She covered her face with her hands. She was crying painfully. "How could you know that? How could you know?" she sobbed.

Rena was staring at her shoes. "Because I . . ."

"Rena!" Lou said sharply.

"I saw it . . . the arm."

"Oh, dear." Maria was still biting her lip. "So you knew all these years. I never wanted you to know."

Rena looked at her mother. Her throat was constricted. "You don't know who did it, do you?" She felt her heart pounding in her chest.

"No." Maria shook her head. "No one knows."

"Can you tell us what happened?" Lou asked.

Maria looked at Rena. "You really want to talk of this, *kukla*?"

"I don't . . . yes, I want you to tell me."

Maria nodded solemnly. "Someday then, I will," she said, "but this is not the time. Your friend is here. This is no way to entertain her."

Rena glanced at Lou. "She's here to be with me while I learn about it, Mom."

Maria looked distraught. She found a handkerchief buried somewhere in her dress and wiped her whole face and her neck. "I still have nightmares." She stared at the flocked wallpaper. "I'll tell you how it was if you really want to hear."

"I want to. I know it's hard for you, Mom, but I need to hear."

157

Maria took a deep breath, then another. "On the day it happened I was baking. I was using the outdoor oven." She smiled weakly at Rena. "They had electricity then at Kaftarei but sometimes I wished they didn't. I liked it the other way, the old way. I liked the lantern lights at night. It always felt so cozy. And I even liked that old wooden ice box. Do you remember that, Rena?"

Rena shook her head. "Not really."

"They had that new stove but I liked baking bread in the old brick oven outdoors. You remember Kaftarei, don't you, Rena? You enjoyed your summers there."

The muscles of Rena's face felt frozen. "You were baking and what happened then?"

Maria's expression became clouded again. "I could hear Stavros out in back with the electric saw. Your grandfather still used the ax, but whenever Stavros came, he cut logs with that noisy electric saw. Afterwards, *Patera* smashed the thing. I don't blame him." She cleared her throat. "Anyway, I was carrying the bread dough outside, on that wooden board we used, and then I noticed that the sawing sounds had stopped. I slid the dough into the oven and then I remember I looked at my watch because I had to time the bread. It was twelve-thirty-five. I was sealing the door of the oven and then there was this burst of noise, electric saw noise, and then a loud bang like a gunshot. I stood a moment and . . . it was quiet then, and then there was some more sawing noise. I wondered what was happening and so as soon as I finished sealing the door, I went to see." Maria's face twisted in anguish. "The saw was on the ground, and so was Stavros.

"I screamed, and then right away Eleni came running. And then *Mitera* came too and *Patera*. Stavros was lying there on his face, face down. Lying in the dirt and blood was pouring out of his head. And his arm . . . oh good Lord, his arm was gone. It was such a terrible sight. I couldn't move. Oh God, what kind of person would do that? *Mitera* went to him first. She turned him over. Oh-h-h. *Mitera* screamed and screamed and then she fell down on the ground.

"They carried Stavros to the porch. I think it was Nikos who helped Stavros' father carry him, our neighbor, Nikos. I covered him. I got a blanket and I covered him up. And they carried *Mitera* inside. Eleni gave her water and I remember fanning her face with a magazine." Maria moved her hand in a fanning motion. "No one knew what to do. There was no doctor in the village and anyway what good would a doctor do now? *Patera* phoned the Triti police — that's the next village. He said that there had been a death, a violent death, and someone should come.

"It didn't take long before Charalampis arrived. Charalampis Kyriazopoulos. Stavros had gotten him his job on the police force. Charalampis always looked up to Stavros the same as everyone did. When that poor boy saw Stavros, he started to cry and grieve almost as much as the rest of us. I remember him stomping around. He was so angry and he was pulling his hair.

"And all this time I was so worried about you, Rena. I wanted you there, with me. I wanted you at my side. Then you came running into the house. Oh, was I glad to see you. You were out of breath and all wet, your clothes were all wet. You must have been swimming in the river again, with all your clothes on this time.

"I held you. I was crying and couldn't stop." Maria was crying as she told Rena this. "I couldn't speak and then you asked where Uncle Stavros was."

Maria continued with great effort. "I held both your hands. There has been a terrible accident, I told you. Your Uncle Stavros has been hurt, *agape mou,* badly hurt. He was hurt so bad, injured so badly, that he did not live.

"Your lip quivered like a frail leaf in a wind storm," Maria continued. "I can still picture it. He's dead? you said. Yes, *agape mou,* I told you, and you pulled away and ran." Maria's knuckles were pushed hard against her chin. "I stayed with Eleni, trying to console her, feeling so bad for her, knowing how deep her pain must be, knowing how I would feel if it had been Antoni." Maria's teeth clamped down on her lip. "And then they brought Antoni. They had found him in his little house. They brought him home and we laid him on the porch next to Stavros."

Maria was limp.

Rena went to her mother, put her arm over her shoulders. "Oh, Mom, how awful." They held each other, crying. Rena felt ripped by guilt for putting her mother through this, for making her remember

159

and relive it. The feelings she had for having been the cause of it, she could not let in just then.

For awhile they sat silently, Rena's and her mother's hands entwined, and then Rena suggested she get them all some wine. Maria brought bread and olives from the kitchen. They sipped Retsina and talked about the restaurant, of winter coming, of Eleni and her grandchildren.

It was Lou who finally brought them back. "Mrs. Stamatis, there are still a few more questions. Do you mind?"

"Go ahead," Maria said stoically. "Maybe then, Rena, you can let it rest. It affected you more than anyone else, you know. Poor angel, you were not our little Rena after that, not until we came to America. Something in you died, I thought, with your father. But then, when we came here, well, then you seemed all right again. I never did understand it."

"Everything seemed different after he was gone," Rena said. She could feel the heaviness.

"Was Rena depressed?" Lou asked.

"Depressed?" Maria shook her head, her lower lip protruding. "I don't know about depressed. She was sad, different. You were into yourself, Rena. And quiet. You stayed at home all the time. And then you got that terrible rash."

Unconsciously Rena's hand went to her neck. "Why? Why did I . . . why did it happen? There has to be a reason!"

"Allergies, *kukla*."

"I mean the . . . Mom, the last time I saw Dad . . . what happened?" Her head was throbbing. "Did something —"

"The last time you saw him was the weekend before. It was a wonderful weekend for all of us. There was a baptism and a big party Sunday night. Then the next morning, you went walking with your father like you always did. You were so happy to be with him."

"And nothing bad happened or anything? Between me and Dad, I mean. Everything was fine?"

"Everything was fine. Yes, of course. Everything was always fine with you and your father."

Rena felt faint.

"Mrs. Stamatis," Lou said, "Stavros was shot, right, that's how he died?"

"Yes, in the head. Maria's knuckles pressed her lips.

"And Antoni?"

"Antoni was hit on the head. When they found him . . ." She swallowed audibly. "When they found him . . . Stavros' arm . . . it was there, there with Antoni."

"I'm sorry, Mom." Rena was crying.

"*Patera* took the sledgehammer to the saw. He smashed it and pounded it until you couldn't even recognize it. Smashed it into a thousand pieces." Maria had twisted her handkerchief into a tight rope.

"Oh, Mom, I'm truly sorry." She felt sick to her stomach.

"We never wanted you to know." Maria held her, consoling her.

Lou watched them, her face full of pain and questions. "Mrs. Stamatis, do you have any idea who the killer was?"

Maria shook her head.

"No idea at all?"

She was working valiantly to compose herself. "There was talk," she said. "Eleni thought it had to do with George's visit, George Dimitropoulos. He came back after all those years and he met with Stavros, something about the paintings, I think. I don't remember now."

"Paintings?" Lou leaned forward, cocking her head.

Still holding Rena's hand, Maria directed her words to Lou. "Stavros had paintings. He collected them — art works. He also had a factory, you know. He was a wealthy man, Stavros was, even before the war, very wealthy for a man barely thirty-five. That's how old he was when the war started. Antoni was twenty-five, the same as me."

Her eyes became watery and she went on quickly. "Stavros had a big collection and Antoni had some paintings too. Some of them disappeared during the Occupation. It may have been that George Dimitropoulos had something to do with that. After the war, George was no longer welcome in our house nor in Stavros' house." Maria laid her handkerchief like a snake on the coffee table.

"And then, years later," she continued, "in nineteen-sixty, that horrible year, Eleni says George came back from America where he

161

lived, came back to Greece and visited Stavros. And the next thing, Stavros and Antoni are dead. The police thought it had to do with the paintings but they could never prove it. No one knows."

"I didn't know about any paintings," Rena said. She was feeling mildly curious.

"There were paintings."

"Did the missing ones ever turn up?" Lou asked.

"I don't think so. No, they must not have or I would have heard."

Lou took a sip of wine. "Were they valuable?"

"I don't know. Rena, ask Eleni these things. She would know."

"So it looks like this George might have been involved in the murders," Lou said. "Did the police suspect him?"

Maria shook her head. "No, it wasn't George. He had a . . . what do you call it, Rena?"

"An alibi?"

"Yes, that's it. George had an alibi. It wasn't George."

"The police checked it out?" Lou said.

"Oh yes, they checked everything."

Rena was deep in her own thoughts. "Mom, Daddy was expected that day, right? At the village?"

"Yes, he was to come by lunchtime as usual, by two o'clock. He came on Saturdays at two. But by two that Saturday . . ."

Lou asked, "What time was Stavros — What time was it when you found Stavros?"

"Twelve-thirty-five. I remember because of the bread."

"That's right," Lou said. "You mentioned —"

"And the police kept asking, asking about the time. I was timing the bread. Why do you ask that?"

"Just trying to piece everything together," Lou said. "Do you know what time they found Antoni?"

"Two o'clock. He was right on time." Maria's lip started to quiver again. "But no, he came early that day. A shepherd saw him. The shepherd said he saw Antoni earlier, at twelve-twenty. That's what the shepherd told the police. He saw Antoni going toward the little house. If only he had just come at his usual time."

"Yes." Lou nodded sadly. "Do you remember what time Rena came to you? When you told her about Stavros?"

"This is like the police. They wanted to know all the times. Yes, I remember. It was one o'clock. Just after the church bell had chimed."

Lou nodded. "And there's one more thing, Mrs. Stamatis." She waited for the older woman to look at her. "Was there anything . . . did any of it have anything to do with birds?"

"I don't understand."

"The deaths . . . the, well, was there anything about birds connected with it?"

Maria shook her head. She looked at Rena. "No, there was nothing about any birds."

"All right, I just wondered."

Maria looked puzzled. No one spoke for a while. "Did I mention about the truck?"

"What truck?" Rena asked.

"Your father's friend's. I think his name was Simeon. Your father came to the village that day in his friend's truck and when we found it, the door of it, the back door, had been broken open. We never found out why. I don't know why your father came in that truck instead of his car and I don't know why the truck was broken into like that. The shepherd saw Antoni . . . saw your father drive the truck almost to the village, then leave it there."

"Did he see who broke into it?"

"No, he was just passing with the sheep, he said, when he saw your father. We found the truck later. Your Uncle Basilis found it, I believe. It was Basilis who returned the truck to your father's friend in Athens. I think his name was Simeon. We offered to pay him for the damage but he would not hear of it."

"And you never found out why your husband came in the truck?" Lou asked.

"No," Maria said. "His car was running fine, an Italian car, Fiat, I think it was."

Rena was exhausted. "Enough of this," she said. "No more. Mom, we'd like to take you out for lunch. And no more talk of the past. What do you say? Where would you like to go?"

They kept the lunch conversation light, Rena expertly dodging questions about her work and why she was never home when Maria called. Lou got to joking with Maria, teasing her warmly.

"Nice girl, that Lou," Maria said to Rena on the side. "Sometimes I think you like girls better than boys." She laughed her sweet, high-pitched laugh and hugged her daughter goodbye. "Come again, soon. You too, Miss Lou, you come, too."

They were silent for the first few minutes in the car. Rena's eyes were fixed on the road. "Well, do you believe me now?"

"I believe they were murdered." Lou turned onto the southbound ramp of Highway 94. "And you still think you did it?"

Rena glanced at her. "Obviously." She stared at the passing cars. "I still have no idea why. It didn't help at all, talking to her." She closed her eyes, leaned her head back. "Unless the Devil made me do it," she added sardonically. "God, I'm tired."

"One more stop before we go to your place."

The building where Rena's aunt lived was near Lawrence and Western, a six-flat. Eleni and her husband owned it and lived on the second floor. Eleni was effusively delighted to see Rena. She was more chatty than Rena's mother and the small talk with her took nearly an hour. There was no refusing the sweets she offered, baklava and *kourambiedes.*

When they finally asked Eleni about that fateful summer day in 1960, at first she wouldn't speak of it. "A tragic accident," was all she would say.

Rena explained that she knew it was not an accident. She told her aunt how important it was that she learn more, and so Eleni spoke. Her version did not diverge in any significant way from Maria's. She, too, was pained as she recalled that day and again Rena felt gnawed by guilt.

"Your sister-in-law said something about some paintings maybe being involved," Lou said eagerly.

"Stavros never told me all his business, just little bits of it as suited him." Eleni patted the edges of her hair. It was silver white and stiffly coiffured. "He was a businessman," she continued, "but

164

also an appreciator of fine art. An unusual man." The quiver of her lip was barely perceptible. "He had quite a collection. During the Occupation, rumors circulated that the Germans were confiscating works of art. My husband removed most of the paintings that he owned. Antoni had some also and I believe he did the same. They and their friend, George Dimitropoulos, hid them away." She spread her palms. "Some of them were never seen again. Stavros suspected George of stealing them. Their friendship ended over it. That's all I know. The paintings were never recovered."

"And George?" Lou asked.

"Emigrated to America after the war. I was glad. It was just as well that he was gone. There was no contact with him until the day before Stavros and Antoni . . . until the day before they died." Eleni was scraping at the edge of one of her long painted fingernails. "When Stavros came to the village," she continued, placing her hands in her lap, "the day he died . . . we were on the porch, just before he went to saw some logs. He told me George Dimitropoulos was in Athens. He had to remind me who he was. It had been so long, I'd almost forgotten. He said George had visited him."

"Did he say what they had talked about?" Lou asked.

"No."

"Did you suspect him in the killings?"

Eleni raised an eyebrow and nodded. "I did at first. He was proven innocent. The police inspector in Athens thought he might be involved, but as it turned out, he was not."

"He had an alibi."

"Yes, and also it didn't make sense, didn't fit, the inspector said. That's what he told me after he investigated. I don't remember exactly what he said, but he was sure George was innocent, that he knew nothing about it."

"A strange coincidence," Lou said. "His showing up like that and then the murders. Do you remember what else Stavros said to you that day just before . . . when you were talking on the porch?"

"Only that he and Antoni had some business to do that afternoon. It was a Saturday, you know. He said they would be gone for awhile — he and Antoni. They would be gone . . ."

Eleni took a tissue from the brass holder on the coffee table. She blew her nose quietly. Lou looked at the floor. Rena looked around the room. It was beautiful, full of tasteful antiques. Eleni had inherited quite a lot when Stavros died. Her new husband had invested well and the inheritance had grown.

"That's the last thing he ever said to me." Eleni wiped her nose again. "That he and Antoni would be gone for a while." She shook her head sadly. The pearls dangling from her earlobes flopped against her neck. "I can't imagine who would do a thing like that, what sort of evil creature . . ."

Rena stared at the brass tissue holder.

Lou asked, "Did your husband give you any idea what the business was that he and Antoni had to do that day?"

"No."

"Is George Dimito —"

"Dimitropoulos."

"Yes, is he still alive?"

"As far as I know."

"Do you know where he lives?"

"Flint, Michigan, last I heard. He would be about my age, sixty-nine. I would think he'd still be alive. You don't plan to talk with him, do you?" She directed the question to Rena.

"I don't know." Rena looked at Lou. "We might."

"Rena, dear, why? What is it that's eating at you now after so many years?"

"The need to know the truth," Rena said sadly. "All of it."

"Eleni," Lou said quickly. "Could you talk a little about Rena's relationship with her father? How things were between them. Was there anything . . . unusual?"

"Unusual? Well, yes . . ."

Rena gritted her teeth. She could feel the beginnings of nausea in the center of her stomach.

"I've never seen a man so devoted to his child. That was unusual. For Antoni, the sun rose and set with you, little Rena. You were the apple of his eye."

Rena nodded. "Yes, I remember it that way. It was good between us." Her nausea turned to sorrow.

"Very good. Ideal, I would say. That man had the patience of Job." She turned to Lou, smiling. "Your friend here was a well-behaved child most of the time but she did do her little mischiefs." Eleni winked at Lou. "Her father was always patient with her, even when the mischiefs weren't so little." Eleni laughed and continued directing her words to Lou. "Whenever the threshing machine was around and nobody was looking, you know what this one would do? She'd climb right up on it and play with all the levers. She just couldn't keep her hands off things sometimes."

Suddenly Eleni's smile was gone and her chin began to quiver. She composed herself immediately. "She played with the saw one time. I had forgotten about that. She took Stavros' electric saw and was cutting limbs off of trees. Antoni scolded her but he couldn't stay angry at her, not for more than a few seconds. He always loved her so, no matter what." She looked at Rena. "What a shame you had to lose him when you were still so young."

Rena nodded mutely.

Eleni patted her hand. "It's good to be with you, Rena. And I'm glad you visited your mother. She told me she hadn't seen you for a while."

"Thank you, Eleni. Thank you for talking about all this. I know it wasn't easy."

"I only hope it helps, whatever it is that's bothering you. You must come and visit us old ones more often."

CHAPTER EIGHTEEN

Rena's house felt welcoming and warmly familiar to her. There was a thin layer of dust on the furniture but the plants were thriving. Casey came, Rena knew. Casey came and took in the mail, cared for her plants, cut the lawn, and continued to be the most loyal of friends. I don't deserve her, Rena thought.

Lou wandered from room to room nodding approvingly. "It looks like you," she said, noting the earth colors, the Mucha prints, the wooden carvings and boxes. "And you look at home here. Show me the back yard before it gets dark. I want to see the famous gazebo."

The flowers were dead, the grass in need of its final cut before winter. It felt good to be home. Rena pulled up a few weeds and then they went back inside.

"What's this?" Lou held a little wire box in her hands.

Rena took it from her. "It's a trap," she said flatly.

Lou nodded. "For the birds."

Rena placed it on a high shelf. "Something to drink?"

"Do you have any tea?"

"Not your kind."

Lou was examining a brass vase. "No one does," she said. "It's my own special brew."

"What's in it," Rena asked, "truth serum?"

"Mm-hm."

Rena laughed. "I think I have some camomile."

"That will do. I want to review what we know so far, weird one, then talk about whether we want to take a trip to Flint, Michigan."

Rena pulled her tongue across her upper lip. "Wouldn't you rather fool around?" She smiled seductively. "I have a water bed."

Lou shook her head, smiling too, and Rena, still vamping playfully, lifted up a corner of her sweater and flashed one naked breast.

Lou grabbed her, laughing, and gave her a giant bear hug. "Let's talk, shameless hussy. Make the tea."

"Yes, owner."

Lou looked seriously at Rena. "Am I still God to you?"

Rena smiled shyly. "You have your moments." She put the water on to heat and Lou looked through Rena's albums and tapes.

"What are you, a lesbian or something? All this *women's music.*" She selected a Kay Gardner tape, *Mooncircles,* and they sat with their tea in the living room.

"I like being here with you," Lou said. "Helps fill things out."

"Yes. My turf."

"You're a complex woman."

"I suppose." Rena suddenly felt very sad.

Lou did not miss it. "Hang in, Rena, it'll work out. You'll end up free. Trust me."

"Right. Freedom's just around the corner."

"You don't sound like you mean that."

"I mean it. We just have different ideas about freedom." Rena looked around at the various objects she'd acquired over the years, the pottery, the antique end table, the collection of boxes. They used to be important. "How odd," she said, "to feel relief by discovering I'm a murderer."

Lou frowned. "I would guess that the relief comes from finally getting in touch — consciously now — with what you've been believing unconsciously for twenty-seven years, and what you've been torturing yourself with for the past few months." She reached for her cigarette pack. "Now you have something to work with. It's no longer a phantom."

Rena said nothing.

"The real relief will come when we find out who the killers really are and when you understand why that ten-year-old in you believed that crap about you being a murderer."

"Crap?"

Lou shrugged. "Let's review what we know." She lit the cigarette. "I'll start with your version. You correct me if I'm wrong."

She blew a thin stream of smoke into the air. Rena watched it circle around the lamp.

"You were a happy kid, bright, vivacious, loved by your parents, very attached to your father. Everything was going along fine until one day in the summer of nineteen-sixty. You were in the village where your grandparents lived and where you and your mother spent the summers. You were looking forward to your father's arrival. You went to the place where he always went first, that little house of his just outside the village. It was almost time for your dad to be there, so you went to wait for him. I wonder what time that was. It had to have been after twelve-twenty because that's when the shepherd saw your dad arrive."

"I remember seeing him," Rena said suddenly.

"Who?"

"The shepherd. I saw him passing by."

"You did? OK, so you must have arrived at the little house soon after your father did, at around twelve-twenty."

"I guess. So what?"

"So it might be important. Anyway, your dad called you inside. Something happened in the little house then that you can't remember, but you do remember that when you left, you were angry. You went to the river where your anger dissipated and you enjoyed yourself. You masturbated. Am I right so far?"

Rena nodded. She was looking at the lovely Mucha on the wall across the room. It was an expensive print. She had hesitated about buying it. Now, she thought, she wasn't so sure she liked Mucha anymore. Too pretty. Too unreal.

"What happened then?"

"We've been over it a thousand times."

"What happened then?"

"I left the river. I went to my grandma's. I found my uncle and I shot him in the head. Then I cut off his arm, the one with the tattoo."

"What about the gun?"

"Oh, right. You know the story better than I do. I got the gun first, from the closet, then I went outside and killed him."

"You never said what you did with the gun after you shot your uncle."

Rena shrugged. "Put it back in the closet, I suppose."

"You don't remember doing that?"

"That's what I did."

"And then what?"

"I wrapped the arm in a piece of tarp and —"

"Where'd you get the tarp?"

"It was there, on the woodpile. They used it to cover the wood. I wrapped the arm in it and I went to the river, to my nest spot."

"And you hid the arm somewhere."

"Yes."

"And as you sat at the river you started wondering whether it really happened, about your uncle, or whether you just imagined it."

"I wasn't sure."

"So you went to find out? Right? You went back to your grandmother's and your mother told you he was dead. That was at one o'clock. We know that now. So you went and retrieved the arm from where you'd hidden it and then went to the little house again."

"That's right. I went back to the little house and that's when I killed my father. I was a real charmer."

"You were. But you had a very active fantasy life." Lou took her shoes off and kicked them aside.

"Now here's my version." She looked at the ceiling as she spoke. "You went to the little house the first time. Your father was there. He got you angry. You went to the river. While you were at the river

171

feeling angry and doing yourself, somebody killed Stavros and then your dad. When you found out your uncle was dead, you ran to be with your father. You found him dead too. Being a basically weird person, you blamed yourself. You thought you did it."

"You're the one with the active fantasy life."

"Let me ask you something." Lou leaned forward. She looked weary. "Kids often believe they're responsible for things they had nothing to do with . . . you do know that, don't you?"

"I suppose."

"Kids often don't think real logically, Rena. And then, as adults, they're stuck with the illogical conclusions of childhood."

"Is that so?"

"I know you don't believe this applies to you."

Rena shifted positions on the soft chair she always sat in at home. "My goal is not to prove I didn't do it. That might be yours, Lou, but I know I killed them. My goal is to find out why. I know what I did. I need to know why."

"Will you try to keep an open mind?" Lou urged.

Rena looked at her. "Sure, my mind is open. You helped me do that. By the way, did I thank you? I don't remember if I thanked you."

"Cut the sarcasm." Lou leaned back again. "It's one of your less lovable traits."

"Minor in comparison."

Lou exhaled loudly. "The only real lead we have is that some long-lost, ex-friend of your father and uncle showed up in Athens the day before the killings. George something."

"Dimitropoulos."

"I think we should try to find him."

Rena felt mildly curious about the man. She crossed the room and went to the phone. She got the Flint, Michigan operator and then the phone number of a George Dimitropoulos. "So far, so good," she said to Lou, dialing again.

"Mr. Dimitropoulos, this is Katerina Spiros. I'm the daughter of Antoni Spiros. Stavros Spiros was my uncle . . . Yes, yes, I imagine it is . . . Yes, a very long time . . ."

172

They talked for a few minutes. George Dimitropoulos was willing to meet with Rena — in fact, almost eager, it seemed. They arranged the meeting for the following day at his home.

Rena and Lou spent the evening relaxing, listening to music, chatting. They ordered a pizza.

At ten o'clock, they decided to go to a bar. Lou had been to *Steady Ground* many times and so had Rena. Lou wondered if they had ever crossed paths. Rena assured her that if she'd seen Lou there or anyplace else, she would not forget.

"Why are you so taken with me?" Lou asked. They had carried their beers to a corner table.

"I have no choice. You own what's left of my life."

Lou tilted her head, looking closely at Rena. "You don't believe that anymore." She kept looking at her. "Do you?"

Rena laughed. "I never did, big shot."

"You did too."

Rena laughed again. "You're not the only one who plays games."

"Bullshit. I don't believe you for a minute."

Rena ran her finger around the perimeter of her beer glass. "Well, I suppose there were periods when I was pretty much under your sway."

"You were totally controlled by me."

"That's a little strong."

"You called me God. You did everything I told you."

"Only because it pleased me."

"Lou, hi. Long time." The young blond woman reminded Rena of Meryl Streep. She looked frail and lovely. She also looked very fond of Lou.

"Hi there, Lucy. Here, sit down." Lou pulled out the chair for her. "I'd like you to meet Rena Spiros. This is Lucy Scott. Lucy's my favorite artist." She turned from Rena, smiling warmly at the intruder. "How are the lithographs coming along?"

"I have one put aside for you," Lucy purred.

"I told you, you have to stop giving them away."

"For you it will always be free." She gave a throaty laugh. "I did sell six of them, though, at the Hyde Park Art Fair. I thought you

173

might come." Lucy had barely said hello to Rena and totally ignored her now.

"I'd like to see what you've been doing lately." Lou turned to Rena. "I think you'd like her work." Rena nodded. Lucy still did not give her a glance.

"How are things in the country?" Lucy leaned very close to Lou as she spoke. "I've been meaning to come for a visit but I've been so damned busy."

"I wish you'd find the time," Lou said invitingly.

"You should come down to Chicago more often, Lou," Lucy crooned. "You know you have a standing invitation to stay with me."

Rena felt her neck hairs standing on end. The conversation became an undecipherable buzz. She felt dizzy. Her hand opened and closed tensely in her lap. A minute later she stood, walked through the bar, and out. She walked east, toward Lake Michigan. She kept going, walking along the shore, then through the park, and toward the zoo.

When Rena didn't return to the table, Lou searched the bar for her. "She's moody sometimes," she told Lucy. "Probably decided to go home."

Lou and Lucy talked and danced until the bar closed.

CHAPTER NINETEEN

They both slept late the next morning, Lou on the hideaway bed in the guest room, Rena in her water bed. They ate breakfast together in the tiny kitchen of Rena's old Victorian house and then they drove to Michigan. Neither spoke of Rena's sudden exit the night before.

George Dimitropoulos was a small, wrinkled, pleasant old man, who welcomed his visitors with wine, cheese, and candy, and told them stories about the Greek community in Flint, Michigan. He referred frequently to Mrs. Dimitropoulos who had died four years earlier. "I never thought I'd outlive her," he said. It was apparent that he was lonely.

"Mr. Dimitropoulos," Rena ventured, after he finished a very long story about the time his candy store was robbed, "you were friends with my father many years ago."

"That's true. Good friends. And Stavros too. I admired that man. He got things done. Made a lot of money too."

"What happened to the friendships? I understand there was some trouble."

George pursed his thin lips. "Trouble indeed. It was because of those damn paintings." He cleared his throat. "Pardon my language. There were some paintings," he continued, "way back . . . it was during the war, the big one, I mean, number two. They disappeared into thin air." He brushed the palms of his bony hands together. "Now, I was never the art connoisseur like the Spiros boys were. I couldn't tell genius from crap. Still can't. But I do know what I like." He pointed to the wall behind Lou. "Picked that one out myself. Cost me twenty-four ninety-five."

The women glanced at the print of snow-capped mountains.

"I helped them hide the paintings. We helped each other out in those days. Had to. It was before you were born, Katerina. That was a good time not to be born. They shot people in the streets, you know. Hung my friend Alexis from his own balcony. We used to have Turkish coffee together in the mornings, Alexis and I. Terrible times those were. Terrible times."

"Yes." Rena nodded solemnly. "What happened then," she asked, "between you and my father and Stavros?"

"It should never have happened." George scowled and shook his head. "We were all good friends but we became suspicious of each other. About the paintings. Nothing against your father, Miss Katerina, but I thought maybe greed had overcome him."

"You thought my father took them?"

"Well, not really. Well, I might have. They just disappeared. There was no explanation." George blew his nose noisily in his carefully folded handkerchief. "Antoni quizzed me. I was insulted at first and then I thought maybe it was a cover, that he was covering up because he took them. I didn't know what else to think. And he thought I was the thief." George shook his nearly hairless head. "How ironic. You see, later, years later, we discovered that it was all a mistake. All those years of bitterness and it was just a mistake. I lost two very good friends for no good reason. Good friends aren't that easy to get, I've found."

"What mistake?" Lou asked.

George turned his eyes to Lou. "No one had stolen them. The paintings were in Petros Xamplas' attic all that time. Can you believe that? For fifteen years, no, it was more like eighteen years.

176

That's where they were all that time. In Petros Xamplas' attic." The old man shook his head. "The ironies of life."

"How did the paintings get —"

"My wife used to say that. 'The ironies of life,' she'd say. Now, I think you have a right to know about the paintings, Katerina. They belonged to your father, after all, some of them, and to your uncle." George refolded his legs, revealing several inches of shiny bluish shin.

"Petros Xamplas thought the paintings were worthless. That's what he told his sister. He put them in the attic with all the other junk and forgot about them. And she didn't want the junk. Do what you want with it, she told him."

"Who are —"

"And finally, it looks like Stavros and Antoni will finally get their paintings back and then the next thing you know, they're both dead." He touched his fingers to his lips. "Oh, I'm sorry, Katerina, I..."

"That's all right," Rena said quickly. "Who is Petros Xamplas?"

George adjusted his glasses. "Nikki Karras' brother." He looked at Rena as if it should all be clear now. "She's a good woman, Nikki is. A widow, you know, since the war."

It was obvious that the story would unfold at George Dimitropoulos' own rate.

"She never did remarry. Many Greek widows don't. Haven't seen her in years. In fact I believe I saw her only once since my wife got sick. That was ten years ago. She and my wife became friends of sorts, not close friends, but they kept in touch. We met her at a party in Chicago. Nice party. Lots of food. That was just a week before we were to leave for a vacation to Greece. It was in nineteen-sixty. We went back to Greece every four or five years, my wife and I. I was very surprised to meet her, Nikki Karras, I mean. It was at a party given by my wife's cousin, Nicoletta. Now that's someone you'd like, Katerina. Nicoletta is an educated woman, a teacher, like you. High school, I think. Yes, she taught in one of those inner city schools. They call them inner city now, you know. We used to call them slums, but words start to change. People get sensitive. Now, I remember when Negro was a perfectly acceptable..."

Rena glanced at Lou who was already looking at her, slightly impatient, but smiling indulgently. Neither spoke. They let George go on. Rena hoped there would be a pause soon and they could continue questioning him. It was nearly evening by the time they got the information they had come for.

In 1942, they learned, Antoni and Stavros and George hid some paintings in the store basement of Gianni Karras who was a friend of Stavros' business partner. Soon afterwards Gianni Karras was killed by German soldiers. When the Spiros brothers heard, they went to Gianni's store to retrieve the paintings. The paintings were gone.

They questioned the storekeeper's wife, Nikki Karras, but she knew nothing about them. The brothers assumed the Germans had gotten them. When the war ended, they expected the paintings would turn up in Germany. They inquired through their connections in the art world but were unable to locate them. Finally, they accused George and the friendships ended over it. Soon after, George immigrated to the United States and he had all but forgotten the whole business until he met Nikki Karras at a party in Chicago in 1960.

"We talked and talked," George told Rena and Lou. "Nikki and me and my wife. We hit it off real well. We talked about Greece, our trips back. We reminisced about the war years too. That's when I realized who she was." He leaned forward, his eyes shining. "What a coincidence, huh? The wife of Gianni Karras."

George asked her about the paintings. She knew nothing about them, but she remembered that two men had come to her soon after her husband's death. Two brothers, she recalled, acquaintances of her husband. They too had asked her about the things in the basement. They didn't say anything about paintings.

"She told them her husband was an alley picker," George continued, "that he collected all kinds of things — broken lamps, tables, car tires, things like that. Junk, she called it." George smiled, shaking his head. "She had no idea what happened to all the *junk* in the basement. That's what she told Stavros and Antoni."

George paused at this point to watch Lou light a cigarette. "Incense of the devil," he said, smiling and pointing to the smoke.

"Clever," Lou said. "So Nikki didn't know what happened to the junk..."

"Right. It wasn't until years later when she was living in America that she learned more. Her brother, Petros, wrote her from Athens asking if she wanted any of the things from Gianni's store. The day after Gianni died, it turned out, Petros had cleared out the basement and stored the stuff in his attic. There seemed to be nothing of value, he told Nikki. She said he could dispose of it as he pleased.

"When she told me this, I got very excited." George was waving his hands in the air as he spoke. "Maybe the paintings are still there, in that attic." His eyes were shining. "So, I told her what happened, that we hid paintings in the basement there, back in 'forty-two.

"Nikki thought her brother had probably gotten rid of all the things by then. He was planning to sell his house, she said, and move to Thessaloniki. That was why her brother asked her about the junk, to see if she wanted any of it. He never did move, though, Nikki told me. He was still in the same house.

George swept his palms over his pate. "I persuaded Nikki to call her brother in Athens and charge the call to my phone. Nikki said if Petros did still have the paintings, they didn't belong to him or to her and that my friends should have them back. She made the call. Petros checked his attic and called Nikki back. There were paintings, he told her. A dozen or so, of different sizes, all carefully wrapped in canvas. "I was really excited then," George said, "as you can imagine. I had Nikki tell her brother that I'd be in touch with him the next week, when I got there, to Greece. Well, when I did get to Greece I decided to go straight to Stavros. I went to his office. He seemed almost pleased to see me even before I told him about the paintings. The years do mellow a person, though Stavros had not really changed. I still admired the man."

George nodded sadly. "I gave Stavros the phone number Nikki had given me and right then and there he called her brother. Petros Xamplas is his name. Petros said, yes, he had the paintings. And then he told Stavros that he'd had a man in to look at them, just out of curiosity, you know, and that he was offered thirty thousand drachmas for the lot of them. That was about a thousand dollars, you know, at that time, in nineteen-sixty. Of course, he didn't sell them. He told the guy, Demos, that he'd think about it. Now Stavros was very upset about this Demos."

George removed his glasses and wiped them carefully on the corner of his folded handkerchief.

"Stavros said he had to get the paintings right away. He took my phone number where I was staying with my sister in Athens and he promised to call me soon, in a day or two. He said it looked like he had some very sincere apologizing to do to me. That's what he said. We shook hands and I left." George looked sadly into Rena's eyes. "That's the last I ever saw him. The next day he was killed."

Rena nodded.

"After I heard, I decided to give Petros Xamplas a call," George continued. "He told me Antoni had come and taken the paintings. He said he knew nothing more about it." George tilted his head, looking into Rena's eyes. "It's quite a mystery, don't you think? The Spiros brothers are murdered and the paintings disappear again."

"Yes, a mystery," Lou said. "Do you have any idea what might have happened to the paintings?"

The old man raised his scraggly eyebrows. "The killer got them, I'd say."

"And who do you think the killer is?" Lou asked.

"That I don't know, young lady. They never arrested anyone. Had to be somebody who knew about the paintings. The police tried to find out but they never did. They suspected everybody."

He looked at Rena. "Even your mother, did you know that? Of course, that was ridiculous. They suspected me too. I'm surprised they didn't think you might have done it, Katerina." He laughed. "I'm sorry. This is nothing to joke about. Nope, nobody knows who did it. Except the killer," he added, and he laughed again.

Rena felt ill.

A half hour later, she and Lou were on the highway heading toward home. Lou was driving. "So what do you think now?" Lou asked. She handed Rena her can of Pepsi to hold.

"What do you mean?"

"George's story."

Rena took a sip of Lou's drink. "It makes me curious. It's kind of interesting."

"That's all?"

"It doesn't change anything, Lou," she said impatiently.

Lou also seemed impatient. "Rena, obviously somebody was after those paintings. That was their motive."

"Motive for what?"

Lou shook her head. They didn't speak for some miles.

"I hear Greece is quite beautiful," Lou said soon after they crossed the Indiana border.

"Mm-hm," Rena replied absently.

"What's it like in the fall?"

Rena looked at her. "Why? Why do you ask?"

Lou smiled broadly. "Because we're going there, of course."

CHAPTER TWENTY

Rena spent most of the next week working. She canned berries, cut back branches in the orchards, dug up bulbs, fed the animals. She also took long solitary walks.

Late one afternoon while Rena was in the orchard, Lou and Darla sat talking in the kitchen. "My hope is that being there, where it actually happened, will jog the memories back," Lou was saying. "The trip to Greece is the make it or break it point as I see it."

"And if you don't make it?"

"I hate to think." Lou leaned forward, her elbows on the table. "At best, I think she'd be stuck with a very constricted life. She could end up institutionalized. Or she might kill herself."

"And if you do make it?"

"Then she'll be free. That's my hope. She's like a prisoner now, of her own guilt-ridden fantasies." Lou picked up the salt shaker and rolled it around in her hand.

"You've grown very attached to her, haven't you?" Darla took the salt shaker from Lou's hand. "You're spilling salt all over the table. If Rena gets free, what then? She might go back to her life in Chicago."

"Yes, of course. I expect she will." Lou pushed grains of salt into a pile on the table.

"But won't you miss her?"

"Sure."

"Love 'em and let 'em go, huh? Like with Rainflower."

"Yes." Lou smiled. "Itsy Bitsy Rainflower. I think of her as a waif who needed a little love, some help with boundaries, and then a shove."

Darla chuckled knowingly. "A gentle shove."

"Of course."

"Are you still sending her money in Colorado?"

"The first of every month. She's doing real well."

"I wonder if she realizes how much you did for her."

"I think so."

"Why do you do it, Lou? I mean, put so much into people."

"Now, why do you think, darling Darla?" Lou leaned back in her chair.

"You like seeing the changes; you enjoy the power."

"Sure." Lou was smiling broadly. "It's very gratifying. Who could deny that? Sure I enjoy it."

"I hate to think where I'd be right now if it weren't for you," Darla said seriously. She tugged on her earlobe. "But, you know, I've always wondered about you, about your motivation. There's more to it than just the enjoyment, isn't there?"

"I could say it's just because I'm a wonderful person."

"You're not bad, but Mother Teresa, you're not." Darla laughed. "You got money, brains, looks. You could travel around the world, do very exciting things, but you stay here taking in stray orphans. Why?"

"You really want to know?"

"I really do."

"Very few people ask. I guess they assume they have the answers. It has to do with self-destructiveness." Lou looked very serious. "When I see that in people, I can't just turn my back on it."

Darla nodded. "Do you know why?"

183

"I think so." Lou brushed the pile of salt into her palm and dumped it in the ashtray. "There was somebody very dear to me who was self-destructive when she was young. It took a long time for her to get over it, much too long." Lou took a cigarette from the pack and tapped it on the table. "No one seemed able to help her. She had to do it on her own and it was a very, very painful, slow process."

"Who was she?" Darla asked.

Lou pointed to her chest.

"You? You were self-destructive? That's hard to believe."

"Between age eighteen and, oh, I must have been about twenty-five before I really came to terms with it. You know my folks have always been political activists. I told you that."

"Dedicated pinkos."

"Right. So dedicated, in fact, that they had no time to raise their children."

"You and your sister."

"Julie handled it much differently from me. She developed what they call a histrionic personality. You know what that is? You met her. You know. She gets all kinds of attention wherever she goes."

"She certainly is colorful."

"And I handled it by joining the Army."

"What do you mean? You joined the Army because your parents were too busy for you?"

"Basically. It took me years to realize it." Lou put the cigarette back in the pack. "I should quit smoking," she said. "I can't tell you how much I hated the Army. If someone were to try to devise an environment that I would abhor the most, they'd come up with the United States Army. But I stuck it out. I stuck it out for four disgusting years. And do you know why? I did it to get even with them, with my parents. I did it to hurt them. Of course, I didn't know it at the time. But, unconsciously, I believed that joining the Army was the one thing I could do that would really get to them. I was so fucking angry."

"I'm sorry, Lou."

"Well, I'm long over it. We're very good friends now, my parents and I. We did a lot of talking when I finally understood what was going on with me. I made them talk and they did, and Julie too. It

184

was like family therapy without a therapist. We all turned out to be each other's therapist. And we all ended up learning a hell of a lot from it. My parents went through terrible guilt for a while, but then that passed. We're close now. But back then, when I was in the Army and for a number of years afterward, I hated them. I wanted to hurt them and I hurt them all right. But, God, Darla, at what a price to myself. I suffered for four miserable years and then for some time after that. I became real aware of how self-destructive we can be. If I could have realized it sooner, I could have spared myself a lot of misery."

"So people like Rainflower and all the others, me . . ." Darla smiled. "And now Rena . . ."

"Self-destructive people. They're definitely my weakness. I do what I can."

"Well, it sure worked for me. I hope it works for Rena. I have to admit it's hard to understand your methods with her, though. I mean, before, all that obedience stuff, that was . . . I don't know . . . it's hard to see why that was necessary."

"I know. It was drastic but it made sense. Part of what I did with her, I learned in the Army, believe it or not." Lou took a cigarette again and lit it this time. "I guess I still have some self-destructiveness left," she said, taking a deep drag, and looking at the cigarette. "I was in Military Intelligence. I was just a clerk, but I learned a hell of a lot about interrogation procedures. In one sense it's vile, the psychological manipulations I learned, but it's one of those ends-justifying-the-means situations."

"I see. So the obedience . . ."

Lou nodded. "What I did with Rena is play on and increase tendencies she already had, the need or wish to be dominated, to have someone else take over. I still don't know why she has that need. Lots of people do. No one seems to really understand it. I have a friend in Madison who's like that. It's not causing her any problems, though. With Rena, it's different. Hers is connected with her father and uncle somehow — her guilt, the domination stuff, her sexual thing. They're all connected. For her it's important to try to figure it all out because it's destroying her. So what I did was to get her so dependent and trusting of me . . ."

185

"Like a little kid."

"Yes, in a way. So trusting that she'd do whatever I want. In her case, what I want is to get her over the guilt that's destroying her. First, of course, she had to become aware of it, to remember what it is that's making her feel she doesn't deserve to live."

"You've succeeded there."

"Yes. She told me what she feels guilty about. Unfortunately her memories are distorted. Hopefully, in Greece we'll be able to straighten things out."

Darla nodded. "I hope it succeeds. I'm still not sure, though, where the Army stuff comes in."

Lou extinguished the half-smoked cigarette. "In Military Intelligence the motives are different, of course, and the tactics more extreme, using deprivation and fear to develop the dependency, but the principle's the same."

"Getting people pliable enough to do what you want and tell you what you want."

"Exactly."

"But in Rena's case, for her own good."

"Right. So I've succeeded in finding out why she feels so guilty. Now I have to get her over the guilt."

"Trish seems to think the guilt is deserved."

"I know. She's as convinced as Rena."

"God, I hope they're wrong."

"They're wrong. Speaking of Trish, she's coming by soon."

"She's very worried about you."

"I know."

"She's always been protective of you. You're pretty special to her."

"She's special to me too. But she's wrong about Rena."

A half hour later, Trish arrived. After a few minutes Darla left them alone. Lou and Trish went into the living room.

"You'd be insane to go to Greece with her," Trish said immediately.

Lou nodded. "I understand your feelings, Trish."

"She's dangerous, Lou."

Lou put her booted feet up on the coffee table. "I know you believe that."

"She's going to get you."

Lou smiled sadly. "I wish it didn't worry you so, Trish. Rena is not dangerous. I've been working closely with her. I'm convinced. I wish you could trust me on this."

"You're not *always* right, you know."

"I'm not?"

"If you weren't so blinded by your need to see her as a good person, and to help her, you'd realize she's not like the others. Lou, I think about it all the time. I've . . . I've put it together in a way that makes so much sense. Will you at least listen?"

"Of course I'll listen. You have a new theory?"

"New elements."

"I'll try to have an open mind."

Trish pushed up the sleeves of her flannel shirt. "Like I said, it's on my mind all the time. I even dream about it. Anyway, here's how I figure it." She took a deep breath. "It begins with her relationship with her father and uncle, OK? Now, both of them were very powerful figures in her life —"

"True."

"She had a love/hate relationship with them, loving the father, hating the uncle . . ."

"Mm-m, I'm not so sure she —"

"Let me finish."

Lou spread her hand, gesturing for Trish to go on.

"But the two of them came as a package. She had to accept both the nice one and the nasty one. Her whole sense of security, even her basic sense of self, got tied up with them. Or at least with her father. It wasn't like a normal parent-child relationship. Her attachment was so extreme it was unnatural. He was the world to her. She told you this, right? That's where I'm getting the data. But then he did something that threatened it all. It happened in the little house. I have a pretty good idea what it was."

"Daddy got *too* affectionate."

"No."

"No?"

187

"Daddy had a woman with him."

"Ah!" Lou raised her brow. "Interesting."

"Rena panicked. She felt her whole world crumbling. She felt terror at first, but then it turned to rage. Cold rage. The evil part of her emerged and she knew what she had to do — get her father's idol, kill the pig brother and rub Daddy's face in it."

"Torture him with it, I believe you said before."

"That's right. Only that wasn't enough. She had to destroy him. And she did."

"You're forgetting a couple things, Trish," Lou interrupted. "What about the paintings? What about the truck being broken into?"

Trish hesitated, frowning deeply. "Whoever was after the paintings might have been in the little house with Rena's father the first time she went there on the day she killed him. Maybe it was a woman or maybe it was a man."

"You're changing your theory."

"I'm modifying it to fit all the information we have. It's a detail. What really matters is that Rena got upset in that little house, very upset. Maybe the person there had threatened her father or maybe threatened to harm Rena. So the father's all upset and maybe he yelled at Rena or hit her. Maybe he told her to get the hell out of there. Whatever it was, she ended up feeling so rejected that she changed, she tapped that awful part of her and ended up killing. Lou, it's not simple with Rena. She's not an evil *person*. The evil is only one layer of her. Alien even to her. But it's a terrible and violent layer. The rest of her is fine — the good layer, the caring, sensitive, moral part of her, the part that cannot possibly accept what she did. That part can't tolerate the reality of her acts. She has a conscience. She feels guilt."

Trish pushed her sleeves up again; they kept slipping down. "The evil part of her tried to kill Rebecca. The evil part of her did kill Pat. That was too much for her to repress. Guilt overcomes her. She feels like her basic self, her core, is evil. She has to kill it. She tries to do it symbolically, killing birds, but that doesn't work. She tries killing herself. You stop her. You force her to remember why she feels evil. She remembers what she did, and then realizes she truly *is* evil. That brings us up to the present. Now the struggle in her continues. If the evil part wins, she'll go on merging with father-uncle substitutes. But if she senses them withdrawing from her, if she feels the threat of losing them, then her sense of self is threatened. When that happens, her response is to kill."

Lou nodded. "And if the good part wins?"

"She'll kill herself."

Lou looked at Trish reflectively, and with affection. "Trish, obviously you're sincere. You think that she's killed and may kill again. But, could you entertain the other possibility? My theory. It's more likely, really, if you think about it. That she didn't kill anyone even though she *confessed* and is convinced herself that she did. Isn't that more likely? How many ten-year-olds murder?"

"Lou, infrequent doesn't mean impossible. I know what those eyes mean."

"Right, the eyes. You're reading way too much into what her eyes looked like."

"I've seen that look before."

"Oh? What do you mean? Where?" Lou's curiosity was tinged with concern.

"My stepfather."

Lou cocked her head, waiting.

"He tried to kill my brother. I was there. I saw it. His eyes looked exactly like Rena's."

"Trish," Lou said solicitously. "You never told me that. What happened?"

"He went after him with a knife." Trish pressed her fingers against her forehead. "They were having a fight, yelling at each other. Then my brother went up close to him, you know real close and threatening like, and he poked my stepfather and shoved him. That's when my stepfather got that look in his eyes. I'll never forget that look. I've had nightmares about it. He ran out of the room and came back with a knife and he went after Teddy. Teddy raised his arm to protect himself. He slashed his arm. The blood got all over everything. It got on my puzzle. It was a farm scene, I remember. There were ducks and cows, and the blood got all over them. My brother ran out of the house." Trish looked at Lou. "He would have killed him if Teddy hadn't run away."

"Oh, Trish," Lou said earnestly, "that must have been awful."

"It wasn't the first time. Before my mom met him, he beat up a guy. She just told me about it a few years ago. There was a car accident. The other guy and my stepfather started yelling at each other and then my father started beating up on the guy and I guess almost killed him except some people pulled him off. He spent some time in jail for that."

"A very violent man. You never talked about him."

"He went to a state hospital after he stabbed Teddy. He was amnesiac about what happened. He was in the hospital for years. My mom said it happened at the hospital too, that he choked someone. Another patient. The guy cussed him or something and my stepfather went for his throat."

Lou shook her head.

"Some people just have that part in them, Lou. Something sets them off and they're gone, they kill."

"I understand, Trish. I understand how it seems to you, but I still see Rena very differently."

"I think the police should be involved in this."

"You're kidding!"

Trish looked deadly serious. "I'm strongly considering talking to them unless you back out of it."

"Trish, I'm . . . come on, this is no way to handle it."

"I don't want you to go to Greece with her. I don't want her around you."

"I know. That's clear."

"I've got to stop you somehow."

Lou nodded. "I appreciate your concern. Truly, I do. But, Trish, you have to accept that I'm going to do what makes sense to me."

"You're blind."

"The police wouldn't touch it. There's no evidence."

"She confessed."

Lou shook her head. "That means nothing. There's no case."

Trish's jaw grew slack. "I know. I checked with Hilary."

"Your lawyer friend, the one who works in the D.A.'s office?"

"She said there's no case."

"Let it go, Trish."

"I can't."

Lou went to Trish and put her arms around her and rubbed her back.

CHAPTER TWENTY ONE

At their next *tea and communing* session, Lou took Rena back to the day of the killings, focusing on her first visit to the little house. "You saw him in the window. You went inside. What did you see in there?"

Rena strained. She shook her head.

"Was your father alone?"

Rena blocked.

"Were you afraid you were losing him?"

Rena cried. The feelings were there but not the memories.

"Let it come, Rena. It's OK to remember. What happened in there? Let yourself remember."

Rena tried. She cried some more and kept trying to remember, but nothing new would come.

In the morning, at Lou's suggestion, Rena called Nikki Karras and got the address and phone number of Nikki's brother, Petros, in Athens. He would be the first contact, Lou said, and hopefully would lead them to others.

* * * * *

Several days before their departure date, Rena went by herself to Chicago. She wanted to say goodbye.

"What do you expect to find in Greece?" Casey asked. They were at *La Creperie,* Casey's favorite restaurant, sitting at a window table. Casey looked tired or, perhaps, worried, Rena thought. "Reasons," she answered.

"You're here to say goodbye, aren't you?"

"Yes. We're planning to stay three weeks. It may take longer though."

"I mean another kind of goodbye."

A sinking feeling hit Rena's insides. "What do you mean?"

"You and Lou. You've decided to stay with her, haven't you?"

Maybe she shouldn't have been surprised but she was. *I'm not staying with anyone, dear Casey. I'm not staying in the world.*

"Lou and I aren't lovers, Case. We're friends. She's helping me. I'm not going to *stay* with her. It's not like that."

"She reminds me of Pat."

"They're very different."

"Yes, but their effect on you is similar. Only with Lou it's ten times stronger."

"It's very different."

Casey played with her salad, took a bite of the sesame cracker. "I have the sense you're never coming back." She looked up, holding Rena's eyes. "That the Rena you were is gone forever."

The Rena that never had the right to be, Rena thought. She felt deep tenderness for Casey, stirrings way inside, the way she'd felt before she met Pat. How ironic, she thought. How sad. Don't love me, Casey, I'm not worth it. Don't care so much, I'll soon be no more. "Of course I'm coming back. I'm the same me, Casey, only I'm just discovering things about myself that I never knew before."

"Discovering what? The memories, you mean? From your childhood?"

"Yes, I'm remembering some but not everything, not quite enough."

"And in Greece you hope to remember more?"

"Yes."

"Can you tell me what you've learned so far?"

The seafood crepes arrived. Rena waited until the waiter left. "That I'm not what I seem," she said. "That I'm not someone you want to know."

"Oh Rena!" Casey's fork banged her plate. "That's ridiculous! What is that woman doing to you? Dammit, don't go to Greece! Stop this. Please. Go back to Dr. Kepper. Come back to me." She was crying.

Rena felt intensely caring and cared about. The surge of loving feelings enveloped her. Too bad, she thought. Oh shit, too bad. She touched Casey's arm, knowing she was not able to console her. Too bad it could never be. Too bad you can never be my love nor I yours. "I can't, Case. I wish it didn't have to be this way. I mean it. More than you can imagine. But I have to go on with what I'm doing. I have to carry it through."

They ate silently, and when they spoke again, it was of other things.

The following night they went to a movie, then to Casey's for ice cream and coffee. On one level, Rena felt light and happy, enjoying her time with Casey, being playful, joking and laughing with her friend. On another level, she was deadly miserable.

"You're not like you were when you were depressed," Casey said, "but you're not OK either. I wish you'd tell me more."

"I'm sorry."

The silence hung heavily between them. They were at the kitchen table. Casey's dog, Oreo, was at their feet. Rena stared at her knuckles.

"Rena." Casey released a long gush of air.

Rena raised her eyes.

"I'm going to ask something." She set her coffee mug down. "I suppose I shouldn't and it's selfish — but I'm going to. Remember when we first met? We were falling in love, right? I know I was in love with you, but you were, too, weren't you? You were, I know you were."

"Yes," Rena said sadly.

"And then when Pat came along — did the love for me just die?"

Rena played with her ice cream. "It got buried," she said. "I couldn't love someone like you. I couldn't let myself."

"But you could love Pat."

"A strange kind of love. I was more possessed by her than in love with her."

"And the same with Lou, right?"

"Yes." Rena stared at her hands again. "Casey, I'm sorry. I truly am." Tears welled in her eyes. "I should never have been with you in the first place, never pretended that I could be someone for you."

"Why do you say things like that?" Casey nearly screamed the words. "What do you mean? You talk in riddles. Why can't you just let yourself love me like I love you?"

Rena did not reply. The tears slipped down her cheeks.

"I'm sorry, Rena. I don't know why I'm doing this. I wish I could just let go."

"I wish I weren't who I am. I wish everything good for you, Casey, and all I bring you is pain."

"Oh, get off it! You may be weird, friend, but I'm not done with you. I'm not letting you close the book, dammit. So you'll go to Greece and who knows what else you'll do, but don't think it's done. There are more chapters. It's not finished yet."

"You've got ice cream on your face."

Casey smiled and shook her head. She reached for a napkin. "Someday you'll just lick it off for me."

The next morning, Wednesday, Rena returned to Lou's house. On Friday, they were to leave for Greece. Thursday evening Trish came by to see Rena. Rena was surprised. She and Trish had had very little contact for weeks.

Trish suggested they go to De Nova to talk. They drove over in the jeep. In the kitchen of the *Big House,* Trish got them each a soft drink, then suggested they go upstairs to the little sitting room.

"Lou's told me everything that's been going on," Trish said as soon as they were seated.

"I know. I told her I didn't mind."

"It's upset me very much."

"I'm not surprised. It must be hard to learn that someone you used to like is not what you thought."

"Very hard."

"So what's on your mind now? Do you want me to tell you it isn't really true?"

"No," Trish said. "I believe it."

Rena nodded.

"I want you to tell me how Pat died."

Rena frowned. "I don't understand. You know how she died."

"The brake fluid leaked out of her car."

"Yes."

"And she tried to avoid backending someone on the highway and went into a viaduct."

"Apparently that's how it happened."

"That's what the insurance report said."

"You read it?"

"A friend of mine did, a lawyer."

"Oh? Why?"

"You used to work on Pat's car, didn't you?"

For the first time since the conversation had begun, Rena felt uncomfortable. "Yes."

"When was the last time you worked on it?"

Rena shook her head. "I don't know. I don't remember. Are you thinking what I think you are?"

"I think so. What do you think?"

"I don't know."

"What happened that morning?"

"That's what I was just trying to remember. I know I went to meet Marla around noon, to go to the Art Institute. We met at the Belmont el station."

"And before that?"

"Pat and I weren't on good terms. She was in one of her moods the night before. She was nasty to me. The next morning I think I was working, preparing a lecture. Yes, now I remember. She was friendly to me then, warm. Trying to make up for the night before, I guess. I was writing at my desk and she came and put her arms around me. She talked about Jessica's barbecue. I wasn't real enthusiastic. She said I didn't have to go if I didn't want to. She said it was up to me. I said I'd go. She talked about the people who would be there. She kept mentioning this Dawn woman."

"That upset you?"

"Yes. She was taunting me, maybe. Acting like she was interested in Dawn."

"Or preparing you."

Rena thought about that. "That could have been," she said. "To break up with me, you mean?"

"Yes."

"Yes, that could have been. Maybe it was teasing — or maybe she was letting me know she'd found someone else."

"Is that what you thought? That Pat was involved with Dawn?"

"That she was thinking about it, at least. I think she was."

"And how did you feel about that?"

"Not good. Wow, I couldn't remember this before. I remember Dr. Kepper, my therapist, trying to get me to remember, but I couldn't. It's coming so easily now."

"So you didn't feel good. What happened then? Did you do anything to her car?"

Rena kept blinking her eyes. "I might have."

"How did you do it? Did you cut the line? Did you use something sharp but not a knife, a chisel maybe or a sharp piece of stone?"

"So they couldn't tell it was done intentionally."

"You didn't want to get caught."

"No."

"She was rejecting you, going to leave you . . ."

"She didn't want me anymore."

"So you made a hole in her brake line."

"With a chisel or a sharp stone maybe. Yes, and the brake fluid leaked out and she crashed and she died. Yes. Oh boy." Rena said nothing for a while. "I wonder if I've killed anyone else. I'm really a delightful person, huh, Trish? Aren't you glad you met me? Jesus, my dad, my uncle, Pat. I'm crazy. It started with my uncle. I know he was the first. I wonder how many others there were."

"What about Rebecca?"

197

"Rebecca's not dead."

"Did you try?"

"To kill Rebecca?" Rena shrugged. "Probably."

"How?"

"Maybe I poisoned her food. I used to do most of the cooking."

"Or maybe you messed with the scaffolding."

"Oh yes, that. I know I felt like killing her when I found out about Barbara, that bitch. They fucked in my bed — right in my own bed — when I was at a conference. I read it in a letter. The twit wrote it in a letter and I read it."

"So you did something to the scaffolding that day."

"The ropes. You count on the ropes when you're up there. If one of them breaks you can lose your balance."

"You could break a leg that way," Trish said, "or a neck."

"She only broke her leg."

"Did you use the same tool to cut the rope, the same thing you used on Pat's brake line?"

"A knife would do."

"So you used a knife."

Rena nodded. "Sure, that's what I used. I never thought she'd leave me. I felt like she was abandoning me."

"So you tried to kill her."

"Half-assed job on that one. There weren't any others that I can think of. Can you think of any others?"

"Four is enough."

"Three dead, one injured. Quite a record, huh, Trish? But why? Why did it start? It all started with my dad. We're going to Greece to find out why. Don't you find me despicable?"

"Yes."

"I appreciate that, Trish. You're a lot more understanding than anyone else. I'm a dead woman. What I did is so beyond recompense that my death is really a joke."

"Why don't you turn yourself in instead?"

"What do you mean?"

"Tell the cops what you did."

Rena shook her head. "No need. I'm going to save everyone the trouble."

"You'd suffer more if you told, if you confessed."

"I suppose I would. They might not kill me though. I have to die for what I did."

"Will you tell Lou what you told me?"

"What part? What do you mean?"

"About killing Pat. About trying to kill Rebecca."

"Oh, that. Sure, I'll tell her."

"Good."

"Do you think I'm crazy?"

"Something close to it."

"Evil?"

"Yes. An evil slice, but that's enough to spoil the whole pie."

"How come you're the only one who realizes it?"

"I don't know. Maybe I'm the only one who knows what it means, what I saw in your eyes."

"My eyes? It's in my eyes? You see evil in my eyes?"

"I did. Not now. Before. When you were going after Lou with the knife."

Rena tilted her head. "After Lou?"

"The day I knocked you over with my horse."

Rena shook her head. "I don't remember that."

"When Helena spent the night with Lou. You remember that, don't you?"

"Oh, yes. Oh, I remember. I thought Lou didn't want me anymore."

"So you decided to kill her."

"Lou too? God, Trish, you're right about that evil slice. Evil slices. Slice, slice, slice them dead. Slice the arm off. Slice the rope. Slice the birds. Slice them dead. What a weird word, *slice*. Slice, slice, slice."

"Don't go to Greece, Rena."

Rena looked at her. "I have to, Trish. I have to go. I have to find out what started all the slicing."

"No you don't. It doesn't matter."

"It does to me. I really loved my father. You always kill the one you love, thus spake *The Slicer*. I loved Pat. I loved Rebecca."

"I'll go with you to the police. We'll get a lawyer for you."

"No need."

"You need a lawyer."

"Trish, you're an alcoholic, right?"

Trish sighed. "So?"

"Was your drinking like my slicing?"

"I don't see the comparison, Rena. You're not making sense."

"Did you find out why you used to drink?"

"Yeah, I think so. I discovered what purposes it served for me."

"I want to find out why I slice."

"My drinking didn't kill anybody."

"My slicing did. All the more reason to find out why."

"I could go to the police myself."

"I suppose you could. Pat was thirty-five years old. That's pretty young to die. My dad was forty when he died. I lived longer than Pat but luckily I won't live as long as my dad."

"Suicide is a cop-out."

"I was going to use carbon monoxide, but you're right, that would be a cop-out. I'll slice my throat, here, my carotid. Slice." Rena drew her finger across the right side of her neck.

Trish winced. "Any way you do it is a cop-out."

"Oh, God. Trish, if I let myself feel anything right now, I'd probably disintegrate."

"Feel it."

Rena smiled weakly. "You sure hate me." She began to cry, took deep breaths through her nose.

"Oh-Jesus-God-in-heaven-Pat-I'm-so-o-rry-y-y!" Rena's scream echoed through the house. She rocked back and forth holding her head. "Slice-slice-slice," she murmured.

"Rena!"

Rena looked up. Her eyes were red, her face wet. She stared at Trish for an eternity, not really seeing her, then she got up and bolted from the room. She ran into the woods, ran blindly.

An hour later, Lou found her by the big oak tree, the one where she had once hung a swing for her niece, the one under which Rena had once built a platform.

"Hi, pal."

"Hi, Lou. I killed Pat too."

"So I heard." Lou sat on the boulder next to Rena.

"I cut the brake fluid line on her car."

"Oh yeah? The day she died or the day before or when?"

"When? I don't know. That's not what's important. I'm not sure when."

"Tell me exactly what you did."

"I took a chisel, my chisel that I keep in my tool box."

"Where was Pat?"

"I don't know. In the house, I guess."

"Where was the car parked?"

"Out in front."

"So you crawled under it and began chiseling away. What did you tell her you were doing?"

"I didn't tell her anything."

"Did you get dirty?"

"I don't know. I suppose."

"Did she wonder why?"

"Maybe she didn't see me."

"Did you happen to kill Kennedy too?"

"Who's she? What do you mean? You mean Kennedy?"

"Yes."

"Don't be absurd."

"You're in the mood for confessing, why leave anyone out? So you cut Rebecca's rope, huh?"

Rena nodded.

"When?"

"That day. On the way to the job, I guess, yes, that afternoon when we were driving to the job."

"She was driving and you went in the back of the van and began slicing away."

"It was earlier."

"The insurance report said a stone or a piece of flying metal cut Pat's brake line."

"It was a chisel."

"Could you have used a stone?"

201

Rena frowned. "I might have. It was either a chisel or stone. Lou, it's hard to remember the details. I had a headache that day. Like a migraine. It makes me forget things."

"Rebecca said the rope got damaged by the van door."

"That's what she thought."

"Were you coming after me with a knife that day you ran away?"

"I thought I was after a bird. I had a headache. I might have been after you. Trish knocked me down. The next thing I remember, some man was taking me into his car."

"So why didn't you tell me all this before?"

"I don't know. I would have if I'd remembered. I want you to know."

"You still don't remember, because it never happened. You feel so guilty that you'll confess to anything." Rena stared at the widespread branches of the old oak. "You and Trish are so different. She can see it, you can't."

"I'm the only one who *can* see."

"Lou, you're so egocentric." Rena smiled weakly. "But it's part of your charm so don't feel bad about it."

"What I feel bad about is all this nonsense."

"Don't you believe in evil?"

"No."

"I didn't either, before. Lou, I'm not right, can't you see that? Something went wrong with me. Very wrong."

"Do you actually remember doing anything to Pat's car?"

"Yes. I remember being angry and then . . . Lou, my mind gets fuzzy when I'm like that. Sometimes I only remember part of what I did. One time I found a cut up bird in my garbage can at home. It surprised me. I remember having a terrible headache that day. I remember having that feeling, that heavy feeling. I was sitting in my chair in the living room sort of dozing and then I got hungry. I went to the kitchen and opened some tuna. I threw the can away, and there was the bird, all in pieces."

"Did you have a headache the day your father and uncle were killed?"

Rena tried to remember. "I don't know. I might have. Do you still want to be with me now that you know I'm even worse than we

202

thought? If you don't I'll understand. I can go to Greece alone, you know. You don't have to —"

"Shut up."

Rena felt the jolt, that little tingle than ran the length of her spine.

CHAPTER TWENTY TWO

On Friday, October 23rd, Rena Spiros and Lou Bonnig boarded an Olympic Airlines jet.

Rena was restless on the flight, itchy — an itch way out of her reach that kept her squirming. When their taxi entered the city limits of Athens and the first buildings came into view, the uneasy feeling peaked.

"What is it, hon? What's the matter?" Lou asked. "Are you all right?"

Rena was staring out the window, rubbing her fingers nervously across the plastic car seat. "I don't think so."

"Deja vu?"

"Yeah, maybe. It just . . . I don't know. It's so familiar, and yet very strange."

The cab took them to their hotel in Plaka, an older section of the city full of little shops and cafes. Rena fell on the nearest bed and was asleep immediately. Lou left her a note and went out to stroll the crowded narrow streets. When she returned Rena lay just as Lou had left her. It wasn't until an hour later that she stirred.

"I love this city," Lou called from the balcony.

Rena stretched and yawned. "I must have dozed off."

Lou brought her a bottle of lemonade. "Are you feeling better?"

"Yeah, I think so." She glanced around the room. It was stark, whites and pale blues, marble floors, scantily furnished. "Not pretentious," she said. She saw Lou's note. She read it. "You went without me."

"You slept for three hours."

"I did? What's it like out there?"

"Come and find out."

They had agreed in advance to spend the first few days sightseeing. After dining on lamb, potatoes and okra in a noisy cafe, they took the tram ride to the top of the Athenian mountain, Leikavitos.

"It's almost as beautiful as San Francisco," Lou said, scanning the lights below.

Rena laughed. "Almost. Tomorrow we should go to the Acropolis. There's nothing like *that* in San Francisco."

"Sure there is. The Palace of Fine Arts."

"Tacky."

"Not so."

"Chauvinist," Rena said.

"Hey, girl, you're not allowed to call me names." Lou pulled Rena by the collar forcing her to stand tiptoe. "Understand?"

Rena could not utter the smart remark on the tip of her tongue, for Lou was not smiling and Rena felt the strange, pleasant, shuddering tingle along her spine and shoulder blades. "Yes," she said softly.

"That's better. What's that over there, all lit up?"

Rena let her breath out. "I don't know. The Parthenon, maybe."

Lou's eyes floated over the panorama. "Where did you used to live?"

Rena shook her head. "I have no idea. In an apartment somewhere. There was a little store on the corner where I'd get candy."

"Maybe your aunt will know where it was. Would you like to go back there, to your old neighborhood?"

"I guess."

"You feeling funny again?"

"A little."

"I'm with you. It'll be OK."

On Monday Rena called Petros Xamplas. He spoke only Greek and Rena's knowledge of the language was so poor that when they hung up she wasn't sure what had been said.

"We need a translator," Lou said.

Fortunately, Rena's cousin, a very bright, soft-spoken woman named Christina, turned out to be fluent in English. She was an archeologist and spent most of her time on the island of Delos. Christina agreed to accompany Rena and Lou on their visit to Petros Xamplas.

On Wednesday the three women went to the home of Petros Xamplas. His wife, after serving them drinks and sweets, stayed off to the side. Petros appeared to be in his late sixties or early seventies, a robust and energetic man. He spoke freely and loudly.

"Yes, I remember your father well," Christina translated, "though I met him only once. He came here, to this house, many, many years ago. I never got to know him for he died the same day."

"He came to get the paintings?" Rena asked.

"Yes. I helped him load them into the truck. Fifteen of them, there were. Then he drove off. He was to take them to the Hellenic Art Museum." Petros emptied his glass, gestured for his wife to refill it. "The paintings never got there." He shrugged. "The truck was found, broken into and empty. Your father was . . . what a shame to die for a few pictures. Such craziness."

"You think that's why they were murdered?" Lou said. She watched Christina translate.

Petros folded his hands over his round belly. He looked at Rena as he spoke. "I thought I saw someone in the back of the truck when your father drove away. I could be mistaken. In the cab. Hiding behind the front seat. I wasn't sure, though." He leaned forward, elbows on the table. "There was a man named Demos. He wanted to buy the paintings from me. They must have been very valuable, much more valuable than what he offered me."

Lou spoke to Christina. "Ask him if he has any idea how we could locate this Demos?"

"None at all," Petros replied. "I think that was not his true name."

Lou continued the questioning. "It was you who contacted him, I understand. Originally, I mean. You called him to assess the value of the paintings. Is that correct?"

"Yes." Petros shook his head. "I wish I hadn't done it but I had no idea . . ." He shook his head again. "After my sister called from America and talked about paintings and I found them in the attic, I was very curious. Are these treasures, I wondered? I must admit, I thought perhaps I might get a reward of some sort. From the owners. From the Spiros brothers. I wanted to know what the paintings were worth. I talked to a friend about it and he said he knew this man who dealt in art. So I called the man. It was Demos."

"Your friend who suggested you call Demos —"

"Died of cancer."

"I see. So you think Demos killed the Spiros brothers?" Lou asked.

"Maybe." Petros rubbed his belly. He looked at Rena. "Is it the paintings you're after, Miss?"

"The story, actually," Rena said. "Answers, truth. Not just art," she added sardonically.

They spent the rest of the day seeing the sights with Christina. Despite the purpose of her mission and the dead feeling inside of her, Rena was able to enjoy the beauty and foreignness of the land where she was born. Christina showed them ruins, took them to Sounion where they swam and ate, bought each of them a small replica of an ancient vase. Lou and Christina seemed to have a great deal to say to each other, Rena observed. She often noticed them leaning against a wall somewhere or sitting on a bench deep in conversation while she looked at the columns or the sea. Christina was nearly as tall as Lou but thinner, almost frail, with large round eyes and hair the color of Rena's.

Rena and Lou slept late the next morning in their Spartan room, had a leisurely breakfast, then went to the Hellenic Art Museum. Lou hoped that someone there would know about the events connected with the missing paintings. Rena felt as if she was just going along for the ride.

They were shuffled from one person to another at the museum. Finally, a young, tired-looking clerk dug up some records. "The file was closed years ago on this," the man said. "The paintings you're referring to were among several dozen the museum hid during the Occupation. There are five listed under *Spiros*. They all disappeared." He moved his finger slowly down the page, his shoulder blocking Rena and Lou's view of the file. "Ten others on the same list, not belonging to us, also disappeared." He looked with mild curiosity at Rena. "Do you have some information about them?"

"No," Rena said. She did not like the man. "I thought you might."

"There was an investigation. Nothing came of it." He closed the file folder decisively.

"My father used to work here," Rena said. "Perhaps someone who knew him, some other employee, is still around."

"Check with personnel," the man said. He turned his back. The man in the pin-neat personnel office found in his files that Antoni Spiros had been an assistant curator from 1950 to 1960. "An excellent employee, high ratings. Seems he became deceased in nineteen-sixty. None of the present employees were here then. I'm sorry, Miss."

Disappointed, Rena and Lou were about to leave when the man remembered a Mr. Oneides. "He's retired now, but he was a curator here in nineteen-sixty. He handled loans and rentals." The man wrote Oneides' name and number on a slip of paper. "He came back and visited a few years ago. I had a nice talk with him. Maybe he can help you. He lives in Rhodes."

Lou was ready to go immediately to the island of Rhodes.

"He may not know anything," Rena protested. They were walking along a wide corridor of the museum, passing life-size sculptures of warriors and robed nobles. "A phone call will probably do." She was much less enthusiastic than Lou about pursuing the mystery of the paintings.

"I think it would be better in person," Lou said. "Besides, Christina says Rhodes is beautiful."

Rena did not respond.

"So what do you think?"

"I don't know." She stared at a marble god with a missing arm. "I think we should at least call him first."

Outside the museum they found a booth and Rena made the phone call to Rhodes. Mr. Oneides was out walking, a woman told her in heavily- accented English. She reminded Rena of her mother. The woman suggested Rena try again in an hour.

"Let's find out about getting to Rhodes," Lou said. "Do you want to fly or boat it? I think we should go by ship." Lou cocked her head at Rena. "We could have a shipboard romance."

Rena stared at her. A taxi she had hailed stopped, waited a moment, then drove off.

"You let the cab get away," Lou said.

"With who?"

"What?"

"Romance with who?"

"With *whom*, you mean." Lou winked at her. "With youm. Me and youm. Yum."

Rena got tingling sensations along her neck and suddenly felt very hot. She's teasing. She doesn't mean it. "You're not my type."

They had begun walking, neither any longer looking for a cab.

"I thought you were mad about me," Lou said.

"That was when I was mad."

"What are you now?"

Rena didn't answer. It means nothing to her, she thought. I mean nothing to her. I'm just a curiosity.

Lou took Rena's chin and turned her face until their eyes met. "Hey, don't funk out on me."

Rena's body responded despite her conscious thoughts. She wished they could go somewhere that moment and be alone and that Lou would want her and be rough with her and fuck her, fuck her

209

brains out. "Maybe Christina would like to take a pleasure trip with you. I'm here on business."

Lou put her arm through Rena's. "Let's go get a drink and talk about this." They found an outdoor cafe. Rena people-watched and listened to the different languages. Besides Greek and English, she heard German, French, and several she couldn't identify. She did not look at Lou.

"You don't talk much about how you're feeling about all this, Rena. About being here in Greece and all. How are you doing with it?"

"Fine."

"How are you doing, Rena?"

"You're repeating yourself."

"We need to commune."

"I'm not in the mood for tea."

"Are you jealous of Christina?"

"No."

"Yes you are."

"I'm not. You have your life, I have mine."

"I see."

"I really don't know anything about you."

"Oh?" The waiter came and they ordered their drinks. "What would you like to know?"

"Nothing."

Lou made an exaggerated pout. "You're not interested in me."

Rena looked at her. The little streaks of gray in Lou's hair were more pronounced in the brilliant sunlight of Greece. Her eyes looked lighter, but her mouth was the same, soft and sensuous. "Lou, don't tease about romance. Don't play with me like that. You and I are together for one reason. The big question. What made the crazy girl crazy? Why did she flip out and kill and mutilate?"

Lou rolled her eyes.

"We both have the same goal. Right? To get answers. Right?"

Lou suddenly looked very serious. "Sometimes I forget," she said. "I really do enjoy your company. Especially lately. You realize that ever since you first talked about your father, you've changed."

"Oh yeah?" Rena's voice was flat.

"Something in you loosened up. You became more of a person, I think, somewhat freer, and a lot less intimidated by me."

"Could be."

"So what's going on now?"

"Nothing. I'm the same as when you got me to realize that I'm a multiple murderer. Nothing's changed since then."

"You're not a murderer."

Rena traced a stain on the tablecloth with her index finger. "You know, Lou, you're where I used to be." She circled around the stain. "Denying part of reality. I've killed three people and you treat me like I'm a regular human being with some little emotional problem. Maybe *you* need some tea and communing."

Lou didn't respond. She did not look happy. The drinks arrived. Lou switched gears and started talking about the different people passing by. She made jokes and speculated about their lives, deciding who were the spies and who the government bureaucrats, and who the tourists from Akron, Ohio. After a while Rena joined in.

When they left the cafe, Rena called Oneides. His English was excellent. Of course he remembered Antoni Spiros who had worked under him for ten years and, yes, he remembered Stavros Spiros and the missing paintings. Yes, a visit would be fine. They could spend the night if they liked, he told Rena. He had plenty of room.

The Oneides villa overlooked the sea. The blueness of the Mediterranean continued to amaze Rena. "It makes Lake Michigan look like mud," she said.

Oneides lived alone and was attended by a housekeeper, Efstathia, who he invited to join them on the veranda. It seemed his employee was also his friend. After a period of light conversation, Efstathia left to prepare the afternoon meal and it was then that Oneides mentioned the paintings.

"There were fifteen," he said, "several of them masterpieces. There was a Goya, a Van Gogh, a couple of nineteenth century French works. Five belonged to the museum. It was my idea for Spiros to hide them. That was in nineteen-forty-two. The board

211

approved, but I felt responsible. I felt guilty ever since they disappeared. When it looked like we had our hands on them again, I was extremely relieved. And then..."

Oneides seemed very tired and weak. Rena assumed his health was poor. He did not continue speaking and she wondered if he had fallen asleep. "Mr. Oneides?" she said softly.

"We hid other paintings around the city. They were all returned." He fanned himself with a paper fan.

"Do you feel all right?" Rena asked. "Would you rather talk another time?"

"Your father was a dedicated employee, Miss Spiros. He loved art. He loved to be around it. He loved some of the pieces like they were his children. You are his only child, aren't you?"

"Yes."

"A shame he died so young. He was a much gentler man than his brother, Stavros. That one was a bull. A bull with brains. But he wasn't tough enough for Giannes Fortes. Fortes finally got him, as I'm sure you know. He was sent to prison, he and a few of his odious friends."

"What? I don't understand."

Oneides wrinkled his brow. "You don't know about Fortes? I thought everyone knew. Well, you were young. Fortes was a smuggler, kingpin in a very successful smuggling ring. A thief. A killer. He died in prison."

"But...are you saying —"

"Your father was to bring the paintings to the museum. They'd been discovered in somebody's attic. Antoni was to pick them up and bring them to the museum. The museum planned to restore and display them, the ones that were ours. How I looked forward to that day." Oneides was staring out to sea. "I don't know what your father and uncle intended to do with theirs. Their value had increased a great deal over the years."

"So my father went to pick them up..."

"Yes. Your uncle and I were at my office, in the museum, waiting for your father to arrive. There was some concern that Fortes was aware that the paintings had been rediscovered and we were somewhat nervous. I was, at least. Stavros seemed calm, but he was not a man to show his emotions. We were in my office waiting and then we got a phone call from your father. Stavros took the call. He was quite distraught, understandably." Oneides was looking very pale. He reached for his drink.

"Do you need anything, Mr. Oneides?" Lou asked.

"No, no, dear. I'm fine. Just old and dying. So Antoni called. He talked to Stavros. There had been trouble, Antoni told Stavros. Someone had tried to hijack the truck. There was fighting. Antoni got rid of the thief and apparently got all the way to the museum and then he was pursued again. Others must have been waiting for him at the museum. Again Antoni got away. He thought he had evaded them. He was calling from the road somewhere, on his way to his village, Kaftarei. Stavros was to meet him there. That was the plan.

"Stavros told me not to worry. He would call the police, he said, and arrange for an escort of the paintings from Kaftarei back to the museum. He left right after the phone call. Well, needless to say, I worried anyhow. An hour or so later your father called again, looking for Stavros. It had occurred to Antoni that taking the paintings to Kaftarei might not be such a good idea. He realized that whoever was after them would probably find out that the brothers are from Kaftarei and might assume that is where Antoni would go. Antoni said he was worried about a confrontation between Stavros and the thieves, fearing Stavros would lose his temper and things could get ugly. He said he had a plan, though, a way to lure the thieves away from Stavros. He, too, told me not to worry. I worried nonetheless. Your father thought he had a good plan." Oneides shook his head sadly. "Apparently he didn't."

"They found him again?"

"The paintings disappeared, Antoni and his brother were killed. What else is one to think?"

"And you think this Fortes did it." Lou said.

"That's right."

"But he was never convicted of it or . . . you say he was sent to prison?"

"Yes. Income tax evasion."

"Oh. Well, the missing paintings . . . there was an investigation, wasn't there?" Lou asked.

"Yes. By the police and also by an agency the museum hired. Nothing was learned. There were two strangers in Kaftarei that day. Several villagers reported this. But the investigators never found out who they were. Fortes had a tight alibi. The investigation came to nothing."

"And he's dead now?"

"Died in prison. Heart attack."

"Do you know anything about a Mr. Demos?" Lou asked.

"If you mean the Demos who wanted to buy the paintings, I'd guess that was Fortes. He used aliases."

Lou brushed a bee from her arm. "What do you think happened to the paintings?"

"I imagine they were dispersed around the world. Sold to private collectors." The bee hovered near Oneides' head. He seemed not to notice.

"But if the paintings were well-known in the art world, wouldn't people know they were stolen?"

Oneides smiled. "Some collectors feel that makes the works even more valuable. They don't display them publicly."

Lou nodded. "I see. What was Fortes' alibi?"

Oneides' eyes again sought the calm blue waters. "That whole weekend he was with family and friends on Santorini. That is what he told our investigators and the police. There were many witnesses."

Rena was staring up the coast. She could dimly make out the two statues of deer that greeted arriving ships at the port of Rhodes.

After lunch, Rena and Lou toured the city. The weather was fine, sunny, mild. The sights were pleasing. They spent the night at Mr. Oneides villa by the sea and for short periods of time acted like vacationers.

CHAPTER TWENTY THREE

Rena's mood kept shifting. For periods she'd slip into gloomy silence and other times be silly and playful and even rowdy.

The night after their return from Rhodes to Athens Lou and Rena and Christina had dinner in a vine-covered outdoor restaurant on the outskirts of the city. Lou was very attentive to Christina; they discussed Christina's work and the Leakys and other anthropologists and Lou talked about a visit she had made to the Aztec ruins in Mexico. Rena felt excluded. Maybe Christina isn't straight, she thought. Maybe she wants Lou. Maybe Lou wants her.

Christina had told them of a nightclub she was sure they'd enjoy, *To Mavro Kardia*. There would be bouzoukia music and dancing. Their plan was to go there after dinner.

"I think I'll skip the night club," Rena said. "I'm feeling tired. I'll just go back to the hotel."

"Oh, Rena. That's too bad." Her cousin touched her arm solicitously. "Maybe we should make it another night."

"No, no, that's all right. You two go ahead."

Outside the restaurant, they got a cab. Rena was dropped off at the hotel then the cab continued on to take Lou and Christina to the night club.

Rena sat on her bed. Her head was buzzing. That feeling again. She lay down but couldn't rest. Her breathing came in quick sharp gasps. She left the room. The buzzing wouldn't go away. Her head ached. She walked determinedly down the narrow streets of Plaka.

The nightclub was packed. It was a favorite haunt of both natives and tourists. Lou's head was bent close to Christina's at the little bench they'd found in the corner. They tried to talk over the din and music but soon gave up. They drank wine, watched the dancing.

After a while the musicians took a break and the crowd thinned. Lou listened intently as Christina spoke of her life on Delos, how much she loved her work, but the emptiness that was there sometimes.

Twenty minutes later the music started again. Another wave of patrons had come into the club. Lou had just suggested that they go somewhere a little quieter when an uneasy buzz began to sweep through the crowd. People started moving toward the exit. Someone screamed. There was pushing, more pushing, yelling. An acrid charcoal smell reached Lou's nostrils. *"Fire,"* someone shouted. A wave of crushing bodies stumbled and shoved its way toward the door. Lou had her hand around Christina's wrist trying not to lose her in the panicking crowd. A woman was down, feet trampling her as the stampede rushed on. Lou pushed people aside, detouring them. She succeeded in forming a space, then stooped for the fallen woman, grabbing her under her arms, pulling her upright.

Rena returned to the hotel. Her eyes were glazed, her head fuzzy. From the balcony she looked north toward Elia Street where the Mavro Kardia nightclub was. The anger had subsided. She felt a little sad but mostly numb.

216

* * * * *

Flames could be seen gulping around the kitchen doorway. Tables were overturned, chairs crushed and kicked aside, broken glass peppered the floor. Lou couldn't find Christina. The crowd on the sidewalk was back at a safe distance watching those still inside squeezing their way, three abreast, from the burning building and out into the air and safety.

Two hours later, Rena was sitting stoop-shouldered on the edge of the bed. At the scratching of a key in the door, she started, then turned her head sharply.

Lou looked exhausted. Rena stared at her, speechless.

"Couldn't you sleep?" Lou asked.

"No." Rena's voice was hoarse.

"What a night!" Lou tossed her bag on her bed. "There was a fire."

"A fire," Rena repeated dumbly.

"At the nightclub. The place was totalled."

Rena blinked. She took in air through her mouth.

"It was madness. I got separated from Christina. I was about to go back in after her and then there she was behind me. Shit, Rena, what a scene! Somebody got a broken arm. Lots of people got cuts and bruises. One guy was knocked out and two French kids dragged him outside. Nobody got burned." Lou was talking rapidly. She collapsed on the bed across from Rena. "It was a miracle nobody got killed. It was arson. An amateur job, they said. They found the gasoline can in the back alley. Some people thought it was terrorists who did it."

Rena stared.

"I doubt it, though. They use bombs." Lou frowned, looking at Rena. "Are you all right?"

Rena nodded.

"Christina's fine. It was frightening, though. It really was. You missed all the excitement."

"You're alive."

Lou smiled.

217

"I'm glad you . . ." The words caught in Rena's throat. She was sobbing.

"Hey, I'm fine." Lou went to her, rubbed her back. "Everything's all right."

"Oh, I'm so glad!" Rena clung to her. "I really am." She pictured the flames. "Let's go home, Lou. It's dangerous here. Let's leave right away."

Lou held her warmly, cradling her, rocking her. "We'll talk about it in the morning, Rena. Here now, lie back, just let yourself relax. That's right. Good. Just letting go . . ."

By morning Rena felt much better. The previous night was a fading blur. They had the hotel *paidi* bring breakfast to their room. After her coffee, Rena actually started to feel good, cheerful, even a little giddy.

"You know where we have to go next," Lou said. "We've put it off long enough."

"It scares the shit out of me." From the tiny balcony Rena watched the throngs on the narrow street below.

"I'm not surprised." Lou was leaning against the iron railing; there was only one chair. "We could hang out in Athens a while longer first, if you want, or go play tourist some more. We could go to Mykonos."

"I want to get it over with."

"All right. Tomorrow, then. Don't you think I should have the chair?"

"Why should you have the chair?"

"Because I'm the boss, I'm in charge."

"Here, boss," Rena said, "sit on my lap, I want to feel you up."

"Rena! Do you want us to be stoned? People hate queers here."

"They only hate boy queers. They think girls are amusing."

Lou rolled her eyes. "And that in the cradle of civilization."

"Come here, I want to cradle your civilization." Rena grabbed Lou and pulled her to her lap. After thirty seconds she pushed her off again. "You're too heavy."

"Call the *paidi* and order another chair."

"There's no phone."

"You're right. This place has no class," Lou teased. "Why did you bring me to a place like this?"

"You brought me, pea brain," Rena said.

"I like it here. It has character. Don't call me pea brain."

Rena pinched Lou's rear.

"I remember when you used to respect me. Do you remember that? And you used to obey me too."

"I remember." Rena wasn't so light-hearted anymore. "That was humiliating."

Lou crossed her arms, smiling. "It served its purpose."

"I'm embarrassed thinking about it."

"You've come a long way since then."

"I liked it." Rena wouldn't look at Lou.

"I know. You have a quirky personality."

"So do you."

"I suppose I do. I might have to assert my authority over you again," Lou said kiddingly.

The rush came, a tingling along Rena's back and in her stomach. She felt confused.

"You want me to, don't you?"

"I don't know," Rena said softly. "Let's take a nap."

"It's not sleep you want."

"You drive me crazy."

"It may happen soon."

"What?"

"You know what. We're getting closer and closer."

Rena turned and faced her. "Let's make love."

Lou shook her head. "Closer and closer but not yet close enough. Let's go to the beach."

"You're a bitch!"

Lou shrugged.

"You're not my type, anyway." Rena was making every effort to break the spell. "You're too butch. Besides, you're too old for me. How old are you, anyway?"

"Fifty."

"You are not."

"Thirty."

219

"Bullshit."

"Let's go to the beach," Lou said.

"How old are you?"

"Sixty."

"Right."

"How do we get to Kaftarei," Lou asked. "Bus? Taxi? Boat?"

"Boat? It's inland, dupa brain. We could go by bus, I think. We used to go by bus sometimes when I was a kid."

"I think Christina should come along. She said she'd be available all this week."

"Oh, yeah?" Rena squinted. "The sleazy whore."

"That's your cousin you're talking about."

"That's my cousin you're lusty about. Do you like her better than you like me?"

Lou laughed. "How old are *you*, Spiros, six?"

"Seriously, Lou, how old are you? I want to know."

"Forty-four," Lou said.

"There's nothing wrong with that."

"Who said there was?"

"She wants to come along, huh? Doesn't she have anything better to do?" Rena stretched her arms over her head and tried to yawn lazily. She was faking it, feeling confused.

"We'll need a translator."

"Maybe we can find some decrepit older person to be our translator," Rena said, "somebody really old, like forty-four, maybe."

"Let's go to the beach."

"Hey, Lou?"

"Rena, I think I should have the chair now."

Rena got up, Lou sat.

"Hey, Lou?"

"What?"

"Do you know how much I wish, desperately wish, that I wasn't like I am, that whatever there is in me that made me do those evil, heinous things never was."

"Rena, don't get into that now."

"I did about the worst thing a human being can do." Rena's mouth curled in disgust. "I don't even deserve to be called a human being. Reptile. That's what I am. No, that's no good either. When snakes and lizards kill, they do it to survive."

"Rena, would you just —"

"I killed Pat because I was afraid she was abandoning me."

"You didn't —"

"It wasn't for survival, not *real* survival. Psychological survival maybe. I thought I couldn't exist without her. Stupid thought. I tried to kill Rebecca for the same reason, I think. The day she fell, I had just found out about Barbara."

"You were afraid she was abandoning you, is that what you're saying?"

"Maybe."

"And you feared your father was —"

"Yes. It's the same feeling. I get the same feeling when I remember how it was in the little house. I had the same feeling last night."

Lou cocked her head, frowning.

"When I heard Rebecca had a broken leg but otherwise was OK, I felt such relief."

"Of course, anyone would. She could have —"

"Why do I have to be like this!" Rena grabbed the railing with both hands. "Oh, how I wish I didn't do it, didn't kill and cause so much pain for so many people."

"You cause the most pain for yourself."

"Took lives, human lives, took them away. Life is so good, Lou. There are so many good things about life. So many reasons to live. I wish I hadn't blown it."

"I wish you weren't so neurotic," Lou said. "Shut up and let's go to the beach."

CHAPTER TWENTY FOUR

Early the next morning, they set off for Kaftarei in Christina's beat-up VW. Rena was quiet on the drive. She sat in the back seat, watching Lou and Christina for a while, then watching the dusty white rocks of the hilly terrain, orchards of gnarled olive trees, cypresses, peasants leading donkeys, red-roofed village houses. It was nostalgic and it was scary. As they neared Kaftarei, Rena couldn't sit still.

"Do things look familiar?" Christina asked.

"I don't know. Yes and no," Rena said. "It's weird."

"Grandma's house hasn't changed much. You probably won't remember Basilis and you never met his wife. They like living here, I guess. I'd go out of my mind with boredom in the village."

"Stop here, will you?" Rena said urgently.

"Why?" Lou asked, scrutinizing Rena.

"The little house. It's up there, I know, past those two hills. I want to go there. Drop me off."

Christina stopped in the middle of the barely-paved road.

"Why don't you hold off a while, Rena," Lou said. "We'll go later. Together. Let's start at your grandparents' house."

Rena's heart was pounding. She stared up the path that led to the little house. "All right. You come with me when I go."

"Of course."

Christina continued driving. She had been only five when her uncles were killed, she had told Lou. Though she had few feelings about it herself, she could understand what Rena was going through. As they continued through the village, Christina waved to several people. Rena's heart wouldn't slow down. Two-thirds of the way in, Christina turned onto a dusty side road, drove several hundred yards and stopped the car.

Rena stared at the house. It was familiar in a vague and murky way. Lou and Christina got out of the car, but Rena did not move until Lou came for her, opened the door, and helped her out.

"Oh God, it feels so strange." She was perspiring despite the mild weather.

A woman in a print dress came onto the porch and ran to them, arms spread, chattering rapidly in high-pitched Greek. She kissed and hugged each of them. Her name was Toula. She was the wife of Basilis, Antoni and Stavros' youngest brother. Three young girls joined them, two talkative adolescents and a silent one. Introductions took place and greetings, with Christina translating for everyone. She finally gave up, laughingly suggesting they use sign language.

Rena walked from room to room in the house. It was definitely familiar yet different from what she remembered. Everything seemed smaller, the kitchen especially. She went out back. The old stone oven was still there. Rena had loved the heavy bread her grandmother and mother used to bake. Behind the oven, through the trees was the shed and the place where the wood pile used to be. She went toward it. Lou watched her from the porch.

This is where it happened, she thought, where Stavros had lain bleeding. She stared at the clumps of grass and bare sandy soil near the shed. There was no sign of blood. The shed was lopsided and crumbling. Rena opened the rotting wooden door and went inside. It was damp and cool. She sat on a fat sack of something and remembered the time Uncle Stavros had locked her in here. She didn't feel much now, just a vague annoyance that he had done it. She remembered she had felt hungry. She remembered seeing his arm reaching finally to unlock the door.

Feelings came then, overwhelming feelings. I cut that arm off, she thought with horror. No, no, I couldn't have. I wouldn't do that.

Rena was shaking when Lou came and led her from the shed.

Christina was inside visiting with her aunt and cousins. Rena did not want to go back in the house. "Let's go for a walk," she suggested, and with Lou at her side she roamed the village. The village square looked different. It was paved now and there were benches.

People greeted them as they passed. *"Hairete." "Kalimera."* Rena recognized no one.

"Let's go to the river. It's this way," Rena said.

"Now?" Lou questioned. "Are you sure?"

"Yes, come on." She was excited.

The water flowed gently, the bank was not as steep as Rena had remembered.

"Where's the *nest?"* Lou asked.

"Up a little further, I think." They came to a section where the river made a gentle curve. "There it is." Rena stepped up her pace. Lou followed.

"This is it. Yes, I'm sure. This is the spot."

In the small recessed cove, a semi-circle of rocks formed a sheltered nook. Soft grass carpeted the ground, and leafy bushes and shrubs sprouted among the rocks.

"This is nice," Lou said.

Rena sat where smooth rocks made a backrest, a natural seat surrounded by bushes. "This is where I used to come."

"I can understand why. It's very cozy." Lou sat next to her, but there was no backrest for her. "A good place to come alone."

"I don't think I ever brought anyone here." Rena looked at the river and the surrounding hills and greenery. "It was my favorite spot but . . . This is the first time I've been here since . . ." She sucked in her breath.

"How is it feeling?"

"I don't know." Rena was a little light-headed. "Overwhelming, in a way. Too many feelings."

Both women were silent. Rena had left the present. The memories were coming, bit by bit, very vivid memories. She had come here many times and most times it was good, but not always.

"It's so clear. I was sitting right here, just like this, only I think I had a dress on. I used to wear dresses. I was mad at Daddy, very mad. I was thinking about it and feeling so angry. How could he do such a thing?" She looked at Lou.

Lou's eyes were riveted on her.

"Lou, I remember! I remember what happened in the little house."

Lou's eyes widened. "Yes . . ."

Tears rolled down Rena's cheeks. "He didn't want me anymore." Her hands were clasped tightly over her breasts. She was sobbing.

Lou waited.

"He pushed me away. He pushed me so hard I almost fell down. He wanted me to go away. My Daddy. He didn't want me anymore." Her pain was excruciating.

"He pushed you."

"I didn't want to leave. I wanted to be with him but he made me go. He didn't want me. I told him I didn't want to go and then that's when he pushed me." Rena could feel the cruel shove. "Daddy never did that. He had such a mean look on his face. I didn't understand why he didn't want me anymore. I felt so frightened and so horrible. Inside my head and my eyes it was stinging and hurting."

"Because he pushed you away."

"So I didn't do what he said." Rena's lower lip jutted out. She was reliving the moments. "He said it was important and I should go right away but I didn't. I came here. I don't want to go tell Uncle Stavros. I don't want to do what Daddy said."

"He pushed you and told you to tell your uncle something."

"Yes. He didn't want me. He wasn't like Daddy. He wanted me to go away. I wanted to stay with Daddy."

225

"That's what happened in the little house then." Lou's eyes were blinking rapidly. "That's what got you so upset? He pushed you?"

"Yes."

"Did anything else happen? Was that all he did?"

"Was that *all*?"

"OK. Yes, of course. You felt terrible about it. You felt rejected, hurt. And angry. So instead of going to your uncle you came here."

"Yes. It's so clear. I was sitting here . . . I remember hearing the church bell. I always stopped to listen. I liked the song it played before it told you the time. I listened to the song and then the gongs. I think there was just one gong."

"It was one o'clock."

"I guess. I was angry and scared and . . . I knew Uncle Stavros would whip me and . . . and then . . . that must be when I decided what I had to do. Yes, that's when I decided I had to go to Uncle Stavros . . ."

"Like your father said."

"No. To kill him. I had to go there to kill him. Oh, God, Lou, what am I? How could I? I killed them because my father pushed me away. Jesus, I'm worse than I thought. For that I killed him." She shook her head. "Just like the others," she said dully. And then she was very calm. "So now I know."

There was a long silence. Rena stared at the river. Finally she spoke.

"I've got my answers." She laughed sardonically. "The reptile can slink away now." She looked steadily at Lou. "I'm going to go now, Lou. For a walk," she added. "Alone, if you don't mind."

Lou seemed nervous. "I mind," she said. "This is not a good time for you to be alone."

"I need to be." Rena was very determined. "Please respect that."

Lou looked at her for a moment, then stood.

Rena closed her eyes. She felt Lou move away.

It was deathly quiet. A long silent time passed and then Rena rose. She seemed to float through the quiet woods, past the two hills.

The little house was the same as it had always been. The brass lamp was on the table near the door. The old sofa was still lopsided and saggy. Rena got a knife from the cupboard and sat on the floor where her father had been. She hoped he'd want her, hoped he could forgive.

"I'm coming, Daddy."

The blade was razor sharp. She didn't even feel it. She lay on the floor, floaty, numb, her blood making a little puddle on the old wooden floor.

It was fine after that. "You took so long," he said. "I waited so long for you." He wasn't mad. He was just like always. They walked in the woods and he wrote poems for her. She was ten again. She would always be ten. Always.

Dreams are strange things, Rena often thought. She had had many dreams of all kinds in her life. There were dreams about being chased, scared, frightened, alone. There were funny dreams. There were peaceful pleasant dreams. There were odd, confused dreams. There were bloody dreams, dreams about birds. There were thought-like dreams and dream-like thoughts. Sometimes it was hard to know which were which. Dreams and thoughts. And truth. Sometimes the dreams were true. Sometimes the truth was a dream. Or the thought was a dream. Sometimes the thoughts were truth; sometimes they were made up. Could truth be made up, Rena wondered? Truth was real. Sometimes the dreams seemed more real than the truth, and the thoughts as real as the dreams. If I think a tree is a tiger, then it is. To me it is a tiger as true as any tiger. And the fear I taste is my fear of a tiger and the blood that pumps fast to help me run is real blood and the terror I feel is real. The dream is real. The thought is real.

* * * * *

227

From the edge of the river where she stood, Lou looked over at Rena. Rena's eyes were still closed. Lou continued watching her.

Finally Rena stirred.

"Are you awake?" Lou called.

Rena rubbed her eyes, hard, with the palms of her hands.

"So you decided to sleep instead of walk."

Rena looked at Lou. "I dreamed I died."

Lou came to her. "How are you feeling?"

"Weird. Numb. I wish I had."

"Can you remember any more? About what happened at the little house?"

Rena shook her head. "There's no more to remember. No need."

"Was anyone else in the little house when your father pushed you?"

Rena frowned. "No. Why do you ask that?"

"Just wondering. I wonder what made him upset."

"He didn't want me anymore. I told you. He wanted me to go away from him."

"He didn't want you there right then. He wanted you to leave, to go tell your uncle something."

"He didn't want me."

"Rena, use your grown-up mind, will you? That's what you believed then, but what really makes sense now? He was upset, very upset. But why? Did he seem frightened?"

"I don't know. It doesn't matter, Lou. Don't you understand? I found out what I needed to know. It's over."

"Wrong. There's a lot more to find out. Let's go." Lou took Rena's hands and pulled her to her feet.

CHAPTER TWENTY FIVE

Lou was worried. The more Rena remembers, she thought, the worse it's getting. Trish's theory came to mind and Lou felt sick to her stomach.

When she and Rena arrived back at the house, Christina was on the porch talking with an old man named Nikos who lived in the next house. He remembered Rena well, he said, as he gave her a hug. Lou shook his leathery hand.

"You've changed a little, not too much," he said to Rena. He laughed with a wheeze. He was nearly toothless, his skin weathered rough, and wrinkled like a fig. "Do you remember me?" He spoke in passable English. "I used to take you on Kitsos."

"Yes," Rena said. "Yes, Kitsos, I remember that. Your mule. I remember now. I would go with you to your fields sometimes." She nodded. "You lived next door."

"I'm an old man now. I don't go to the fields anymore and I'm glad of it." Nikos laughed his wheezy laugh. It reminded Lou of her grandfather. "Where is your husband?" Nikos asked Rena.

"No husband," Rena said.

Lou smiled to herself.

The old man shook his head. "Maybe you only loved your father." He laughed again and asked Christina if there might be some coffee handy. "After your father died, you were not the same," Nikos said. "You became a sad sack. Do you remember that?"

"Kind of." Rena touched her head. "I have a headache," she said. "I'm sorry but . . . I'd like to talk with you some more, Nikos, but later, all right? I think I need to go lie down now. Nice seeing you again."

"Do you want me with you?" Lou asked.

"No, I just need to lie down for a little while."

Lou wasn't sure it was safe to leave her alone.

"A terrible thing, those deaths," Nikos said to Lou after Rena had gone. "So you're from America?"

"Yes, the Midwest. Farm country."

"I've been a farmer all my life. Except for four years. For four years I lived in your New York City. The Biggest Apple. I worked in my cousin's restaurant. I did not like it there in New York City, never got to like the noise and too many people. People not kind to each other, not taking care of each other. So I came back. You like it here in my country?"

"Very much," Lou said. "Rena and I came here to find out more about the killings."

Nikos looked uncomfortable. "So many years ago."

Christina returned with coffee for both of them. It was the thick Turkish kind which Lou couldn't stand. She took it anyway and set it on the little table on the porch.

"I gave her two aspirins," Christina said. "She's lying down."

Lou nodded. "You were here the day it happened?" Lou said to Nikos. "The day they were killed?"

"I was here. I helped carry Stavros onto the porch."

"Did you hear anything?" Lou asked. "Before they found Stavros?"

Nikos raised his gray bushy eyebrows. "I heard the saw."

Lou nodded.

"It was so long ago. Why does Rena want to poke into it now?"

Lou hesitated. Christina and Nikos waited. "Rena's troubled by it," Lou said.

"Mm-m." Nikos took a slurpy sip from the demitasse.

"She was a child. She felt somehow . . . responsible for it . . . for their deaths. Children do that sometimes. She has terrible guilt feelings about it."

"Responsible? Rena? How foolish." He shook his head. "She had nothing to do with it."

"I know that. I only wish *she* did."

"Well, tell her!" Apparently it seemed very simple to Nikos. He was quiet a while, staring at his cup, then at Lou. "Tell her two men did it, strangers from outside."

"She wouldn't believe it," Lou said.

Nikos seemed very pensive.

Lou was having serious trouble holding onto her optimism. She was beginning to doubt that Rena would ever be free. "It's destroying her life."

Nikos was quiet, clearly deep in thought. "That shouldn't be. She seems like such a sweet girl. I always liked her when she used to visit here. She was always very polite to me. She liked my mule. She shouldn't be suffering. The Spiros family has suffered enough."

"I agree, but she *is* suffering. The guilt feelings are destroying her."

Nikos shook his head sadly. He drained his cup then sat thinking some more. "Tell her there was a witness, that someone saw it happen."

"I wish there were."

He looked at Lou. "Well, *I* was there that day."

"But you didn't —"

"I was watching." He hesitated just a moment, then added, "I saw the killers."

Christina's eyes widened.

Lou leaned toward Nikos. "You saw?"

Nikos cleared his throat. "Yes. There were two of them. Two men."

"What did you see?" she asked eagerly.

"They did something to Stavros after they killed him."

"Cut off his arm," Lou said.

"Ah, so you know about that." He rubbed his scraggly cheeks. "Yes, that's what they did. With that saw Stavros had. Rena's grandfather never did get another saw after he smashed that one. It was a good saw too, light and fast."

"And there were two of them, two men, and you saw them do it?" Lou's heart was pounding.

"Yes. They took the arm with them. Wrapped it in a cloth from the wood pile. They took it to Antoni's little house. Did you know that?"

Lou was trying not to show her excitement. "So, what happened? Why did they kill him?"

The old man had his eyes closed. Finally he spoke. "They argued. Stavros was furious. He towered over the other two. You tell Rena this, Miss. I saw all of it. Yes, you tell her I saw everything that happened. They argued and then one of the men shot Stavros."

"Can you tell me exactly what happened?" Lou asked. Her palms were sweaty, her heart drumming against her ribs.

Nikos looked at his shoes. They had a coating of dust from the road. He wiped them on his pants. "I've always been a curious man," he said. "Like to know what's going on with the people around me. I knew Stavros was there cutting wood and then I saw these two men come by and, well, to tell the truth, I just went a little closer where I might be able to hear them, just out of curiosity, you know. My wife always said I'd get in trouble some day because of being so curious. Nosey, she called it."

"You heard their conversation?"

"I did."

"What did they say?"

Nikos leaned back on the old wooden chair. "I never told anyone. Probably should have, but I never did. Never told the police."

Lou nodded. "What did you overhear?"

"They talked about the cargo," Nikos said. "They said the word cargo a lot. They talked about getting the best price and about going fifty-fifty. Stavros suggested that. It sounded like they were making a deal. There was something about an art museum and overseas contacts. To tell the truth, I didn't quite understand it all. Then one of the men said Stavros should come with them to Kalamata. Stavros had told them the cargo was in Kalamata. They insisted Stavros come with them. Things got very heated. The man said Stavros had to come with them. They kept arguing back and forth." Nikos stared at the porch floor. "And that's when Stavros got shot in the head," he added quickly.

Christina flinched as she heard the words.

"I couldn't believe what they did next," Nikos said with a wheeze. His eyes were bright. Suddenly he seemed to be enjoying telling the story. "With the saw. Cut the arm clean off. Just like that. Quicker than cutting wood."

"What happened after that?" Lou was rubbing her palms on her jeans.

"They wrapped the arm and left. Went to their car. I stayed where I was. Hiding. Then my wife called to me. She had that sound in her voice. When I heard that I knew I better go right away. I had left a pot boiling on the stove. Ooh, she was mad! I was cleaning up the mess when I heard screams outside. It was Maria. I went out there and . . ." Nikos' eyes narrowed. "You know, that might be why Rena got all confused about this, thinking she was responsible, like you said. Yes, it was probably Rena I saw."

"You saw Rena? What do you mean?"

"I remember seeing a child, one of the village children, I figured. I never thought it might be Rena, but maybe it was."

"Right after the murder, you mean?"

"Yes, when I came outside after Maria screamed, I saw someone scrambling up the back road, a youngster. I couldn't tell who it was and I didn't give it much thought with everything else that was going on. Maybe it was Rena. Maybe she saw something."

Lou was blinking rapidly, picturing what Nikos was describing, trying to digest it all.

"Anyway," Nikos continued, "I helped out as much as I could. It was terrible. But then it got even worse. An hour or so later, someone came and told us Antoni had been murdered. I went with Costas — that's Rena's grandfather, God rest his soul — I went with him to the little house. Antoni was lying on the floor, poor fellow. He had been hit in the head, probably with the lamp that was on the table. That's what the police said."

Christina looked faint. Lou took her hand.

"Stavros' arm was there. What a sight!" Nikos searched his pockets but apparently didn't find what he was looking for. He wiped his nose on his sleeve. "I'll never forget that sight. I can still picture it." He looked straight into Lou's eyes. "It's not a pretty story but Rena should know it. Those two men were the killers. You tell her."

"I'll tell her," Lou said. "Nikos, you said you never told the police —"

"Never told anyone. Except my wife."

"Well, why not? Why didn't you? It could have helped in the investigation."

Nikos was shaking his head. "I didn't want to get involved."

Lou was appalled. She tried lamely to cover it.

"It was my wife," Nikos added quickly. "She told me eyewitnesses to murder end up murdered themselves."

"You were afraid."

"My wife. She was afraid."

"I see."

"I would have told what I saw if they arrested the wrong people. I would have told then, but as it turned out there was no need."

Lou didn't respond. She was experiencing a mix of feelings. Disgust was one of them.

"You tell Rena what I told you. No need to tell anyone else, Miss. You know what I mean?"

"Your wife might think there's still some danger," Lou said sarcastically.

"My wife is gone, Miss. Dead these eight years now. No need stirring people up is what I mean. You tell Rena because she needs to hear it. I'll tell her myself if you want. She needs to know. No one else does." He turned to Christina. "You know what I'm saying, Christina?"

"Yes, I understand."

"Thank you," Lou said to Nikos.

234

He took Lou's untouched cup of Turkish coffee from the table. "Don't mention it," he said, and gulped the coffee down.

Rena listened open-mouthed.

"It fits. It all ties together," Lou said at the end. "These guys were after the paintings. Fortes' men, most likely. One of them could have been Fortes himself. They killed your uncle and father and stole the paintings from the truck. It all makes sense."

Rena said little as Lou spoke and when Lou finished she insisted on hearing it from Nikos. They sat in the kitchen of his plain little house as he told the story once again. He told of seeing the two men, listening to their conversation. "Stavros did not want to go with them. There is no need, he said. They were arguing about it." Nikos paused for a long time. "Stavros must not have seen the gun," he said at last. He looked at Rena. "They shot him in the back of the head."

"And you saw it?" Rena said.

Nikos looked Rena in the eye. "I did," he answered firmly.

Rena shook her head. "But that's not what happened."

"I saw what I saw," Nikos insisted.

"Rena, the man saw it," Lou said.

Rena did not respond.

"That's the way it happened, Miss Rena." Nikos waited for her to look at him.

Rena nodded feebly.

"So now you know. You just go on about your life now, you hear?" Rena nodded again.

"I'm truly sorry you had to lose your kin that way," Nikos said. "But it's best that you know just how it happened. And now you do." He rubbed his jaw. "I saw what I saw, all right? That's the way it happened."

"That's the way it happened," Rena repeated, numbly.

"That's right." Nikos smiled and seemed to relax.

Lou thanked Nikos again and led Rena back to her uncle's house.

"How could it be?" Rena repeated over and over again. "I was so sure." They were in the living room.

"You were angry so you imagined killing the ones you were angry at."

"But . . . it seemed so real."

"I know, Rena. Kids do it all the time. Adults, too. *A thought-murder a day keeps the psychiatrist away.* Have you ever heard that? You were expressing your anger in a safe way, but then that horrible coincidence. Someone actually *did* kill the people you were wishing dead."

"I don't know."

"And then you believed your wish had caused it. You believed that your fantasy had actually happened."

Rena pictured herself at the river. "I remember that after awhile I wasn't angry any more. I started masturbating and forgot all about being angry at Daddy. I felt loving towards him again."

Lou nodded.

"And then I got worried that I wasn't doing what he said."

"Going to your uncle."

"Yes. So I went to find him. I went to find Uncle Stavros."

"To give him the message, right?"

Rena's brow wrinkled. "Maybe so."

"Not to kill him."

"Maybe I went to give him the message. I went to Grandma's to find him and —"

"And you found out he was dead."

"I remember Mom holding me and crying. I felt so awful."

"You thought you had done it. You thought the fantasy you had at the river was real."

"It must have been just a fantasy?"

"That's right. Part of it at the river, then you elaborated on it after you found out your uncle was dead."

"All fantasy."

Lou nodded vigorously. "And then you ran to find your father."

"He would hate me for what I did."

"That's what you thought. But when you got to the little house . . ."

236

"When I got there —"

"He was dead. Your father was already dead." Lou's face looked pained. "It must have shocked you terribly, Rena."

"There was so much blood." Rena could picture it clearly. "He was on the floor."

"Yes, he was already on the floor when you got there."

"Maybe he was. Maybe he was already dead. I would never hurt Daddy, never, never, never!"

"That's right," Lou said softly.

Rena took several deep quick breaths. "I went over to where he was. I . . . I picked up the lamp. Yes, it was lying across Daddy's hand. I picked it up. I put it on the table and then I went back to Daddy and I took his hand. I took his hand in my hand and I held it next to my cheek." She was picturing it as if it were just happening. "I kissed Daddy's hand."

Rena was crying and so was Lou. "Oh, Rena, you poor baby." Lou's arms were around her.

Rena clung to her. "He was my best."

"I know, Rena."

"Oh, God, why did he have to die?"

They did not speak for a long time. Finally, Rena leaned back on the chair. Her face was splotchy red and wet. "He was murdered by those men."

"Yes. Like Nikos said. You had nothing to do with it."

"I didn't do it."

"No, you didn't. Your father and uncle were killed by smugglers, Rena, by black market art dealers."

Rena's hands were clasped in front of her. "Nikos saw it." She turned to Lou. "But, Lou, I don't know. I was so sure."

"You were ten years old."

Rena nodded. "I couldn't murder anybody. I could never hurt my father."

"That's right, Rena. But you could fantasize about it. And that's what caused all the trouble for you. You thought the fantasy was true."

Rena stared into space. "I didn't kill them."

"No."

She was breathing loudly through her mouth. "I have to let it sink in."

"Yes." Lou stroked her arm caringly.

"It . . . it . . . I don't know. I was so sure."

"You were so wrong, my sweet."

Rena suddenly seemed alarmed. "But, Lou, what about Pat? What about Rebecca?"

"What do you think, Rena? You tell me."

"I don't know."

"Do you actually remember doing those things? Damaging Pat's car? Cutting Rebecca's rope?"

"I don't . . ."

"You said it was fuzzy, the memories were fuzzy. You didn't actually shoot Stavros but you did have a fuzzy fantasy-memory of it nonetheless. The same with your father, Rena, and the same —"

"— with Pat."

"Yes. A fantasy-memory."

"And Rebecca. It's all fuzzy."

"Yes, because it wasn't real."

"I didn't do it."

"But your guilt made you susceptible to believing you did."

"I didn't kill them."

"That's right."

"I didn't kill anyone." Rena was staring blankly. "Then I'm not evil. I'm not a lizard. I'm not a killer. I'm not crazy." She looked at Lou with tears in her eyes.

They reached for each other. The embrace was strong and warm.

Rena began blinking rapidly. "If I didn't . . . well, it . . . it changes everything, Lou."

"Exactly."

Rena's head felt light. She was gripping Lou's hand. She let the new truth sink in further. I didn't do it, she thought. Nikos saw the men. It wasn't me. I didn't kill my father. I didn't kill my uncle. Someone else did it. It wasn't me. I didn't kill Pat. It was an accident. I didn't kill anyone.

She looked at Lou. "Then I'm free," she whispered, her eyes glistening.

Lou nodded. Her eyes, too, were wet. She was smiling and Rena smiled back through her tears.

"I'm not evil."

"Not at all."

"I can live. Lou, I thought I had to die, but now . . . I don't have to die. I can live. It's all over and I'm truly free. Just like you said, Lou."

"Just like I said."

CHAPTER TWENTY SIX

It took a lot of talking for Lou to convince Rena that it wasn't yet time to leave Greece.

"There are the birds," she said. "We still have no idea what that was all about."

"It doesn't matter," Rena insisted.

It was late at night. They were in the same bedroom that Rena had used during her summers at Kaftarei. The room was small but had a new double bed and a cot. Rena was stretched out on the bed.

"And there are other things," Lou said. "Aren't you curious? We still don't know what you were supposed to go tell Stavros that day, the message from your father."

"I don't see what difference it makes. We know the important thing." Rena sighed happily. "It's ending so differently from how I thought it would."

Lou gave her the thumbs up sign. "But, I'm still curious," she said.

Rena sighed again. "And I'm satisfied. The other things don't matter. I want to get home and see if I'll feel it there."

Lou tilted her head. "Feel what?"

"You know, the . . . the freedom! I want to really *feel* it!" She pressed her open palms against her chest.

"I thought you said —"

"Oh, I do feel relief. Yes, for sure. It's like a huge weight taken off me. *That* I'm real aware of. But the whole hugeness of it just isn't sinking in. I don't have to feel guilt. I'm not a murderer. I'm not evil. I have a life to make and so much to think about. I know all that, but I don't *feel* it, not like I want to. Maybe at home, I will."

Lou nodded. "I imagine it will be a bit by bit process," she said. She was sitting on the little woven chair by their window wearing only her Artemis Singers T-shirt, lavender underpants, and a pair of shoes.

"I still feel like me. I don't know . . . I mean . . ." She smiled warmly at Lou. "In some ways, it's just like you said. I . . . it's great. Like I can begin liking me again." She looked at Lou very seriously. "I owe you a lot. I would have been dead if it weren't for you."

Lou nodded. "I'm glad you let yourself go along with me."

"Me too." Rena was silent a moment. "I couldn't help it though, you know. I couldn't resist . . . you . . . what you wanted me to do."

Lou moved to the cot and bent to take off her shoes. Rena watched her strong fingers pulling on the laces. "About not feeling it enough . . ." Lou looked up at Rena. "Maybe it just doesn't work that way. I mean, after all, for twenty-seven years, you thought you were an evil being. You repressed it pretty well. When you left Greece you left most of it behind. You had your first *rebirth,* so to speak."

Lou tossed her shoes aside. Rena watched her movements.

"But the repression wasn't complete. I think it affected your self-concept, and it certainly affected you sexually."

"Sexually?" Rena felt herself beginning to blush. "You think so?"

Lou nodded. "You couldn't have orgasms unless your partner dominated you."

"Yes, but . . ."

"Like your Uncle Stavros did. To get your father's love you had to please your uncle, right? Isn't that how it was? They were very

241

connected in your mind — your father's tender loving and your uncle's authoritarianism. They weren't separate for you. It was like a package deal. To get the love of your father, you had to accept your uncle's domination."

"Yes, that fits. That's how it was."

"And you used to masturbate while daydreaming about your father."

Rena nodded. She was feeling quite uncomfortable.

Lou sat up straight, looking right at Rena. "I think in your mind, in your ten-year-old mind, a link was made between sexual feelings, guilt, and obedience."

Lou stood. Rena stared at the rippling leg muscles.

"You were supposed to be pleasing your uncle by bringing him that message which would also please your dad." Lou was talking excitedly. "But instead you were pleasing yourself, fantasizing about killing them, masturbating while thinking of your dad. Then they got killed and you concluded that you were responsible." Lou put her foot up on the woven chair. "You know what I think? I think it worked like this . . ." She put her foot back on the floor and leaned forward, her arms resting on her bare knees. "Your father told you to do something. You disobeyed. You were enjoying yourself sexually instead of obeying your father. He gets murdered. You think you did it. You repress that idea but you feel terrible guilt. In your mind guilt becomes connected with sexual pleasure. Then later you can only allow yourself complete sexual pleasure when you earn it, overcome the guilt, by being obedient."

Rena nodded but was not sure she fully understood.

Lou continued. "You probably would have been a total basket case if you hadn't been able to repress most of it. The rash was one price you paid."

Rena was feeling a little dazed. "The rash?"

"Psychosomatic. Overall, though, you were a psychologically-healthy enough kid to manage to go on once the repression took place. Leaving Greece helped with that, I'm sure. But, like I said, you didn't come out unscathed. You ended up with the sexual quirk."

Rena listened with fascination. It did make sense. Lou seemed so wise the way she could put it all together.

Lou continued. "You could only be orgasmic with a lover who would play out the roles for you, someone who symbolized both your father and your uncle. She had to be kind and loving like your father, but powerful and demanding like your uncle. Only with someone like that could you feel free enough to let go sexually."

Lou was gesturing freely as she spoke. Rena still felt dazed.

"Do you see what I mean? You were making amends, pleasing Uncle to get Dad, pleasing the tyrant to get the tenderness. At the same time you were also making amends for your ultimate act of willfulness — the fantasied murders — by submitting to someone else's will. Powerful, dominating women who were also capable of tenderness were a turn-on to you. They reproduced the dynamics of your father and uncle."

"Complicated," Rena said. "I don't know. Pretty convoluted. It does make sense, but . . . I mean, I didn't have a sexual thing going with my father, you know."

"That's not what I'm saying. You weren't overtly sexual with him."

"You've changed your mind about that."

"Yes. Apparently it wasn't literal, but the association was there for you. Sexual pleasure connected with guilt connected with making amends and re-enacting your childhood situation through seeking lovers who would both dominate and love you."

"You sound like a shrink."

"It fits, Rena."

"So why women rather than men? I supposed you got that figured out too."

Lou laughed. "That's another story."

"So tell it."

She laughed again. "I haven't the slightest idea."

"I thought you knew everything."

"Not quite."

"Well, what you said does make sense, though. It's a lot to digest." Rena leaned back on the bed, hands behind her head. "You love figuring things out, don't you."

"Yes, of course. Doesn't everybody? But we still don't know all of it." Lou was leaning against the wall, her arms folded in front of her. "I wouldn't be surprised if just understanding this isn't enough for you to totally change — to change all the inside stuff. Understanding that you didn't kill anyone is a major step, of course. Maybe it is enough. We'll see."

Rena thought of Casey. "I'd like to be free to go and *come* with whom I want." She chuckled.

Lou seemed not to have heard her. She went and sat on the edge of the bed. "You built a whole structure on top of a false premise, built part of your self-concept on a major distortion." She was gesturing continuously as she spoke. "It's like building a house on a crooked foundation. All the beams then have to be distorted, too, to compensate for the messed up foundation. So now the foundation is straightened out, but you still have to correct all the beams. Get it?"

"My attraction to domineering women is a crooked beam?"

Lou smiled. "In your case, I think so. Maybe what you now realize will change that. I don't know. Killing the birds was another crooked beam, I suspect. That urge stopped after you remembered about your father, didn't it?"

Rena thought about it. "Yes. You're right. After that communing session when I remembered that I'd killed him, or thought I did, then I went into your chicken coop — to test it, I think. That feeling wasn't there. I didn't want to do anything to the birds. It didn't seem necessary anymore."

"So maybe the bird-killing was a symbol or substitute somehow for —"

"Or a way of trying to take care of the guilt. I know it always seemed I'd feel better if I could just cut them open."

"Why would that be?" Lou was tapping her finger on the bed. "I don't get it, do you?"

"I know I felt that if I could just get inside that bird and find ..." Rena shook her head.

"Find what?"

"I don't know." Rena was sitting on the edge of the bed, her feet on the floor. "But I do know it felt crucial to cut them open, like that would resolve something, or make amends somehow."

244

A knock on the door startled both of them.

"Come in," Lou called.

"Am I interrupting something?" Christina opened the door a crack and remained outside. "I just wanted to get my book."

"Come in, come in." Lou reached over and got the book from the side pocket of Christina's overnight bag. "You're reading Kazanzakis, huh? I've got some books you might enjoy even more."

Christina's face colored. "Everyone's gone to bed," she said, taking the book from Lou without looking at her.

"Oh, did you want to sleep now?" Rena asked. "We can —"

"No, no. I'm going to read awhile in the front room. I know you two are talking. You go ahead."

"We'll be going to bed soon," Lou said. "Whenever you're ready, just come on in."

Again Christina's faced reddened and she quickly left the room.

Rena was staring at her hands. She felt a little dizzy.

"Where were we?" Lou asked. "Oh, yeah. The birds. Your reasons for cutting them open. So we still don't know how that connects with everything. We know that Pat's death set it all off — started the depression and the bird killing." Lou rubbed her chin. "Maybe you believed you killed her, you know, poked that hole in her brake fluid line. I don't think so, though. I think you might have felt responsible, but I don't think you had that idea about doing anything to her car until Trish suggested it. What do you think?"

"I don't know. I sort of went numb after she died."

"You know what it might be. If Pat symbolized your father and uncle —"

"Yes," Rena said. "Then when she died —"

"Of course!"

"It was like killing them all over."

"Exactly!"

"I was angry at her. I wasn't *obedient.* I rebelled. I did what pleased me rather than what she wanted. I stayed out rather than —"

"Yes, rather than getting home in time to go to that barbecue with her."

"And the next thing I knew, she was dead."

245

"And you felt responsible, just like with your father and uncle."

"So the old guilt feelings came pouring back." Rena's whole body was tight.

"They got de-repressed," Lou said. "Pat's death set it all off. Yes, of course. That's it. You were reliving it. You believed you were responsible for her death and that re-contacted you with the belief about being responsible for your father's death and your uncle's."

"But I didn't actually remember it."

"No, it was too awful to really remember it. Just the feelings were there. The guilt. The sense of being evil." Lou tapped her fingers on the bed again. "But why the birds? That's the remaining unknown. We need to keep looking." Her eyes were glowing.

"You know what's weird?" Rena said. "Even though I can see all this, even though I know I didn't kill anybody, and that my sexual . . . *quirk*, as you call it, was related to my father and uncle . . . even though I know all this, I still . . ." She stood and walked across the room.

"What, Rena?"

"It isn't changing how . . . there are still some pretty crooked beams." She was looking at Lou longingly.

"You mean . . ."

"I still feel the same about you. You're a father-uncle symbol too, you know."

"Yes, I know."

"And I still feel . . . the same."

"You have to work it through." Lou laughed. "I suggest you do the work in therapy with Dr. Kepper." She was looking very seductively at Rena. "However, sometimes actions speak louder than . . ." She stopped talking and moved to Rena. She put her arms around her, tightly, and covered Rena's warm mouth with her own.

Rena's whole body responded. She felt gushy and weak and hot. She pulled away. "Christina could come in any minute."

"True," Lou said, putting her hand on Rena's waist and slipping a finger inside the waistband.

"Let's go for an early morning walk tomorrow."

Lou nodded, her eyebrows raised.

"We'll go to the nest, bring a blanket. We'll go at sunrise."

"Sounds perfect." Lou gave Rena one more kiss, a light one this time.

Rena was beaming.

Lou smiled back at her. "I know what you're thinking."

"I know you know."

"It's been a long time coming, hasn't it?"

They both laughed at the unintentional pun.

CHAPTER TWENTY SEVEN

Rena awoke first. Christina was next to her on the double bed, breathing deeply, her lips partly open. Slowly, silently, Rena crept from the bed. Daybreak was near. She stood over Lou, who was still asleep, and felt a tremendous surge of excitement and happiness. She touched her cheek. Lou stirred, then was immediately fully awake.

"Make some coffee," she whispered.

There was not a soul on the street nor on the path to the river. By the time they arrived at the nest, the sun had crested. Lou spread the blanket. "I remember I said this is a nice place to come alone. Even better with a friend, I think." She looked at Rena very affectionately. "Sit, my sweet, let us break our fast."

"How about a bite to eat first," Rena said, giggling.

They had fresh bread and feta cheese and olives and grapes, looking at the river, looking at each other, talking softly. Lou covered the thermos and put the coffee aside. She took Rena's hand.

She spread the long smooth fingers across her palm. The knuckle skin formed series of interlocking crescent moons. Lou

248

kissed each knuckle, then with her fingertip, traced a path up each of Rena's fingers. She brought Rena's hand to her face and retraced each path with the tip of her tongue, licking sensually the little web of skin between the fingers. Rena watched, her head tilted, smiling. Lou took the thumb fully into her mouth, pushing it against her inner cheeks then drawing it up against the roof of her mouth, sliding her tongue back and forth along the length of it. Lou's cheeks and tongue and the roof of her mouth made a warm wet surrounding womb for Rena's thumb.

Rena continued watching her, her own tongue vicariously sucking and tasting.

Lou turned Rena's hand over and looked at the palm. With the tip of her slippery tongue, she traced one of the lines. "A long life," she said. She followed another palm line. "Love." And a third. "And freedom." Placing Rena's hand against her cheek, Lou closed her eyes and moved Rena's smooth fingers slowly across her face.

Rena picked up the movement, tenderly, lightly stroking the soft skin of Lou's face, along her full lower lip, slowly, softly brushing the tips of Lou's teeth with her fingertip, then following the contours of Lou's mouth with all of her fingers, above her lips, along her nose, to her cheeks and her eyes. She explored the soft skin of Lou's eyelids, the hard bone around them, feeling all the textures; then she let her fingers sink into the jungle of Lou's thick hair.

Lou's head fell back as Rena continued stroking her hair and her forehead and temples. Rena leaned over her, lowering her head until her mouth touched Lou's brow. The sweet scent of Lou was mixed with the smell of mint growing nearby. With her lips, she continued the meandering over Lou's face, kissing softly each eye, cheek, her parted lips, the little mole, her chin, her neck. Lou shivered as the warm air of Rena's mouth and the soft moistness of her lips danced along her throat.

Side by side they lay on the blanket in the grass at the nest by the river. A light breeze rippled over their skin. Lou's hand was on Rena's shoulder feeling the fabric of Rena's blouse, then going in at the neckline, caressing the warm skin of Rena's chest, lightly flowing her fingers over each breast. Rena's hand moved up and down Lou's

249

side, dipping at the waist, rising at the hips, moving slowly, tenderly down the outer thigh as far as she could reach, then back up.

Lou shifted and leaned over Rena. Rena looked into her eyes. The kiss began as softly as the caresses, as softly as the soft fingering and tonguing, but grew as Rena's lips parted and Lou's tongue entered her smooth mouth, tongue against tongue, tongue finding every little place, along the inner mouth and inner lips. The kiss grew stronger, harder, hands moving faster, more urgently along the contours of each other's body.

There were more kisses. Soft ones, soft, tender surface ones. Deep ones, hard, entering, sucking. Their mouths still pressed deeply together, Lou's fingers found Rena's belt and soon the ends fell free, and she undid the button and lowered the zipper. Crouching then, Lou tugged on Rena's jeans, slipping them down over her hips, down to her knees. She brushed her lips over Rena's knee, then upward along the top of Rena's thigh, up to where one leg joined the other, the joining place hidden by pale blue cotton which Lou kissed, from the narrowest part, up, until the underpants ended and there was flesh and Rena's navel which Lou circled with her tongue.

"Shall I take my shoes off?" Rena asked.

"I will," Lou said, and removed a shoe and sock.

Bent over on her knees, Lou touched the top of Rena's ankle with her lips, moved downward towards her toes, then up again, above the ankle to where there was more flesh, and nipped softly with her teeth. She removed the other shoe and sock, and caressed the newly freed foot with both hands. She pulled Rena's jeans all the way off. She moved her head along Rena's legs until her cheek rested on Rena's soft belly.

Rena caressed Lou's back, down the center, back and forth, and along her neck, and ran her fingers over Lou's ears and through her hair. She could feel Lou taking hold of her underpants, and the slow slide of them down her hips. She helped kick them away.

Lou undid the buttons of Rena's blouse, pulled the cloth aside and lay her head on Rena's chest, one cheek then the other, caressing Rena's breasts with her cheeks, as her cheeks were caressed by Rena's breasts. Rena savored the softness. Lou raised her face, looked at Rena a moment, her eyes bright, then slowly lowered her mouth over Rena's breast, pulling the nipple tenderly inside and rolling it around and around with her tongue. Rena felt the heat grow all through her.

With her tongue, her mouth, the lip-covered edges of her teeth, Lou continued toying with Rena's nipples which had grown firm and erect, as her hands gently kneaded the flesh of Rena's breasts. One hand wandered downward along Rena's thigh, to the hair-covered triangle. Her fingers teased softly at the door as she moved her head up, finding Rena's mouth, taking it to her own hungrily, one finger slipping closer to the entrance down below, the kiss continuing above, two fingers finding the slippery wetness and slipping in, her tongue dancing inside Rena's mouth, her fingers dancing inside Rena, faster and faster.

Rena felt herself rising, felt the heat shooting within her, radiating across her spine and in her cunt, rising and rising. Lou continued the rhythmic movement of her fingers following Rena's rising, leading her, following and leading. Panting, her back arched, Rena suddenly sighed and relaxed. She could hear the gurgling slosh of the river passing them by.

Lou paused, kissing Rena tenderly along her jaw line, stroking her thighs and the edges of her buttocks, nibbling her earlobe, kissing her neck. Then her hand returned, one finger this time, along the edge of Rena's clitoris, gently stroking, slowly, then faster, as Rena's breathing quickened, more and more and more, until again Rena's back flattened and she lay quietly.

"What would you like?" Lou whispered, her breath warm in Rena's ear. "Shall I . . ."

"No," Rena said, "here, let me . . ." She turned onto her side, her hand going to Lou's waist. "Let's get rid of these." She undid Lou's pants and helped her out of them. Lou was naked except for her shirt which Rena also removed. "Mm-m, nice," Rena murmured, running her hands from Lou's shoulders, across her breasts, to her hips, thighs, then down to her crotch.

Lou was on her back, Rena lying partly on her, partly next to her, her hand playing around the edges of Lou's cunt, then centering, and continuing as Lou moaned and raised herself, pushing against Rena's fingers which moved more and more rapidly and targeted and faster until Lou's arching body rose more and Rena's fingers flew until Lou, too, flew and gasped and held Rena tightly for a long, long time. Slowly she descended, but Rena, at once, began again to play in the wetness and again Lou rose to it, rising all the way, a throaty moan and a little joyful laugh emerging with her full climactic peaking.

They held each other warmly, Lou clothed only in a fine layer of perspiration and Rena's arms, Rena still partially covered by her shirt. Lou's eyes were on the sky, her fingers sneaking towards Rena's groin. Rena's face was nestled in Lou's neck and she murmured something low and gurgly as Lou's finger reached the spot. In a flash, Lou was moving down, her head lowering along Rena's body, her chin brushing the hairs, her lips whispering over Rena's silky cunt. She spread Rena's legs.

Slivers of dancing sunshine decorated Rena's glistening labia and Lou touched with her gaze and then her fingers the deep rose fleshy narrow mounds and crevices. She licked the rays of sun sparkling on Rena's clitoris and sucked them, sucking the hardening little rod, pulling it gently into her mouth, circling it with her tongue, circling, vibrating, as Rena's hips moved with Lou's mouth, moved with her arousal. With tongue and lips, Lou continued, while her hands fondled Rena's buttocks and hips and belly, continuing, urging Rena on and on, until Rena's tense muscles loosened and grew lax and she tugged Lou gently to her, kissing her, tasting herself on Lou's mouth, holding her tightly.

"You're wonderful," Rena declared.

Lou chuckled, blowing softly on Rena's neck. "Do you mean that?"

"Oh, I do. You're so . . . really gentle and sensitive . . . so loving and tender and . . ."

"Does that surprise you?"

Rena raised herself up on one elbow. "Where are the cigarettes?"

Laughing, Lou reached for her jeans, got the pack. "Does it?" She lit one for each of them.

"What?"

"Surprise you that I'm gentle and tender and all that."

Rena blew a cloud of smoke and watched it float toward the sky. "Maybe a little."

"It's not what you expected."

"I love how you seem to just love being with my body . . . just into every part of it."

"You enjoyed it?" Lou asked. "Making love with me?"

"Oh, yes . . . a lot."

"But not in the way you expected."

Rena drew deeply on her cigarette.

"Unless my perception is highly off," Lou said, "I believe you didn't quite go all the way, or *come*, as they say."

"It felt wonderful."

"But not . . ."

Rena wrapped her arms around her knees. "Lou, I have absolutely no complaints, absolutely . . . you're a wonderfully tender lover."

"Which doesn't turn you on."

"I was turned on," Rena said defensively.

"Part way."

Rena looked away.

"You wanted it to be different, didn't you? You wanted me to dominate you, to top you, to take your body like it was only mine, like I own it, own you."

Rena shrugged.

"Isn't that it?"

"I guess," Rena said softly. She was hugging her knees. "I had these fantasies, millions of them, since the first day I met you, and they grew and grew. I wish we could have . . . I wish I'd found out about . . . that I was *free* back in Wisconsin, back when . . . "

"When I owned you?"

"Yes." Rena turned to face her. "I wish I could be free, free of the guilt like I am now, finally, and still . . . still have you . . . be with you like . . ."

Lou shook her head. "Freedom has its price," she said, smiling.

"You're really not what I thought you were."

"Oh?"

"I thought you were powerful, not just . . ." Rena looked off to the river.

"Not just what?" Lou said.

"I don't know." Rena stared at the grass. "Nice. Ordinary."

Lou snickered. "I see. Well, we do understand where that's coming from, don't we? The old father-uncle stuff."

"I'm sick of that psychological bullshit."

Lou's eyes narrowed. "You know, I could . . ." She grabbed Rena by the jaw and held her firmly. Her eyes were fierce and fiery, they penetrated Rena. She was not smiling. "I could do whatever I want with you, couldn't I?"

Rena felt a tremendous surge of chilling excitement shoot from Lou's fingers down her neckline to the pit of her stomach. She gasped. "Yes," she answered.

Lou did not loosen her hold. "I could make you kneel and crawl and serve me. I could take whatever pleasure I want from you in whatever way I want it."

Rena's lips were quivering above Lou's grasp. She did not speak.

"Isn't that true?"

"Yes," Rena whispered. She could not meet Lou's eyes.

"And take you roughly, fuck you, possess you, use you."

"Yes, anything you want. You can do what you want with me." Rena's heart was pounding madly. "I want you to do anything you want . . ."

Lou's hand softened on Rena's jaw, the grasp turning into a caress. "But Rena, I did what I want. That's what I want. I don't want to dominate you. I don't want the power to . . . I liked it the way it was here at this wonderful nest. That's what I wanted."

Rena nodded sadly. "I see." She pulled up a long blade of grass. "Well, I understand, I mean, that's fine. That's more . . . normal, I guess, or whatever and . . . really, I understand. You . . . you really are amazingly sweet. I'm not going to stop adoring you." She gave Lou a big hug, then reached for her jeans. "God, look at the sky, it's so clear."

"Yes, very clear," Lou agreed.

CHAPTER TWENTY EIGHT

The house was jumping with activity when they returned. Christina and two of the children were rolling dough for noodles; Rena's Uncle Basilis was in the back working on the tractor; Toula was helping Antonia, the quiet one, with her homework which was due that morning, while two neighbor women sat with them at the table. Rena was tempted to join her uncle at the tractor, but instead showed Lou how they cut the noodle dough into tiny squares. Lou soon tired of the task and went outside.

"Your friend is very interesting," Christina said, pushing the rolling pin over a new wad of dough. "I've never met anyone like her."

"She's one of a kind," Rena agreed.

"A very independent woman."

"Yes, I suppose she is."

"You, too, Rena."

The children were talking and giggling in Greek, laughing at how fast and unintelligibly their relatives spoke English.

"I wondered why you never married," Christina continued, "but now I think I know."

"Oh, really?" Rena held the knife still.

"*I* will never marry," Christina continued. "Many men have tried to be with me."

Rena nodded attentively.

"I thought I just had no interest, you know, in such things, you know . . . romance and love and . . . sex."

Toula came into the kitchen speaking to the children, shooing them on their way.

"They must go to school now," Christina said. "I always loved school. I was a very dedicated student. People thought that's all I was interested in."

Toula joined them in the noodle-making and they talked of life in the village and of their relatives, with Christina translating.

An hour later, Rena found Lou reading on the balcony. "I'm ready," she said.

Lou put the book aside. "Lead the way."

The walk took them through the village and a short distance beyond it and then on a path past the two gently rising hills topped with cypress trees.

As soon as the little house came into view, Rena stopped. "It's falling apart," she said sadly.

They went closer. The window glass was missing, the door rotted and hanging from rusted hinges. The chimney had caved in. "That's the tree where the swing was," Rena said. Her eyes were tear-filled. She approached the entrance and swung the creaky door. "Oh, what a mess."

Lou walked inside. "Looks like it's been home to a number of different species." She sidestepped a dry pile of dung.

"All the furniture's gone," Rena said sadly. "It hardly even seems like the same place." She looked at the filthy sink, the rotting cupboards, then back at the main room. "That's where the couch was," she said, and then, looking at the floor next to it, added, "and that's where . . . where I found him." Her eyes scanned the room. "The lamp's gone."

"Where was the table where the lamp was?" Lou asked.

"Right here, by the door." Tears streamed down Rena's face. She ran outside.

Lou found her leaning against a tree. "So, this is where the swing was." Lou patted the tree. "This is where you were swinging that day."

"Yes," Rena said softly. "I was swinging and singing." Her eyes were closed, her head back, resting on the tree trunk. "And then Daddy came to the window, right there." She pointed. "I can still picture his face. I was surprised to see him."

Lou waited but Rena did not continue. "And then . . ."

"*Sh-h-h,* he said, and he made a gesture for me to come inside the house."

"So you did . . ." Lou began walking to the door.

Rena followed.

". . . And you went inside, and . . ."

They were in the house again.

"And Daddy gave me a hug, a great big giant hug. *Kukla mou,* he said. He always called me *kukla;* that means doll. And then he said . . ."

Lou waited excitedly.

". . . He said, *There is something important I want you to do for me, for me and Uncle Stavros.* I can hear his voice." She looked at Lou.

"Go on."

"He went to the table. Yes, over there. And he leaned over. He didn't sit down. And he wrote something. Sometimes he wrote me little poems, funny ones, cute little silly poems. I thought that's what he was doing, but when he finished, he rolled the paper up real tiny and . . . yes, and then he took his knife from his pocket and he opened it up and . . ." Rena was breathing heavily. ". . . And he went over there, to the mantle and he took . . . it was a bird, a statue of a bird." Rena's eyes were narrowed in concentration as the remembering continued. "I don't know what kind of bird it was. It had pretty colors, I remember. He cut it open with his knife."

Rena's eyes widened as she heard herself. "It was a real bird," she continued, "a stuffed one. He cut it open, a slit, and he put something in it. And then he said I should go quickly to Uncle Stavros and tell him that the secret is in the bird."

Lou stared wide-eyed at Rena.

"But daddy, won't you tell me a story. He looked so angry and mean. *No! No story today. I mean it, Katerina. Go! Get out of here. Go quickly to Uncle Stavros. The secret is in the bird. Tell him that. Now go!"*

Rena was shaking her head. "I didn't want to go. And that's when he . . . he pushed me away. He shoved me real hard and I almost fell down. Daddy never did anything like that before. Never anything mean like that. He pushed me away from him. He didn't want me anymore."

Lou nodded. She gave Rena a hug, held her and rubbed her back. "Poor little girl. How painful that was."

"I thought he didn't want me anymore."

"Yes, that's what you thought."

Neither of them spoke for a while. Rena stood quietly thinking. *"The secret is in the bird."* She smiled. "So that's what it was all about." She looked at Lou. "Isn't that something!"

"You were after the secret."

Rena nodded slowly. "That must be it."

"That's why you cut them open."

The two women looked at each without speaking for a long time. Lou finally broke the silence. "So, when Pat died . . ."

Rena shifted gears, quickly making the connection Lou was making. "When she died, I felt so guilty and . . . and it got all mixed up with my father's death and . . . you know what I think? I think I must have figured I could make amends somehow if I could find the secret . . . the secret in the bird." Rena's eyes were wide. "Do you think that's it?"

"That's what it sounds like." Lou said. "Fascinating. You were trying to appease your guilt."

"How absurd, really," Rena said.

"Well, yes, logically," Lou said. "It was symbolic though. It made sense symbolically."

"I guess."

Lou gave Rena another warm hug. "We're getting the answers, girl."

Rena thought of Dr. Kepper and her tablecloth story. Lou's eyes were glowing. "I wonder what happened to the bird."

Both women stared at the empty, dirt-caked mantle.

"My father liked that bird a lot," Rena said, as they walked back to her aunt and uncle's house. "He wrote a poem about it once."

"How did it go?" Lou dodged a fallen limb.

"I can't remember. Something about its noble wings, and gliding over fields. I don't really remember the words."

Basilis was on the porch. The youngest of the Spiros boys, he was now in his fifties. Rena thought he looked a little like her father. Lou went to get Christina to translate and then they asked Basilis if he remembered the stuffed bird Antoni had in his little house.

"He kept it on the mantle," Rena said.

"Oh yes, the pheasant." Basilis pursed his lips, nodding. "Your father tried to save its life but was unable to, and then he had it stuffed. Yes, I remember. Your mother kept it in the back bedroom after your father died." Basilis smiled kindly at his niece. "You have a good memory."

"Whatever happened to it?"

"It's in the closet," Basilis said. "On the top shelf above the blankets."

Lou seemed even more excited than Rena. Basilis brought the pheasant onto the porch and began fumbling with the plastic wrapping. Lou helped him. Some of the feathers were missing, others fell to the floor as Lou turned the bird over and began to feel around the abdomen. She found the slit. Rena was breathing over Lou's shoulder as Lou extracted a slender tube of black plastic, a pen cap. "There's paper inside," she said.

Rena took the pen cap. Using her pocket knife, she pried the paper out. Everyone watched as she unrolled it. The words were clearly legible. She handed it to Christina. "What does it say?"

Christina held the yellowed note flat against the porch railing and read it, first in Greek, then in English. *"Villains on my tail. I will lure them away. The paintings are safe with Uncle Aristotle."*

Christina looked at Rena. "Did Uncle Antoni write this?"

259

"Yes."

"Do you know what it means?"

"Yes, I know what it means." She and Lou exchanged glances. "But I don't know who Uncle Aristotle is. Do you?"

Christina shook her head. She asked Basilis.

"My mother's brother," Basilis replied. "She had a brother named Aristotle, but he's been dead for thirty or forty years. He died of tuberculosis."

"There's no other Uncle Aristotle?" Lou asked. "Who else could he be referring to?"

"Stavros had a tomb built for him," Basilis said. "For some reason, he didn't want him in the earth."

"A tomb!" Lou shouted the words as Christina finished the translation. She was looking excitedly at Rena.

Rena turned to Christina. "Ask him where the tomb is."

Basilis replied, "About ten kilometers from here. At the cemetery just outside of Triti. It's the only decent cemetery in the area. Our parents are there, too, and so is —" He stopped. Christina translated, Basilis watching Rena.

"My father?" Rena said.

"Yes, and Stavros."

Rena laughed sadly. "They're together," she said. "Both of them, and the paintings."

"Is that what the note means?" Christina asked. "That the missing paintings are in Aristotle's tomb?"

"I think that's what it means," Rena said. "It's all making sense now." She was squeezing the pen cap between her fingers. "Those bastards must have figured my father would come to his village. They came here and they found Stavros. They tried to make a deal with him and ended up killing him. Then they must have seen Dad in the truck and Dad probably spotted them and ran to the little house."

Lou was nodding vigorously.

"My father knew they were coming. He knew it when I was there at the little house, when he put the note in the bird."

Christina stared at the paper.

"So your father had already hidden the paintings before he arrived at the little house," Lou said. "He knew the thieves were after him."

"He tried to lure them away," Rena said.

"Yes, that was his plan, apparently. And he sent you to tell Stavros in case . . . so Stavros would know. But the killers had already gotten to Stavros." Christina looked from one to the other as they spoke.

"I bet I know what happened," Rena said. She grimaced. "I bet when they found my father in the little house, after I had left, I bet they showed him the arm . . . and . . ."

"Trying to scare him into telling them where the paintings were."

". . . And then my father . . . I bet he flipped out. God, his brother! He loved him so much."

"So he attacked the killers," Lou said.

"And they —"

"Yes, they hit him, hit him on the head, and the secret died with him." Lou rubbed her chin. "The paintings may still be there," she said.

The ten kilometer drive felt like fifty. The caretaker showed them to the vault. It was simple and solid, its corners of Ionian columns in bas relief. The caretaker unlocked the door and stood outside while the three women entered.

A marble coffin rested on a raised platform. Between it and the east wall, leaning against the wall and against each other, were canvas-wrapped packages of various sizes, tied with old twine.

"I'll be damned," Rena said. "I wonder if they're still in good condition."

Lou carefully unwrapped one of the smaller packages as the other women watched. The caretaker peeked around the edge of the portal.

Lou held up the painting. It was a Delacroix. A young child, a female, sitting on a man's knee, both figures looking very happy.

Rena stared at the pair in the painting. "This one must have belonged to my father."

"I imagine the museum will know," Lou said. "We need a Brinks truck."

"What you got in there?" the caretaker called.

Christina translated the question.

"Tell him family papers," Lou said. "Let's lock these back up in here and get to a telephone."

Before they left the cemetery, Rena visited the grave of her father. Flowers grew around it, wild and beautiful. She stood there a long time looking at the silent stone and the flowers.

The truck that came the following day, though not owned by Brinks, was armored and well-guarded. Lou and Rena and Christina followed it to the Hellenic Art Museum in Athens and spoke with the curator, Mr. Tatoulis. He checked the records. All the papers were in order and, he added, a reward was due those who recovered the museum's paintings.

The procedures took the rest of that day and part of the next. When they were finished, ten paintings, those belonging to Rena's aunt and mother, were to be shipped to the Art Institute in Chicago for safe-keeping, and the other five restored to the Hellenic Museum where they belonged. The reward, a check for eighty-five hundred dollars, was given to Rena and Lou.

"Want to go around the world?" Lou asked, holding the check.

"I'd rather go home," Rena said.

CHAPTER TWENTY NINE

Rena and Casey talked for hours. Casey needed to hear it all, every detail. She was fascinated, though her heart ached for what Rena had been through.

"Isn't the human mind amazing. You wrapped up the idea in a tight little package and stored it away in the back of your mind for years. But it's like the package had a couple of strings sticking out from it."

They were in Rena's living room snuggled under a blanket on the sofa. The wind whistled outside the windows. It was snowing.

"One of the strings," Casey continued, clearly intrigued by her own analogy, "got pulled when sex was involved."

Rena put her cheek against Casey's. "Pull my string."

Casey pulled Rena's earlobe. "Another one got pulled when Pat died."

"You have sexy nostrils."

"It's fascinating. And you knew just enough about the package to know you didn't want to unwrap it."

Rena traced a path on Casey's nose. "They go out and around and then they attach right here just perfectly."

"You couldn't do it alone. *I* couldn't help you. Dr. Kepper could only help in a limited way. You needed something else, someone who you could trust and depend on completely and look up to and . . . you needed someone who would be like your father to you. That's what it took to get you to do it, to unwrap the package. Don't you think, Rena? Is that what Lou represented and why you were able to —"

"Can I stick my tongue in your mouth?"

Casey pulled the blanket over their heads. "You can stick your tongue in my anything-you-want."

Rena stuck her tongue in Casey's ear. "Mm-m, honeydew ears. Delicious. What does your neck taste like?"

Casey squirmed as Rena nibbled.

"I'm so hungry," Rena said. "I want to eat you upstairs. I love to eat in bed."

Casey uncovered their heads. "You know what?"

"What?" Rena cupped Casey's breast beneath the blanket.

"I'm scared."

Rena cocked her head. "Really? Why?"

"I don't know. It's just . . . I can't believe this is really happening. That you're back, really back, and free, and with me, and . . ."

Rena stood and pulled Casey with her. "Come into my parlor."

Casey chuckled. "Are you a spider?"

"Maybe," Rena murmured. "Are you a fly?"

"I'm flying."

They made love fast and slow and lovingly. "You fit perfectly in my arms." Rena was still puffing. "Isn't that amazing? I guess we were meant for each other."

"I guess we were. I want to go down on you again."

"I want you to."

They were atop the down-filled quilt on the heated waterbed. Casey opened Rena's legs, kissed and nibbled her thighs. She rolled her index finger and her middle finger around in her mouth, moistening them until they were almost drippy, then walked them around Rena's vulva, lingering at the entrance, going in, exploring

264

leisurely, then doing the same with her tongue. "Mm-mm, num." She licked and sucked as Rena writhed with pleasure and happiness. Taking Rena deeply into her mouth, sucking, sucking, and Rena gasping, clinging, twisting, soaring, soaring, though she did not fly to the height.

It was three a.m. when the lovemaking came to a satisfied exhausted stop. Rena felt content, happy, loved, safe, having shared the closeness, the excitement, the pleasure, and having shared Casey's orgasms, though she had none of her own. "It doesn't matter," she insisted. "Truly trivial. I couldn't be more satisfied." She kissed Casey's neck.

"I'm loving you, Rena." They were wrapped together. "I'm very happy."

"You are wonderful, Casey Grant. Thank you for being. Thank you for hanging in. I love you."

Less than a week into the new semester at Rena's college, the Art Institute notified her that the paintings had arrived. Rena's mother insisted that Rena keep them. "If anything should be yours, it is those paintings," Maria said repeatedly. "I know your father would have wanted that. I want it. Do with them what will make you happy. I love to think of you as a wealthy woman. Sell them, if you please. Buy yourself a nice big car and a new house with a swimming pool. Whatever you want, my *kukla*."

Collectively the four paintings were valued at six-hundred and twenty-five thousand dollars. The magnitude of it overwhelmed Rena. And when, as a reward for recovering the paintings that belonged to her, her Aunt Eleni gave her an additional fifty thousand dollars, and would not hear Rena's protest, Rena could only sigh and look aghast.

"I thought I would just return to my old life," she told Casey.

"With some new additions," Casey said.

"I'm going to keep teaching."

"Good. You enjoy it."

"It feels great to be back at work. I'm getting the new questionnaires together."

"Displaced rural women?"

"Mm-hm. You're my pearl of a woman. I love you."

"Will it go to your head? Being rich?"

"Probably. There's something I've been meaning to mention to you."

"Mention away, darling." Casey put her screwdriver down and gave Rena her full attention. "It's about the paintings. I gave two of them away — to Lou."

"Oh." Casey picked up the screwdriver again.

"I thought you might not like it."

"It's your decision."

"She saved my life."

"Yes. I . . . sure, I understand. Rena, are you still — How are you feeling about Lou these days?"

Rena handed Casey the washer she needed. "She'll always be special to me. Always. But I'm in love with you."

"Yes, you are, aren't you?" Casey was beaming. "And you know what? I knew it all along. Even when you were with Pat and blew me off the way you did, even when you were depressed and then so enthralled with Lou . . . I always knew we'd get together. It's so right. It had to be."

"I agree. We're very lucky lesbian dykes."

"We're lucky people. Let's have a party."

They embraced passionately, hands going to each other's crotches. Rena got very aroused, felt very excited and joyful being with Casey, but never in all their lovemaking did she experience the full pleasure and release of sexual climaxing. It bothered Casey more than Rena.

Lou was very busy with her counseling work in town. She'd neglected her practice during her "Rena period," and was back into it full swing. It felt good having her house to herself again. The only pea under her mattress was Trish. When Lou had told her what they'd learned in Greece, Trish had not been in the least convinced that all was well with Rena Spiros. "I don't buy it," she had said. "I know what I saw and what I sense. No way was it all fantasy."

Trish made Lou go over and over the story. She wrote frantically as Lou spoke and then went away until the next day. "To put it all together," she had said.

"But," Lou had objected, "the evidence is overwhelming."

"The evidence is open to interpretation," Trish had responded.

The next day when Trish returned, she and Lou were barely seated at the dining room table when Trish began presenting her case. "I'll start with your so-called eyewitness," she said, scoffingly. "By his own admission, he isn't exactly Mr. Morality and Truth."

Trish had laid out a sheet of paper on the table, but she didn't look at it. "You get this old guy feeling sorry for Rena, telling him she thinks she's responsible for the killings. He believes this is absurd so he says what he says because he figured it would help Rena. No skin off his teeth to lie for a worthy cause."

"Oh, come on. He obviously told the truth."

"The guy very likely did witness *something* that day," Trish responded, "but not the actual murder." She scratched vigorously behind her ear. "The part I'm not really sure of is whether Rena actually buys his story or not."

"Well, my friend," Lou replied warmly, "unlike *some* of my favorite people, Rena has now seen the light." She looked intently at Trish. "Trish, I heard him. The man was credible. What he said was true. He saw Stavros murdered by two men."

Trish's eyes flashed. "He seemed credible to you because he said just what you wanted to hear, Lou."

Lou shook her head. "He had details of the conversation. And it all made sense. Those two men were after the paintings. They tried to make a deal with Stavros but Stavros balked at part of it. They argued and ended up killing him. Nikos had all the details."

"His story's full of holes." Trish glared her determination. "Do you think a person who just watched someone get offed and mutilated is going to go into his house and start cleaning up the goddamn kitchen? I mean, really, no matter how much of a nag his wife is or how intimidated he is by her, he's not going to do that."

"Sure he is. He was operating on automatic."

"He watches his next door neighbor get murdered and he never says a word, doesn't tell the police. What kind of a creep is the guy?"

"A frightened one."

"We believe what we want to believe, I guess," Trish said. "Or what we *need* to believe. I think I'm in a better position than you to be objective about this."

Lou started to say something.

"Sh-h," Trish said. "Listen. Here's how I figure it. This Nikos guy is hanging around his kitchen cooking a batch of feta cheese or whatever and he hears that his neighbor has company. Being a nosy s.o.b. he sneaks outside for a ringside seat. He listens to their conversation, hears them talking about cargo and stuff. They argue and he's getting a voyeur's kick out of it. Then his wife screams for him to get his ass inside. He splits. In the meantime, the boys finish their negotiating and the two guys leave to go get the paintings where Stavros told them they were hidden — a town called Kalamata."

"Correction: They didn't believe Stavros, about the paintings being in Kalamata, and that's why they —"

"Wait!" Trish glared. "You're right that they might not have believed him. They wanted Stavros to come with them to Kalamata, but when Stavros refused they decided to go without him. They could always visit Stavros again if it turned out he had lied to them. So they make their exit, but no sooner are they gone than Rena arrives. She's in a frenzy, feeling totally rejected by her father because she'd just been with him in his little house and he gave her a shove and told her to get lost. She has Grandpa's gun. She sees Stav by the woodpile and she raises the gun sight to her demented eye and fires. Then she grabs the saw and slices off her uncle's arm as a gift for Dad. She wraps the arm in the tarp and flees. That's when Rena's mom arrives on the scene. In the meantime Rena is off somewhere stashing the arm and the gun and probably cleaning the blood off herself. Rena's mother gets an eyeful of dead Stavros and screams bloody murder. This brings the neighbor back out. He sees the corpse and, naturally, he *infers* that it was the two guys who did it. What else would he think? He didn't see Rena do it, though he did see her running away afterwards."

"He saw some village kid."

"Right, Rena the village kid. The little lizard slipped in and out, struck and slithered away. Now when this kind-hearted Nikos hears from you a quarter of a century later that sweet, pretty, half-orphaned Rena dear is tearing herself apart with guilt about the killings, he does what he thinks is his good deed. He tells his story."

Lou started to interrupt, but Trish pushed on. "Except he embellishes it a bit. He says he saw more than he actually did. He says he saw the actual murder even though he didn't." Trish sat back triumphantly. "That's what I think of your eyewitness."

Lou shook her head.

"Rena did it," Trish said adamantly.

"What an imagination you have. Trish, I hate to bother you with facts, but what about the paintings? I take it you at least don't deny that a couple of men were in the village trying to get the paintings."

"Of course they were there. Their presence is not in dispute. They made a deal with Stavros, apparently agreeing to split the profits from the paintings. Stavros told them the paintings were somewhere in the town of Kalamata. So they give up on trying to get Stavros to come with them and they leave. They're on their way out of the village to go to Kalamata when they see the truck, the one Rena's father used to transport the paintings. Since they already suspect Stavros might be lying about the paintings being in Kalamata, they break into the truck figuring the paintings might be there. The truck's empty. We know — though they didn't — that the paintings were already hidden in the tomb."

"You really think you can twist the facts until they fit your ridiculous obsession," Lou spat scornfully.

"Try to keep listening." Too excited to sit, Trish got up and began pacing as she spoke. "Now I have to backtrack a little, back before Stavros was killed. Soon after the two art smugglers got to the village, Rena's father arrived. He thought he'd gotten there first, before the crooks, but he hadn't. They were already talking with Stavros, which is just what Rena's father didn't want to happen. He left the truck where they'd see it to lure them to him. OK, so Antoni is waiting at the little house for a confrontation with his pursuers. But who shows up instead?"

269

Trish, who had been walking circles around the dining room table, now stood directly in front of Lou. "Little Rena. This is the famous *first visit* to the little house." She started pacing again. "He tells her to get the hell out of there. She feels totally rejected and devastated. She flips out and decides to kill her uncle. Which she does. Then she goes to the river and feels miserable until she masturbates and cheers herself up. She wonders if she really did kill her uncle. Remember, the kid is in a real deranged state. She goes to her grandmother's to find out if Stavros is dead and her mother tells her he sure is. Oh, no. Now she's sure her dad will be very annoyed at her. She runs to him. He's still nervously awaiting the arrival of the art thieves and again tells her to get out, but this time he also tells her to bring the message to Stavros. *The secret is in the bird.* She leaves, totally rejected and totally crazy. She goes and retrieves the severed arm. She returns to the little house and shows her prize to Daddy. Daddy collapses in a state of shock and she bangs him over the head with the lamp."

Lou was nodding. "Beautiful," she said. "Masterpiece fiction."

Trish sat again at the table. She fingered the slip of paper, but said nothing.

"Rena never talked about *three* trips to the little house," Lou said.

Trish smiled sardonically. "Rena twisted a number of details, didn't she? And forgot others. He rejected her once; she killed the uncle. He rejected her again; she went and got the arm, freaked him out, then killed him. It's as good a theory as yours." Trish leaned back. "Interestingly," she added, "if Nikos had told the cops what he actually saw, that he saw the two men arguing with Stavros, those men might have taken the rap for what Rena did."

"Oh, silly Trish. Your story is absurd." Lou shook her head slowly back and forth. "You really are obsessed. What do you have on that piece of paper?"

"A chart." Trish had her palm resting on it. "It's called, *The Crucial Hour.*" She looked at Lou. "It documents who was where when and proves Rena had the opportunity and means to do the killings. We already know she had the motive."

"Let me see that." Lou reached for the paper. She read it silently for several minutes. "You're right up to a point," she said, "but then you deviate pathetically from reality. I should make my own chart. Let me show you where you're right and where you're wrong."

They both hunched over the paper.

"*Twelve noon: Stavros is at his parents' house,* you say. *Rena is playing somewhere in the village. Antoni is en route from the cemetery to Kaftarei. The crooks are en route to Kaftarei.* I agree with all this," Lou said.

"Next, *Twelve-ten: Crooks arrive at Stavros' parents' and start talking with him; Rena is still hanging out somewhere in the village; Antoni is still on his way.* No problem with this." Lou had her finger on the page to mark her place.

"Next entry: *Twelve-twenty: Antoni arrives at the outskirts of the village, parks the truck and goes to his little house.* Right, that's what the shepherd said. *Stavros is still with the crooks and Nikos is eavesdropping. Rena is on her way to the little house.* I have no problem with twelve-twenty," Lou said. She looked at Trish. "This is clever. I like it."

"Thank you, Lou," Trish said sarcastically.

Lou went on to the next entry. "*Twelve-twenty-five: Rena is at the little house being told by her father to go away.* OK, I agree, but you left out that he's also telling her to take the message to Stavros."

"No, that comes later," Trish said.

"Our first disagreement. And we were doing so well. For twelve-twenty-five, you also have *Stavros still with the crooks,* and *Nikos still spying on them.* That's fine. Ah, but here we diverge again. You say at twelve-thirty *Nikos goes inside his house.* This is wrong, Trish, he went inside later, after the murder, at twelve-thirty-five."

"What's five minutes between friends?" Trish said.

"Now from this point on our versions really diverge." Lou got a pen from the holder on the table. "You have for twelve-thirty-five that *Rena arrives at her grandparents and kills Stavros.* This is a rather significant error." Lou began to write on the paper.

"Don't mess up my chart."

"I only want to improve it, Trish."

"Don't write on it."

"All right." Lou put the pen aside. "In fact, Trish, at twelve-thirty-five, Rena, rather than killing anyone is over at the river at her very pleasant nest spot. She's there being angry and masturbating and fantasizing and all that."

"How much you wish that were so."

"The rest of your twelve-thirty-five seems OK except for the major omission — the crooks killing Stavros. That should go right here." Lou tapped the paper with her finger tip. "Then you have the two crooks leaving Stavros and heading out of the village. I agree. And you have Antoni at the little house awaiting the arrival of the crooks. I agree with this too." She looked at Trish. "You know, some people would find this chart business boringly obsessive."

"They wouldn't make good detectives."

"At twelve-forty, you say that the crooks find the truck, search it, and leave town. Tsk-tsk," Lou chided, "another major omission. The crooks stop at the little house before they leave town, Trish. You left that out. They stop at the little house and they show Antoni his brother's arm. Only instead of being compliantly talkative as the crooks had hoped, Antoni attacks them. And they kill him."

"Nope," Trish said. "At that point Antoni still has a little while yet to live. He's still at the little house waiting for the crooks who end up never coming. They're already on their way to Kalamata hoping the information they got from Stavros is accurate."

Lou shook her head. "And also at twelve-forty, you have Rena busily hiding things. A gun. An arm. And cleaning blood off herself. No, Trish, at twelve-forty Rena is still having fantasies at the river."

"She doesn't go to the river until twelve-forty-five," Trish said.

"Now you skip to one o'clock when you have Rena going to her grandparents and seeing if Stavros is dead. This is true. Her mother attests to it. See, we do agree on some things. But you think Antoni is still at the little house, alive, and nervously awaiting the arrival of the crooks. Unfortunately, in fact, by one o'clock the crooks have already arrived and Antoni is quite dead. You, on the other hand, think he died between one-ten and two. You have Rena returning to the little house between those times. *Antoni pushes Rena and tells her to go deliver the bird message to Stavros.* And then *Rena —* you

272

don't have this part down but I'm sure you're seeing her eyes looking very evil at this point — *Rena takes the lamp and bludgeons her father to death*. In fact, Trish, Rena does go to the little house sometime after one and before two. She finds her father already dead. The end."

Trish sighed. She was feeling very alone. "Like I said, the facts are open to interpretation." She took her chart, folded it and put it in her pocket. "The crooks may have had the motive, opportunity and means to kill Stavros and Antoni, but so did Rena, Lou. You think the two art thieves did it. I think Rena did."

"Rena did nothing."

"She did Stav and her poor daddy," Trish retorted, "and then, years later, she did Pat."

"You can't really believe all this," Lou said impatiently. "You certainly must know that the crap about her killing Pat was complete and total fabrication — yours. Rena was so suggestible and guilt-laden she would have confessed to anything at that point. You told her she killed Pat and how she did it and she simply nodded."

"She killed them," Trish said.

"You're dead wrong," Lou replied.

"You could have been," Trish spat. "Dead, I mean. Because of being so wrong about her." She sighed. "Well, in a way it doesn't matter. You made it back from Greece. That's the important thing. Believe me I was relieved to see you." Trish brushed the hair back from her narrow forehead. "I guess her attachment to you never got to be quite like the others — Rebecca and Pat. And I think I know why."

"Oh, really? Trish, you know so damn much. So tell me why."

"Because you never made love to her."

Lou smiled victoriously.

"I don't believe it!" Trish shook her head vehemently. "If you did, she'd be here right now. She'd be so attached to you, you'd never get rid of her — and live to tell about it. You really made love with her?"

Lou nodded.

273

Trish sat silently, thinking. "How'd you do it? I mean, were you, you know, did you do the dominating stuff? Did you top her?"

Lou raised her eyebrows. "Do I ever kiss and tell?"

"You didn't. Of course, that's why. I bet she was disappointed. You were smart, Lou. If you'd have done it her way, you'd be in big trouble." Trish shrugged. "I wonder who the next one will be. She'll meet some other powerful dyke one of these days and it will start again."

"You and I used to see eye to eye on things," Lou said, smiling.

"That's when you weren't half blind," Trish rejoined.

"I think we're at an impasse, friend. Think about it some more. Put all the data together more rationally. Then we'll talk again. Maybe you'll change your mind."

"I won't change my mind."

A few days later, Trish called on Lou once more. "I have to admit," she said, "that you do have a lot of rational support for your perspective."

Smiling, Lou offered her a cup of coffee.

"It *is* very unlikely that a ten-year-old would murder. I'll grant you that." Trish blew into her cup.

"Good."

"And even if Rena *were* so inclined, it *is* unlikely that she could have pulled it off. For one thing, wielding a power saw couldn't be easy for a ten-year-old kid. They're pretty heavy."

"That's right."

"And even if she were physically capable of doing the killing, and psychologically capable, how could she pull it off with no one the wiser? Surely, there would have been some giveaway. Blood on her clothes, for example. Or evidence that she had gotten rid of a bloody set of clothes or washed them out. Something. And her confessions — fabrications. A ten-year-old fantasizer makes more sense then a ten-year-old murderer."

"I agree."

"And furthermore, we have a much more probable explanation for the deaths of her father and uncle."

"The art thieves."

"Yes. They had motive and opportunity. Clearly someone was after the paintings. We know that for sure. It isn't far-fetched to believe those people would kill to get them."

"Not far-fetched at all," Lou concurred.

"And then there's the grand finale. The eyewitness. He completely corroborates your version."

Lou nodded.

"And what's the evidence on the other side?" Trish continued. She sipped her coffee. "Not much. We have Rena's first confession, about killing her father and uncle. Now retracted. We have her second confession, about Rebecca and Pat, elicited by me in a leading way while Rena was highly vulnerable and suggestible. So the confessions don't mean much. Then we have my theory to explain motivation."

"That she was so upset when she believed her father didn't want her anymore..."

"Yes, but enough to kill?"

"Not that upset... unless that evil —"

"Yes, her eyes," Trish said. "That's a biggie. Demented eyes." She pictured Rena's eyes and couldn't help shuddering. "But that's certainly not solid, court-admissable evidence," she said matter-of-factly.

"It's pretty subjective."

"So, OK," Trish said. "What's the logical conclusion? What does the evidence suggest, the preponderance of evidence? That Rena Spiros is no killer."

"Exactly." Lou was smiling warmly at Trish.

Trish shook her head. She took another drink of coffee. "But I know she did it!"

Lou rolled her eyes.

"I know she's dangerous." Trish swung her arm, almost knocking her cup over. "Or was, at least. *Was* dangerous. Maybe not anymore. Maybe now that she believes she's innocent, the evil in her is smothered. Maybe she'll no longer get hooked by dominating women and so no longer be susceptible to evil murderous impulses

275

if she fears her love object is going to leave her. Maybe that's all over now."

Trish was nodding vigorously, no longer aware of Lou's presence. "Even if it is over though," she continued, "shouldn't she be punished for what she did — killing three people, for Christ's sake, and injuring a fourth? Should she just be free to live, never prosecuted, no longer bothered by any guilt?"

Trish stared intently at the floor. "But what good would punishment do? Revenge? That sucks. Would spending time in jail or a mental institution serve any useful purpose, do any good for anyone? Only if she's still dangerous," Trish answered. "Only then would confining her make any sense. Is she still dangerous?"

Lou said nothing as Trish continued her monologue.

"Probably not. If she's no longer attracted to dominating women, to those father-uncle symbols, then she probably no longer is dangerous. I suppose it's OK then for her to just live out her life and for no one, not even her, to know she's killed."

Trish, finished, felt exhausted. Her cup was empty.

"More coffee?" Lou asked. "This is very hard for you, isn't it?"

"I think I'm done with it. This helped. It helped to talk it out."

"Good. I only wish that —"

"And I really want to let it go. I'm tired of Rena Spiros. Would you like to play a game of backgammon?"

"I'll whip your ass."

"You'll eat those words."

CHAPTER THIRTY

A group from De Nova came to Chicago for Casey and Rena's party, including Lou. Trish was not among them. De Nova was well in the black now and everyone knew where the money had come from.

"We probably would have lost everything if it hadn't been for you," Pete told Rena. "Now we're even going to expand, cultivate more fields, build more cabins. Did you know that?"

"Yes, I heard." Rena was dressed in sleek black pants and a loose white shirt. She had consciously tried to look very sexy for the party. "You know, though, that it was Lou's doing. I gave her the paintings and it was her choice to —"

"I know, I know, but we love you. We're naming the new apple grove *Rena's Rows.*"

Rena laughed. "That's neat." She could see Lou from the corner of her eye. She felt the quickening of her pulse. "I figured she'd use the money for De Nova."

Suddenly there was a sharp squeeze on the back of Rena's neck. "Well, well, so this is how it ends," Kate said, still keeping her hand on Rena's neck.

Pete moved away. Every room of the house was crowded with women. Music filled the air and there was dancing upstairs.

Rena felt uncomfortable with Kate. "How've you been?" she asked.

"You gave her your fortune."

"That doesn't concern you, Kate."

"Ha-ha-ha! I should have known it wouldn't be any different with you. Well, did you get to fuck her at least?" Kate lit a cigarette and offered Rena one.

Rena accepted the cigarette, but said nothing.

"You still have the hots for her, don't you?"

"Have you tried the punch?" Rena asked.

"You'll never get over her. I warned you. How's Casey?"

"Casey's fine. I'm fine. You're the one with the problem, Kate."

"Yeah, yeah, I know. There she is now. I bet you'd like nothing better then to go off somewhere with her and drop your pants."

"You're projecting."

"That, too." Kate laughed. "Welcome to the club."

Lou joined them then, standing between them, a hand on each of their shoulders. Kate grew suddenly subdued. "Hi, Lou." Her voice sounded almost sweet.

"They're watching dirty movies upstairs," Lou said. "So you bought a video recorder, eh, Spiros?"

"They're not dirty, they're erotic," Rena said.

"Oh, right." Lou laughed. "I keep having trouble telling things apart."

"Like giving and getting," Kate said. Her voice was no longer sweet.

"Well, Kate, hello." Lou chuckled. "At first I didn't recognize you. I thought you were one of the people at the party."

"I am one of the —"

"You're looking very fetching this evening, Miss Rena." Lou took Rena in from head to foot.

Rena hoped the dim lights covered her blush. She had seen Lou only twice since their return from Greece. Once, she and Casey had visited De Nova for the day. Lou had been with a crowd of other women. Rena had felt drawn to her, but almost shy. The other time was in Chicago. Lou had called her from a bar and Rena came and met her for a drink. Lou had seemed very at ease, but Rena felt foolishly nervous and excited to be with her again. The conversation had been light and brief. Other friends of Lou's came and Rena had soon left.

Strangely, Lou had been on Rena's mind more and more as time passed. The fantasies, the sexual ones, had returned, despite the growing love between herself and Casey. They're separate, she thought, the two relationships. I love Casey. Lou . . . I don't know, there's still something there . . . something unfinished.

"You're looking rather hot yourself for an older person," Rena said. She was not feeling the flippancy.

Kate laughed. "Oh, that's rich. *Older person.* Great." She walked away.

"*She* hasn't changed any," Rena said.

"And how about you? How are you doing?" Lou touched Rena's lips with a celery slice.

Rena's lips parted and Lou slipped the stalk into her mouth, slowly, sensually.

Rena took a bite. "I'm OK," she said.

"Teaching's going well?"

"Yes."

"And Casey?"

"Real well." Rena looked to the side.

"But?"

"What do you mean, *but?*"

Lou narrowed her eyes and looked deeply at Rena. They had moved to the corner of the living room. "I don't know. Something's going on."

Rena shrugged.

"Does it have to do with me?" Lou asked.

"Egotist."

"Does it?"

279

Rena shrugged again. "Could be."

"Tell me."

"Well, no . . . I don't think . . . no, there's no need."

"You're being mysterious. Am I supposed to guess?"

"No. How are things in Wisconsin? Made any unusual decisions for anyone lately?"

"How are you feeling towards me?" Lou asked, still penetrating Rena with her eyes.

"Disappointed." Rena's hand went to her lips. She looked flustered. "No, I didn't mean . . . I don't know why I said that."

"Disappointed about what?"

Rena shook her head.

"About the way it was at the nest with us?" Lou asked. "The lovemaking?"

Rena knew the soft lighting was not sufficient to conceal the flush that was rising from her neck up across her cheeks. "I don't know what you mean," she stammered.

"That's it, huh? A real letdown. All those turn-on fantasies and all you got when the moment finally came was your basic tender screw."

"I think I need to go tend to things in the kitchen."

"Stay here!"

Rena didn't move. She was pressed against the drapes in the corner by the window.

"Rena, I think you ought to go back to Dr. Kepper. There are still things that you haven't —"

"What a big front you put on," Rena blurted.

"Front?" Lou looked more curious than upset.

"That's right. You're great with coming attractions but when it comes to the main feature, you're a dud." Rena turned away, then turned right back. "Oh, I'm sorry. I didn't . . . I've had a lot to drink." She began to move away.

Lou stopped her. "A dud, huh?"

"No, I didn't mean that. You're an excellent lover, Lou, very . . . you're just fine. Everything's fine. Why the hell are we talking about this?"

"You want to change the subject?"

280

"Yes. Change the subject, will you?"

"Did you get the letter from Christina?"

Rena leaned on the back of the sofa. "My cousin Christina? No, I didn't get any letter."

"You will. She's writing to let you know she's coming."

"Here? To Chicago? To the States?"

"To Wisconsin."

Rena's face darkened. "Oh, I see. She's coming to Wisconsin. She'll stay with you, I assume."

"That's right. I know you didn't talk to her much while we were in Greece, but she and I had several very important conversations. She's a bit confused about herself. Thought she was an old maid type. Resigned to a less-than-fulfilling emotional life. Now, she's not so sure. She thought coming to the States might help her resolve it."

"*She* thought! You had nothing to do with encouraging her to think that." Rena's voice dripped with sarcasm.

"I didn't *discourage* her."

"You bitch!"

"What?" Lou glared at her. Several people turned to look. "Let's go upstairs."

"There are people up there too," Rena said softly. "Just forget it."

"I don't just forget it when someone calls me a bitch — correction, when *you* call me a bitch."

"We could go down to the basement."

The basement had a partially finished room with a couple of old easy chairs and a table. They sat across from each other.

"OK, go on," Lou said.

Rena's mouth was an angry line. "It makes me sick that you're getting involved in Christina's life. Why are you doing it?" Rena turned her head. "As if I have to ask."

"You really do have an ax to grind with me, don't you?"

Rena started to cry. "Oh, God, I feel awful. After all you've done for me and I treat you like this. Shit." She tried to smile. "Look, I'm sorry. Please try to forget we had this conversation. Let's go back upstairs."

"I'm sorry you're upset."

"I know. I'll be fine. I think it's just the alcohol and all the people here and . . . I don't know. I'll be fine." She was standing. "Come on, let's hug and make up."

They hugged each other warmly.

"It really is good to see you," Rena said. "I'm still dealing with a little re-entry, but I'll be fine. Come on, I've got this wonderful pasta stuff that should be ready to come out of the oven now. I'll get you some."

The party was a great success. Rena drank a little more than she should have and was hung over the next day, but she and Casey agreed it was one of the best parties they'd ever been to, if they did say so themselves.

In the weeks that followed, Rena and Casey continued growing even closer. It seemed that the problems stemming from the past were gone. Rena felt free and happy and very very lucky.

And then she met Veda.

It was late February at the racquetball courts. Rena and her friend, Joyce, finished playing and turned the court over to the next players, two women. One of them was tall, dark complexioned, had a deep resonant voice, moved like a panther, and held Rena's eyes with her own black ones for several seconds. Rena was gone, enraptured. The excitement made her woozy. It was happening again. Everything else became background.

She went to the viewing area above to watch the woman play. The panther won every game as Rena knew she would. Rena couldn't move. Joyce left. Rena remained, transfixed, staring, fantasizing, her heart pounding. She tried to make herself leave, but she could not. When the women finished playing, Rena followed them to the locker room and started a conversation which she and Veda continued over coffee at a nearby shop. Rena was unable to stem the growing infatuation. Veda responded to Rena's obvious interest and they made a date for the following Saturday.

CHAPTER THIRTY ONE

Two nights later, Rena and Casey were going north on Lake Shore Drive after a movie. Casey was driving. "Where are you?" she asked.

"What?"

Casey laughed. "You've been distracted all evening. What are you thinking about?"

Rena felt herself flush and glanced at Casey to see if she had noticed. The fantasies wouldn't stop. It was Veda, then Lou, Veda again. "Oh, I don't know, just daydreaming."

"My place or yours tonight?"

Rena pulled the zipper of her jacket halfway down. She felt hot. "Would you mind just dropping me off, Case? I'm tired . . . I don't know, a little . . . a little crabby, maybe. I feel like being alone tonight."

"Oh? OK, hon." Casey moved to the right lane and took the Addison exit. "Do you want to talk about it?"

"Talk about what?"

Casey glanced at her. "Did something happen with you and Joyce the other day?"

"Joyce?"

"Yes, when you played racquetball. You've seemed a little upset or something since then."

"No, nothing happened." Rena tried to laugh. "She won two out of three. My ego can't take it."

"Bullshit. Really, Rena, what is it? I know something's bothering you." She was driving very slowly on Clark Street. A car pulled around and passed her.

Rena was silent for a while. "There's something I have to do Saturday. Yes, something is bothering me, Casey. I don't feel ready to talk about it." Rena felt her stomach tightening. "I will, but . . . it's something . . . I'm just not ready yet."

"You have to do something Saturday?"

"See someone. Oh shit. Look, I hate being mysterious, but I have to ask you to just . . . just let me take care of something. I . . . it's for both of us, but I just can't talk about it yet."

On Saturday, Rena drove to Wisconsin.

"I've missed you," Lou said. She took Rena's down jacket.

Rena could feel her stupid heart jumping around under her ribs as Lou's hand brushed hers.

"Look," Lou said, "I got a nice fire going for us. Want a drink?"

"Yes." Rena sighed deeply. "I think I need some tea."

"Tea?" Lou, still smiling, scrutinized her. "Hm-m. Maybe I should have built the fire up in the womb room."

"This will do." Rena sat on the sofa. "Actually, I'd rather have a Pepsi if you have any."

Lou brought their drinks. "So, what's going on? You said on the phone you needed to discuss something."

"Right." Rena hadn't been looking at Lou. She turned to her now. "Shouldn't we make some small talk first?"

Lou laughed. "Do you want to?"

"No."

"So, go ahead, then. Make big talk."

Rena sighed. She lit a cigarette, took a sip of Pepsi. "I met a woman."

"Oh?"

"I feel like I did when I first met you."

"Oh-oh."

"I'm scared, Lou. I'm afraid of what's going to happen."

"What's going to happen?"

"I can't do it to Casey. God, not again! I don't want to, but I'm afraid I'll have to. I can't get her out of my mind. Her name is Veda. She's . . . God, she's . . . I just feel overwhelmed by her, like . . ."

"Yes, like before, with the others."

"Right, you and the others. It ended with Rebecca because she ended it. It ended with Pat because she . . ."

"Yes. Because she died."

Rena drew on her cigarette. "It hasn't ended with you."

Lou was silent.

"In my fantasies about Veda, about her . . . dominating me, having power over me, you know, that stuff . . . it gets confused. She becomes you and . . . but, Lou, I'm in love with Casey, I really am."

"I believe it, Rena."

"I don't want to fuck it up. And yet . . . oh, shit! I thought it would go away. After my party . . . you remember, our talk and . . ."

"Yes, I remember."

"Well, after that, you were out of my mind but then I met this Veda and it all came crashing back. I think it's hopeless for me. The crooked beam, remember?" She laughed half-heartedly. "I've been thinking of talking with Casey, of telling her I don't think it can work with us. God, I don't want to do that. I love her so much, but sexually, I . . ."

Rena lapsed into a sad silence. Lou waited.

"I've been thinking maybe I could have both." Rena looked beseechingly at Lou. "I don't know if that's possible, but . . ."

"Both?"

"Casey and . . ."

"And Veda."

"No, not Veda. You! It's you I want. Veda's just a . . . Lou, don't you understand? Even though everything is going so well for me, there's this . . . like a gap, something missing or unfinished that . . ."

"And you think I can fill the gap."

Rena nodded. Her palms were slippery wet. "It's like this terrible need . . . a . . . a craving, a yearning . . ."

"That you want to satisfy with me."

"Yes."

"Sorry, Rena." Lou's tone was cool. "Maybe you should act it out with this Veda, or if you don't want that, work it out with Dr. Kepper."

Rena's shoulders slumped. She turned her back. "You don't give a shit about me," she said, pouting.

"Oh, God. Don't baby out, huh?"

"Kate said you were like this."

"Oh yeah, like what?"

"That you use people, stir them all up, get what you want, then dump them." Rena was facing Lou, sitting on the edge of the sofa seat. "You don't care where they are when you're finished with them. Especially if you have someone else lined up. A couple more weeks and *Christina* will be here. You'll have her so why should you give a shit about me."

Lou rolled her eyes. "Rena, you're acting like a jerk."

"People-user."

Lou laughed.

"It came out real well for you, didn't it?" Rena spoke loudly. "Your fiefdom, De Nova, is thriving, thanks to the money you wheedled out of me. And you're getting a new victim to experiment on, a foreign model this time." Rena's face was red with rage. "Oh, you're doing fine. As usual. Kate was right."

"That's enough, Rena." Lou's jaw was tight, her eyes hard.

"You know what the funny part is, though." She was standing, several yards away from Lou. "What's so funny about it is that you, Lou Bonnig, *power* personified, turn out to be a goddam pussy. The truth is, you're afraid of power. Real power. It scares the shit out of you!"

"Sit down, Rena."

286

"Fuck you, Bonnig. You can't tell me what to do, you chickenshit bitch! You're afraid — afraid to really — you're weak, Lou. Really, a phony. You're nothing but a phony, weak, lily-livered coward —"

"Shut up!"

"Truth stings, doesn't it? Lying, sissy, coward. Big tough Lou. Watch the bully cringe when it really comes down to it, when her bluff is called."

"You're pushing it, Rena." Lou, too, was standing.

"Ah, are you scared, baby, chicken, yellow-belly, pussy?" Rena came up to her threateningly. They stood face-to-face.

"Your behavior is disgusting," Lou spat.

"Your phoniness is disgusting, you power-pussy." Rena poked Lou's chest with her finger.

Lou grabbed her wrist. "That's it. I've had it." Her tone was as cold as her eyes. "So you think I'm afraid, do you? *Power-pussy*, huh?" Her lip was curled in an angry sneer. "I ought to give you a real taste of my power, little girl. Maybe I will. You've pushed it a bit too far. You've irritated me, Rena, and that's dangerous." She held Rena's wrist tightly. "You think you want it all, don't you? And you want it from me. You want it so bad. You want the whips and ropes and chains. Is that right? Is that what you want, my little bottom? Maybe you'll get all of that, Rena my dear. What else? Hot wax? Is that part of your little fantasy? Leather and handcuffs? Is that the power you want? OK, you want to play with power, you got it!" Lou released her wrist. "Get on your knees!"

Rena obeyed immediately, looking up at Lou fearfully. The crotch of her corduroys was gushy wet.

CHAPTER THIRTY TWO

Lou ordered Rena to stay in the living room. Rena felt frightened of what she had provoked, and at the same time, breathlessly eager for it. Lou returned in a few minutes with a bottle of beer. She draped herself onto the big armchair, her blue jean clad leg slung over one arm. She looked at Rena who sat on the floor several yards from her. "I own you," she said matter-of-factly.

Rena nodded and looked away.

"You've had a lot of fantasies about this, haven't you?"

"Yes." She could not look at Lou.

"I want to hear them. All of them. In detail. Come over here, next to me."

Rena hurried to Lou's side, sitting on the floor next to Lou's chair. Lou rested her hand casually on Rena's head and took a slug from the beer bottle. "Speak, girl. Start with the very first one. I want to hear them all."

Rena's mouth was dry. She ran her tongue over her lips. "Fantasies about you?"

"That's right. About me. Start with the first one."

Rena smiled, remembering. "It was at the *Big House*. I was there waiting for you, that first night. You were going to come and play poker. I was waiting at the window. You were going to show me the photographs and I started to imagine how you would talk to me . . . that you would tell me what to do and that I would have some trouble doing it exactly right, and then you would . . ." Rena was staring at Lou's leg as she spoke, excitedly aware of Lou's hand on her head.

"And then I would what? Go on. No hesitation. You're to tell me all of it." Lou's fingers tightened slightly on Rena's hair. "Understand?"

"Yes," she whispered. The current shot from Lou's fingertips, down Rena's neck and through her body. "That you would . . . punish me . . . for not doing it right."

"I see. Yes, you *need* to be punished."

Rena closed her eyes, nodding.

"Why?" Lou demanded. "Punished for what?"

"I . . . for . . . for . . . I don't know."

"Yes you do. Tell me, Rena. Say it!"

"For what I did to them . . . for . . ."

"For what?"

"For killing them." She looked at Lou, eyes wide, shaking her head.

"You still —"

"No. No, I know I didn't but . . ."

"But it feels like you did."

"It's so stupid."

Lou nodded. "I think only your top layer is convinced of your innocence. It didn't get down to the core yet."

"I need it."

"Yes, you do. You should have been punished before, severely punished. Punished for your disobedience. Punished for those evil thoughts. You need it. You have to pay."

Rena's breathing was rapid.

"Isn't that right? That core part of you craves that punishment."

"Yes," Rena muttered breathlessly.

"You were bad."

"Yes."

"Of course," Lou said. "All right, go on. How would I punish you? Keep talking."

Rena talked for several minutes. "All right," Lou said. "Enough. I get the picture. Take your shoes and socks off," she ordered.

Rena obeyed immediately, not even forming a silent question about Lou's purpose or intent.

"That's good," Lou said. "You weren't good back then, though, were you? When you disobeyed your father?"

Rena's mind flashed to the nest.

"Now you'll pay."

"Yes." Rena's tone was breathy again, her voice pained.

Lou tossed Rena's jacket onto the floor next to her. "Now go out back and cut some branches. Nice flexible ones. Some thick, some thin."

Rena's mouth was open.

Lou grinned at her, nodding. "Strip the bark off," she added. "When you've got three or four good switches ready then get your tender little ass back here to this room and take off your clothes."

Rena was still sitting on the floor. Lou's eyes bore into her, shrinking her.

"This is it, Rena."

Rena nodded with fear and anticipation. Lou turned and left the room.

Rena pulled on her jacket and hurried outside. The cold air stung her cheeks and the frozen ground bit at the soles of her feet. She dashed to the barn where the tools were, found the small red-handled saw, the one she'd used in the past for pruning, and headed toward the woods.

Her feet were red and pinched from the cold when she brought the branches into the kitchen and, leaning over the sink, began shaving off the bark.

This is it. Lou's words echoed in her head. Finally, she thought. She swung one of the whips through the air listening to the whistle, wondering what it would actually feel like to have it slap against her skin, wondering if she could go through with it, knowing that she had to. She took the switches to the living room and laid them near the wall. She was picturing the rose tattoo.

She took off her jeans, her sweater, her T-shirt, her underpants, then stood near the fire, staring at the whips.

At the sound of footsteps, Rena's breathing quickened and when Lou entered the room, her whole body became tight. Lou wore a black tank top that clung to her breasts, and faded jeans that hugged her legs and rear. Around her waist was a black silk scarf. Rena's mouth opened as she looked at her and she felt unspeakably vulnerable. Her heart pounded and her mind was racing, full of doubts and fear, full of excited anticipation. She tried to make herself smaller, less noticeable. She could see Stavros' bushy-browed frown.

Lou moved toward her. Rena shuddered. Lou was next to her, reaching for her. She grasped one of Rena's nipples, lightly at first, then tightly until a tiny moan came from Rena's lips.

"I can do whatever I want to you." Lou reached to Rena's crotch and traced the triangle of hair with her middle finger. "And you have to take it. You have to pay the price."

Rena inhaled in quick gulps. Her mouth was powder dry, her heart pounding. She glanced to the left where the switches lay on the floor. Lou's eyes followed hers.

"You can't wait, can you?" Lou gave her a quick light anticipatory tap on her behind and Rena's muscles and bones liquified. "Over there." Lou beckoned toward the staircase.

Lou followed her, stopping to pick up the switches. She removed the scarf from her waist and tied Rena's wrists together. She tied the remaining tail of the scarf to the bannister, high up so that Rena's arms were stretched above her head, her back to Lou. Then Lou went upstairs.

Rena shivered as she waited. It was not cold that caused the shivering. Her body was warm, burning warm. She tugged on the bonds, wondering if she could free herself if she wanted to. She tested it, stretching her fingers toward the knots, but they would not reach.

"You can't get away." Lou stood above her on the stairs. She had added a black leather jacket to her outfit. "You really are totally in my control, Rena." Slowly she descended, the boots thudding on each stair, until she stood next to Rena. "You've been in my control before, but it was different then, wasn't it?"

Rena nodded.

"It wasn't quite enough then. This is the way you wanted it, isn't it?"

"Yes," Rena said. Her voice was hoarse. The scarf pulled on her wrists. Her body felt safely immovable. She could see that Lou had one of the switches in her right hand, and then could feel it gently sliding along her buttocks.

"I'm going to whip you now," Lou said softly. "You can't stop me." She patted Rena's rear. "I wonder if you can take it. You know you deserve it and you think you want it, but I wonder if you can really handle it."

Rena's brow was coated with perspiration. She wondered the same thing.

"You can beg me to stop but I will continue."

Rena felt the shudder up her spine.

"You can plead for mercy, but that will not move me."

Rena was trembling.

"If you find in your core that you have had enough, tell me that it's finished, that it's truly done, and then I'll stop. Just say, *It's finished.*" Lou came right up next to Rena and raised her chin with the handle end of the switch. "What will you say if you've truly had enough, if you need me to stop?"

"It's finished," Rena croaked. "I'll say, *It's finished.*"

"That's right."

Lou released Rena's chin, but kept her eyes captive. Grinning. She moved a few steps back. Rena's fear and anticipation intensified. Her tied hands rested on the bannister as she leaned forward, her feet apart, her naked body ready. Her heart beat blood rapidly through her tense muscles, her synapses snapped their electrical charges to every nerve. This was the moment. The finale. Uncle Stavros had prepared switches once. Finally it would happen.

The first blow stung her butt. She let out a sound that was a mix of fear and joy, pain, relief and release. She wasn't sure if it actually hurt. Her uncle was there, angry, stern. She couldn't believe it was happening. The second snap of the switch deepened the reality. Yes there was pain, but not ordinary pain. Not stubbed toe pain or dental probe pain. There should be another word for this — hot, consuming pleasure-pain, longed-for pain. With the third blow, Rena stopped thinking about words. The world of things and thoughts was gone.

Sensation took her away, transporting her. She entered the timeless, boundless whirl of pure feeling. It was OK to feel it. Expiation. Freeing pain. Her mind flamed with visionless pictures, deep colors, reds and violets. Lightning flashes came.

Her father was there. More and more, relentlessly, it continued, and the impact grew. She was totally engulfed, her head was spinning. She felt woozy, liquidy, hot. Liberated and filled. Filled, complete, intensely vibrantly alive and free at last. She seemed to hear music. There were a dozen suns rising and setting simultaneously. Every inch of her skin, every internal organ and every nerve was feeling it, overwhelmed by it. Her mind seemed to leave the earth. She floated upward, up, higher and higher. The music was soft and inviting. She floated over hills, rocky hills with olive trees and cypress. From high above the trees she saw them both. They were waiting for her, but as she came closer, one of them began to fade. Her father hugged her tightly, warmly, and she knew she was totally safe. He told her Uncle Stavros was gone. He said Stavros had gone away now and would not be back and that it was good. Everything was OK now. Rena understood. He was gone and it was over. Her father had his tablet of paper and he wrote a poem for Rena, telling her each line as he composed. Then they recited it together and laughed and hugged each other and Daddy told her that some faraway day she would come again and they would be together forever.

Rena felt the loosening, a total freeing. She was floating again, floating happily, free and happy. She only became aware of a world when she felt someone rubbing her wrists and supporting her limp body, moving her to the living room, laying her on something soft in front of a beautiful fire.

Strong hands smoothed cool cream over the hot skin of her buttocks. Lou's hands. Loving hands, caressing her, soothing her, slowly bringing her back from the middle of the past and the future to the beginning of now. The fire blazed and crackled.

Lou leaned over her. "Are you here?"

Rena's mouth was wide and slack. There were tears in her eyes. She could not speak.

"What's happening?" Lou asked. She stroked Rena's brow.

"Oh God . . ." Rena gasped for air, struggled for words. "It . . . it all happened." She sighed deeply. She looked at Lou. "It was you and then it was him. Both of them. It was total . . . he beat me, Stavros . . . that was you . . . yes, then held me . . . he said it was OK . . . it was you, my father." Rena was crying.

"It all happened."

"Yes."

"Atonement."

Rena nodded, wiping her eyes. "And forgiveness." She was sitting up now, looking for her cigarettes.

"Mm-m. Very powerful stuff."

"Powerful, climactic, freeing. It's amazing." Rena stood. She got her sweater and wrapped it around herself. She lit a cigarette and offered Lou one.

Lou shook her head. "I quit. Haven't had one in two weeks."

"Hey, good for you. Oh, wow, I'm flying." Rena raised her arms and danced about the room.

Lou went to the sofa. "Remember in Greece," she said. "Remember after you realized you weren't a murderer . . . how you talked about expecting some tremendous, powerful feeling, but that it wasn't there?"

Rena nodded vigorously. "Yes, that's it! It's here!" She bubbled. "This is the feeling. God, exactly. You know me so well." She went to Lou and hugged her lovingly and let the happy tears come. "You're wonderful."

Lou shrugged, smiling modestly. "You're not so bad yourself, Spiros."

Rena sat next to her on the sofa. Lou stroked Rena's knee.

"I think it's over." There was a new glow in Rena's eyes.

"It may well be," Lou said.

"It's such a good feeling. Light. Like I don't feel like I have to . . . to make up for anything, set anything right."

"You took care of it."

"*You* did."

"I helped."

"I owe you so much. I made you do it. You didn't want to but I made you."

"You convinced me it needed doing," Lou said. "I didn't have to do it."

"But you did. You're something very special, Lou Bonnig. Was it awful for you?"

"As a matter of fact, it was damn hard, one of the hardest things I've ever done."

Rena took Lou's hand.

Lou said, "You know what helped? I have a friend in Madison who talks with me about this kind of thing . . . power games . . . dominance and submission, and the sexual highs she gets. I think knowing her helped me take this step with you. She's a very committed feminist, but also one of the least rigid people I know. She went through hell for a time . . . trying to reconcile her needs with her philosophy. She ended up neglecting neither and accepting that some people will never make room for the apparent contradiction."

"Have you . . . Did you and she . . ."

"She talks with me about it, that's all. It's not my thing. There are other women she acts it out with."

"And it doesn't bother you, her involvement in it?"

"No. Yours we came to understand. You needed to. Those impulses in you were not what you wanted. They were ego-dystonic. It was something for you to be free of."

Rena nodded, closing her eyes a second, feeling very happy. "And your friend?"

"A different story entirely. She used to think she needed to understand it, but then she let go of that. She feels no more need to figure it out than I do to figure out why I'm a lesbian." Lou watched Rena extinguish her cigarette. "I like being a lesbian. It's mine and I enjoy it. It harms no one and I have a perfect right to be what I am, no matter how many people believe differently. My friend in Madison likes playing top and bottom with her similarly-inclined friends. It's her and she likes it and it harms no one and it's no one else's business, no matter how many people believe differently."

"I like how you think."

"Me too. If there's one thing I've learned, Rena, it's to live and let live. When someone clearly needs and wants my intervention in her life, and I think I can help, I'll do what I can. If they're doing OK with where they are, then I butt out, but fast."

"Even if what they're doing is politically incorrect?"

Lou laughed. "Save me from the judges."

"But people like your Madison friend are reproducing the oppression of the patriarchal power-over mentality." Rena smiled. "Did I say it right?" She laughed. "Freedom is so damned complex. People are. Life is. I can't believe we're having a political-value discussion right now."

"And you with no clothes on."

"This is as naked as I've ever been."

"I think it is."

"And I look at you now, Lou, and you know what I see? I see Lou Bonnig. Just Lou."

Lou raised her eyebrows.

"Do you know what I mean? I feel like I'm seeing you for who *you* are, not who I needed you to be. This is a first. Who you are is quite a bit, by the way," Rena added. "Lou is a lot. You're very real to me just being you."

"No more symbols, you mean?"

"It really feels gone. Done."

"No more Vedas?"

"Not a flicker. I think of her now and feel nothing. I don't get that little tingling feeling . . . that . . . no, nothing." Rena grabbed her T-shirt from the floor and put it on. "I do still feel some tingling, though. Maybe there's one compulsion I'm going to keep. It's one I hope never goes away." She began putting on the rest of her clothes.

"Casey?"

"Exactly. I can't wait to see her. Lou, you are my salvation. I love you. I'm going now."

"Beat and run, huh?"

Rena giggled. Lou laughed heartily.

Rena and Casey talked long into the night. Casey understood. The complex mystery, still complex, seemed no longer so mysterious to either of them.

"All the strings are tied up now," Casey said.

Never had Rena felt so connected. She slept peacefully, holding Casey close to her. For the first time ever, she was totally, fully, consciously in love.

The next day the light, safe, free, solid feeling continued as Rena taught her classes, lunched with colleagues, analyzed her latest data, lived her life. Born again, Rena thought, the loaded phrase echoing in her mind and making her smile.

That night, they made love. It was tender and long and sensual and soft and mutual. For the first time in Rena's life, for the first time while loving another, and while making love that involved no controlling, no power games, no topping, Rena Spiros experienced a very pronounced, definite and extremely delightful orgasm. And then another.

"That's nice," Casey cooed, cuddling her lover lovingly. "I sort of thought you would eventually. It's better this way, don't you think?"

Rena kissed Casey's neck playfully. "It's better this way. You put things so well. Have I told you I love you?"

"Not in the last thirty seconds."

"I loved you every one of those thirty seconds." The parakeet chirped. "Do you think she's jealous?"

"She knows you love her too." Casey rubbed her knee against Rena's thigh. "God, you're sexy."

"Don't call me God."

"I think I'm getting turned on again."

"God, you're horny."

"Don't call me God," Casey murmured, but the words were swallowed by Rena's enveloping lips.

* * * * *

Rena lay awake that night long after Casey was deeply asleep. Her eyes were closed, her fingers touching the little scar on her neck, the *X* with the two dots.

It's all right that I'm alive. She felt loose and dreamy. It's all right for me to be happy. I did what I had to do. Her breathing was deep and slow. No more, never again. The past is past.

Yes, no more, her father seemed to say. It *is* all right, *koukla mou.*

I suffered. I paid. It's all right now. It's done.

Done and finished, he said. He was always like that with Rena, always loved her so, no matter what.

She was drifting off, swinging and singing. The bird flew over her head toward the river then landed by the nest. Her father drew wings on a piece of paper and put the wings on Rena. She flew after the bird. It was a pheasant. At the nest, the bird laid an egg for her. She held the egg in both her palms. It was still warm. She held it for a long time knowing it was life, held it so long that when she finally took the egg to her uncle he was gone. Rena looked up over the hills and saw him. He waved to her. Behind him was her father and there was Pat. Lou held the olive branch, waving it over Rena, smiling, and Rena reached and took Casey's hand.

A few of the publications of
THE NAIAD PRESS, INC.
P.O. Box 10543 ● Tallahassee, Florida 32302
Phone (904) 539-9322
Mail orders welcome. Please include 15% postage.

CHERISHED LOVE by Evelyn Kennedy. 192 pp. Erotic
Lesbian love story.   ISBN 0-941483-08-8 $8.95

LAST SEPTEMBER by Helen R. Hull. 208 pp. Six stories & a
glorious novella.   ISBN 0-941483-09-6   8.95

THE SECRET IN THE BIRD by Camarin Grae. 312 pp. Striking,
psychological suspense novel.   ISBN 0-941483-05-3   8.95

TO THE LIGHTNING by Catherine Ennis. 208 pp. Romantic
Lesbian 'Robinson Crusoe' adventure.   ISBN 0-941483-06-1   8.95

THE OTHER SIDE OF VENUS by Shirley Verel. 224 pp.
Luminous, romantic love story.   ISBN 0-941483-07-X   8.95

DREAMS AND SWORDS by Katherine V. Forrest. 192 pp.
Romantic, erotic, imaginative stories.   ISBN 0-941483-03-7   8.95

MEMORY BOARD by Jane Rule. 336 pp. Memorable novel
about an aging Lesbian couple.   ISBN 0-941483-02-9   8.95

THE ALWAYS ANONYMOUS BEAST by Lauren Wright
Douglas. 224 pp. A Caitlin Reese mystery. First in a series.
                                             ISBN 0-941483-04-5   8.95

SEARCHING FOR SPRING by Patricia A. Murphy. 224 pp.
Novel about the recovery of love.   ISBN 0-941483-00-2   8.95

DUSTY'S QUEEN OF HEARTS DINER by Lee Lynch. 240 pp.
Romantic blue-collar novel.   ISBN 0-941483-01-0   8.95

PARENTS MATTER by Ann Muller. 240 pp. Parents'
relationships with Lesbian daughters and gay sons.
                                             ISBN 0-930044-91-6   9.95

THE PEARLS by Shelley Smith. 176 pp. Passion and fun in
the Caribbean sun.   ISBN 0-930044-93-2   7.95

MAGDALENA by Sarah Aldridge. 352 pp. Epic Lesbian novel
set on three continents.   ISBN 0-930044-99-1   8.95

THE BLACK AND WHITE OF IT by Ann Allen Shockley.
144 pp. Short stories.   ISBN 0-930044-96-7   7.95

SAY JESUS AND COME TO ME by Ann Allen Shockley. 288
pp. Contemporary romance.   ISBN 0-930044-98-3   8.95

LOVING HER by Ann Allen Shockley. 192 pp. Romantic love
story.   ISBN 0-930044-97-5   7.95

MURDER AT THE NIGHTWOOD BAR by Katherine V. Forrest. 240 pp. A Kate Delafield mystery. Second in a series.
ISBN 0-930044-92-4   8.95

ZOE'S BOOK by Gail Pass. 224 pp. Passionate, obsessive love story.
ISBN 0-930044-95-9   7.95

WINGED DANCER by Camarin Grae. 228 pp. Erotic Lesbian adventure story.
ISBN 0-930044-88-6   8.95

PAZ by Camarin Grae. 336 pp. Romantic Lesbian adventurer with the power to change the world.
ISBN 0-930044-89-4   8.95

SOUL SNATCHER by Camarin Grae. 224 pp. A puzzle, an adventure, a mystery — Lesbian romance.
ISBN 0-930044-90-8   8.95

THE LOVE OF GOOD WOMEN by Isabel Miller. 224 pp. Long-awaited new novel by the author of the beloved *Patience and Sarah.*
ISBN 0-930044-81-9   8.95

THE HOUSE AT PELHAM FALLS by Brenda Weathers. 240 pp. Suspenseful Lesbian ghost story.
ISBN 0-930044-79-7   7.95

HOME IN YOUR HANDS by Lee Lynch. 240 pp. More stories from the author of *Old Dyke Tales.*
ISBN 0-930044-80-0   7.95

EACH HAND A MAP by Anita Skeen. 112 pp. Real-life poems that touch us all.
ISBN 0-930044-82-7   6.95

SURPLUS by Sylvia Stevenson. 342 pp. A classic early Lesbian novel.
ISBN 0-930044-78-9   6.95

PEMBROKE PARK by Michelle Martin. 256 pp. Derring-do and daring romance in Regency England.
ISBN 0-930044-77-0   7.95

THE LONG TRAIL by Penny Hayes. 248 pp. Vivid adventures of two women in love in the old west.
ISBN 0-930044-76-2   8.95

HORIZON OF THE HEART by Shelley Smith. 192 pp. Hot romance in summertime New England.
ISBN 0-930044-75-4   7.95

AN EMERGENCE OF GREEN by Katherine V. Forrest. 288 pp. Powerful novel of sexual discovery.
ISBN 0-930044-69-X   8.95

THE LESBIAN PERIODICALS INDEX edited by Claire Potter. 432 pp. Author & subject index.
ISBN 0-930044-74-6   29.95

DESERT OF THE HEART by Jane Rule. 224 pp. A classic; basis for the movie *Desert Hearts.*
ISBN 0-930044-73-8   7.95

SPRING FORWARD/FALL BACK by Sheila Ortiz Taylor. 288 pp. Literary novel of timeless love.
ISBN 0-930044-70-3   7.95

FOR KEEPS by Elisabeth Nonas. 144 pp. Contemporary novel about losing and finding love.
ISBN 0-930044-71-1   7.95

TORCHLIGHT TO VALHALLA by Gale Wilhelm. 128 pp. Classic novel by a great Lesbian writer.
ISBN 0-930044-68-1   7.95

LESBIAN NUNS: BREAKING SILENCE edited by Rosemary Curb and Nancy Manahan. 432 pp. Unprecedented autobiographies of religious life.
ISBN 0-930044-62-2   9.95

YANTRAS OF WOMANLOVE by Tee A. Corinne. 64 pp.
Photos by noted Lesbian photographer.   ISBN 0-930044-30-4   6.95

MRS. PORTER'S LETTER by Vicki P. McConnell. 224 pp.
The first Nyla Wade mystery.   ISBN 0-930044-29-0   7.95

TO THE CLEVELAND STATION by Carol Anne Douglas.
192 pp. Interracial Lesbian love story.   ISBN 0-930044-27-4   6.95

THE NESTING PLACE by Sarah Aldridge. 224 pp. A
three-woman triangle—love conquers all!   ISBN 0-930044-26-6   7.95

THIS IS NOT FOR YOU by Jane Rule. 284 pp. A letter to a
beloved is also an intricate novel.   ISBN 0-930044-25-8   8.95

FAULTLINE by Sheila Ortiz Taylor. 140 pp. Warm, funny,
literate story of a startling family.   ISBN 0-930044-24-X   6.95

THE LESBIAN IN LITERATURE by Barbara Grier. 3d ed.
Foreword by Maida Tilchen. 240 pp. Comprehensive bibliography.
Literary ratings; rare photos.   ISBN 0-930044-23-1   7.95

ANNA'S COUNTRY by Elizabeth Lang. 208 pp. A woman
finds her Lesbian identity.   ISBN 0-930044-19-3   6.95

PRISM by Valerie Taylor. 158 pp. A love affair between two
women in their sixties.   ISBN 0-930044-18-5   6.95

BLACK LESBIANS: AN ANNOTATED BIBLIOGRAPHY
compiled by J. R. Roberts. Foreword by Barbara Smith. 112 pp.
Award-winning bibliography.   ISBN 0-930044-21-5   5.95

THE MARQUISE AND THE NOVICE by Victoria Ramstetter.
108 pp. A Lesbian Gothic novel.   ISBN 0-930044-16-9   4.95

OUTLANDER by Jane Rule. 207 pp. Short stories and essays
by one of our finest writers.   ISBN 0-930044-17-7   6.95

SAPPHISTRY: THE BOOK OF LESBIAN SEXUALITY by
Pat Califia. 2d edition, revised. 195 pp.   ISBN 0-9330044-47-9   7.95

ALL TRUE LOVERS by Sarah Aldridge. 292 pp. Romantic
novel set in the 1930s and 1940s.   ISBN 0-930044-10-X   7.95

A WOMAN APPEARED TO ME by Renee Vivien. 65 pp. A
classic; translated by Jeannette H. Foster.   ISBN 0-930044-06-1   5.00

CYTHEREA'S BREATH by Sarah Aldridge. 240 pp. Romantic
novel about women's entrance into medicine.
    ISBN 0-930044-02-9   6.95

TOTTIE by Sarah Aldridge. 181 pp. Lesbian romance in the
turmoil of the sixties.   ISBN 0-930044-01-0   6.95

THE LATECOMER by Sarah Aldridge. 107 pp. A delicate love
story.   ISBN 0-930044-00-2   5.00

ODD GIRL OUT by Ann Bannon.	ISBN 0-930044-83-5	5.95
I AM A WOMAN by Ann Bannon.	ISBN 0-930044-84-3	5.95
WOMEN IN THE SHADOWS by Ann Bannon.		
	ISBN 0-930044-85-1	5.95
JOURNEY TO A WOMAN by Ann Bannon.		
	ISBN 0-930044-86-X	5.95
BEEBO BRINKER by Ann Bannon.	ISBN 0-930044-87-8	5.95

Legendary novels written in the fifties and sixties,
set in the gay mecca of Greenwich Village.

VOLUTE BOOKS

JOURNEY TO FULFILLMENT	Early classics by Valerie	3.95
A WORLD WITHOUT MEN	Taylor: The Erika Frohmann	3.95
RETURN TO LESBOS	series.	3.95

These are just a few of the many Naiad Press titles — we are the oldest and largest lesbian/feminist publishing company in the world. Please request a complete catalog. We offer personal service; we encourage and welcome direct mail orders from individuals who have limited access to bookstores carrying our publications.